"PROTEST NO MORE, LITTLE ONE!"

"Does it matter how we came to be together? You are here, I am here, the bed is here. You felt warm and soft beside me."

She backed away a step, only to come up against the cold stone wall. *"Monsieur,* I'm . . . I'm afraid you don't understand. One of us has made a mistake."

"The only mistake, *ma petite,* would be for us to waste the hours left until dawn. Come back to bed. It is cold without you."

"No. I can't . . ."

His hands—large, warm, callused hands—drew her close until her breasts flattened against the solid wall of his ribs. His mouth captured hers with a strong, soft heat and Celine discovered something far sexier than this man's voice or his body. *His kiss.*

She never had a chance to think of a protest, to think at all. Before she could stop herself, her arms slid around his back and she was holding onto him as much as he was holding her.

Other **AVON ROMANCES**

Beloved Pretender *by Joan Van Nuys*
Dark Champion *by Jo Beverley*
Flame of Fury *by Sharon Green*
Master of My Dreams *by Danelle Harmon*
Outlaw Heart *by Samantha James*
Passionate Surrender *by Sheryl Sage*
Touch Me With Fire *by Nicole Jordan*

Coming Soon

A Gentle Taming *by Adrienne Day*
Scandalous *by Sonia Simone*

And Don't Miss These
ROMANTIC TREASURES
from Avon Books

Angel Eyes *by Suzannah Davis*
Fascination *by Stella Cameron*
Fortune's Flame *by Judith E. French*

Forever His

SHELLY THACKER

AVON BOOKS ⬦ NEW YORK

FOREVER HIS is an original publication of Avon Books. This work has never before appeared in book form. This work is a novel. Any similarity to actual persons or events is purely coincidental.

AVON BOOKS
A division of
The Hearst Corporation
1350 Avenue of the Americas
New York, New York 10019

Copyright © 1993 by Shelly Thacker Meinhardt
Inside cover author photograph by Jim LaMoore
Published by arrangement with the author
Library of Congress Catalog Card Number: 93-90404
ISBN: 0-380-77035-0

First Avon Books Printing: December 1993

AVON TRADEMARK REG. U.S. PAT. OFF. AND IN OTHER COUNTRIES, MARCA REGISTRADA, HECHO EN U.S.A.

Printed in the U.S.A.

RA   10 9 8 7 6 5 4 3 2 1

Dedicated to the memory of
Kathleen Thacker, Olive Thacker,
Lucy Taylor, and Margarette Menard,
special ladies who touched so many lives
with love and joy.
I miss you.

Time is too slow for those who wait,
too swift for those who fear,
too long for those who grieve,
too short for those who rejoice,
but for those who love,
time is not.

HENRY VAN DYKE

Prologue

Artois Region, France, 1299

Rain pelted down from the iron-gray sky, choking the first tentative rays of morning sunlight and turning the trampled battlefield to treacherous mud. Unarmed and unescorted, Sir Gaston de Varennes walked slowly past the two assembled armies, his dark mood matched by the roiling clouds overhead, his pace slowed by pain from the freshly bound wound in his side—and by the agonizing knowledge that the action he was about to take would haunt him for the rest of his life.

He stopped a few paces short of his destination, his body tensing as he stared at the hastily erected tent and its drooping white-and-blue pennant. The downpour deepened the autumn chill in the air, sluicing off his helm and soaking through his surcoat and chain mail until he felt the cold to the raw depths of his soul. The drenching rain could not wash away the scents of smoke and blood that hung heavily in the air.

He turned a narrowed gaze on the men gathered around—his own forces on the right and his enemy's on the left. The tent's festive colors struck a sharp contrast to the somber, grit-smudged, determined faces of these warriors whose weapons lay at their feet. The steady ping of raindrops upon discarded blades and shields and battle-axes made strange music in the uneasy silence.

As he studied his own ranks—loyal knights who had served his family for years, men who had fought valiantly beside him these two months—Gaston saw the message vivid in each pair of eyes: despite the fact that they were

1

badly outnumbered, despite their almost-depleted supplies, they would fight on if he but said the word.

One word and they would battle until the death of the last man. Until they had claimed some measure of justice from the soulless whoreson who had by treachery taken lives and land from the house of Varennes.

Gaston felt as if he were being ripped in half. His warrior's heart was one with theirs, pumping fire through his veins, searing him with a longing for steel and vengeance. Never had he felt more like the symbol emblazoned on his surcoat: a black lion on a silver field. A dark predator stalking the shadows.

But the leader in him knew the foolishness of continuing this battle with winter's bite in the air, with his forces and his food stores already dangerously depleted. He could not so heedlessly spend the lives of those who depended upon him.

Nor could he defy the man who had called him to this place. The one man in all the realm who could force a halt to this war.

Clenching his jaw, he turned, thrust aside the tent flap, and entered the torchlit darkness where unwelcome peace would be met.

It took a moment for his eyes to adjust to the flickering light. He removed his helm and straightened to his full height, his dark hair brushing the top of the tent. A rough-hewn table and two chairs had been placed in the center of the small pavilion.

The table, he noted, was round, traditional symbol of honor among knights, a table to be used for the making of noble bargains and the sealing of vows of friendship. The sort of table that he himself found use for only rarely. On the far side of it stood the Duc Alain de la Tourelle.

Gaston fastened a murderous expression upon him and saw his own hatred mirrored back tenfold.

By nails and blood, how many weeks had he fought to get within blade's reach of this cur? In every melee, Gaston had battled like a madman, trying to win a clear path to that pale visage with its keen blue eyes and wild crop of red hair. He had never quite managed it.

Now his palm itched for the pommel of his sword and his muscles went taut with ready violence. The deep slash in his side throbbed, but he barely felt it through a haze of frustrated fury.

Holding his enemy's gaze, he stepped closer to the table, ignored the chair that had been provided for him, and tossed down his helm. It landed with a clatter.

"Varennes," Tourelle said with a humorless smile, leaning forward and bracing his arms on the thick oak, "as our host has not arrived yet, mayhap you and I might come to an understanding, without his interference. The claim I have upon the chateaux and the lands I have taken is—"

"Your *claim* is a lie." Gaston yanked off his mail gauntlets and threw them down beside his helm. "The lands you took by treachery mark you as a thief, and the lives you took mark you as a murderer."

Tourelle sneered. "You are a strange one to accuse another man of knavery, Blackheart."

Gaston ignored the familiar gibe. "Is that why you dared attempt such blatant theft?" he asked scathingly. "Did you truly believe that the arrant son would offer no resistance?"

"It *is* surprising that you could tear yourself away from dicing and comely wenches long enough to lead men into battle," Tourelle shot back. "But we waste time. The claim I have through my mother's line is both ancient and valid. As for the tournament which went awry—"

"Tournament?" Gaston snarled. "It was not a tournament but an ambush. Exactly as you planned it to be. You lured my father and brother with your challenge to tourney for glory and ransoms—and they never suspected that a lord who had sat at our tables and broken bread with us and spoken of honor and friendship for years would so suddenly prove himself a knave!"

"They knew the risks when they agreed to the tournament," Tourelle countered. "You all did. With a hundred men on each side fighting over a ground of fifty miles for three days from morning until dusk—it is to be expected that there may be breaches of the rules. 'Twas a fair combat."

"My father and brother were too skilled and experienced to be killed in a *fair* combat. What you hoped was to wipe out the entire Varennes male line." Gaston narrowed his eyes. "How long had you been planning it, Tourelle? Years?"

Tourelle straightened, his mien all innocence. "Had it been my intent to kill every last one of you, Varennes, you would not now be standing before me."

"Aye, how disappointed you must have been when I did not arrive."

"And where *were* you, Blackheart? Why did you not join them? Why did you break your word?"

Gaston's temper slipped its leash as Tourelle's barbs found their mark and brought an unwanted rush of grief and guilt. "Allow me to make clear one vow that I *will* keep," he said with a feral smile. "The souls of my murdered father and brother demand justice. My brother's widow demands it. The villagers whose homes and fields were ransacked and burned demand it. The women who were brutally raped demand it." Gaston thrust himself away from the table. "I vow that I will reclaim all the lands you have stolen and make you *pay* for the blood upon your hands!"

Tourelle reached for his scabbard, only to find it empty. With an oath, he launched himself over the table. Gaston crouched into a fighting stance.

"Hold!" A booming voice rang out behind them before they could land a single blow.

They froze, turning to find that their host had arrived at last—and his expression at the moment reflected naught of the name his features had earned him: King Philippe the Fair.

Slowly, Gaston dropped to one knee, bowing his head. "Sire." Beside him, Tourelle did the same.

"Rise, Sir Gaston," the King commanded, his voice deep with anger that rivaled the thunder outside. "Rise, Duc Alain."

Gaston straightened, but did not flinch from his lord's wrathful gaze or stormy tone; he could not pretend remorse he did not feel for a war he did not regret.

"You will both be seated," the King ordered flatly, sweeping off his fur-lined velvet mantle, spattering rain across the small tent.

Gaston moved slowly, reluctantly, but obeyed without a word, as did Tourelle.

The King came to stand at the table, an equal distance between them, glaring from one to the other in turn. "I have sent missives to you both and they have been ignored," he began in a quiet voice all the more ominous for its softness. "More than a fortnight past, I declared again that there would be peace between you, and yet you fought on. Did you both believe that I hold your past service in such esteem and your present counsel so valued that you could *defy your King?*" He slammed a fist on the table with such force that any lesser wood than oak would have split asunder.

"Sire," Tourelle said. "My claim—"

"Silence!" Philippe demanded. "I will hear no more of claims and thievery and tournaments gone awry. I have decided the matter, and there will be *peace.*"

"My liege, one cannot make peace with a viper," Gaston insisted.

"It is the way of these times, Gaston," the King assured him with a bitter laugh. "One finds oneself making peace with all manner of creatures. I married my own sister to the English King not two years past to seal a treaty of peace."

"Sire," Tourelle bit out, clearly displeased at being likened to a viper . . . or to an Englishman. "It is *I* who have been wronged in this. I did not start this war. I merely defend myself. This knave attacked my lands without warning!"

"And what would you have done in his place?" Philippe snapped. "A mere knight engaging a *duc* who possesses much larger holdings and more men? His strategy of surprise was his only hope of succeeding. It is not with polite, mild ways that Sir Gaston has earned the name The Black Lion, Alain. And it is no accident that I have come to depend upon his military counsel. You would be wise to remember that."

Any pride Gaston might have felt at the King's words vanished when Philippe turned his furious gaze upon him.

"But it is the *wise* knight," Philippe continued, "who knows to stop when his lord so commands!"

"My liege, had you been here, I would have been able to explain," Gaston said. "I fear you do not fully grasp—"

"Nay, Gaston, it is you who do not grasp this situation. With unrest along the Flemish border but a day's ride distant, I require strong, *obedient* vassals here in the north, ready to defend my holdings from attack. Men with no quarrels between them." He glanced from one to the other, then drew himself up to his full regal height. "We can no longer be Aquitaine and Orléans and Touraine and Artois, each region for itself, each man for himself. It is time for us to put aside the old ways and old wars and stand together as France. To fight together as France!"

Silence followed his declaration, broken only by the pounding of the rain overhead. If his words were meant to replace hatred and enmity with loyal fervor, Gaston thought darkly, they failed.

The King's expression hardened. "It is not necessary that either of you understand. It is only necessary that you obey my commands. And *there will be peace* between you!" He folded his arms over his chest. "I have decided it thusly: you, Alain, shall have a portion of the lands that you claim through your mother's line—those bordering the Oise River and westward."

Gaston bit back an oath and clamped his hands on the arms of his chair to keep from surging to his feet in outrage. That amounted to half of his brother, Gerard's, holdings!

"You, Gaston"—the King shot him a quelling glance—"will have returned to you your rightful inheritance: the chateaux that belonged to your father and brother, with all the lands and vassals entailed to each, but for that portion which I have just transferred to the Duc."

Gaston found but small satisfaction in that—though he did enjoy the strangled sound of protest that Tourelle couldn't quite contain.

"My liege!" Tourelle sputtered. "Varennes is not capable of managing such holdings! Nor is he deserving of them. The only chateau he possesses now is one that he *stole* during a—"

"And to seal this peace and assure that there shall be no future trouble between you," Philippe continued calmly, talking right over him, "Gaston will marry your nearest female relative, Alain."

Both men leaped to their feet with vehement protests before the King had even finished his sentence.

"Nay, my lord, you cannot ask this!" Tourelle cried.

"It is impossible," Gaston declared, stunned by the unexpected command. "My liege, you have already promised me the hand of Lady Rosalind de Brissot." He slanted a scornful look toward Tourelle. "Precisely so that I may join her lands with mine and protect my holdings and my people from the marauders who plague our region."

"Aye, Gaston, I did promise her to you, along with her dower lands. Half the Artois region, if you will recall. Mayhap you should have given some thought to that before you disobeyed my order to end this war."

Gaston felt his gut clench. He could not lose Lady Rosalind! He needed her lands and her knights now more than ever. His father's and brother's chateaux lay far to the north; he could not hope to hold them unless he had the reinforcements and the power that the de Brissot lands would bring him.

"Sire," Tourelle said patiently, "it pains me greatly to agree with this barbarian, but he is right in this instance—it is impossible. He cannot marry a maiden of my house because there are none available. My daughters are married. My sister died years past. I've no unmarried cousins—"

" 'Twas your ward I thought of, Alain. Christiane de la Fontaine."

Tourelle flinched as if he'd been struck. "Not Christiane!" he spluttered. "She is an innocent, sire. Raised from the age of three in a foreign convent. She is soon to take her sacred vows and join the cloister. I cannot hand her over to this . . . this—"

"This *barbarian* wants naught to do with a woman of

his enemy's house," Gaston said tightly. "Especially some impoverished novice fresh from the cloister without a blade of grass to her name. Sire, you must believe me. Tourelle is *not* what he pretends to be, and you are placing a weapon in his hands. He will only use this girl to accomplish what he has wanted all along—the death of the last male heir of the Varennes line. I will no doubt find her blade in my back as soon as the wedding vows have been spoken!"

"Enough! Both of you!" the King snapped. "Alain, you will send for Lady Christiane immediately."

Shaking with suppressed fury, Tourelle replied through gritted teeth. "The convent is many weeks distant, sire. In Aragon. With the snows hard upon us, by the time a messenger can be sent, I—"

"You will go there and fetch her yourself," Philippe commanded. "Mayhap a journey through the snow will cool your anger and give you time to consider the wisdom of obeying your King without question when next he gives you an order."

A deafening crack of thunder sealed his words. For a long moment, the pounding storm made the only sound in the small tent.

"Sire," Gaston said at last, his determination no less fierce than before, "I will wed this Fontaine girl because it is what you command, but I vow to you, I will have done with her and marry—"

"You savage son of a cur," Tourelle hissed. "If you harm so much as one lock of Christiane's hair, I will—"

"I'll not harm her. I'll not even *touch* her. I'll not consummate the marriage and I will *prove* to the King that you are the murdering knave I have claimed!" Gaston turned back toward Philippe. "And when I have done so, my liege, I ask that you grant me an annulment, that I might marry Lady Rosalind. And that you return to me the rest of my brother's lands."

"Enough!" Philippe looked exasperated and disgusted with them both. "You may seek to prove whatever you wish. You may bed your wife or not as you wish. But from this moment onward, neither of you will raise so much as a dulled table-blade against the other!" He bestowed a royal glare upon each of them in turn. "You, Alain, will forfeit all of your lands *and everything you own* if Gaston is harmed in any way—and the same holds true for you, Gaston, if aught befalls Alain or Lady Christiane!"

His expression would have turned lesser men into cowering pups. The message was clear. The matter was closed.

"As you command, my liege," Gaston grated out.

"Aye," Tourelle agreed.

The King gave them a frosty smile. "At last, my two most valued and troublesome vassals have chosen to obey my orders. Pray that I never have to journey all the way from Paris to deliver them in person again!" He picked up his sodden cloak and flung it about his shoulders. "Alain, you will bring the Fontaine girl to Gaston's chateau by the end of December. The wedding will take place on the first day of the new year—and I shall attend myself to ensure that naught goes awry."

He spun on his heel and pulled aside the tent flap, muttering under his breath as he stepped out into the storm, "And may God protect the unfortunate maiden who is about to be dropped into this den of wolves."

Chapter 1

Artois Region, France
New Year's Eve, 1993

Coming here had been a huge mistake.

Celine Fontaine sat perched on the edge of a crimson brocade Louis XVI chair, a Baccarat crystal champagne flute clutched in one shaky hand, her lungs unable to steal a single full breath. The *grand salon*'s warm air, heavy with the competing scents of Saint Laurent and Lagerfeld and Gucci, seemed too thick to breathe. The crowd ebbed and flowed and chattered around her, but Celine had never felt more alone.

She had been a fool to think she could handle this.

Any second now, it would happen. She would lose control. Give in to the shivers of terror that iced through her and dissolve into a trembling heap on the expensive Kilim rug on Aunt Patrice's marble floor.

She could imagine her horrified mother dashing to her side, kneeling over her, shaking her head. *Darling, darling,* she would say. She always addressed Celine that way, as if her troublesome middle child needed that second "darling." *Darling, darling, your doctors said you were fully recovered. They said there wouldn't be any long-term psychological effects.*

Her family would finally be forced to call out the men in the white suits. Or whatever the French equivalent was.

Celine tried to picture what a French straitjacket might look like. Impeccably tailored, she imagined, choking back a hysterical little laugh that bubbled up inside her. Maybe with a Louis Vuitton logo on the lapel or gold Chanel buttons.

She should have stayed home. Alone in her studio on Lake Michigan. Along with her art and her antiques and her cats and her secret.

She kept telling herself she was safe here. Nothing and no one could hurt her in Manoir La Fontaine. The family's ancestral chateau, nestled in a small town north of Paris, had always been her favorite place in the world. She had spent all her childhood and teenage summers here, had always looked forward to the annual reunion over Christmas and New Year's.

The only one she had ever missed was last year's. Because she had been in the hospital. Because of her headline-grabbing disaster with Lee.

A twinge of hurt mingled with the terror that made her heart beat painfully hard. Thoughts of Lee would only make everything worse. She forced the name to the back of her overcrowded mind.

She had insisted on coming to this year's reunion despite her surgeon's protests, not only because she wanted to please her family, but because she thought she might find tranquility in this place.

But she couldn't calm down. Nothing could soothe her unreasoning panic. That's what her doctors had called this "unfortunate side effect." Panic attacks. Quite understandable in the circumstances, they informed her. The episodes would fade eventually, they assured her.

But it had been a year now, and they hadn't faded. She hadn't had an attack in weeks, had dared hope she might finally be past them—but the fear that had become her shadow that violent night last December seemed to follow her everywhere. Even here.

Celine kept a carefree smile pasted in place as she glanced down at her watch, at the tiny gold hands moving inexorably along diamond-flecked numerals. Eleven-fifteen. In forty-five minutes it would be midnight. Thank God. She would clink a few glasses, kiss a few relatives, find Uncle Edouard and Aunt Patrice, make her apologies. Make her escape.

Calm down, calm down, calm down.

Her doctors had prescribed tranquilizers, but she refused to take them. She didn't want to trade one problem for another. Didn't want to become one of those desperate, high-strung, Valium-popping society women she met too often.

She had always hated pills, and seven weeks in the hospital had left her with a strong distaste for anything medical: sedatives, needles, nurses, IVs, EKGs, and the most dreaded initials of all, PT. Physical Therapy.

She lifted the champagne flute to her lips, took a sip, and tried to swallow past the knot of terror in her throat. She had to make it through this. Slowly, forcefully, she returned her attention to the conversation around her.

The room hummed with French, Italian, upper-class British, and the American accent of her father's branch of the family. The popular topic among her intellectual relatives seemed to be some astronomical event that was supposed to happen tonight. A lunar eclipse or something. But, seated beside her, two of her cousins were nattering in low tones about their latest romantic liaisons on the Côte d'Azur.

Celine felt grateful that everyone was acting absolutely normal toward her. She had even dressed carefully tonight, choosing a low-cut, form-fitting black Donna Karan dress that practically screamed *I am perfectly fine.* She wanted everyone to believe that. *She* wanted to believe that.

She had promised herself she would tell her family the truth before they all flew home.

To top off the dress, she had chosen a favorite hat from her collection: a sixties pillbox in a particularly florid shade of pink, accented with a pair of antique brooches. She wore her blunt-cut red hair in a tight chignon, purposely revealing flawless makeup and her most cheerful smile. No one should be able to tell that anything was wrong.

Celine glanced at her watch again. Forty-three minutes until she could escape to her room.

Aunt Patrice and Uncle Edouard had laid out a lavish New Year's Eve buffet on lace-draped tables; party guests chatted between nibbles of escargots bathed in butter and

garlic, savory *bricelet* crackers topped with caviar—
beluga, of course—and tiny sea-urchin *soufflés d'oursins*
served in the shells. Celine hadn't eaten a bite.

Forty-two minutes.

Brilliant light from chandeliers and candelabra glowed
along the dark Renaissance paneling. The festive room
overflowed with thousands of tiny white rosebuds fashioned into swags and arches. Aunt Patrice had placed the
decorations with typical Fontaine humor: one wreath hung
over the marble fireplace, on the portrait of a dour ancestor who had been guillotined during the French Revolution. He did not look amused by his new hat of flowers.

Forty-one minutes.

"Marie, Dominique, I'm sorry," Celine said suddenly,
sitting forward and interrupting one cousin's description of
her polo-loving playboy. "I'm absolutely starved. Got to
get something to eat. Please excuse me." She set her glass
on the low table beside her; the slender crystal clattered
and wobbled dangerously between a nineteenth-century
urn and a bronze statuette.

Celine pretended not to notice. She stood up. She had to
move. The heart-pounding urge to run was overpowering.
With a few quickly muttered *pardonez-mois*, she made her
way through the crush of guests toward the buffet table.

She could feel concerned glances turning her way as she
picked up a plate and tried desperately to keep from shaking.

She knew what everyone was thinking. That she was
young. Rich. Pretty. That she had her whole life ahead of
her. That it was time for her to put last year's "unfortunate
incident" behind her and get on with her future.

What they didn't know—what no one knew—was that
she might not have a future at all.

Holding that secret inside left her alone in her fear, but
saying it aloud would be too terrifying to bear.

"There you are, Celine. I've been looking for you. Feeling all right?"

Celine tensed as her older sister, Jacqueline Fontaine
O'Keefe, appeared at her side. "I'm fine, Jackie," she re-

plied with a smile. *Perfectly fine. I feel better physically than I ever have in my life. That's the irony of it.*

She kept her thoughts to herself and moved down the table.

"Glad to hear it. Love the hat. Is that a new one?" Jacqueline's voice burbled with laughter and too much Dom Perignon. She kept right on talking without waiting for an answer. "I'm not here to hover, promise. Just the opposite, in fact. I'm appointing myself your personal social director for the evening."

Celine groaned inwardly and tried to look like she was intently deciding between the lobster and the frogs' legs.

"I've found you the dream date of all time," Jacqueline continued. "Six feet of pure gorgeous. Blond hair, green eyes, killer bod. I told him about that August '92 *Elle* cover and he's dying to meet you."

Celine frowned. "I wish you wouldn't go around reminding people of that. It's bad enough when they bring it up on their own." She put a spoonful of marinated salmon on her plate, wishing for the umpteenth time that she had never agreed to pose in nothing but a few strategically placed baobab leaves.

"It's okay, Celinie-Beanie," Jackie said in the same tipsy tone. "I told him you gave up modeling last year for a career as a finer artist."

"Fiber artist."

"Right. Anyway, I'm not taking any ifs, ands, or buts this time. This guy's got 'wild romantic fling' written all over him. God knows you deserve one."

Celine sighed. "That's true," she agreed, chastising herself even as she said it. She knew she should correct the "flighty, footloose" image everyone had of her; she preferred to think of herself as *free-spirited* and *independent.* Maybe she didn't have the scholarly bent and the get-to-the-top drive of the rest of the Fontaine clan, but she wasn't flighty.

And definitely not footloose. She was not the wild-romantic-fling type. On the contrary, she was perhaps the last twenty-three-year-old virgin left on the planet. She had never found Mr. Right, or even Mr. Right Now.

But she didn't like being teased about her old-fashioned streak, any more than she had liked being teased about her grades as a kid. Or her height. The nickname "Celinie-Beanie"—short for Celine-the-beanpole—had always stung.

"He sounds great, Jackie." Keeping her smile in place, Celine moved down the table, taking a wafer-thin slice of her favorite Port Salut cheese, two crackers, and a dozen fat *fraises des bois,* wild strawberries covered in chocolate. She decided to try a little humor, which usually managed to deflect her determined sister. "I'm afraid I'm just not in the mood for a blond. Now, if he had a great smile and dark hair, say in a Tom Cruise-Sylvester Stallone sort of way—"

"Oh, please. This guy's perfect for you. He's not a cop, a lawyer, a reporter, or a surgeon. I asked."

Celine tried to laugh at Jackie's attempted joke. Her sister knew those were her four least-favorite professions, after the past year. "Then how about 'I've got a headache'?" Celine deadpanned.

"I'm not taking no for an answer." Jackie stole one of the strawberries from Celine's plate and took a bite. "Honestly, Celine, you're going to hurt my feelings if you keep turning down every man I try to set you up with. You don't know what you're missing."

Celine followed her sister's gaze across the room to where Jackie's tall, handsome husband, Harry O'Keefe, stood talking to some of their British cousins. He balanced a Perrier in one hand and their three-year-old son, Nicholas, on his shoulders.

Celine's eyes suddenly misted and she turned aside before Jackie could notice. *Yes, I do know what I'm missing,* she thought, a wave of sadness choking her. *I might never have what you have. A husband. Children. I might not have enough time left.*

She started to shake uncontrollably.

Oh, God, not here! Not now!

It was the moment she had been dreading. She was going to burst into hysterical tears in front of everyone. Embarrassment urged her to flee, but the roar of her heartbeat left her paralyzed with panic.

She felt rather than saw Jackie take the plate from her hands and set it aside. "God, Celine, I'm being about as sensitive as a runaway train. It's Lee, isn't it? You still haven't gotten over Lee." She steered Celine toward a nearby Louis XIV settee and shooed a pair of partygoers out of the way so her sister could sit down.

Trembling, Celine forced a smile, blinked, and blessed whoever had invented waterproof mascara. "No, I wasn't . . . I wasn't thinking about him."

Jackie put an arm around her shoulders and gave her a hug. "Oh, sweetie, don't try to be brave. Go ahead and cry. When I think of the way that schmuck demanded his ring back while you were still in the *hospital,* for God's sake—"

"Darling, darling, are you all right?"

Celine winced as her mother appeared from behind her in a cloud of Chanel No. 19. Francine Fontaine started patting Celine's cheeks as if her daughter had fainted.

"Y-y-yes, M-M-Mother," Celine managed between pats. "I'm fi—"

"It's Lee," Jackie supplied. "She can't stop thinking about him."

"No, I—"

"Oh, my poor darling, darling girl." Francine stopped patting, came around the settee, and sat down. Snatching up Celine's hand, she squeezed it in both of hers. "Don't waste one more tear on that horrid man. He wasn't worthy of you!"

If Celine's stomach hadn't been churning with anxiety, she might have laughed. A little more than a year ago, her mother had used that same tone to *insist* that she accept Leland Dawber III's marriage proposal. Her entire family had agreed he was perfect for her: a no-nonsense, take-charge type who would give her the direction she needed. Lee had a villa in Rome, a chalet in Switzerland, a successful chain of hotels, and an answer for everything.

And she had always wanted a husband and children. Much more than she wanted a career, though she could hardly admit such an old-fashioned idea to her family of Nobel Prize nominees, business moguls, and assorted overachievers.

Lee had swept her off her feet so completely, she had started to believe she was in love with him, that he might finally be the one. Especially when he had surprised her by slipping an engagement ring on her finger, that night last December, after they had run through Chicago's Lincoln Park like a couple of kids and made angels in the snow.

But that evening hadn't ended the way either one of them had expected.

Leland Dawber's abrupt departure from her life a few weeks later had come as a surprise to everyone. Especially to her. She had really believed he cared for her—until he abandoned her when she needed him most.

"It's . . . it's not Lee," Celine said, trying to catch her breath and calm down.

"Then what is it?" Jackie prodded.

"It's . . . I'm . . ." Celine barely managed to stop herself before it all came tumbling out.

Everything her doctors had told her before she left the States.

Unexpected complication, Ms. Fontaine . . . one more surgery . . . important that we don't delay. They had couched it all in their best bedside manner, but she had gotten the point: the surgery would be risky, but if she didn't have it, she would die.

The bullet fragment embedded deep in her back, the one they had thought best to leave in place, the one so tiny she couldn't feel it, was shifting, slowly. Dangerously close to a major artery. Before long, it would kill her. Perhaps not this month or next month, they said, but within a year. Surgery was her only hope.

She was scheduled to enter the hospital in two weeks.

"I'm . . . I'm tired," Celine said quietly, glancing from her sister to her mother. "That's all. Just tired. Still having a bit of jet lag, I guess."

She couldn't tell them. Not tonight. Her family had just recovered from the unpleasantness she had brought into their lives last year. She could at least let them enjoy their holidays. Another day or two would be soon enough to break the news.

"Oh, darling, darling, are you sure that's all it is?"

"Yes, Mother. I think I'll call it a night and go up to bed. Give my apologies to Uncle Edouard and Aunt Patrice, will you?" Celine kissed the air on either side of her mother's cheeks before turning to Jacqueline. "And kiss little Nicholas good night for me?"

"Of course. But are you sure you don't want to stay even a few minutes longer? At least until the eclipse begins?"

"No, I'll let you scientific types tell me all about it tomorrow. I'm not into eclipses—I'm a *finer* artist, remember?"

"*Fiber* artist," Jackie corrected softly, hugging her. "I'll make sure Harry gets some pictures for you. You get some rest." Her voice dropped to a conspiratorial whisper. "And if I run into a guy with a great smile and dark hair in a Tom Cruise-Sylvester Stallone sort of way, I'm sending him up."

"Absolutely." Celine flashed what she hoped would pass for a tired-but-happy smile before she all but bolted from the settee. "Good night, Mother. Good night, Jackie."

"You think I'm kidding?"

Already making her way into the noisy crowd, Celine barely heard her sister's parting comment.

She dashed past startled guests and caterers and servants until she reached the oldest part of the chateau. Away from the crush, she started to feel a little better. *Come on, Celine,* she admonished herself, slowing to a more dignified walk. *Where's that famous Fontaine fortitude?* She stopped in the middle of a deserted hallway to catch her breath.

Sometimes it seemed God had given so much fortitude, determination, genius, and all the other Fontaine characteristics to her many relatives, He had run out by the time she came along. All she got was the famous Fontaine flaming-red hair.

No, no, no. She squeezed her eyes shut, trying to shake off the familiar feelings of inadequacy. Maybe she didn't fit in, but that didn't make her a failure. Maybe she hadn't found her place in the world just yet, but she would some-day. And she wasn't going to get there by giving in to self-pity. Or panic.

Opening her eyes, she slipped off her Italian leather pumps, squared her shoulders, and padded down the slate-floored passageway that led to her room. The halls seemed eerily quiet tonight, the silence punctuated only occasion-ally by the distant echo of the New Year's Eve celebration.

She had asked to stay in the oldest part of the mansion because it was quiet here. And this wing had long been her favorite. Some of her earliest childhood memories were of these rooms, the Gothic architecture, the faded tapestries.

She paused to look at one of the hangings highlighted by a museum-style lamp. Her family's tapestry collection had been one inspiration for her becoming a fiber artist. The pieces were unique: medieval in materials and tech-niques, but almost modern in their colors and designs. She loved the idea of creating something so special and lasting.

Sighing, she turned and continued down the hallway. She could hardly blame her family for not taking her new career seriously; she had claimed to be equally committed to opening her own restaurant, modeling, and becoming a personal fitness trainer. Each had lasted less than a year.

In time, they would realize this was different.

And she would have time. Plenty of time. In two weeks she would have the surgery, and she'd be okay. There was nothing to be afraid of. Really.

Holding tight to that thought, Celine glanced up as she passed under an arch, at another of the chateau's decora-tions, her personal favorite: the entwined letters G and R, carved over every doorway.

Family legend had it that one of the original owners of the chateau, a knight by the name of Sir Gaston de Varennes, was responsible for that bit of artwork.

Sir Gaston, it seemed, had been quite a ladies' man—until he had met and married his wife, whom he loved so much, he had had her initial engraved with his in every castle he owned; the romantic gesture appeared in several chateaux in the region. The wife's name either had never been recorded or had been lost over the years, because the identity of "Lady R" remained a mystery.

A wistful smile curved Celine's lips as she turned down another hallway; as a child, she used to pretend that she was Lady R, that she rode with her handsome knight on a white charger through a world of pageantry and colorful tournaments and lavish banquets. And ladies with great hats.

Her smile faded. Some dreams died hard. She was *still* holding out for that kind of man: gentle, sensitive and sweet, soft-spoken and thoughtful. The perfect, chivalrous knight, devoted to his lady fair.

Not the sort of man who would leave her when the going got tough.

This time the thought of Lee brought anger and determination as well as hurt. It hadn't been fair of him to blame *her* for the incident in Lincoln Park. Maybe it had been her romantic, impulsive idea to go make snow angels at midnight—but if he hadn't fought with that gang of armed teenagers who demanded his precious BMW, she might not have been shot.

Carjacking, the media had called it. One violent moment that had changed her life and threatened to steal her future.

Her vision suddenly blurred as she passed beneath another arch and glanced up at the engraved G and R. What if this were the last time she saw the cherished hallways and tapestries of Manoir La Fontaine?

What if she weren't alive to return next year?

Celine ran the last few steps to her room. Blindly, she closed the door behind her and dropped her shoes, willing away the fear. Her heart was hammering again, and her head ached.

She rubbed her temples. Sleep. That was what she needed. In the morning she would feel better. Stronger. Able to face the truth. Able to tell her family. She wouldn't think about it now. Not tonight.

She left the lights off, savoring the cool darkness after the bright lights and noise of the *grand salon*. Leaving her shoes where they lay, she crossed unsteadily to the dresser. She unfastened her earrings and watch and dropped them on the polished top.

She could hear celebrations outside, in the streets surrounding the chateau, the citizens of the town of St. Pol singing and laughing and setting off fireworks. It must be almost midnight.

Unpinning her hat, she stepped over to the windows, into the light from the full moon that poured in through the stained glass. Looking down, she watched the snow falling softly, the twinkling lights of the houses surrounding the chateau, the blinking neon that advertised night spots in the town below.

There were a few dozen people perched atop the ancient, crumbling chateau wall, some holding cameras and telescopes aimed skyward. Celine leaned her forehead against the glass, letting the moon's silver light wash over her.

Silver. Gold. Below, she could see the chateau's outdoor heated pool and tennis courts and guest villas, and the Mercedeses and Bugattis and Aston Martins that crammed the courtyard.

Wealth. She had always taken it for granted. But her family's wealth couldn't protect her anymore.

Daddy couldn't buy her way out of this.

Her head begun to pound more fiercely. She turned away from the window. If she was going to get any sleep tonight, she would have to take an aspirin, no matter how much she hated pills.

Crossing to her armoire, she tossed her hat into the jumble of brightly colored fedoras and berets and plaid tams on the top shelf. She unzipped her dress, pulled it over her head and slung it across a hanger. Wearing only her gold silk teddy—a lacy little nothing she had picked up for six hundred dollars in Milan—she bent down and rifled through the clutter of boots and shoes on the bottom of the armoire, looking for her purse. She might have an old aspirin in it somewhere.

She found the large, hot-pink leather bag, carried it back to the bed, and sat down. Her fingers encountered passport, plane ticket, wallet, sunglasses, camera, sightseeing guidebook, a rolled-up Chicago Cubs baseball cap, and a chocolate Toblerone bar with a few bites left. No aspirin.

She closed her eyes with a shoulder-slumping sigh.

Outside, she could hear the crowd counting down: *"Six . . . cinq . . . quatre . . . trois . . . deux . . . un—Bonne Année!"*

Happy New Year.

She started to cry. It was a stupid thing to cry over, not being able to find an aspirin, but she couldn't stop the sob that had welled up inside her.

It was just so typically Celine: ready to fly around the world at a moment's notice, but unprepared for anything as simple and mundane as a headache.

It was a moment before she realized the laughter and songs outside had stopped, changed, turned into a cry of awe.

Celine opened her eyes—and gasped the same sound of wonder as she looked out the window.

The moon was slowly turning black. Disappearing into darkness! Mesmerized, she stood and stepped toward it, breathless at the sight of the night sky engulfing the lunar glow.

Suddenly a ray of the silver-blue light struck through the window. Like a prism, the stained glass condensed it into painful brilliance. Startled, blinded, Celine threw up a hand to cover her eyes, dropping her purse, falling backward.

But there was nothing beneath her.

The bed had disappeared!

Falling, she flailed wildly. There was nothing around her! Nothing to grab onto. A strange heat shimmered through her body. It felt like she was made of a million particles of fire. She opened her mouth. Screamed. She didn't hear the sound. She was falling into darkness and couldn't breathe. *Because there was no air.*

Chapter 2

Celine came awake with a start, suspended for a moment in the confusing fog between sleep and consciousness. She lay motionless in bed, groggy, unsure whether she was dreaming . . . but what she felt couldn't *possibly* be real.

Because what she felt was an arm around her waist. A burly, muscular, masculine arm.

Not daring to move or even breathe, she widened her eyes, blinking, trying to tell whether she was still asleep. She couldn't see. The room was pitch-black. There was no moonlight. No glow from the lights outside. No light at all. Like there had been a power failure.

But she was definitely awake.

And definitely not alone.

And that bare arm was definitely attached to a bare man!

Even as the shock of it stunned her, she felt a tingle of awareness chase down her body: warm breath dusting the nape of her neck, a broad, hairy chest pressed against her back, a muscled leg thrown over hers. *And nestled against her hip . . .*

Celine sat up with a yelp of panic and outrage. "Who are you and what are you *doing* in my room?" she cried, trying to untangle herself from his heavy limbs.

The man mumbled something she couldn't make out, in weary-sounding French, and recaptured her easily with his arm. Pulling her close again, he kissed her bare shoulder and settled back to sleep with a sigh.

"Stop that!" Celine demanded in fluent, frantic French, realizing she had spoken English the first time. Her heart

23

hammering, she wriggled and twisted and finally extricated herself from his embrace. She threw aside the blankets and half fell out of bed. It seemed much higher than it had before.

The man groaned. *"Chérie,"* he murmured painfully, "you make far too much noise. Stop tumbling about the floor and get back into my bed."

Celine scrambled to her feet, away from him, so terrified that her throat had closed off. It was difficult to understand what he was saying. His words were strangely accented—perhaps because his voice was muffled by the pillow and fatigue. And liquor.

Who was this naked man in her bed?

Thoughts of rape and kidnapping and various other violent crimes chased through her head. She turned to run—and slammed her knee straight into a large, square piece of furniture. It tripped her and sent her sprawling with a shout of mingled pain and surprise.

"Saints' breath," the man grumbled in that same hungover tone. "If you must cry out so loudly, *petite,* at least return to bed and let me give you reason."

For a second, Celine couldn't answer his outrageous request because she was biting her bottom lip and holding her knee. Where had that big wooden trunk come from? She didn't remember it being in her room before! And what was the crunchy stuff beneath her—like straw—all over the floor? She couldn't see it. Or the bed or the man or anything. It was too dark. And there was a strange scent in the air, like cooking herbs.

Between painful, frightened little gasps of air, she finally managed to say something. "D-don't you come near me! I'll—I'll scream!"

Even as she threatened that, she knew screaming wasn't going to do her any good. She was the only one staying in this wing of the chateau; everyone else was at the party in the *grand salon.* And the walls were so thick that no sound would get past these corridors.

Not even a bloodcurdling cry for help.

"Chérie, you speak so quickly, I cannot understand half of what you say." The man's muddled tone turned curious.

"You felt too softly rounded to be Isabeau . . . and too long of leg to be Yvonne or Babette. Are you the new wench who works in the kitchens?"

Celine got to her feet, her heart racing. If she couldn't see him in the darkness, he couldn't see her, either—and she wasn't going to give away her position by talking.

"Or mayhap one of the guests at the feast?" he mumbled into his pillow.

She began making her way quickly but cautiously around the bed toward the door, stretching her hands out in front of her to feel for obstacles, shivering. God, it was freezing in here!

"Fie, but I cannot . . . remember taking a wench to my bed at all last night," the man continued, his voice thick with equal parts alcohol and confusion. "Though it was worth celebrating the eve of the new year, with Tourelle and his party so long delayed." He rolled over with a heavy, tired chuckle. "Mayhap they are all lost in the snows somewhere. Gone forever. Never to be seen again . . ."

Celine didn't even try to make sense of his drunken ramblings. Her silent escape had carried her halfway to the door. But she was so concerned about large obstacles, she neglected to be careful of small ones.

She tripped on a stool and landed hard on the stone floor. Pain shot through her ankle, wrenching an exclamation from her lips.

"Saints' blood, demoiselle," the man gritted out, the words muffled as if he had pulled a pillow over his head. "If you do not cease your clamoring, I shall toss you out on your shapely derriere!"

Celine tried to stand and to think of some threat that would keep him away from her. "If you lay one hand on me, I'll . . . I'll . . ." Her ankle wouldn't support her weight, and her efforts to get up only landed her painfully on that part of her anatomy he had just described.

As for her unfinished threat, it only seemed to amuse him.

"You shall . . . mete out some dire punishment?" His intoxicated voice was now laced with laughter. She could hear him sitting up. "Allow me to offer a suggestion that would be most effective: kiss me into submission."

He got out of bed.

She remembered vividly that he wasn't wearing a thing.

"Don't! Don't come near me!" she cried desperately, tearfully, helplessly, holding up one hand as if that would be enough to hold him off.

To her surprise, she heard him stop and sit back down on the mattress. She still couldn't see him; though her eyes were adjusting, he was still nothing more than a black shadow in the darkness.

When he spoke, he sounded a bit more sober and serious. "Do I frighten you, *petite?*" he asked with genuine surprise. "Why?"

"Why?" she echoed incredulously. Despite the fact that he had backed off—for the moment—she was so terrified of this naked stranger who had invaded her room and her bed that her head swam dizzily and her tongue seemed incapable of forming anything more than that one stunned syllable.

"Chérie, was I . . . rough with you last night?" The words were reluctant and edged with a sharpness aimed at himself. "I was well into my cups at the feast, but I cannot believe I would . . . Saints' breath, I apologize, demoiselle, if I was less than gentle." He stood up again. "Allow me to—"

"No!" she squealed. To her surprise, he stilled again.

He didn't sit back down, but he didn't make another move toward her. "I only intend," he said softly, "to make up for whatever drunken behavior last night left you so fearful of me that you would injure yourself trying to get away."

He stayed where he was; incredibly, he seemed to be allowing her the next move.

Celine couldn't begin to figure out what was going on. Nothing in her life had prepared her for such a bizarre encounter. "I—I have no idea what you're talking about and I don't care! I'm . . . I'm getting up and I'm getting out of here. I'm going out that door, and if you try to stop me, I'll—"

"I would never do aught to force a woman, *chérie,*" he assured her quietly. "Leave, if that is what you wish."

Her mouth dry and her heart in her throat, Celine managed to get to her feet, slowly, painfully. She couldn't move much farther than that. She hobbled one step and stood there, swaying unsteadily, teeth chattering, unable to run if her life depended on it—which it just might.

After a moment, his voice sounded again from the darkness.

"Do you wish me to carry you out?" he offered lightly.

Celine realized just how ridiculous her predicament was. As he was so subtly pointing out, if he intended to hurt her, he could do it in a second and there was nothing she could do to stop him. "No," she insisted stiffly. "I'll ... I'll be fine on my own." She took only one limping step, and even that made her inhale sharply with pain.

"Mayhap I could hold the door for you?"

His teasing tone made her laugh. She couldn't help it. He had had ample opportunity for rape, kidnapping, murder, or anything in between by now; instead, he was keeping his hands to himself and tossing out one-liners.

"I can't believe this," she whispered. "I can't believe I'm standing here laughing with a naked stranger in my room."

"The room is mine, *chérie.* As is every other in the chateau."

He must be much more drunk than he sounded, Celine thought; he was having delusions of grandeur. She tried to calm down and think. He hadn't made any threatening moves toward her. Yet. Perhaps there was some rational explanation for all this. She limped two steps and reached for the lamp on her dresser.

The lamp wasn't there.

Neither was the dresser.

Her fear returned in a rush. "What is going *on?*" she asked in a small voice.

"Alas, I am no more certain than you, *chérie.* I do not remember taking you to bed last night." He yawned and stretched and sat back down on the mattress. "Though I cannot say I regret it. Noisy though you may be, you felt most pleasing curled beside me."

He chuckled, a low sound that did an odd little dance down Celine's back and made her suddenly, uncomfortably aware of the warm spot on her shoulder where he had kissed her.

"You did *not* take me to bed!" she corrected.

"Truly, *ma petite?* It was you who seduced me, then?"

"No! I—"

"Come seduce me again." He fell back on the pillows.

"Absolutely *not!*" Celine groped her way along the wall, trying to feel her way to the door. "Look, whoever you are, it sounds like you had too much to drink at the party. Maybe there was a power failure or something and you wandered into the wrong room by mistake."

A power failure. That made sense. It would explain why there wasn't a speck of light. Or heat. The air was so cold, it gave her goose bumps and stung her throat every time she inhaled. The furnace must have gone out.

He sighed and yawned again. "As I told you before, demoiselle, the chamber is mine."

It took Celine a moment to realize that the wall felt strange: her hand encountered nothing but cold, clammy, bare stone. The paintings and tapestries that had hung in her room were missing. She tried to find the light switch. It wasn't where it was supposed to be, either.

Suddenly her cheeks heated with an embarrassing thought: maybe he was right about this chamber being his. Maybe *she* was the one who had stumbled into the wrong room!

She didn't remember getting into bed. In fact, the last thing she remembered was looking through her purse for an aspirin, then stepping toward the window as the moon went black. Rays of silver-white light had glanced off the glass and blinded her, sent her reeling, then . . .

She couldn't remember anything after that. It was entirely possible that she had staggered out of her room, into the maze of corridors—and into the room of another party guest.

She turned back toward the stranger she couldn't see in the darkness. "Monsieur," she said tentatively, a bit chastened. "Perhaps I'm the one who made a mistake. I—I don't remember—"

"Nay, protest no more, little one," he interrupted, his voice easing into a low, coaxing tone. "Does it matter how we came to be together? You are here, I am here, the bed is here. You felt warm and soft beside me."

He paused, and she could almost *feel* him remembering—because she was remembering, too: what it felt like to lie snuggled against him.

He spoke again, his voice even deeper, softer, just a notch above a whisper. "Come back to bed, *chérie*. I will seduce you this time."

"No!" Celine squeaked, not sure whether she was objecting to his command or to her body's reaction. She was shivering, and not because the room was so cold. That tone he was using sent an unexpected electricity through her, tingly currents that ran from her fingertips to her bare toes and back again in a heartbeat. It left her trembling. It also made her vividly aware of just how little she was wearing: nothing but her silk-and-lace teddy.

She backed away a step, only to come up against the cold stone wall. "Monsieur, I'm—I'm afraid you don't understand. One of us has made a mistake—"

"The only mistake, *ma petite*, would be for us to waste the hours left until dawn."

That confident voice reached out to Celine through the shadows and cold, wrapping around her, warm and rich and dark as sable. She swallowed on a dry throat. Who the heck *was* this guy? A voice like that should belong to a hypnotist. To a deejay whispering above love songs on late-night radio.

To a suave playboy who could easily seduce unseen women in the darkness.

Celine froze at that thought, remembering her conversation with her sister earlier. Maybe this man wasn't here by mistake after all! "Oh, God," she whispered in shock and dismay, "did my sister put you up to this? I can't believe she would really— Listen, I don't know what she *told* you about me, but I am *not*—"

"Again you speak in riddles, *chérie*. I know naught of

you but that you felt good beside me. Very small and soft and good. Come back to bed. It is cold without you."

"You're only cold because it's freezing in here!"

"I must have been too deeply in my cups to light the hearth last night. Or too eager for you to bother." He chuckled. "It is naught. Come here to me and we will light a fire of our own."

"No! I can't—"

"Then I will come fetch you, shy demoiselle."

Celine could hear him getting out of bed. "No! Wait!" She turned and ran but barely made it two steps before her ankle gave way and she fell, hard.

Before she could do more than utter a sharp cry of pain, he was beside her. He had moved almost silently despite the crunchy stuff on the floor. The man lifted her to her feet—and into his embrace.

"Shh, sweet, you have naught to fear. Are you hurt?"

Celine couldn't answer. The sensation of being held against him stole her voice, her breath, her *mind*. She could not see him in the darkness, but she could feel him.

Oh, God, could she *feel* him!

His hands—large, warm, callused hands—drew her close until her breasts flattened against the solid wall of his ribs. She gasped at the contact, her heart thrumming wildly; the textures of her lingerie only intensified the friction of his body against hers—heat and muscle sliding across silk and softness and lace.

He stroked her temple, her jaw, then gently pressed her head to his chest. The fact that he had moved so quietly belied his size; she was tall, but he towered over her. A dense mat of hair covering broad, flat muscle roughly pillowed her cheek. His other arm flexed across her back, holding her, soothing—an arm that was hard and brawny and probably strong enough to bend steel pipe; she could only guess, because he was being very careful with her. He smelled of woolens and woodsmoke, and of a tangy, masculine spice that she sensed was not some expensive designer cologne, but him.

Celine didn't know which surprised her more: that such

a powerful man could be so gentle, or that she had stopped shivering.

She no longer felt cold or terrified. It was ridiculous—insane!—to feel safe in the arms of a naked stranger, especially one with the build of a world-class weight lifter ... but she did. She couldn't explain it. She only knew that she hadn't seen him at the party or anywhere before. No man like this could walk around without drawing the stunned attention of every red-blooded female over fourteen!

"I—I ..." She struggled to find her voice and answer his question, but couldn't think over the thunder of his steady heartbeat beneath her cheek. "Wh-what did you ask me?"

"It was naught, *ma petite.*" He laughed again, and she felt as well as heard the easy, pleasant sound this time. His voice, however, sounded strained, unsteady, as if he were just as affected as she by the unexpected currents flowing between them. "Fie, but I am hard put to remember who you are. I truly do not recall taking a woman to my bed last night—certainly not you. Even drunk, I would remember making love to you."

"We *didn't* make love," she said breathlessly. "That's what I've been telling you all—"

"It matters not. You are here now and we shall remedy the oversight. Tell me, are you one of the beauties who came to the feast with Edric and his party from Languedoc?"

"No, I'm ..." She lost her voice again. His hands were moving, to her shoulders, down her back, to her waist in a slow caress. "I'm ... from Chicago."

He lowered his head to hers. "I know not this land 'Chicago,' " he whispered, his breath warm against her lips. "But let me sample the sweetness of one of its fair flowers."

His mouth captured hers with a strong, soft heat and Celine discovered something far sexier than this man's voice or his body. *His kiss.* She never had the chance to think of a protest. To think at all.

She had been kissed before, but never like *this*.

It was neither awkward and teasing nor forceful and overpowering, but long, slow, confident, and devastating.

It was as if he were binding them together, deftly drawing her soul into his.

He tasted of wine and strong spices and the virile promise of shared pleasure. Of strength and tenderness beyond anything she had ever imagined. Her knees gave way. He held on to her effortlessly. His lips melded gently to hers . . . then gradually parted.

He angled his head, deepening the intimacy, and Celine made a small sound in the back of her throat. She didn't know what it was; she had never made a little cry like that before, almost feline, somehow . . . restless. Wanting. It seemed more like a plea than the objection she had intended. Her hands pressed against his ribs, but instead of pushing him away as she knew she should, she found herself exploring the corded muscles she encountered there, entranced by the unfamiliar angles and hardness. She felt his breathing quicken, heard a moan shudder out of him, deep and masculine.

Before she could gather up the scattered confetti of her senses, she felt herself slipping deeper into the kiss. Into him. Into this stranger in the darkness who teased her and laughed with her, touched her, awakened her, electrified her in a way no man ever had.

Before she could stop herself, her arms slid around his back and she was holding on to him as much as he was holding her.

His kiss became bolder, more intense. The first touch of his tongue against hers dragged a soft moan from her lips. She felt his arms tremble, as if he were fighting for control. His tongue flicked against hers, retreated, then returned, sliding, seeking. She tasted him, breathed him, felt hot needles of unfamiliar hunger. His bristly five-o'clock shadow rubbed roughly against her chin and jaw.

If ever she had had cause for nervousness, uncertainty, fear, it was now—but that was not what she felt.

She felt longing, she felt tenderness, she felt . . . *right*. She wanted this. As if she had been waiting her whole life.

And in her heart, she knew that she had.

She felt *alive*. More alive and whole than she had for as many months as she could remember. She nearly sobbed with the joy of it. She must have made some sound, because he broke the kiss and lifted his head.

He didn't say anything for a moment. Neither of them did. They just stood there, clinging to one another in the dark, breathing hard. The heat between them was so tangible it felt as if the furnace had been turned on, full blast.

After a second, the sensual fog that he had spun around her cleared a bit. "Wait," she whispered. "I—I can't . . . I mean, I don't—I'm not—"

"Nay, do not pull away." He lowered his head, nibbled at her lower lip, then nudged at her chin, urging her to tilt her head back. "You are all I could wish, little flower. You are fire and softness and you taste of a sweetness beyond any I have known. Stay with me," he asked. *"Touch me. Let me touch you."*

"Please, I—I think I should tell you . . . I mean, no matter what my sister told you, I'm not what she . . . I'm not . . ."

"Not what?" he urged.

"I'm not . . ."

"Not *this?*" He kissed her again, more powerfully this time.

A moan escaped from Celine's throat at the feel of that hot, deep joining of his mouth and hers, the rough stubble of his beard abrading her sensitive skin. The feelings radiating from deep within her, the pent-up yearnings, the wild fever, all constricted into an ache, focused in the center of her body. Her hands grasped his rock-hard arms and she grasped wildly for reason as she felt herself tumbling over the edge. *I can't do this! It's insane! I don't know this man! I can't even see him!*

But when he finally raised his head and ended the sweet torment he was lavishing on her, she slumped against him.

He held her easily, gently.

"My God," she whispered.

"Heaven," he promised.

"But . . . I don't even know your name."

"Gaston." His mouth claimed hers again, demanding her response with a kiss that sent the last shreds of sanity whirling away. His name barely registered, except for a brief, fleeting thought that it was old-fashioned. Uncommon. A name not heard much anymore.

His hand stroked upward, his fingers tracing over her back, her shoulders, and the silk and lace and spaghetti straps of her teddy. "Saints' breath, but 'tis strange, this garment," he murmured against her mouth. "This land of yours, this 'Chicago,' must be a far place to have such wonders as this that I have never seen. You must tell me of your home." He kissed her again, laughing. "*Later.* For now, let us greet the new year properly."

Celine was surprised that he had never seen a teddy before. She also meant to ask how it could be that he had never heard of Chicago, but instead found herself sighing in agreement. "The New Year."

He nipped a hot rain of little kisses down her neck. "I can think of no better way to celebrate the dawn of the first day of a new century."

Celine's mind was spinning, but not so much that she missed what he had said. "New century?"

"Aye, the first day of the year of our Lord 1300."

Celine stiffened.

Her heart pounded so hard she couldn't breathe.

The darkness, the cold, the strange furnishings, the straw on the floor, his unusual speech, his old-fashioned name—

"What did you say?" she sputtered, pulling out of his arms.

"*Chérie,* mayhap it is you who drank overmuch last night, if you have forgotten already the reason for the feast. This day is the first of January, 1300."

Celine stumbled away from him, barely aware of the pain in her ankle, gasping for breath as she felt her way to the far wall, over to the left, to the window.

Or where the window was supposed to be.

She found a pair of wooden shutters.

"Are you unwell, *chérie?*" Gaston asked, a hint of irritation creeping into his voice.

Celine tore open the shutters. The stained glass was there; she yanked it inward on its hinges and a blast of cold air poured into the room, along with a spill of silver light. The moon above looked normal, clear, full—

But the city was missing.

Celine stared, opened her mouth, couldn't utter a sound. Cold dread knotted her stomach. *The town of St. Pol had vanished!* Where there had been buildings, paved streets, people, motor scooters, neon, noise—there was now only silent forest.

Her gaze fell on the courtyard below. The Mercedeses and Bugattis and Aston Martins were gone. The neatly plowed circular drive was gone. The guest villas. The tennis courts. The swimming pool. One entire wing of the chateau was missing!

There was only the stone keep. A smooth blanket of new-fallen snow. The moat. The wall—which didn't look crumbling and ancient, but solid and new.

The first day of January, 1300.

This couldn't be happening! It was a dream! A nightmare!

"Chérie?"

Celine turned at the soft query.

It wasn't a dream. And the man coming toward her out of the shadows was certainly no nightmare.

As he stepped into the shaft of moonlight that framed her from behind, she saw him from the ground up: first his feet, then a pair of strong, lean legs sprinkled with dark hair, then heavily muscled thighs, then . . .

God!

Cheeks scalding, she immediately lifted her gaze to a broad, deep chest, matted with that same dark hair, impossibly wide shoulders . . . and she felt smaller and more fragile than she ever had in her life as he came completely into the light, the moon illuminating a full six sinewy feet of bronzed, taut, hard male.

His face was every bit as powerful and chiseled as the rest of him. Handsome in a rough way, with that bristly five-o'clock shadow, a mane of tousled hair as dark as his voice, and eyes that . . . She had never thought of anyone having potent eyes before, but that's what they were. Potent. Made for sending seductive glances across crowded, smoky rooms. He stopped just inside the edge of the light, smiling at her, a dazzling smile that crinkled the corners of those thickly lashed, hypnotic, coffee-hot eyes.

"Demoiselle, if you keep running out of my arms that way, you are going to greatly damage my confidence as a lover."

Celine swayed dizzily. "Did you say you were . . . but you couldn't be . . . not *that* Gaston!"

"Sir Gaston de Varennes," he confirmed, a note of pride in his voice. His smile widened. "Did you not realize that you were about to make love to the lord of the chateau?"

Celine felt the blood drain from her face. She clutched at the wooden shutter, but felt herself sinking to her knees.

Gaston was at her side in an instant, moving in that quick, silent way. *"Ma petite,* what is it that upsets you?" His voice was husky with concern as he helped her to her feet.

Celine looked up at him, but as he saw her face closely in the light for the first time, his expression changed. His smile disappeared. He stared at her eyes, at her hair.

Suddenly, his hand came up to touch the loosened chignon at the nape of her neck—and this time his fingers were faster than they were gentle. He had it unknotted in seconds. Her hair fell freely in its natural, chin-length blunt cut.

Just as quickly, he released her and stepped back. His eyes narrowed with disbelief.

"You are the Fontaine woman!" He snapped the words more like an accusation than a question.

Celine blinked, confused by the sudden change in his attitude—but at the same time relieved. At least he knew who she was. She was not losing her mind. Maybe there was some explanation for this after all.

"Yes," she replied. "Yes, of course—"

He cut her off with a particularly short, nasty-sounding oath. "I should have *guessed* Tourelle would attempt such treachery as this!" He grabbed her by the arm.

"Wait a minute!" Celine cried in astonishment. "What are you doing? I don't understand! What's going *on?*"

"Do not pretend ignorance, demoiselle. You know your purpose here," he replied sharply. "You are to become my wife this day."

Chapter 3

"**H**ow did Tourelle spirit you into my chamber?" Gaston demanded, tightening his hold on the Fontaine girl's wrist, glaring down at her in the moonlit darkness. "What was his plan? Why did he wish me to bed you when he wants this match no more than I?"

She seemed unable to speak, or move, or do anything but stare at him, wild-eyed and trembling. She almost crumpled, but he held her upright—and tried to ignore the fact that his body felt heavy and hard with wanting her. He could not cool the desire she had roused in him. *Damn* her.

By nails and blood, apart from her burnished red hair, his unwanted bride was not at all what he had been told to expect. She looked naught like a convent-raised innocent; she looked like a fallen angel, created to sate a man's needs, to fire a man's body with hell's own heat and heaven's own pleasure. She had appeared out of the darkness like a fantasy plucked from midnight dreams and sent floating in on a ray of moonlight.

He ground out an oath, struggled to right his thoughts—and instead found his gaze fastened on the indecent garment she wore. It shimmered over lush curves, concealing and revealing and tantalizing. Her tall, slim form fitted to his perfectly. Her kisses still burned on his mouth, on his memory.

The urge to carry her to the bed and lose himself in her heat almost overpowered him. Almost made him forget his vow to leave this girl untouched; if he compromised her, it would make their betrothal binding and an annulment impossible.

Which would end his plans for vengeance and justice.

"Answer me, woman," he ordered in a low, taut voice,

fighting the desires that threatened his control. "How did you steal past my guards?"

"I . . . I'm . . . I . . ." She gasped for breath, then started sobbing. "Oh, God, I've finally lost it! I'm having a nervous breakdown! This can't be happening! *It isn't real!*"

It was difficult for him to understand her words—especially when she was crying and talking at the same time. From what he could make out, she seemed to doubt his identity. "I assure you, I am as real as our betrothal, Lady Christiane." He tightened his grasp to underscore his point.

"But you can't be! I can't—Chris *who?*"

"Do not think to play games with me," he warned sharply, walking her backward into the stone wall. "You have already admitted to being the Fontaine woman. Now you claim not to recognize your own name?"

"I am not 'Lady Christiane'! I'm not Lady anybody. My name is Celine. Celine Fontaine. I'm from America. From Chicago! There's been a mis—"

"Lies will not save you," he snapped. "You are Lady Christiane de la Fontaine, ward of the Duc de la Tourelle. You were to arrive last week from a convent in Aragon for our wedding. We thought the snows had delayed you."

She gaped at him as if he were speaking a foreign tongue, then started shaking her head. "I don't know what you're talking about! I don't know any *duc* and I've never been in a convent and I don't even know where Aragon is! I am *not* Christiane—"

"Then how do you explain your hair?" His hand came up to touch her short red tresses—and before he could stop himself, he had buried his fingers in the silken strands, hating himself for wanting to feel it, hating her for making him want to feel every inch of her. "What woman but a novice would cut her hair off in such a way?" he growled. "And what of your speech? If you are not from Aragon, then explain your strange accent. And how did you come to be in my chamber, in my *bed?* Wearing *this!*" He touched the plunging bodice of the shameless bit of silk; she gasped and squeezed her eyes shut, shuddering as if terrified that he meant to do more.

Gaston clenched his jaw. Tourelle obviously had had time to think and plan during his long, cold journey to Aragon; he had evidently decided it would be well to have a marriage tie to the Varennes lands as well as the claim through his mother's line. The girl could protest her innocence until her last breath, but the garment she wore was clearly intended for seduction—even if she had lost her nerve and decided to run when the moment was at hand.

"Explain yourself, demoiselle," he taunted, sliding his hands under the slim ribbons that held the garment up. He could snap them both with one flick of his fingers.

Her long lashes fluttered upward and a shiver coursed through her, whether from fear at being discovered or in response to his touch he knew not. Her tongue darted out nervously to wet her lips and a newly sharpened blade of desire speared through him. Her slender form stiffened; he knew she could feel his body's response to hers. The mutual awareness only intensified his physical hunger for her—which made him angry.

His scowl made her drop her gaze from his. "I—I can't explain how I got here because I don't know how it happened," she whispered after a moment. "You have to believe me—I know this sounds insane ... m-maybe I *have* gone insane ... but when I stepped into this room to go to bed, *the year was 1993.*"

Gaston exhaled through his teeth, willing away the havoc her lithe body and soft voice wreaked upon his senses. "Do you mistake me for a fool?" He glowered at her with a look he usually reserved for enemies on the battlefield. "What I believe, demoiselle, is that you are every bit as treacherous and cunning as your overlord."

Her expression reflected an almost painful mingling of fear and confusion. "I don't *have* an 'overlord'! I'm not who you think I am! I don't know what I'm doing here or how I got here or—" She shut her eyes again. "Oh, God, this can't be happening! It's got to be a dream. *It's got to be a dream!*"

Tears suddenly spilled onto her cheeks, tiny drops of shimmering crystal in the moonlight. Gaston released her before he could give in to the mad impulse that seized him . . . a tender urge to take her in his arms and comfort her.

He spat an oath and spun away, forcing aside the foolish, gentle feeling, along with the fierce desire she had ignited. Stalking to the far side of the room, he snatched up his clothes from where he had dropped them the night before, donning them by feel in the darkness.

He could not allow this wench to ply her feminine wiles on him. Nay, he knew himself too well. Women besotted him as easily as gaming and drink; they bewitched him, rendered him senseless. He had counted on Tourelle's ward being a dull, naive little novice, easy to resist—not this stunning, sensual creature.

Pulling his woolen leggings on with impatient motions, he devised a plan. He would *not* be forced into marriage with this lying red-haired beauty. Her feigned madness was no doubt part of some scheme she had devised with her overlord.

Or mayhap the wench *was* insane, as she had claimed. He jerked his fur-lined surcoat over his head, picked up his belt, and fastened it with a yank. Saints' blood, she certainly raved like a madwoman. Mayhap that was why her family had banished this girl to a distant, foreign convent at such a young age. To rid themselves of a lunatic.

By nails and blood, sane or not, he was not going to take the wench to wife—not now that he had evidence of Tourelle's treachery. He shoved his boots on, picked up his knee-length woolen tunic, and turned toward Christiane again.

She had fallen to the floor. She knelt in the rushes beneath the window, crying, one hand over her eyes, the other braced upon the stone as if she needed something solid to hold her up.

Unbidden feelings struck him with a suddenness that was like a fist in the gut. She looked so small and pale in that ribbon of bright moonlight, fragile as a snowflake that would melt at a single harsh word. She roused confusing, conflicting instincts in him, urges to ravish and protect, to—

He strangled every single emotion he felt.

Every bit of weakness.

He flung the tunic at her feet. "Garb yourself, woman."

She flinched and raised her head. Their gazes locked and burned across the brief distance between them. A second later she snatched up the garment and held it against her, as if realizing only then how indecently clothed she was. How naked to his eyes. How much intimacy they had shared a moment ago.

How close they had almost come to sharing the deepest intimacy a man and a woman could know.

"Do you believe me?" she asked hopefully. "Will you help me?"

It took a moment before Gaston could tear his eyes from her parted lips long enough to answer. "What I believe, demoiselle," he said harshly, "is that you would say or do anything to save yourself, now that you have been discovered. But it is too late for your pleas. You are the evidence I needed that Tourelle is a lying viper who intends not peace but treachery by this marriage."

He crossed the chamber until he stood towering over her. "And as soon as I present you to the King, he will end this farce of a betrothal. Let us go and awaken him."

Celine's heart pounded so hard she couldn't hear anything over the roar of her own pulse. Gaston barely gave her two seconds to put on his heavy, scratchy shirt before he pulled her out into the hallway. He grabbed a torch from an iron sconce on the wall and took a firm grip on her upper arm as he headed into the darkness.

She had no choice but to go with him, limping, barefoot, the stone corridor cold beneath her feet, her hair a wild tangle that clung to her tear-dampened cheeks. He walked quickly, without regard for her injured ankle, making her keep up with him.

Her mind and body had gone almost numb with confusion and fear. But beneath the terror, some part of her brain was still working. She was vividly aware of her surroundings: the biting cold of the air, the heat of the torch in Gaston's hand, the rough cloth of the shirt she wore, the tangy, masculine scent of him that clung to the fabric.

All her senses told her in no uncertain terms that this wasn't a dream.

But if it wasn't a dream, then what in the name of God was it?

She was still in Manoir La Fontaine—but she *wasn't*. There were too many things missing from the hallway. Things that had been there only hours before—moments before?—when she had walked to her room. *Things that couldn't have just disappeared.* The brilliantly colored tapestries. Paintings and statues and gilt-framed mirrors. Carpets. Lights. The letters G and R carved over the doorways. Antique tables. A phone. All vanished.

At the end of the corridor, Gaston thrust open a door and led her down a spiral stair. One that hadn't been there before. It made her feel disoriented and dizzy all over again. She stumbled on the smooth stone steps, but Gaston held her upright and kept moving downward. Then her memory supplied the reason she had never seen these stairs before: the chateau had been bombed in World War II and this section had been destroyed.

The steps beneath her feet, connecting the upper floors to the ground level of the chateau, *hadn't been there since 1942.*

The thought sent her mind and senses reeling. Anxiety knotted in the back of her throat and choked off her breath. If Gaston hadn't been firmly in control, she would have tripped and fallen. Her lungs burned for air, but she couldn't even manage to inhale.

When they reached the main level, Gaston turned abruptly, opened another door, pulled her into a shadowed room lit by torches. He finally stopped. Celine's eyes widened.

She gasped a shuddery throatful of air—then started to hyperventilate.

It was a cavernous chamber. A . . . a huge . . . *great hall*. Like something out of a movie. Camelot. Robin Hood. As they stepped inside, there was a sudden din of dogs barking and men rousing themselves from sleep.

A fire burned in an enormous hearth at one end. Huge axes and swords hung on the walls. There was straw all over the floor. Long wooden tables and benches were strewn about. And people were strewn about, sleeping on pallets along the walls. On the floor. On the benches and tables. All of them wearing clothes like Gaston's. And there were metal mugs and wooden plates and food scraps and discarded bones scattered over the floor. And dogs sleeping next to and half on top of people. It was cold and damp and drafty and it smelled like smoke and beer and roasted meat and it was all unmistakably . . .

Real.

Celine felt her legs give way and a dark gray fog closed in from the edges of her vision. She almost fainted, but Gaston kept her on her feet, shifting his grip to hold her up with an arm around her waist.

"Do not think a display of feminine weakness will sway me, demoiselle," he said coldly. "You will face your King and explain yourself to him."

Celine didn't reply. She couldn't. All she could manage in that moment was to focus on just . . . drawing . . . her . . . next . . . breath. Gaston's arm around her felt solid and strong, and she couldn't keep denying what she was seeing, hearing, smelling, feeling, breathing. She was standing there . . . *not* dreaming, *not* crazy.

In the year 1300.

Gaston let her go and she swayed unsteadily. He threaded his way through the sleeping people. Many had already heard their lord's arrival and were getting to their feet. Others sat up at the sound of Gaston's voice, groaning, looking groggy. He shook some of them by the shoulders. "Awaken!" His words echoed off the distant ceiling. "Our guest from Aragon is arrived at last!"

Celine found herself almost instantly surrounded by men and women rubbing the sleep from their eyes and looking at her with bleary—and decidedly hostile—stares.

"Matthieu, Royce," Gaston said to two of the men as he pushed his way back to her side through the gathering crowd. "Rouse the guards and search the grounds. It seems our friend Tourelle has some scheme in mind, for he sent his beloved Christiane in alone. The cur no doubt lies in wait nearby to see whether his ruse has succeeded. Find him."

The men hurried off, and others with them. Celine realized with a sinking feeling that the faces of the people surrounding her had become even less friendly. She tried to get her careening mind and wild heartbeat under control. She had to pull herself together. She had to get these people to believe her!

"W-wait a minute," she said, forcing words past her dry throat at last. "I'm not who you—"

"Save your lies." Gaston took her arm again. "Mayhap they will amuse the King. Let us see what he thinks of your sudden arrival, my *innocent* Lady Christiane." Pulling her with him, he turned and headed toward the rear of the chamber, his people moving aside to clear a path.

A strapping blond teenager ran ahead to open a door on the far side of the hall, near the hearth. Celine's panic meshed with a fresh wave of shock as the significance of what Gaston had said sank in.

The King?

As in the *King of France?*

He led her through the door into a side chamber. This one had a smaller fireplace, a large glass window on one side, and two men sitting on stools in front of yet another door. They were dressed differently from everyone else, in white-and-blue velvet tunics. Both were dozing but scrambled to their feet when Gaston entered.

"Milord?" one of them queried. They blinked at her, looking her over from short hair to bare toes with curious expressions.

"My betrothed is arrived," Gaston said dryly. "And as you might tell from the state of her garb, all is not well. I would speak with the King."

"Please, please listen to me!" Celine's voice was as thready as her pulse. She tried to unfasten herself from Gaston's hold. "I am *not* your betrothed!"

None of the men paid any attention to her. The guards were obeying Gaston's request. One opened the door behind their stools and disappeared, while the other shooed out the throng of whispering, uneasy people who were trying to crowd in from the great hall.

When the room was emptied and the door closed, Gaston finally let her go, leaning against a nearby trestle table. He smiled at her, a smile that was predatory, triumphant—and much more unpleasant than the openly hostile stares the people in the hall had given her. Somehow, that one look made her feel more alone and afraid than any of the other mind-numbing blows she had suffered tonight.

"Stop looking at me that way! Please, you don't understand! I'm not—"

The door on the other side of the chamber suddenly swung open and Celine turned to find herself facing a tall, fair-haired man not much older than Gaston. Only the velvet shirt and leggings he wore set him apart from the rumpled, weary bunch in the hall. His blue eyes narrowed as they fastened on her. "Lady Christiane?"

"Sire, I ask pardon for disturbing you at this hour." Gaston stepped forward and dropped to one knee. When Celine didn't move, he yanked her down beside him. "Apparently, my liege," he continued, slanting her an irritated glance, "this *innocent* is so unschooled in worldly ways that she does not know enough to bow before her liege."

"Leave us." The King motioned curtly to his guards. He kept studying Celine as Gaston rose. She was trembling too hard to get up until the King took her hand and helped her to her feet. "Milady, what strange garb is this you wear?" He turned his gaze to Gaston. "And where is Tourelle?"

"Precisely what I would wish to know, sire," Gaston said darkly, not giving Celine a chance to speak. "I have my men searching for him even now. I awoke not an hour ago to find my betrothed in my bed, wearing a garment so shocking I will not shame her by forcing her to show it to you. Tourelle obviously thought to trick me into compromising her."

Celine felt a cold lump in her stomach as she found herself the object of yet another angry glare, this one more regal and intimidating than any of the others.

"Is this true, Lady Christiane?" the King demanded.

She summoned what shreds of courage she could. "I'm . . . I'm *not* Lady Christiane. My name is Celine and I—"

"She feigns madness, sire. She claims to be from a place called 'Chicago'. But she admitted to me that she *is* the Fontaine girl. She cannot explain how she came to be in my bed. And one has only to look at her and hear her to know her identity."

"Aye," the King agreed, nodding. "She looks most like the description I received. But why would Tourelle wish you to bed her? He was as much opposed to this marriage as you."

Celine tried to get a word in, but they talked right over her.

"True, sire—or so we believed. He obviously had time to devise a plan while journeying here from Aragon. Had he managed to overcome my vow not to bed her, the betrothal would have been binding and an annulment impossible." Gaston folded his arms over his chest. "My new wife would inherit all, were some untimely fate to befall me. Tourelle no doubt intended to bide his time and make it seem accidental, to avoid your wrath. He probably promised the wench some reward for her role in it."

Celine gaped at him as he related his theory. At least now she understood why he had so suddenly turned furious at finding her in his bed! Because he had sworn *not* to make love to her—to Christiane, that was. He thought she was involved in some enemy's plot against him.

Both men looked at her expectantly.

"Well?" Gaston prompted when she didn't say anything. "Do you still insist on your deception? Do you still claim you are from this place that does not exist?"

She glanced from one glowering male to the other, her heart hammering. She was finally being given a chance to squeeze a word in edgewise and explain—but how could she?

How could she explain the way she had suddenly appeared in Gaston's bed? She didn't understand it herself! She could only guess that it had something to do with the lunar eclipse. That ray of blinding moonlight had somehow snatched her world from beneath her feet and landed her here.

But how could she make them believe she was from almost *seven hundred years in the future?* She had no proof. No way to convince them. No one to back up her wild-sounding story.

Swallowing hard, she dropped her gaze to the rush-strewn floor, looking at her bare feet. "No . . . I—I mean . . . yes . . . I . . ." Her voice dissolved into a whisper as the full truth of her predicament hit home. "I'm . . . I'm from a country that won't even be discovered for almost . . . two hundred years."

It overwhelmed her to think about it. She had no idea how to get home. No way to get help. No way to get in touch with her family. She was in a time when there were no phones, no electricity, no cars, no planes. No refrigeration, no running water, no sanitation, no technology, no medicines—

Celine started to hyperventilate again.

No doctors.

At least no neurosurgeons.

And if she didn't get home fast, she was going to be in far worse trouble than she was in now.

Her mind reeled. How long did she have? Months? Weeks? How long before the bullet fragment in her back shifted enough to kill her? If she didn't return to her own time and have the operation she needed . . .

She was going to die.

"Do you see, sire?" Gaston asked with satisfaction when she didn't say anything more. "She is caught in her scheme and cannot admit to it. Tourelle does not want peace. He wants my blood. Since you have prevented him from getting it by war, he will be equally happy to obtain it by treachery—using her as his weapon."

"I am not so sure, Gaston," the King replied. "Lady Christiane, how did you come to be here? Where is the rest of your traveling party?"

"I . . . I don't know. I don't know how I got here or anything else." She raised her head, tears sliding down her cheeks. "Except that I'm not who you think I am. I'm not Christiane. My name is *Celine* Fontaine. Please, you must believe me. I'm from . . . from a place that's far away and I *have* to get home."

"Hmm." The King raised one eyebrow. "Gaston, there is a possibility you have not thought of. Mayhap it was not the snow that delayed her arrival—their caravan might have encountered some misfortune along the roads. She acts most like one whose memory has been affected by a blow to the head."

Gaston's expression revealed what he thought of that idea. "If that is true, sire, how did she find her way here alone? Nay, she must have had someone instructing her."

The King sighed heavily. "It is no matter. The bride is arrived and the wedding will proceed."

Celine inhaled so sharply the cold air hurt her lungs. "No! I can't—"

"My liege!" Gaston protested. "You cannot ask me to marry her now! Knowing that there is at least suspicion—"

"It is mysterious how she came to be here, aye. But there is no point in delaying. You are here, your betrothed is here, does it matter how you came to be together?"

Celine blushed furiously and Gaston grimaced at the King's choice of words. "But, sire, surely we should await Tourelle's arrival to have the truth of the matter."

"The truth of how she came to be here will not change what I have decreed shall be," the King replied hotly. "All is in readiness and I must return to Paris this day. Before I leave, I would see peace assured. The wedding shall take place as planned this morning." He turned to go back to bed.

"My liege!" Gaston said in a rough-edged voice. "I will wed this girl as you command, but I vow to you again that I will not consummate the marriage. I will expose Tourelle for the murdering bastard he is—and then I will have an annulment. I *will not rest* until I have both vengeance and justice. At any cost!"

The King spun on his heel, his eyes full of fury. "You tread upon the limits of my patience, Varennes. One step more and I will call it treason! The *cost* of your vengeance may be all that you hold dear."

"Excuse me!" Celine finally managed to interrupt the masculine bluster. "But you both seem to be forgetting something. I am *not* going to marry anybody."

The two men turned to her with looks of surprise, as if the chair or the table had just spoken.

"Milady, you have no voice in the matter," the King stated in a patient tone one might use with a child. "The decision has been made by your overlord."

"By my—my—" Celine stuttered, a wave of feminist pique overwhelming the fear and confusion and everything else she felt. "For the last time, I don't *have* any overlord! I'm not Christiane and I'm *not* going to marry him!"

"I would not force the lady against her wishes," Gaston offered gallantly.

"You will *both* do as your *King* wishes! We shall end this foolishness once and for all. Go, both of you, and garb yourselves properly for your wedding."

She never had a chance to get away.

No chance to run.

And she wasn't sure *where* she would run if she did. Into the forest? In the snow and freezing cold? She had no idea how many miles it might be to the nearest town. How would she survive? She had never exactly been the L. L. Bean type; her family had always teased that Celine's idea of roughing it was a hotel without cable TV.

And even if she could get away, what kind of people might be out there? What might they do to a woman found alone?

Those thoughts chased round and round through her head as she stood at the entrance to the chateau's small chapel, shivering and alone, facing row after row of un-friendly faces.

This wasn't a great choice—but it was her only choice.

The animated hum of voices, all speaking that stilted-sounding old French, died down as she stepped forward.

She wore a faded yellow velvet gown, grudgingly loaned to her by one of the maids who had helped her dress. It was too tight and too short, and more than one pair of eyes dipped to look disapprovingly at her immodestly displayed figure, at her ankles, and at her red silk slippers.

They clashed with the dress, but they were the only ones big enough that the women had been able to find.

Or maybe the women had just told her that. She sus-pected they had done it on purpose, to let her know ex-actly how unwelcome she was.

She didn't have a hat or a veil or anything in her hands. No one had offered so much as a single dried-out flower;

she had nothing to hold on to to steady her shaking fingers. Her head pounded as hard and as painfully as her rapid heartbeat. She stood there, unable to move, staring at the man who waited at the end of the aisle.

This unpredictable giant who hours ago had touched her, kissed her, caressed her in a way that still made her tremble, then sworn he would never do so again.

This dark lord who despised her.

This man she was about to marry.

A shaft of morning sunlight streamed in through the stained-glass windows behind him, bathing his tall, angular form in swirling jewel tones. The brightness only made him look all the more shadowy and forbidding.

She took a step. One tentative step toward the raven-haired knight dressed all in black, with a black lion embroidered on his tunic and his black mood showing clearly in his hard features. His eyes—those potent, smoky eyes—captured hers, willing her away, wishing her to drop through the floor and disappear.

On that, she thought desperately, they were in total agreement.

She took another step, trying again to think of some way out of this. A few minutes of wild pleading with the serving women had made her realize that she had better stop sounding like a lunatic. She had no way to prove she was from the future—and no idea what people in this time might do to someone they considered mentally unstable. Images of being carted off to some medieval asylum or burned at the stake as a heretic finally made her shut up.

Everyone from the King to the page boys believed her to be Christiane. For now, she had decided, she had better keep quiet and play along. She had no choice; while she couldn't begin to figure out how the lunar eclipse had landed her here, some part of her sensed that she might have to go *out* the same way she had come *in*—through the window in Gaston's bedchamber upstairs.

At least she wouldn't have to sleep with him. She was grateful for that. Not only did he dislike her—Christiane, rather—he was adamant that he had no intention of consummating their vows.

All she had to do was get through this for a few days, she told herself, taking another step forward, then another, her throat dry as a dust storm.

All she had to do was hold out until the *real* Christiane showed up—which should be any minute now, from the sound of it—and they would discover what a huge mistake had been made. By then, she would have figured out some way to convince them who she really was. Then they would help her find some way to get home. Until then . . .

Until then, she was on her own. She would have to rely completely on herself.

For the first time in her life.

She reached the end of the aisle and knelt beside Gaston, feeling the heat—and the resentment—radiating from his large form. The ceremony was a blur, an endless drone of Latin interrupted only by everyone's impatience when the priest had to repeat each word she was supposed to say, one at a time.

She barely remembered Latin from her lessons in private school, but she was quite sure one of the words she said had something to do with "obedience."

She grated it out and told herself it didn't matter, that this was a temporary arrangement and she wasn't really Christiane . . . so it didn't really count.

The next thing she knew, Gaston was taking her left hand and slipping a ring on her finger. The gold band felt hot from being held in his hand. Her skin tingled with sensitivity where he had touched her for even that brief second. The weight of the ring seemed awkward and unfamiliar. Heavy.

The mass went on endlessly, until her entire body ached with stiffness and she was sure her knees had rubbed permanent hollows in the stone floor. Everyone in the chapel was joining in a responsive prayer when a harsh whisper from Gaston startled her.

"You have not won yet."

"What?" she whispered back.

Not moving his head, he slanted her a steely glance. "You and Tourelle have not won yet. I promise you, wench, you will regret your part in this if you do not cooperate with me. I mean to have done with you anon and I *will* marry Lady Rosalind."

The name arrowed straight into Celine's memory.

Lady Rosalind.

Lady R.

The woman whose initial he would someday carve with his above the chateau doors. Celine surprised herself by whispering her thoughts aloud. "The woman you love."

"Love?" he replied scathingly. "Love is a weakness for fools who know no better. Whatever I may feel for Rosalind, it is certain what I feel for *you*. Contempt."

Whether it was something in his voice or something in her, Celine felt another unexpected emotion welling up from the tangled knot inside her. Jealousy. "As if you're Sir Perfect," she muttered under her breath. "If you're so chivalrous and devoted, what were you doing seducing some unknown woman last night?"

"You will find I take my pleasure where I will—a habit which I have no intention of changing. Ever."

"Fine. I don't care. It will keep you away from me."

"On that we are agreed. I intend to apply for an annulment with haste. And you, my deceitful little wife, will help me obtain it. If you do not, I vow that you will discover for yourself why some call me Blackheart."

Before Celine could reply, the priest cleared his throat.

Only then did she realize the prayer had ended. Everyone must have overheard the last part of their conversation. Her face burned.

"Sir Gaston," the priest repeated patiently, shifting to French. "You have been pronounced man and wife. It is time to kiss the bride, to seal your vow."

Gaston turned her to face him, his dark eyes blazing, his fingers burning right through the worn velvet of her yellow gown. As his mouth brushed over hers, Celine couldn't help the quick clenching of her heart, the heat swirling through her, or the uncomfortable question flitting through her mind.

Which vow?

Chapter 4

This wasn't exactly the kind of medieval pageantry she had always imagined.

Celine felt queasy as she stared down into the plate before her—a "trencher," everyone called it. A square, stale piece of bread that soaked up juices from the chunk of half-charred meat a servant had plunked on it. Beside it sat a bowl of thin soup with bits of something unidentifiable floating on top, and a platter with two partridges, roasted whole.

At least she *thought* they were partridges; she didn't want to guess what other sort of birds they might be.

The greasy smells alone were enough to make her stomach clench, never mind the tense, stultifying silence that held the room captive.

The great hall overflowed with people celebrating the wedding feast, but only the occasional clink of a knife on a metal platter, the splash of more wine being poured, or a hushed request for salt broke the tomblike quiet. The hearth crackling at her back was the loudest sound in the chamber—and the only warmth.

Celine and her new *husband*—she had to force herself even to think the word—had been sitting beside each other on a dais, not speaking, for what felt like hours. Gaston slouched in a huge carved chair next to hers, satisfying his apparently ravenous appetite, occasionally glowering at her over the edge of his battered metal goblet.

She mostly kept her eyes on her trencher, thinking about what the King had said before he departed. His Majesty had left for Paris after wolfing down only a few mouthfuls of food, offering one last warning to the newlyweds: they were to do no harm to each other, "lest the offending parties forfeit their holdings."

Celine wasn't exactly sure what that meant, but it sounded ominous. *Do no harm?*

She darted a nervous glance at Gaston.

He was tearing into his partridge, using his knife and bare hands to rip it to pieces with quick, brutal efficiency.

A shudder ran through her. He wouldn't actually *harm* her, would he? A few hours ago, she hadn't thought so . . . but as she watched him make short work of that poor little bird, his blade flashing in the firelight, she again questioned her sanity in agreeing to this marriage.

But it was too late for second thoughts.

Swallowing hard, she turned her gaze to the people sitting at trestle tables arrayed below the dais. They ate with their fingers or knives, wiping their hands on the tablecloths; forks apparently had yet to be invented. Huge, wolfish-looking hounds wandered among the tables, snarling over scraps, bones, and other refuse that littered the rushes.

The noise of slobbering, fighting dogs killed whatever was left of Celine's appetite. She tore off a corner of her trencher, squishing it between her thumb and forefinger into a little cube. As she toyed with her food, she became aware of the stray glances and whispers being cast her way. It looked like she was the main topic of interest among the velvet-garbed guests.

They were no doubt discussing her unusual height, her odd accent, the way she had stumbled through her vows during the wedding ceremony, her decidedly un-nunlike attitude. All of it seemed to be explained away by other guests, however, with knowing looks and a single mouthed word: "Aragon."

Wherever it was, Aragon was apparently as distant and foreign as Borneo to these people.

Or about as distant and foreign as this place was to her.

She couldn't help wondering whether the awful food was intended to make her feel unwelcome, like the faded yellow dress and scarlet shoes she wore.

Celine dropped her gaze to her lap, feeling heat prickling at the back of her eyes. What if she were stuck here? What if she couldn't get home?

What if she didn't *live* long enough to get home?

In that moment, she would've given anything to hear her mother call her "darling, darling." To have Jackie tease her. To be smothered by parental lectures about her impulsive, flighty ways. Would she ever see them again? They must be frantic over her sudden disappearance. By now they probably had the CIA, the FBI, Interpol, and the French Sûreté all out searching.

But the best cops in the world wouldn't be able to track her down here. There wasn't going to be any daring rescue. Not unless she rescued herself.

Blinking back the tears, she sat up straighter. She couldn't allow herself the luxury of getting depressed. She had to focus on making it through this and going home. It was a race against time—and she had no idea how much time she had. How many days or weeks before the bullet fragment in her back shifted enough to kill her.

But she knew the clock was ticking.

"Our wedding feast is not to your liking, my lady wife?"

Startled by Gaston's low voice, Celine dropped the piece of bread she had been toying with. She turned a wary glance on him. "The food is . . . not what I'm used to," she whispered, mindful of how her voice carried.

He stabbed the little partridge again and ate a chunk of meat from the tip of his knife. "You were accustomed to finer fare at your convent in Aragon?" he asked with a skeptically raised eyebrow, chewing.

She hesitated, trying to imagine whether nuns would have better food, guessing the answer by his attitude. "Uh . . . no," she said after a moment. "I mean . . . not really." She had been playing her role for only a few hours, yet she was already finding it wearying, having to constantly think of what the real Christiane would say, what she would do. "This is just . . . different from what I'm used to at home."

Gaston poured himself more wine from a nearby flask. "Do you miss your home already? I would think a wench such as you would be pleased to escape an impoverished cloister for the comforts of a chateau."

"I am not a wench, and I wish you would stop calling me that. And yes, I miss my home," Celine replied tartly. After a heartbeat, she added under her breath, "And as for my being impoverished, my father is one of the most renowned and wealthy heart surgeons in the world, and he flies—"

"Your father *flies?*" Gaston laughed so hard he almost choked on his wine. *"Ma dame,* your father died years ago, without a sou to his name. And never have I heard of him working as a barber-surgeon. Or having wings."

Celine bit her bottom lip. She would have to be careful not to let pride run away with her; if she couldn't keep her temper from getting tangled up with her tongue, she would find herself the newest resident of the nearest asylum. She was supposed to be trying to fit in. She was supposed to be Christiane—an innocent young thing who had spent her entire life sheltered behind the walls of a poor convent. "I . . . I meant—"

"If only you had inherited his gift of flight," Gaston said dryly, slouching lower in his seat. "There is naught I would like better than for you to fly away and be gone."

Celine was uncomfortably aware that the dozens of guests in the hall were hanging on their every word. "Please believe me, monsieur, that's exactly what I want, too. I'd like nothing better than to go *home.* Unfortunately, it looks like we're stuck with one another, for now."

Gaston leaned forward in his chair, slowly lowering his goblet to the table. He looked at her with a curious expression, eyes glittering. "If you truly mean what you say, there is no need for us to be 'stuck with' one another at all. All you need do is go to the King and reveal whatever it is Tourelle is planning. You can be home within the month."

Celine looked away. "I can't explain anything to the King. Not for the reasons you think—I just can't. You've got to believe me. I'd get out of your life right this second if I could. Really. I'm *not* in on any plot against you."

"You are not?" His voice dropped a note lower. *"Ma dame,* mayhap I have misjudged you. Mayhap you have been forced into this against your will."

Celine turned toward him. His face was only inches from hers, his expression one of seeming misgiving and gentleness that made her stomach feel all fluttery—even as she told herself she couldn't trust him. "Yes, actually, in a way I was."

He smiled, a low-beam version of his knee-weakening dazzler. "Then, if you do not wish to be here, you would agree to help me obtain an annulment?"

Celine almost said yes—then stopped herself. If she agreed to that, she would no doubt be sent packing in the wink of one of his dusky lashes. She would find herself alone and vulnerable in a world she knew nothing about. For now, Gaston was her only protection. "I'm . . . I'm not sure that would be—"

"Come, *ma petite,*" he coaxed. "Do not allow loyalty to Tourelle to sway you. Your faith in your overlord is misplaced. Have you forgotten so quickly the lessons learned in your convent? It is not always easy to choose good over the temptations of evil—but you *know* the right course to choose in this: admit the truth before the King."

Celine's heart beat unevenly. There was something unnerving about hearing him say the word "temptations." And it seemed ironic, to say the least, for a man who looked darker and more dangerous than the Devil himself to be offering her a lecture on good and evil. "I . . . I can't."

He leaned closer, his voice as persuasive as it had been last night in his bedchamber. "Has Tourelle threatened you in some way? Do you fear him? I will protect you, Christiane. I will escort you home to your convent personally and see that you are well guarded. With our marriage annulled, you will be free to take your vows and join the cloister. Is that not what you wish?"

She turned away, unable to withstand the urgency in his gaze. "You don't understand."

"Nay, *chérie,* I do not. I do not understand why you would be so stubborn when it is within your power to end this with but a few words." He reached out and gently placed a finger beneath her chin, turning her face toward him. "Stand with me before the King and admit what scheme Tourelle intends. It is best for us both. Our liege will forgive you your part in this. *I* will forgive you. You will be safe."

Safe? Celine could hardly steal a breath, feeling the warmth of his touch, the contrast of his rough, callused finger against her skin that had been softened by years of pampering and expensive facials. His eyes held hers, and Celine felt herself falling deep and then deeper still into those hot, lavish-lashed pools of darkness. Danger and drowning waited within, yet tempted and compelled at the same time. "Gaston," she whispered, "please don't ask me to—"

"Has he promised you some boon for your part in this?" he replied, leaning even closer, his breath warm against her mouth. "Jewels? Wealth? Is that what you seek, rather than life in a convent? I will double whatever he has offered. Do what is *right* and you will want for naught."

He was so urgent, so persuasive, Celine almost wished she could do what he asked of her. She clenched her fists in frustration against the worn velvet of her gown. It was impossible. She couldn't explain Tourelle's plot to the King. She had never even met this supposed "overlord" of hers. Even if she tried to make something up, it wouldn't sound plausible.

And if her marriage to Gaston were annulled, she would be banished from the chateau. She wouldn't be able to stay close to that window in the upstairs bedchamber—which just might be her only way back to her own time.

"I can't!" she cried, pulling away from his touch. "I can't explain why, but I can't say anything to the King and I can't agree to an annulment!"

Gaston stiffened. The softness in his expression vanished and he straightened with a jerk. "Your misplaced loyalty to Tourelle will be your ruin, *ma dame.*"

Celine didn't know what upset her more—the sharp emphasis he put on the word "ruin," or the fact that his eyes, his voice, his words shifted so quickly from warmth to cool malice. "You weren't thinking of me at all just now, were you?" she accused hotly, incensed that Gaston's easy, powerful charm had almost reeled her in when she should know better. "You don't care what happens to me. You were just saying what you thought I wanted to hear."

He smiled again, but this time it had a cold, cynical edge. "You wound me, *chérie*. I wish to do what is best for us both."

"Best for *you*, you mean. What kind of knight are you, anyway? What about honor? What about chivalry?"

"What of them? As I warned you, *ma dame*, refuse to help me and you will discover how I earned the name Blackheart." His expression hardened. "I was one of the good Christians who took part in the slaughter of two hundred Saracens at Jaffa in 1290. I returned home and became a mercenary purely for the booty and the bloody love of battle. I stole the very castle you are sitting in now by cheating in a tourney. I have oft found honor and chivalry to be most inconvenient. You would do well to remember that. And you would be wise to change your mind. Quickly. Do what I ask, speak to the King, and get as far from me as you can."

Celine could only gape at him, numbed by the litany of his ruthless past—and by the threat in his tone. This was *not* the kind, sensitive, noble knight of her childhood dreams. Meeting the real Sir Gaston was a very rude awakening indeed.

He kept staring at her, as if he were unused to meeting with defeat, as if he could force her by sheer, overpowering will to do what he demanded. "You will not succeed in your scheme," he grated out. "And you will live to regret any harm you bring to this place and my people."

"There *is* no scheme and I'm not going to harm anyone," Celine replied in exasperation. "The only thing I want to succeed at is *going home.*"

"Aye? Then let us drink to that." He stood suddenly, the force of the movement pushing his massive chair back several inches. The whispers of conversation in the hall instantly fell to a hush.

"My friends and loyal retainers," he began, lifting his

silver goblet, "I wish to offer a *salut* to my new bride." He turned to Celine, his eyes piercing. "Short may her stay be, and swift her departure." He drained the cup and thrust it back down onto the table so hard that a reverberating clang sounded and the metal edge marked the wood.

An uncomfortable silence deepened in the hall.

"She is not to be trusted," Gaston continued, his hand still on the goblet. "Nor is she to be left alone at any time. Etienne!"

A tall youth came forward from one of the tables—the blond teenager Celine had noticed last night. He dropped to one knee before the dais. "Sir?"

"I appoint you to keep watch over my wife. Whatever she may be planning, we will not make it easy for her to carry out."

"Aye, milord."

"And while she is here—however blessedly short a time that may be—she will fill some useful purpose. She will work as a servant."

A gasp went through the hall; apparently the thought of a knight's wife—enemy or not—being forced into menial labor was utterly shocking.

Celine felt her cheeks grow hot. She bit her tongue to keep her pride in check. Let him try to humiliate her. Let him make her work like a dog. She wasn't going to get upset.

Gaston glared down at her, as if expecting some protest. She looked back at him mutinously and tried not to feel the sting of this treatment, tried to tell herself he had every reason to be suspicious of her.

He gestured with the metal goblet. "You will do whatever Yolande"—he pointed to a slender, dark-haired serving woman of about forty—"bids you to do."

Celine remained silent. Didn't even nod.

He leaned down until his face was only inches from hers. "I mean to keep you well busy, my lady wife—too exhausted to venture anywhere near my bed. You will come begging for quarter anon. Are you certain you do not wish to reconsider your stubborn loyalty to Tourelle? Will you not go before the King and admit the truth?"

"I can't tell the King anything because I don't *know* anything," she insisted. "That *is* the truth."

He shrugged. "The battle is joined, then." Filling his cup, he turned back to his people and raised it again. "I promise you all, mark me, that this marriage will be ended as swiftly as possible, and that Lady Rosalind will soon be mistress of this castle!"

Everyone seemed to brighten at this. A few people were barely able to restrain applause. As for the looks directed at Celine, the ones that had been hostile since her arrival, they subtly changed.

Now they were both hostile and smug.

Gaston snagged a flask of wine and stepped off the dais, leaving her alone at the high table. *"Au revoir, ma dame. Sleep well this night—if your conscience so permits."* His bootheels echoed dully on the rush-strewn stone floor as he exited the chamber.

Celine sat frozen, smothered by the ensuing silence in the crowded, cavernous room. *Her* conscience? How could he talk about her conscience when *he* was the one being so awful? Everyone stared at her with wide eyes, clearly expecting her to burst into tears or race after her husband and beg for mercy.

Slowly, silently, she unfastened her fingers from the folds of her skirt, pushed herself back from the table, and stood, looking from one expectant face to another.

Then, chin high, she began clearing the dirty dishes.

Alone in his solar, the private audience chamber off the great hall, Gaston looked glumly into the bottom of the goblet he had emptied many times over the past hours. He swirled the cup with a flick of his wrist, watching the last few drops of golden ale shimmer over the silvered metal in the hearth light.

He had finished the entire flask of wine sometime after the sun had set, then switched to a stronger mead in an attempt to lose himself in drink. It did not succeed.

He had built up too great a tolerance over the years. Years he had spent fighting in hostile lands. Fighting as a mercenary here at home. Fighting to take and hold this castle. Sometimes it seemed his entire life was made of naught but blood and blades.

'Twas difficult to believe that he was now a landed lord, with many chateaux and men at his command, and influence that reached all the way to Paris.

Gaston de Varennes. The Black Lion. The mercenary called Blackheart. The younger son, who had cheated and fought his way to every bit of glory he had ever possessed, now had more wealth, more power, more duty, and more responsibility than he had ever imagined in his life.

He kept hearing Tourelle's words to the King echoing through his head: *Varennes is not capable of managing such holdings! Nor is he deserving of them.*

And he did not know if it was true.

He knew only that he had no choice. Most of what his father and brother had worked for was now his, and soon he would reclaim the rest. And avenge them both.

'Twas a cruel trick, to have battled for so long, gained so much, come so close to having the justice he sought—only to be forced into marrying a wench who could undo it all. A minion of his enemy. A she-cat in the guise of an "innocent" novice, sent to sink her claws into him and then end his life when he expected it least.

He smiled humorlessly as he gazed down into the goblet. Fate, it seemed, would not allow him to set aside his weapons. Not now. Mayhap not ever. He must keep fighting . . . and truth be told, he was tired of battle. Bone-weary tired. A pox on his fierce reputation. He had planned to spend this time of his life strengthening his holdings, learning to tend to his lands, making sons, and watching them grow tall and strong. After a lifetime of destroying, he had looked forward to discovering what it was to build, to create.

Never had he imagined spending his wedding night this way.

Were it Lady Rosalind who wore his ring, he would be getting himself an heir even now.

But as he looked down into the cup, watching the wash of gold over silver, he frowned, perplexed. For it was not a fantasy of gentle Rosalind's petite form in his bed that tormented him.

His thoughts were filled instead with the shimmer of a strange, topaz-colored garment, lace and silk as liquid as the ale, immodest and enticing over curves generous enough to stir a man to recklessness. He could not banish the image of flashing bright eyes, rich with unusual color—not quite blue, not quite gray, like a stormy clash of clouds and sea. A sweep of silky, short red hair. A mutinous little chin lifted with pride and defiance.

Defiance. Saints' breath, but that confounded him. Never in his life had he met with such complete resistance to all his skills of persuasion and will. She had not offered a word of protest when he took the outrageous step of declaring her a servant—but there had been an unmistakable spark in her eyes. It went beyond stubbornness or disobedience.

She had looked at him, not with anger or hatred as he might have expected, but with . . . disapproval. Disappointment.

He suddenly tossed the cup aside, sending it clattering across the scarred oak table. The devil take the wench. And her overlord as well. The sooner he had done with her, the better.

A tentative knock sounded at the door.

"Come," Gaston commanded, straightening, half expecting his wife, mayhap come to use a few midnight wiles to try to win some mercy from him.

Instead it was Royce Saint-Michel, the captain of his guard.

"Milord? I was unsure you would still be awake." The tall, dark-haired man stepped inside and closed the portal behind him, stamping his feet and brushing snow from his broad shoulders; he so resembled Gaston that they were sometimes mistaken for brothers.

Gaston waved him to a seat, oddly disappointed that he would not face another duel of wills with Christiane. "I wished to hear of your search before I slept. But it would seem from your expression that we shall find more answers in our cups this night than you have found in the village." He slid the flask of mead and an empty chalice across the table.

"Aye, sir." Royce settled his large frame on the opposite bench, unfastening the silver clasp of his sable-lined mantle and letting the garment fall to the floor. He picked up the flask with a nod that was equal parts fatigue and gratitude. "I fear I have naught but mysteries to report."

That gave Gaston a sinking feeling in his gut, but he allowed his friend a moment to thaw and pour a drink before explaining his comment.

As Royce filled his cup, the Spanish blade at his waist and the jewel-inlaid gauntlets he wore flashed in the firelight. The young man always flaunted the expensive garb in the same way he had taken up arms at the age of fourteen: in sheer defiance of the world. As the son of a peasant, he had no right to wear either weapons or finery, but he had "obtained" much of both along the coast of Castile, during two years of his life that he never discussed.

For boldness and blade-skill, he had few equals. Gaston would never forget watching Saint-Michel talk his way into a tourney, where only those of noble blood were usually allowed to take the field. After seeing this peasant's son, then barely twenty, defeat a dozen older challengers, he had offered him the highest place in his guards.

"You found no sign of Tourelle anywhere?" Gaston prompted at last.

"Nay." Royce shook his head, finishing a long draught of ale. "No one in the village has seen a caravan, or a single blessed nun, or one red hair of Tourelle or any man answering such a description. They say no strangers have passed this way for a fortnight. And though it was difficult to tell how many travelers there have been upon the roads, I doubt that anyone with a lesser mount than a destrier could have ridden them. The snows are too deep."

Gaston frowned. "So Lady Christiane came here alone, through the worst winter storm we have seen in years, on roads that no palfrey could have managed? Without being seen by anyone? It is impossible. She could not have made her way into the castle without assistance."

"Indeed, milord, she could not. But that is yet another

mystery—there was no trace of her entering the castle at all."

Gaston raised an eyebrow. "I am in no mood this night for jests, Saint-Michel."

"It is true, sir." The young captain sighed heavily. "Once the guests had arrived, the drawbridge was raised, with our men posted along the ramparts, and the King's guards as well. All had been told to watch for Tourelle's party, but they saw not a soul venturing near the curtain walls. And within the castle grounds . . ." He paused, running a hand through his thick, damp hair, clearly disturbed that he could make no sense of this puzzle. "Sir . . . I checked for myself, and there were no footprints. The fresh snow was unmarked. Even beneath the window of the bedchamber where you slept . . . I do not know how she came to be there, unless she flew."

Gaston felt an unearthly chill chase up his back as he remembered her strange comment at supper: *My father flies . . .*

He shoved the idea aside just as quickly. He would not let the treacherous wench and her insane lies play havoc with his logic. "She must have known of our secret sally port," he declared flatly.

"Nay, sir. I thought of that as well. The lock had not been disturbed. She did not slip inside that way." Royce shook his head, frowning; as the one responsible for securing the castle, he seemed deeply unsettled at being unable to find out how an intruder had gotten all the way to his lord's bedchamber. "I am sorry, milord. I cannot explain it."

Gaston couldn't explain it, either, but there *had* to be some logical answer. She was not an angel who could wing her way past raised drawbridges and armed guards. He tried to think, to remember the moment he had first noticed her in his room. Had she come through the door? The window?

All he could remember was falling asleep alone . . . and awakening to find her nestled beside him.

Christiane's voice again drifted through his thoughts. He remembered vividly the claim she had made while trying to explain herself: *When I stepped into this room to go to bed, the year was 1993.*

Madness. Lies. He shook his head to clear it. "I must have an answer, Royce. If she has found some secret way to slip inside, we can wager that Tourelle knows it as well."

"But, sir, even if she *could* have gotten inside—past the drawbridge, the guards, and through the bailey without leaving a mark in the fresh snow—how did she manage the portcullis? She could not lift a gate made of solid oak and iron." Royce pushed himself away from the table and stood, then paced to the hearth and back again. "Even a child could not fit through the small openings in it. Certainly no woman with such ample—" He suddenly broke off and froze, his gaze dropping to his boots, color rising in his face. "I . . . uh . . . meant—"

"Nay, do not apologize," Gaston said lightly. "My men would have to be blind not to notice the lady's generous . . . attributes. It bothers me not, Royce. She may be my wife, but she means naught to me." He dismissed the odd tightening in his gut as a reaction to too much drink and poor food, not a jealous response to another man noticing Christiane.

Royce nodded, but still seemed uncomfortable. He quickly returned to the hearth, stoking the flames as he continued his musings. "If she could not have slipped inside last night, that means she must already have been inside when the celebrations for the eve of the new year began. Mayhap she disguised herself, entered with some of the guests, and secreted herself somewhere until all had gone to bed."

"Mayhap," Gaston agreed, though he did not quite believe that, either. When one played host to the King, one did not let unknown persons wander in through the gates; the guards had stopped and identified each guest and his retainers before allowing them entrance. Such a tall, striking beauty would not have slipped past unnoticed.

But it was the only explanation.

Gaston rubbed one hand over his eyes. "The fact that we can find no trace of the lady's arrival only underscores what I have said from the beginning: she is cunning, skill-ful, and *not* to be trusted."

"Aye, sir. We shall have to keep a close watch on her." Royce leaned back against the stone hearth, crossing his arms over his chest. A grin slowly crept across his face. "While we see how she fares at the scrubbing of floors."

Gaston grimaced. "Told you, did they?"

"Aye. Even the guards at the gates were speaking of it by the time I returned. I am sorry to have missed her *adoubement* as a serving maid. They say she began her du-ties at once."

Gaston slanted him a disbelieving glance. "You jest."

"Nay, milord. They say she cleared as many trenchers and platters as she could carry, then asked that young Etienne direct her to the kitchens that she might wash them."

Gaston almost laughed. "I trust she did not mean to wash the trenchers." She had more spirit than he had given her credit for. Damn.

Royce shrugged. "Poor Etienne had no idea whether to bow to his new mistress or correct her. Are you sure it was wise to put him in guard of her?"

"The lad will stick to her like porridge to a plate."

"Aye." Royce nodded in hearty agreement. "That is what concerns me. He can be a bit of a feather-wit, that one, when it comes to a pretty face."

"He must learn to be a man, to let his *reason* rule his actions, not some foolish passion for a female. It will serve him well to learn at a young age how to manage a woman, beautiful or not. And I doubt she will be so fair after a few days of washing, spinning, cutting wood, fetch-ing water—"

"Milord, you could make the lady clean stables, and even with straw in her hair and the smell of horses about her, she would yet be fair enough to fell a man with a sin-gle glance." Royce's grin widened, and he added quickly, "My apologies for my boldness, milord. You said it both-ered you not?"

Gaston was annoyed to find that it *did* irritate him that Royce had taken such notice of Christiane's beauty. He covered the unwelcome feelings with laughter. "Someday, Saint-Michel, you will go too far."

"Without a doubt, milord." The younger man nodded sagely, like a pupil absorbing a lesson—but he did it while managing to look as unrepentant as the Devil himself. Then he broke into laughter as well.

The chamber reverberated with the deep sound of their humor, breaking the tension of the unanswered questions about the enemy in their midst. As it died down, they fell into another silence until Royce came back to the table and poured the last of the ale into their cups. "Milord, I would offer a *salut.*"

"To my new bride's attributes?" Gaston asked dryly.

"Nay, sir." Royce lifted his goblet, his expression suddenly solemn. "To your inheritance. With your marriage this day, you have come into rightful possession of what should have been yours months ago, what we fought to win back from Tourelle: the chateaux of your father and brother." He raised his cup higher. "I drink to you and to them, God rest their souls. You are three of the most honorable men it has been my privilege to know in this life."

Gaston felt his throat close, caught off guard by the unexpected homage. Royce was like that; he could be flippant one moment, deadly serious the next.

Never in his life had Gaston thought of himself as "honorable." Nor had he counted himself in the same rank with his father and brother, on that score or any other. In truth, he had not allowed himself to think much about them at all these past weeks, keeping his mind fastened on reclaiming the chateaux, the lands, his inheritance . . .

And now he had that. But his father and brother were gone. The last of his family. All he had left was their half-empty castles and a sister-in-law who wouldn't even speak to him.

He had gained much . . . and lost far more.

He forced down the grief, lifting his goblet. "To my father, Sir Soren, and to my brother, Sir Gerard."

He and Royce clicked metal against metal and drained the last of the ale.

"And by all that is holy," Gaston continued when his

cup was dry, wiping his mouth with the back of his hand, "I will make Tourelle pay for their murders. Nay—" He held up a hand. "I will not allow you to blame yourself, Royce."

Royce choked back whatever he had been about to say, but Gaston knew what he was thinking. Royce had been the one who had found them—lying only yards apart from each other in a field, looking as peaceful as if they had fallen asleep, each with a single mortal wound. When no witnesses had come forward, Tourelle and his men had been quick to cast suspicion Royce's way, since he had been the first to find them—and he was not of noble blood.

Royce succeeded at holding his tongue for only a moment. "But the blame *is* mine, sir. They told me they were riding off alone. I should have suspected some trap. Tourelle had been acting strangely all day. I should have warned them—"

"There is but one knave in this, and I will see that he answers for what he has done." Gaston looked into the empty bottom of his cup again, at the play of gold over silver. "And my new wife shall help me."

Now Royce looked genuinely puzzled. *"Help* you, sir?"

"Aye," Gaston said confidently. "She will come to her senses with haste. Within a se'nnight, she will be begging to tell the truth and give her overlord away."

"But how shall you accomplish this? And in only seven days, milord?"

"Because, Saint-Michel, the lady believes she knows how ruthless I can be. In truth, she has had merely a taste of me." Gaston indulged in a wicked grin as he rubbed the smooth cup ever so gently between his hands. "She will get her first full draught on the morrow."

Chapter 5

God, she would kill for a shower. Celine lay on the straw mattress in her bedchamber, too exhausted to sleep, too sore to move a muscle, so tired she couldn't even think . . . except to imagine how wonderful a shower would feel right now: a hot, stinging spray that would tingle on her skin and steam up the room and soothe her muscles until they felt warm and relaxed. She sighed in longing.

A shower. Complete with her favorite herbal shampoo and silky conditioner and perfumed bath gel to wash away all the grit from hours of work after the wedding feast. And then a few minutes in her whirlpool. Just a few. Oh, what she wouldn't give for that. And a fluffy cotton towel still hot from the towel-warming rack in her bathroom.

And, best of all, her own bed to slide into . . . with its satiny-soft, three-hundred-thread-count sheets, her thick eiderdown comforter, her feather pillow . . .

Celine moaned softly. God, she wanted to go *home*.

Her entire body ached, right down to her fingers and toes. And her back. She couldn't stop worrying about whether the soreness in her lower back was really from the long hours on her feet . . .

Or from the bullet fragment.

It might be a relief to be put out of her misery right about now, she thought with black humor. Even the most grueling step-aerobics class had never made her feel this wiped out.

All night she had done everything Yolande had asked, without one complaint. She had scrubbed platters and bowls and knives until her skin was raw from the harsh soap. She had helped move the trestle tables and benches against the walls, cleared the hall of dirty rushes, swept the floor clean, and washed it, using a bucket and brush and more of the strong soap until the stone gleamed.

Then she had gathered new rushes from a storage shed outside, untied the bundles, and spread them out with a sprinkling of herbs. They had made the place smell surprisingly good, as "meadow-fresh" as any room she had ever sprayed with potpourri-in-a-can.

As the evening wore on, the servants had gotten fed up with having to show her how to do every little thing. When darkness fell, she had been assigned to go from room to room lighting the oil lamps and candles that sat on stone sconces jutting out from the walls—but Celine didn't have the most distant idea how to use the pieces of flint and steel they had handed her.

Her best effort had ended up sending the flint flying in one direction and the steel sailing in the other, bringing laughter even from poker-faced Yolande. The woman had finally relented and sent Celine around with a small torch. Her eyes still felt dry and bleary from all the smoke.

By midnight, when she thought she would surely be allowed to trudge to bed, she had instead been handed over to the cook, to assist in baking breads and meat pies for the next day.

At least she had been able to show some skill there; she hadn't trained at the Cordon Bleu for nothing. She might not know her way around a cauldron, but she had run one of Chicago's finest restaurants for a year and a half. She made a pastry crust to die for. All the newspaper reviewers had said so, before she closed her little bistro to pursue a career in modeling.

Celine rolled over, trying to find a comfortable position on the bed, groaning as a muscle in her leg cramped in protest. She rubbed at her calf, laughing to keep herself from crying; if all of this weren't so awful, it would almost be funny. Like Cinderella in reverse. A rich princess transformed into a servant.

She had never realized until now just how much she

was used to living a life of ease, to having people around to take care of life's bothersome little chores.

People to take care of her.

At least there had been one positive note to the night's ordeal: Gaston slept downstairs, in his own room, the one he had given up during the King's stay. Celine slept in one of the small upstairs bedchambers. She hoped that the distance and her duties meant she wouldn't be seeing much of her surly husband.

Even better, her room was just down the hall from the bedchamber Gaston had been using the night she arrived. As soon as she figured out how to return to her own time, her window of opportunity—as she had started to think of it—would be just a few steps away.

She pulled the heavy woolen blankets closer, sighing with equal parts hope and misery. The room was not uncomfortable, really. A fire blazed on the hearth, and the homespun cotton sheets felt almost soft against her bare skin.

When the cook had escorted her here, Celine had asked for something to wear to bed, but the woman's incredulous look told Celine she had made yet another mistake. Medieval people, it seemed, slept in the buff. Too exhausted to debate it, unwilling to sleep in her grubby gown, she had stripped and kicked off her red slippers.

At that moment, an image from *The Wizard of Oz* had danced through her head: perhaps all she had to do was click the heels of her ruby slippers three times and say, "There's no place like home." The crazy thought left her laughing until her sides hurt.

Then she had tried it.

With a wry little smile at the memory, Celine curled up on one side, watching firelight lick at the dark stone walls. She murmured the words again, under her breath. "There's no place like home."

She whispered the phrase over and over, until her eyelids drifted closed and sleep finally claimed her.

It seemed as if only minutes had passed when Celine felt a hand on her shoulder, shaking her awake, though when she opened one reluctant eye to a slit, she saw that the fire on the hearth had burned almost out. "No," she groaned, rolling away and pulling a pillow over her head. "Please ... have to ... sleep."

The hand touched her again.

Tickling her bare shoulder this time.

A large, masculine hand.

"It is time to awaken, my lady wife," a familiar voice rumbled. "Your many duties await you."

Celine sat up with an exclamation of surprise—remembering too late that she had gone to bed naked. She gasped and grabbed the sheet to her chin, but not before Gaston, standing beside the bed, had gotten quite an eyeful. "What ... what ..." she sputtered. "What are you doing in my room?"

He smiled down at her, a slow, lazy grin, his gaze lingering on that part of her anatomy she had just concealed with the sheet. "You seem to be forever asking that question of me, Christiane. And my answer is ever the same: the room is mine. I own all that is in this castle."

His eyes finally rose to meet hers. His quiet, firm voice and the way he had said "all" made her uneasy. The dying embers on the hearth cast his angular features in a faint golden glow; she couldn't read the expression in his gaze. Celine shivered, and told herself it was because the room had become chilly. "I didn't mean ... I ..."

Without warning, he sat down on the bed. She forced herself not to flinch away, though he looked particularly large at the moment, a dark presence dressed all in black, blending with the shadows of the room. He wore a tunic that fit him like a glove. The cloth sharply outlined the breadth of his chest and the massive size of his biceps. A second, sleeveless tunic, embroidered with his crest—a crouching lion—hung loosely over the first. A cloak lined with silver fur swept back from his brawny shoulders. It fastened with a heavy chain at his neck.

Celine found her gaze on that spot, his exposed throat: the smooth curve of bronzed skin over muscle, encircled by the chain links. Her own skin tingled, suddenly and unexpectedly, a little rain of sensation that ran from the nape of her neck right down to the soles of her feet. "I—I thought I wouldn't be seeing you," she blurted. "I mean ... you appointed Yolande and your squire to be in charge of my work."

"It occurred to me that I should take a more personal interest in your duties."

Celine didn't like the sound of that. And she didn't like the uncomfortable feelings coursing through her, the intense awareness of how vulnerable she was beneath the white sheet, the way her eyes were slowly drawn to his hands. They rested on the bed. On either side of her legs. He wore black leather gauntlets that matched his cloak. "I ... I only just ... I've only had a little sleep."

She chastised herself immediately for saying that. She had promised herself she would stand up to whatever work he dished out to her. She wasn't going to be the weak, wimpy female he seemed to expect.

"You may stay abed all day if you wish," he said, leaning to one side, resting his weight on one elbow. The bed ropes creaked with his movement. "I imagine you must be sore after working through the night."

Before she knew what he was doing, he had snagged the bottom of the sheet and pulled it up, exposing her bare legs to the knees.

"Wait a minute! What—" She tried to sit up, too late. He had already captured one of her feet in his gloved hands—and she couldn't wriggle out of his grasp without exposing even more of her nakedness. She froze, her breath coming in short, sharp little puffs.

"*Ma dame,* I only wish to do what is best for you," he said, all innocence.

His gauntlets were soft and warm, the leather worn smooth by years of use, his fingers incredibly strong as he started massaging her foot, his thumbs pressing into her sole with small, circular motions.

Celine bit her bottom lip to repress a little moan of pleasure. "P-please stop that," she requested as calmly as possible.

He kept right on working over every knotted little muscle, rubbing and kneading with perfect, gentle pressure. "I would not be accused of mistreating you, Christiane. If you are too fatigued to work this day, you may sleep as long as you like."

Celine couldn't speak; she was too busy holding her breath, trying not to let him know how absolutely wonderful it felt to have him do what he was doing.

After a long, slow massage, he released that foot and shifted to the other. A small sound escaped her.

His gaze leaped to hers, that small grin playing about his mouth. "I could arrange for a bath as well," he offered. "A large tub of hot, steaming water, here in your room. Would you like that?"

God, this wasn't fair. He was using really underhanded tactics now. *And he had practically read her mind.* She released a slow breath, not trusting a word he said for one second, but not wanting to end his tender attention to her aching feet, either. "And all I have to do in return is . . .?" She already knew the answer.

He tilted his head to one side, sending a lock of dark hair tumbling over his forehead. The look was incongruously boyish for a powerfully built man dressed all in black. "It is simple, Christiane. All you need do is admit the truth. I will escort you to the King personally. Simply agree to speak to him, and you need never lift another finger here."

Wrapping both arms around herself to hold the sheet in place, Celine sighed and managed to move her legs beyond his reach. "As I've told you before, and as I will probably tell you again, *I can't possibly do that because I don't know anything.*"

His gaze sharpened. He didn't try to recapture her. "Christiane, do you not see by now that your stubbornness serves you ill? You will give in now, or you will give in later," he said quietly, "but you *will* give in."

Celine just stared at him in unyielding silence. She wasn't going to argue it with him. He wouldn't believe her, she couldn't convince him, and that was that. All she could do was face up to whatever annoyances he heaped on her until she managed to get out of here and go home.

"Very well." He shook his head, looking almost genuinely regretful—though it was impossible to tell with him what was real and what was false. "Then you've no time for sleep or a bath, my lady wife, for your duties await. But I would have you remember, this is your choice, not mine."

"Fine." She started to get out of bed.

He didn't move.

She stopped, her cheeks warming. "Would you at least turn around, please?"

He remained where he was, half reclining on the bed, looking very much like the lion on his tunic: all casual power, poised and ready to pounce even as he relaxed. His smile looked a little hungry. "Do I cause you discomfort?" he asked softly.

Celine swallowed hard. He was at it again, using his sensual skills on her—not to seduce or persuade this time, but to intimidate. He thought she was an apprentice nun, a girl who had spent her whole life in a convent. He *wanted* to make her uncomfortable. Wanted to make her run from him like a frightened rabbit, so shocked by his behavior, so fearful of what he might do, that she would say anything to anyone to be free of him.

Well, she wasn't going to be intimidated. She knew he had strong reasons to avoid consummating their marriage; he wasn't going to touch her, and she wouldn't be shocked by anything else he might do.

"No, monsieur, you do not," she said lightly, remaining where she was. "I thought I might make *you* uncomfortable. I wouldn't want to be accused of trying to seduce you again. Believe me, it's the furthest thing from my mind."

"Is it really?"

"Yes. So, if you would turn your back—"

"Trust me, little nun, I am not so taken with your charms that a single glance will set me ablaze."

"Fine. As long as you remember that this is your choice, not mine." Celine finally let go of her white-fingered grip on the sheet and got out of bed, turning her back on him.

She hoped he couldn't see her blushing in the low firelight; she could feel a wash of color chasing down her body, all the way from her cheeks to her belly.

Moving quickly—but trying not to *look* as if she were moving quickly—she picked up her yellow velvet gown from where she had tossed it last night and pulled it over her head. She did her best to appear casual, as if she got dressed in front of a strange man every day.

Her hands felt awkward as she wrestled with the dress. Her clumsiness was caused by last night's dish-washing, she told herself, not by her silent male audience. She tried to fit into the too-snug gown, but getting it over her bust and hips required a bit of wriggling, which only made her blush all the more furiously.

The entire time, she was intensely aware of Gaston's gaze on her back, tracing over every bare inch of her. Damn the man, anyway. He was enjoying this. It only made her that much more determined to ignore him.

"How did you come to have the scar on your back?"

Celine flinched, froze, then continued dressing. "You wouldn't believe the truth if I told you." She finally had the gown on, and laced it up the back, at least most of the way; she sure as heck wasn't going to ask for help.

"You have lived all your life in a convent." He persisted. "How did you come to be injured? An accident of some sort?"

"Yes, you could say that. An accident. Nothing that need concern you."

"I am not concerned, little wife," he replied quickly. "Merely curious."

Putting on her red slippers, Celine turned around, her chin raised a notch. Gaston hadn't moved an inch. He was still draped across the bed. That grin—she was starting to find it arrogant—still teased at his mouth.

But his body had gone taut, tense, utterly still.

And his eyes . . .

His dark eyes held that *potent* look again. As if he were made all of flame, as if anything that chanced to touch him would be burned to a cinder.

Celine's knees felt weak. She barely managed to remain standing.

She supposed she had realized what was happening to her, at some point, she wasn't sure when: all these funny tingles, the flutters in her stomach, the way she blushed at the drop of a hat, the unsettling warmth that melted through her at one brush of his fingers. Much as she hated to admit it, she was attracted to her macho medieval husband on some deep level that was beyond her power to control.

But she hadn't believed that she affected him in the same way, until now.

Until she saw it etched so clearly in the way he held himself; saw it blazing so fiercely in his eyes.

It all lasted only a breathless second before he relaxed, the heat vanishing beneath cool control. He stood up, moving silently and easily as he picked up something from the floor beside him. Another cloak. He must have carried it in with him.

"You will need this," he said in a low tone that played over her nerves. "Today you work outside."

That snapped Celine out of her daze. *Outside? In this weather?* Forcibly suppressing a groan, she squared her shoulders and tried to take the cloak from his hands.

Instead he took a half step around her and settled it over her shoulders himself. When he fastened the silver chain beneath her chin, the back of his hand brushed the sensitive skin under her jaw. She shivered.

"Are you cold already, *ma dame?*" he whispered teasingly. "You may change your mind at any time." He lowered his cheek to hers. "Save yourself from me."

"That, monsieur, I can't do."

He chuckled, low and confident. "Then follow me."

The first hint of dawn faintly lit the eastern sky as Celine followed her tall, dark, and irksome escort out of the castle. Her muscles ached with every step, and her breath formed a frosty puff of white as she yawned.

Even though she had been outside briefly last night, gathering rushes, it still made her feel disoriented to see how different everything looked. In her time, there had been floodlights, garages, ornate little gardens, walkways, paved drives; now nothing but snow and a scattering of hand-hewn buildings of various sizes loomed out of the darkness.

Even the air felt different. *Tasted* different. Clearer. Colder. Every time she inhaled, the sharp bite of it filled her lungs. It almost made her dizzy, as if it contained too much oxygen or something. Even when she had gone skiing with her cousins at Chamonix or Val d'Isere, she had never breathed air this . . . clean. It was a far cry from the diesel-and-lead-flavored stuff she was used to in Chicago.

All right, score one for the Middle Ages, she thought grudgingly.

Huddling deeper into her cloak, she trudged after Gaston. She didn't comment on the fact that she hadn't been offered any breakfast. She could hold out until lunch, for one of the meat pies she had slaved over last night.

Meanwhile, she wasn't going to show any weakness. She wouldn't give this big hunk of obstinate male striding in front of her the satisfaction. She couldn't do what he kept demanding, and the sooner he realized that, the better. Maybe when he figured out that turning her into Cinderella in reverse was *not* going to get him the confession he wanted, he would give it up.

He led her to one of the large huts that hugged the inside of the massive stone wall. It was a sturdy-looking structure, with a thatched roof, wooden walls, and a little fenced yard attached. Etienne waited in front of it, watching while a pair of small boys herded a flock of chickens and fat geese into the open-air pen.

The squire smiled as they approached, bowing. *"Bonjour,* milord. And to you, mila—" The greeting hung unfinished as he looked at Gaston uncertainly.

"You may call her milady," Gaston said. "She is, after all, my wife"—he turned to Celine with a cool smile— "for the moment." He gestured to the inside of the hut. "There you are, wife. You may begin your work."

"Work?" Celine echoed, peering into the dark, malodorous little building with a sinking feeling. There were rows of wooden benches built into the walls on all four sides, floor to ceiling, covered with nests. The smell of the place was so strong it made her eyes sting.

"The interior requires a thorough cleaning and the nests need to be replaced with new ones. When you are finished here, there are the dovecotes and falcons' mews to attend to."

Celine felt ill. It would take all day. If she didn't faint from the smell first. Or get frostbite before she ever finished; her feet were already numb. She rounded on Gaston. "This time, monsieur, you go too far."

"I am sparing you the kennels and stables," he said magnanimously, leaning on the wooden rail fence. "And you may accept this task or not, as you please. The choice is entirely yours."

Celine clenched her fists within the folds of her cloak, watching the chickens and geese scramble about, squawking and flapping their wings. The closest she had ever been to a goose at home was the down in her pillows. "I'm *not* in on any plot against you. I wish you would believe—"

"Do not be so quick to be stubborn. You will never manage this, little nun. You know you will not. And I can think of many more duties whenever you finish here. You will not outlast me, Christiane."

Gritting her teeth in frustration, Celine bestowed a silent, unflinching glare on him. Damn the man!

"Say the words," Gaston prodded. "You want to say them as much as I want to hear them. Such simple words, Christiane: 'I wish to tell the truth.' Say them to me and free yourself."

Celine gathered her cloak more tightly around her and turned to Etienne. "What am I to do first?"

"The old straw must be cleaned out, milady." He ducked into the shed and came back with a small, ineffective-looking pitchfork, which he handed to her with an unhappy expression.

Gripping the tool tightly in her bare hand, Celine turned to Gaston. "You'll have to excuse me, monsieur. I'm burning daylight."

She turned on her heel and stalked into the dark shed.

The overpowering odor smothered her senses; she tried not to inhale too deeply. Behind her, she could hear Gaston chuckling at her strange comment. She didn't care if he understood it or not.

He walked away, his boots crunching in the snow. "Watch her well, Etienne, and when she is done"—he raised his voice, for her benefit, no doubt—"take her inside to Yolande. I will leave instructions for further duties."

Celine felt her resolve flagging already; left with no target for her righteous indignation, she could feel the full force of total exhaustion pressing down on her. She couldn't have had more than an hour's sleep. The thought of just curling up in a snowbank and falling unconscious was tempting.

Instead, her stomach growling, her strained muscles stiff and painful, she gripped the rough wooden handle in her dishwater-raw hands, stabbed a forkful of hay, and tossed it aside.

"That man is the most *arrogant*"—she skewered another forkful—*"insufferable"*—she picked up the pace—"pigheaded ... insensitive ... underhanded ... overbearing ... annoying ... tyrannical ..."

It took several minutes for her to run out of adjectives.

She set the pitchfork aside, breathing hard from the brief exertion. To her surprise, she had already cleared a respectable amount of hay. And she felt a little better. Smiling with satisfaction, she wiped away the perspiration beading her forehead. She couldn't outlast him? Ha!

Etienne peeked into the hut during the momentary silence. "Milady?" he asked a bit timidly. "Is there aught I can do to help?"

"I don't think your lord would like that, Etienne."

"I do not think he means to make you suffer," he said with staunch loyalty. "Sir Gaston treats all women with great care. He is always most chivalrous."

"Chivalrous?" Celine stopped in her hay-pitching, looking pointedly around the reeking hut, then back at the lanky teenager. "I think we can safely say that isn't true."

"He would not do this if you would agree to what he asks."

"I can't give the King information that I don't have," she said wearily, tired of repeating that. "I can't explain why, but no matter what Gaston does to me, I will never be able to tell him about Tourelle's plan. It's impossible."

Etienne went a little pale. "Then I fear for you, milady."

Celine stopped her work again and straightened, a tiny tremor going through her. First the King with his warning—now Gaston's own squire. Why did everyone seem convinced he might do some sort of harm to her? "Etienne, he wouldn't actually . . . I mean, if he's as chivalrous as you say, he would never . . ."

"In this situation, I cannot say," Etienne said ominously.

Celine tried to convince herself that Etienne was saying that on purpose, to make her afraid of Gaston so she would give in and confess. But a lump settled in the pit of her stomach.

"Why, Etienne? *Why* does he hate me so much?"

"Because of what happened to his father and brother," Etienne supplied matter-of-factly.

Celine shook her head, not understanding. "What happened?"

"Everyone knows."

"I don't."

He peered at her with a look of surprise and suspicion.

"Etienne, if it's such common knowledge, there's no harm in telling me, is there?"

"You truly do not know?" he asked warily. "You were never told?"

"No. I don't know about anything that happened before I arrived here on New Year's Eve."

He considered that for a moment. "Mayhap it is as everyone has been saying—your caravan was attacked in the forest and you lost your memory due to a blow to the head."

"Perhaps. I have no memory of what happened, in the forest or before." That was true enough. "Please, Etienne—remind me?"

He brightened a bit. "Mayhap the truth will persuade

you to change your mind about your stubbornness, and spare you from this onerous work. Very well, milady, I will tell you. Milord's father and brother were killed last autumn, during a tournament with your overlord, the Duc de la Tourelle. Sir Gaston believes it was murder."

Celine gasped, unable to speak for a moment. His father and brother *murdered.* "But . . . why would he believe it was murder?" she asked, confused. "What if it was just an accident? Weren't there people there to see it?" She thought of all the movies she had ever seen, of knights in bright armor charging one another on opposite sides of a fence, with ladies and nobles watching from nearby pavilions with colorful pennants.

Etienne looked at her strangely. "No, of course not. It was a *tournament,* milady. Not a joust."

She mirrored his uncomprehending look. "Perhaps you had better explain to me what that means, Etienne. I . . . uh . . . can't seem to remember."

"A tourney is much like a battle," he said impatiently, as if even a child should know. "Two teams of knights fight for days, over a field many miles wide, even through towns and forests. The knights seek to win prizes and ransoms and fame for their battle prowess—but it is not unknown for men to be badly wounded or even killed. The Church condemns it as a most un-Christian sport."

Celine gaped at him; that sounded nothing like the festive events she had always seen in movies. "So . . . that's how Gaston's father and brother were killed? In this mock battle?"

"Nay, milady. Their bodies were not discovered until the tourney was over—" He stopped suddenly, as if unsure he should be revealing such details. "The circumstances were . . . suspicious. Especially as the Duc was the one who had issued the challenge to tourney, and made immediate claim on their castles and lands when their bodies were found. I fear that if milord had been there as well, he would have—"

"But why *wasn't* Gaston there?"

Etienne paused, glancing at the ground. "That is unimportant, milady—I must tell you the rest of what happened." He raised his head, eyes suddenly blazing. "Tourelle acted as if the spoils were already his to claim. He ravaged the Varennes lands, ordered his men to ransack the villages, to take all the food and valuables they came upon. And Tourelle himself ... some of the villagers' wives and daughters ..." He hesitated, turning red.

"They were raped?" Celine whispered.

He nodded. "Tourelle and some among his knights used them most brutally. That, Sir Gaston will not let go unpunished. He is not like most noblemen—he cannot abide the abuse of *any* women, no matter their rank." The young man folded his arms over his chest, a muscle flexing in his jaw. "And there is more, milady. Mayhap you wondered why your wedding feast was so meager. It is because milord gave away a great deal of his winter food stores— much more than he could spare—to the peasants living near his father's and brother's chateaux, because theirs was taken. So do you see, milady? If you did not know any of this, if Tourelle kept it all from you, do you see now the sort of man he is? Do you understand?"

"Yes," Celine whispered. She understood a great deal. She felt her empty stomach churning with repugnance for this man she had never met: a powerful *duc* who would steal, murder, brutalize defenseless women, use force against those weaker than himself.

She understood, too, why Gaston hated Tourelle so much.

Why he hated *her* so much.

And she realized with a numbing sense of defeat that he would *never* trust her. Never believe she was from seven hundred years in the future. No matter what she said. He would think her wild story was all part of some plot to kill him.

But mixed with that emotion was something more ... a sense of surprise and wonder that Gaston was so concerned, so generous, with all his people, regardless of whether they were peasant or noble. Never in her life had she had to worry about where her next meal was coming from ... but here, it seemed, winter was something to be dreaded. Lives could hang in the balance of autumn's harvest. Gaston had made a major sacrifice to help others less fortunate than he. She doubted that his egalitarian ideas were at all common in this time.

"Th-thank you, Etienne," she said at last. "You have . . . explained a great deal."

Etienne brightened. "So you will go before the King and reveal the truth?"

"Etienne . . ." Celine shook her head sadly. "Believe me, if it were in my power to see the Duc punished for what he has done, I would. But . . ." She was tired of saying, "It's impossible." She was tired of everyone being suspicious of her. "Let me promise you this, Etienne: I *swear*, by everything I hold dear, that I'm not in on any scheme with Tourelle, and I will not bring any harm to Gaston or anyone else here. Even though I can't speak to the King, I'll do whatever I can to help. And I'll leave just as soon as I possibly can, so your lord can marry his Lady Rosalind. How's that?"

The young man's hopeful expression wavered. "I pray, for your sake, milady, that it will be enough."

A thunder of hoofbeats interrupted them as Gaston and a half dozen of his men rode past, heading for the gate, all bristling with longbows and quivers full of arrows and dangerous-looking pikes. Gaston glanced her way, wheeled his mount, and brought the huge beast to a rearing halt a few feet from her.

"Have you changed your mind yet, my lady wife?" he called from atop the prancing war-horse.

Celine couldn't answer for a moment. The sight of him mounted on his night-black stallion made an impact that stole her breath away. He cut a magnificent figure, like an image from a tapestry come to life, a warrior lord ready to do bold and reckless deeds. Rays of morning's first light bathed his broad shoulders, struck sparks from his weapons, glistened on the embroidered black lion crouched on his tunic and the silver fur that lined his swirling cloak. He controlled the wild-looking stallion with ease, his gloved hands gentle yet strong on the reins.

A memory of those hands caressing her ever so briefly this morning left Celine shivering with heat and cold. She wet her lips and found her voice at last. "No, monsieur, I have not."

A cynical smile curved his mouth. "Then I trust you will have come to your senses when next I see you." He set his heels to the stallion's flanks and galloped off after his men, thundering over the lowered drawbridge and into the dense forests beyond.

"Wh-where are they going?" She couldn't tear her eyes from the spot where he had disappeared.

"To the hunt, milady. The castle has need of food. They will be gone for several days."

Several days. Celine knew she should be relieved to have her husband away for that long . . . but she wasn't.

God help her, she wasn't.

Chapter 6

"Your final duties of the day await you upstairs, milady, in your bedchamber."

It took a second for Yolande's words to penetrate what
was left of Celine's consciousness. She wasn't sure what
time it was, but she hadn't finished cleaning the goose and
chicken pens, dovecotes, and falcons' mews until long after dark. The roaring fire on the hearth in the great hall
couldn't even begin to thaw her.

Every minute of the day's labor was etched permanently
into her aching back and frozen feet and raw hands. She
never wanted to see another feather as long as she lived.
As soon as she got home, she was going to have every
down pillow and comforter she owned replaced with polyester. Good old-fashioned polyester.

Leaning on a trestle table for support, she blinked at
Yolande in weary confusion, not sure she could keep
her eyes open much longer. "My . . . bedchamber?" she
echoed.

"Aye, milady. Sir Gaston left specific instructions."
Yolande's round face, as usual, betrayed no emotion; the
woman carried out her duties with all the warmth of a drill
sergeant.

She turned to lead the way upstairs, and Celine followed
without further questions. One foot in front of the other. It
was all she could manage. She had no energy left for anything so demanding as an intelligent reply.

All she could feel was dread, heavier and colder than
the frost-encrusted cloak she wore. What new tasks had
her relentless husband thought up to bend her to his will?
Emptying and refilling every mattress in the place straw

by straw? Scrubbing the blackened hearth in her room until it gleamed? Dangling out the window on a rope and scraping ice off the castle walls?

You win. She ached to say it with every trudging step down the darkened stone corridors. *You win, you win, you win.* But she couldn't say that. He asked for the impossible, she couldn't give it to him . . . and he despised her for it. This battle between them wouldn't end until she escaped to her own time.

If she could escape to her own time. If she lived that long. Was the ache in her back really from the grueling work, or from something she didn't want to think about? She could almost hear a clock ticking in her head, ominous, relentless. Precious minutes, hours, days slipping away. *Tick, tick, tick.* Like the timer on a bomb—and she had no idea when it might go off.

She hadn't had two spare minutes to figure out how the lunar eclipse had sent her here and how she could get home. And it didn't look like she would be getting a day off anytime soon.

When they finally stopped before her door, Celine almost sank to her knees in supplication. A little rest. An hour's sleep. Just an hour . . . Yolande stepped into the room, but Celine stood swaying in the doorway, gazing with bleary longing at the bed.

"Thank you, Gabrielle," Yolande said. "I see we are almost ready."

Celine forced her eyes fully open and glanced to her left, where a young serving girl was pouring buckets filled with water into . . .

A tub.

A huge wooden tub, filled with water so hot that a fog of steam rose above it. Celine's reddened nose only now caught the scent of fragrant herbs and dried flowers rising on the tendrils of heat: lavender and thyme and roses.

"I . . . I don't understand." Celine couldn't let herself take a step toward that luscious paradise of warmth and water. It was a mirage, an illusion, a trick. Gaston was purposely tormenting her. "So who's getting a bath?" she asked in a shaky voice. "I suppose I have to help scrub the backs of half the household?"

"Nay, the bath is for you alone, milady. By Sir Gaston's order." Yolande held out a small cake of soap. The serving girl finished with the buckets and went to hang a length of thick white linen on a rack before the fire.

Celine felt like crying. It was too good to be true. She stayed where she was, suspicious. "Why would he allow me a bath, after everything he's put me through?"

Yolande frowned, which gave her stern features an even more dour expression. "In truth, I wondered as much myself, but it was not my place to question. Mayhap he does not wish to be accused by the King of mistreating you." She shrugged, holding out the soap. "Hurry, milady, before the water grows cold."

Celine didn't know why Gaston was granting her the bath he had teased her about this morning. Maybe he was trying to keep her off-balance, never sure of his next move. Maybe he genuinely regretted making her work so hard all day. Maybe he really was as chivalrous as Etienne claimed. Maybe he . . .

She didn't care. She went for the tub like a bargain hunter heading for the clearance table at Neiman-Marcus. The wooden edge, worn smooth by years of use, came up to her waist. A veritable garden of rose petals floated on the surface. She grasped the side, leaned over, and inhaled a deep breath of scented steam. Sighing, she slanted a look at the towel warming before the fire.

How could he have known what she wanted, down to every detail? If she had any sense, she would be worried about that. The man had practically read her mind. But she was too tired, and the steam was already starting to defrost her stiff muscles—and as the feeling returned to her limbs, so did every little ache and pain.

"Oh, Yolande." She held on to the tub and sank to her knees, resting her head on her forearms. "Please tell me this is real. Tell me you're not going to snatch it away at the last minute."

"Hmph," Yolande muttered, helping her out of her stiff

cloak. "It is real, milady. And naught more than you deserve, after your work this day."

The serving girl came over to help unfasten her cloak
and unlace her gown. Celine gratefully wriggled out of the
filthy garments, hopped up on a stool, and went over the
edge of the tub with a rather unladylike splash. Her cold
skin and raw hands stung as soon as she hit the water, but
she dunked herself and came up with a smile as the heat
melted through her muscles. Slicking back her hair, she
settled against the side with a long, deep sigh of relief. Not
even her favorite ten-thousand-per-week spa in Palm
Springs had ever felt this good.

Closing her eyes, she enjoyed the heat for a blissful moment before she snagged the floating soap and started
scrubbing away the mud and feathers and stench that clung
to her skin, working up a frothy lather.

"Do you like the soap, milady?" Yolande asked. "It is a
blend of wood-ash and oil of rosemary. I bought it at the
village fair this Michaelmas past."

"Yes, it's very nice, thank you," Celine replied with
smile, sniffing the fragrant little cake in her hand. It was
generous of Yolande to loan out her own personal soap . . .

Only then did Celine recognize the change in Yolande's
attitude: the woman wasn't acting at all hostile anymore,
or even wary.

Come to think of it, neither was the other servant,
Gabrielle, who was applying herself to washing Celine's
hair.

"Is that warm enough, milady?" Gabrielle asked as she
poured a half bucket of water down Celine's back to rinse
out the soap. "I could run to the kitchens and heat some
more, if you wish."

"No, that's fine." Celine wiped the lather from her eyes
and blinked at the pair of them through the bubbles.
"Yolande, what am I to do after this?" she asked cautiously. There had to be some reason for this sudden
about-face; before now, everyone had made her feel about
as welcome as a homeless bag lady at a black-tie-only soi-
ree.

"Sleep, of course," Yolande said matter-of-factly. "Sir

Gaston ordered only that you were to have this bath. Other than that, he left your duties up to me until his return."

"I see. And what did you have in mind?"

"Well . . ." The older woman pursed her lips. "Everyone was most taken with your cooking, milady—though I did not have any myself. I was displeased to learn that the cooks had given you such free rein in the kitchens. I feared you might poison us all."

Celine gave her a pained expression. "I'm not the dragon lady everyone thinks I am, Yolande. I'm not here on any devious mission and I'm not going to harm a hair on anyone's head."

"Aye, well . . ." The woman didn't seem ready to make up her mind on that just yet. "Whatever the truth may be, no one heeded my warnings. There's naught left of what you made. The meat pies, the breads, the odd flat pastry with cheese and onions—"

"Pizza," Celine clarified. "And if I could get my hands on some tomatoes, I'd show you what a real one is supposed to taste like."

"And the delicious small, flat sweet cakes you made, milady," Gabrielle interjected. "What do you call them?"

"Cookies. Ginger snaps, to be exact."

"*Cookies,*" Gabrielle repeated reverently. "Even Yolande liked those."

Celine turned to Yolande with a raised, soapy eyebrow. "I thought you didn't eat anything I made. I'm dangerous, you know. Poison and all that."

"Aye, well . . . after several hours . . ." Yolande cleared her throat. "When it became clear that no one was dying . . ." She cleared her throat again, then slowly, grudgingly, smiled. "Gabrielle said they were delicious, and near forced one down my throat."

"But then you ate a half dozen more when you thought no one was looking," Gabrielle pointed out.

Celine looked from one to the other, shaking her head in pleasant surprise. "I'm glad everyone enjoyed my cooking." She smiled. "I know this winter is difficult for you, and I only want to help, for as long as I'm here. Please believe me."

"I believe you," Gabrielle declared. "You must have been *so* tired last night while you were cooking, yet you made such wonderful dishes for us. After the way we had treated you." She shook her head in wonder. "How did you manage to make such heavenly foods when our stores are so meager?"

"It's not what you have, but what you do with it. I trained with some of the best chefs in France," Celine said casually, "and they taught—" She suddenly remembered who she was supposed to be. "That is . . . I, uh . . . studied cooking at . . . at the convent in Aragon. Traveling cooks came by and, uh, gave us lessons."

Great. That was about as believable as Elvis having lunch with aliens at a McDonald's in Kalamazoo.

Luckily, neither of the women questioned it. They both had visions of ginger snaps dancing in their heads.

Yolande was still smiling. "I believe it would be wise to put your talents to their best use—since Sir Gaston has left your duties to me."

"Aye, most wise," Gabrielle agreed, nodding eagerly.

"I suppose . . ." Celine said slowly, sensing that she had some leverage at last. "Perhaps we could make a bargain: I'll make meals that will knock your . . . uh . . . slippers off, if you'll agree to give me something in exchange."

"What might you wish?" Yolande asked, still a bit suspicious.

"A little time off." She thought for a second, then added, "And a bath, like this one. Every day."

"But you will become *ill* if you bathe so frequently!" Gabrielle protested.

Celine shook her head. "I'll be fine. It's the custom where I come from. All I ask is some time to relax and a bath. And maybe some new clothes. Do we have a deal?"

Yolande considered the offer for all of three seconds. "Why not? Your bargain is met, milady." Turning, she shooed Gabrielle toward the door. "Come, let us leave Lady Christiane to her bath and her bed. She needs her rest. She shall have a busy day in the kitchens on the morrow. *Bonsoir,* milady."

"Bonsoir." Celine sank back in the hot, soapy water

with a smile, feeling happier than she had since her arrival. Her stay here might just prove bearable after all. A little free time to puzzle out her problem, a hot bath at the end of every day, decent food, decent clothes ... if she played her cookies right, she might even negotiate herself a nifty hat or two. A soufflé would probably win her an entire new wardrobe.

She wondered, for a moment, whether it was wise to introduce *too* many modern dishes to these people—but she didn't think pizza and pastries were going to change the course of history.

Besides, the real Christiane would be arriving soon, and everything would get straightened out; then everyone would *have* to believe her story about being from 1993. And now that they were learning to trust her, they would be more willing to help her return home. With a sigh, she submerged beneath the surface of the water.

Where the heck *was* the real Christiane, anyway?

Four days later, Celine hurried across the bailey—she had learned that was the term for the open ground between the castle and the curtain walls—wearing her new leather boots, embroidered green tunic and leggings, and an ankle-length cloak lined in soft marten fur. A matching hat topped off the ensemble: a cute little number that was sort of like a sailor's hat, pinned to a length of fabric that went beneath her chin and kept her cheeks warm. Gabrielle called it a "barbette." Celine hoped she could take it along when she returned home; it would make a beautiful addition to her collection, not to mention a nice souvenir of this ...

Adventure? Disaster? Escapade? She wasn't sure what to call her present situation. Whatever it was, she hoped it would be over soon—and today, her hopes were higher than ever.

In the four days since Gaston had been gone, Celine had made quite a few improvements in the kitchens. She started by introducing something she couldn't believe hadn't been invented yet: cooking spoons. With a little help from the castle's armorer and carpenter, she also "invented" a few other items, things that would have been right at home in her great-grandmother's house, from rolling pins and wire whisks to a spring-loaded chopper. It wasn't quite a Cuisinart, but it certainly speeded things up.

While the cooks were eagerly soaking up her culinary lessons, she persuaded them to boil any water used for cooking or drinking, and to wash their hands before preparing every meal. They found these tasks bothersome, but gave in when she insisted; being lady of the manor did have some advantages.

Seeing her success in the kitchens, Yolande had indulged Celine's wish to help in other areas of the castle. The laundresses were pleased to find their job much easier with washboards and a simple wringer and wooden clothespins; they could now hang laundry to dry on lines inside, rather than outside on tree branches.

The seamstress was thrilled with her new seam ripper, pinking shears, and rotary cutter, and was putting her head together with the armorer over Celine's sketches of a rudimentary treadle sewing machine.

The sentries were happiest of all, once Celine had shown them how to convert leather wine flasks into hot-water bottles: they filled them with water and a few embers from the fire, and wore them inside their cloaks to keep warm while patrolling the walls.

She found the lack of electricity frustrating but not insurmountable. A few of the things she had in mind—like gaslights and central heating and running water—would just take longer to figure out. She explained all of her "inventions" the same way she explained her cooking skills and the fact that she preferred to wear a tunic and leggings rather than a gown: she insisted it was all quite normal at her convent in Aragon.

Most people were too pleased to question their good fortune. A few still harbored ill will, but others were starting to call her brilliant.

Brilliant. That was quite a novel sensation, having people respect her not for her looks or her wealth or her pedigree—but for her skills and intelligence. She had always been the underachiever in a family of geniuses, always the one who never quite measured up.

Here she could really make a difference. Change people's lives. Make things better, easier. It was irresistible, being needed; the more she helped, the more she wanted to help.

Maybe she had gotten a little *too* carried away by the feeling, but now she was turning her attention back to her own problem. There was someone she wanted to meet.

Snow sifted down from the sky as she crossed the bailey, sparkling like the sugar she had dusted across an angel food cake for last night's dessert. Yolande had given her the afternoon off, and Etienne—the Eternal Shadow, Celine was starting to call him—had granted her request to take a walk alone, as long as she agreed not to go near the gate.

Celine moved briskly, heading for the huts at the rear of the chateau where many of the servants lived. With a few subtle questions over the past days, Celine had learned just who in the castle might have knowledge of astronomy or the moon. Always the answer was the same: Fiara.

The name was always whispered quickly, as if it inspired dread, and people weren't willing to elaborate more than to say that Fiara was a mystic of great knowledge and power. Celine hadn't even been able to find out if the person was a man or a woman, only that Fiara lived in the servants' quarters. Which was exactly where she was headed now.

But as she made her way through the snow, a noisy disturbance near one of the outbuildings drew her attention. It was caused by a group of children. Celine almost hurried past—until she noticed what they were doing: they were gathered around a little girl of about ten, who faced them with a tear-streaked face while they taunted her.

"Thickhead," one called.

"Heathen," another shouted.

"Hag," a third put in.

"Stop it!" Celine cried above the noise.

The children quieted instantly, turning to look up at her as she stalked over, drawing herself up to her full height.

"You wouldn't like it if someone called *you* such awful names, would you?" That logic had always worked with her nephew, Nicholas. She might be seven hundred years in the past, but kids, she suspected, were kids.

"But she *is* a heathen," one little boy insisted.

"We do not want her here," another chimed in.

"Well, since she *is* here, don't you think it would be better if you all tried to get along? No matter what her beliefs are?" Celine crossed her arms. "I don't think I could teach new games to boys and girls who weren't nice to one another," she said lightly.

That seemed to make an impact.

"No more *friz-bee?*" one asked in dismay.

"No more *glissades et échelles?*" another gasped.

There were soon many chastened and worried little faces in the group. Chutes and Ladders had proved to be a special favorite. Ping-Pong had also gone over well. Celine was considering an indoor version of miniature golf.

"I was going to show you something called Pictionary tonight." She shrugged. "But not if I hear of you being unkind to someone again."

The little girl who had been the object of the kids' teasing soon found herself surrounded by a chorus of apologies. One by one, the children left, promising to be good and pleading for more after-supper games.

Celine sent them away with pats and reassurances, unable to resist tousling a few mischievous heads. When they were gone, she went over and knelt beside the little girl, who kept her face lowered and didn't move. Tear-tracks streaked her red cheeks. She had blond hair, tied in a long braid down her back, and a blue dress and mantle that were patched in places.

Celine felt her heart turn over. "I don't think they'll bother you anymore," she said softly.

The girl sniffed, her lower lip quivering.

"You're new here, aren't you?" Celine tried again. "So am I."

"I know."

Celine smiled. At least she had a bit of a conversation

going. That was encouraging. "No one liked me much, either, when I first got here." She reached up, cautiously, and dried the girl's cheeks with her gloved hands. "But now I think they're warming up a bit. Sometimes it just takes a little time."

The girl shook her head. "They will never like me. I am different."

Celine's heart gave another tug. How many times in her life had she said those same words herself? She had always been different. Taller than any girl in her class. Too skinny. Never as good in school as her brother and sister. Never quite able to measure up to what her parents wanted her to be. "You know, when I was about your age, everybody teased me, too. Because I was so tall. They called me Beanpole, or Beanie."

The girl finally glanced up from beneath a fringe of dark lashes, examining Celine with startling blue eyes. "You *are* rather tall," she said gravely.

"I am." Celine nodded, laughing. "My name is . . . Lady Christiane. What's yours?"

"Fiara."

"Fiara?" Celine almost choked, gasping and saying the name at the same time. *"You're* Fiara?"

"Aye, and I already know who you are. You are not Lady Christiane, you are Celine. The lady of the moon."

That declaration almost knocked Celine over. She gaped at the little girl, speechless. A strange tingle shivered up her back, raising the fine hairs at the nape of her neck. "What . . . who . . . *who told you my name?"*

"No one. You are the lady who came here on the moonlight. On the eve of the new year. The moon brought you here." She cocked her head to one side. "Your back . . . there is something odd . . . does it hurt very much?"

Celine's heart started to hammer. "How do you *know* all that?"

"I know many things." The girl bit her lip and dropped her gaze. "That is why no one likes me. I should go now." She turned to leave.

"Wait." Celine caught her arm gently. "Please. If you . . . if you know the moon brought me here, do you know *how* it brought me here? Do you know . . . how it might send me back?"

The girl paused, as if thinking, then shook her head. "I am not sure. My mother knows more than I, but I am not allowed to speak of her."

"Could *I* speak to your mother?"

"She is not here. She lives in a village, far away. She sent me here to live with my aunt b-because . . ." She let the sentence trail off and bit her lower lip once more, as if unsure she should finish.

"You don't have to tell me. You don't even have to say where she lives. Could I send a message to her?"

"I do not see her often. I have to go now."

Celine let her go but followed, feeling desperate. "Please, if there's any way I could speak to her—it's *very* important."

Fiara kept walking. "You are a very nice lady of the moon. I will try. Would you like a kitten?"

"W-what?" Celine stuttered, caught off guard by the sudden change of subject.

"A kitten. My cat had kittens." The girl stopped in the middle of the bailey and turned to face Celine with a tentative smile. "I will call one of them for you. The black-and-white one, I think."

Fiara didn't move. She didn't say a word or make any sound at all, but just stood there with that shy little smile hovering on her lips.

A few seconds later, a small black-and-white kitten came bounding through the snow toward her.

Fiara scooped it up and cuddled it, rubbing her cheek against it, making a little purring sound. Then she handed it carefully to Celine. "He will stay with you now," she stated.

Stunned, Celine didn't know how to respond. She took the kitten, trying to hide her surprise at Fiara's actions. *A mystic of great knowledge and power,* everyone had called her. "Th-thank you," she managed at last.

"I will come see you if I can think of a way to send a message to my mother," the little girl promised. A second later, she vanished around the corner of one of the out-buildings, leaving Celine alone with her gift.

The kitten, purring so hard its fragile body vibrated with sound, was sinking its tiny claws into her arm as it tried to climb closer into the warmth of her cloak. Celine glanced at it with a frown, trying to disengage the little beast.

He had a streak of black above one eye, like a raised eyebrow, and another sooty patch beneath his nose.

Celine couldn't help but smile. The resemblance was just too striking. "There's only one name for you," she declared. "Groucho."

The furry, miniature Marx brother mewed in reply and settled into the crook of her arm as she turned and headed back to the keep, her heart swelling with hope—*real* hope—for the first time since she had arrived here. Someone believed her! Someone knew the lunar eclipse had brought her here! Okay, so it was only a little girl—but it was a start.

If she could just figure out some way to evade her Eternal Shadow and meet with the girl's mother . . .

"Lady Christiane!"

Celine lifted her gaze from Groucho to see the object of her thoughts running toward her from the direction of the castle. "I'm coming, Etienne."

He reached her first, panting. "Milady! You must come back to the keep at once—"

"Why, Etienne? What's—"

"Sir Gaston and the hunting party have returned! Everyone is telling milord what you have done, and he is most angry. He is also wounded, which does not improve his humor." He took her arm. "Come! We dare not keep him waiting."

Chapter 7

Wounded. Celine froze in place, unable to move when Etienne grasped her elbow. Her heart seemed to be beating strangely. "What do you mean, Gaston is wounded?" She squeezed little Groucho so hard he hissed and sank his tiny claws into her arm.

"An injury suffered on the hunt. His anger is of greater concern." Etienne tugged her forward. "Never have I seen him in such an ill humor."

Celine knew that idea should strike fear in her heart and make her want to run in the opposite direction—but it didn't. She wasn't thinking of herself, but of Gaston. *Wounded.* She couldn't explain the emotions that gripped her, yet she didn't stop to question them; she needed no urging now from Etienne to hurry back to the keep.

Near the front entrance they passed servants who were leading away the hunters' horses and carting off the catch, several deer and a huge bristly boar. Celine barely glanced at them—except to notice that Gaston's black horse had great smears of red on its saddle and down its right side.

By the time she and Etienne rushed inside and reached the great hall, she was ahead of him, her pulse pounding out of control.

A crowd of retainers, servants, and the men who had gone on the hunt had gathered around the dais before the hearth all talking at once. It was impossible to hear what was being said amid the clamor of anxious voices. She couldn't see Gaston. Was he stretched out on the floor? Was he too badly hurt to stand? She blindly handed Groucho to one of the younger serving girls and started pushing her way forward with Etienne, asking those in front of them to move aside.

Suddenly Gaston's voice boomed above the noise—and Celine felt a wave of mingled surprise, relief, and dread at his words.

"What do you mean, you allowed her to *cook?*"

"But, sir, she has done no harm," a male voice insisted.

"Milord, you must taste this wondrous delicacy she makes, called *quiche,*" Yolande said.

Celine finally managed to nudge her way to the front of the gathering. Her heart slowed only slightly when she saw that Gaston was seated in his carved chair before the hearth, looking whole and healthy—except that his right leg was wrapped in a scarlet-soaked bandage.

"Are you all right?" she blurted breathlessly.

The crowd's chatter dropped to murmurs as Gaston turned his glowering attention on her.

He swept her from head to foot in a single glance, his eyes darkening, his fingers tightening around the arms of his chair. An unfamiliar expression flickered in his gaze, just for a second before it vanished. A cold, cynical smile curved his lips.

"I see that you have made excellent use of my absence, you treacherous, scheming, murderous little wench."

Celine flinched, taking an involuntary step backward, startled by such an unexpected attack. What in the world had she done that made him so furious?

He didn't give her a chance to speak before he turned his anger on Etienne. "What do you mean by letting her wander around the grounds *unescorted?*" His voice grew louder with each word until this last was a bellow that shook the rafters.

"M-milord, she has worked most diligently these past days, and she has proved both helpful and trustworthy—"

"Trustworthy?" Gaston snapped. "Has everyone in my command lost their senses? What knavery might she be carrying out while you are all busy filling your bellies?" He cast another glare at Celine. "And why is she going about garbed as richly as royalty? From where did she get these . . ." He gestured at her leggings and tunic. A muscle

in his jaw worked and he seemed unable to speak for a moment. "These masculine garments?"

"I made them for her, milord," Yvette, the seamstress, said. "In gratitude for a favor she bestowed upon me. She created the most wondrous devices which cut fabric so quickly and easily—"

"Saints' blood." Gaston's expression was getting stormier by the second. He flicked a glance at Etienne. "Is this how you repay my confidence, lad? I appointed you to guard her—and you have all but handed her my chateau and all I own."

"Nay, sir! I have watched her most carefully. This afternoon is the first that she has been alone for even a moment. She has done naught that could be considered at all threatening, milord. In fact—"

"Of *course* she has not. It is all part of her plan. I am gone but four days and everyone here has forgotten who and what this woman is! She is *Tourelle's ward!* Sent here to ease us into unwatchfulness, that she may better carry out her lord's plans."

"Excuse me!" Celine finally managed to interject. Stunned by his overblown anger, she could only attribute it to the fact that he must be in great pain; he was roaring at them like a wounded lion. "Could we please argue about me later? You need to have that injury looked at."

Gaston's jaw clenched. He speared her with an icy glare. "You have no need to act the attentive wife. You may have woven some spell over my people, but you will find me a better adversary!" He thrust himself to his feet, though the movement obviously caused him pain.

Celine bit back the urge to respond in kind. He was furious enough without her provoking him further; his every move must hurt. "I am *not*—"

She broke off abruptly.

I am not acting. That was what she had been about to say.

"I . . . I . . ." She gazed up at him, feeling desperately confused. He was standing there snarling at her, his weapons gleaming at his waist, his hair ruffled from the wind, four days' growth of beard on his cheeks, blood soaking his clothes, more angry and dangerous-looking than she had ever seen him—and she wasn't the least bit afraid. Not for herself. All she could feel was concern for him. It didn't make any sense, yet it was the truth.

But he wouldn't believe that. "I'm ... I'm merely curious about what happened," she said at last. "Were you gored by a boar?"

The captain of his guards, the man everyone called Royce, chuckled from behind Gaston. "Nay, milady, naught so dire as that. It was an injury suffered when we stopped at a tavern."

The murmurs of conversation around them died down, as if everyone knew what Royce meant by that.

Celine didn't get it. "A tavern?"

"Aye," Gaston said. "To celebrate our successful hunt with a bit of drinking—and a bit of wenching."

His answer landed a cold punch to the pit of Celine's stomach. She was sorry she had asked. Gaston's blunt comment told her more than she wanted to know, but he kept right on explaining.

"I suffered the injury while falling out of a lady's bed. I was in a hurry to enjoy myself, and undressed so quickly that I was less than careful about where I left my weapons. When I rose from the bed—"

"He tripped in the dark," Royce continued for him, barely able to restrain his laughter. "It became quite a melee after that—he had to call for assistance, and the lady in question was so stricken that she insisted on helping, and then we arrived on the scene. It was more difficult peeling her off him than binding the wound ..."

The men in the room were chuckling by now, but Celine's cheeks were burning, her insides knotting up, three words spiraling through her mind: *How could he?* He had been married less than a week, and he had already—

But why was she even thinking of it that way?

What was wrong with her?

The vows they had spoken hadn't meant anything. To either one of them. This marriage wasn't real. It was a colossal mistake, a trick of time. She was going to catch the first moonbeam out of here, back to 1993. What did she care if he slept with another woman or a dozen other women?

She told herself it was just the way he was boasting of it so publicly. Gaston had every reason to hate her: he believed she was Tourelle's ward, an enemy, a threat to his life, to his people. But this was a new low, even for him—and she didn't understand why he was doing it.

Anger and jealousy and hurt and a tumult of other emotions squeezed into her throat, choking off both voice and air. It was ridiculous to feel this way! He had never been anything but honest: he despised her and he had no intention of curtailing his lusty ways. He had told her so when they said their vows. She didn't care about him. *Why should she feel hurt?*

She could have faced him and everyone in the hall without flinching—except for the looks she was getting from the women.

The men were too busy listening to Royce and guffawing over their lord's escapade to notice, but the women were looking at Celine with expressions of sympathy, even pity.

Celine would have far preferred the hostility they had bestowed on her a few days ago.

Gaston kept staring at her, as if waiting for some kind of reaction. She returned his gaze evenly, forcing down all the crazy emotions tangling inside her with every bit of strength she possessed.

"You are bleeding all over your great hall, milord," she said coolly. "I suggest you have the wound tended."

"Then fetch some water and linens, *wife.*" He spat out the word as if it were poison. "You will tend me in my chamber."

Gaston stalked from his bed to the hearth and back again until he had trampled a path in the rushes that carpeted his chamber. He barely even sensed the pain in his leg; a storm of pure black fury blotted out all else. Fury at the woman he had married.

Not because of the changes she had wrought in his absence, or the way she had tricked his people into her grasp in a matter of days, or even the outrageous masculine garb she wore.

Nay, he felt furious because of the strange little leap his heart had made when he saw her again.

What bothered him even more was that the incident at the tavern hadn't happened quite the way he had told it.

He stopped before the hearth, bracing his arms against the stone, hanging his head. He kicked a charred chunk of wood back into the flames.

He had not bedded the tavern wench.

By God's breath, he had had every intention of doing so, had traded smiles and jests with her half the night, then taken her to his room. It was all a familiar ritual, a sport of seduction that usually ended with him feeling happy and satisfied.

But once alone with her, he had been surprised and annoyed to discover that he felt no real desire for her. At first he had feared there was something wrong with him, something physically wrong. Her kisses had left him cold. He had removed his boots and weapons and started to undress, fully intending to take her to bed, when he had suddenly, inexplicably, changed his mind.

His injury had occurred when he turned a bit too quickly in the darkness, tripped, and cut his leg on his own carelessly placed sword.

That infuriated him more than anything. Never in his life had he been careless with a weapon—but his mind had been such a muddle, filled not with thoughts of the woman who was offering herself to him, but with images of Christiane's form and face and . . .

Fie, but this accursed wife of his was dangerous! She had seized such a hold on his senses that he had lost interest in other women. Lost control over his own *thoughts.* He was utterly unable to explain it.

When Royce and his men had arrived on the scene, they had jumped to the wrong conclusion, and Gaston had let their mistaken belief stand. Even now he was unwilling to examine too closely what had happened.

All he knew was that he was . . . *drawn* to Christiane by some force he could not name and had never felt before, in such a way that he found the company of other women unappealing.

The maddening truth of the matter was that he suspected the tavern maid had caught his eye only because she had red hair.

Like his wife.

The wife he must not take to his bed.

He straightened and lurched away from the hearth, prowling to the window, tearing open the shutters. A blast of wintry air poured into the room. He inhaled deeply, welcoming the cold, hoping it would freeze the fire burning in him even now.

The sizzling desire that had ignited within him the instant he laid eyes on Christiane again.

God, the sight of her wearing that outrageous garb—the cloth clinging to her long legs, showing every curve of calf and knee and thigh. He had been parted from her but a few days, yet he had felt like a lost Crusader taking his first draught of water after wandering a foreign desert. Her breasts had seemed more lush than he remembered, her waist smaller, the tilt of her chin more impudent, those sea-storm eyes—

By nails and blood, this was intolerable! He slammed the shutters closed and turned away, pacing, trying to force the images from his mind.

This was dangerous. Deadly. If she were to discover that she had such a potent effect on him, it could prove the perfect weapon in her hands.

He had to hide these unwanted . . . unwanted . . .

He searched for the right word, then, finding it, grimaced.

These *feelings* for her. Bury them beneath a stronghold of defenses.

A sudden, unbidden memory of his brother invaded his thoughts: Gerard and the mad passion he had had for his wife, Avril. The pair had spent every day, every hour, every breath together almost from the moment they had met. Gerard had called it "love." A woman's word. Gaston had recognized it for what it was: an all-consuming desire that had so turned Gerard's head around that he . . .

He had become softened by it. More husband than warrior. He had allowed his fighting edge to be so dulled by his *feelings* for Avril that he had been less of a knight, that one second when it counted most. Had he been more cautious, more wary, more *himself* that day at the tournament, he might still be alive.

Their father might still be alive.

It was a mistake to feel passion for one female above all others. A lethal mistake. Gerard's death was proof enough of that.

Gaston sat on the bed, running a hand through his hair. He must rid himself of this foolish desire. Rid himself of Christiane. She was Tourelle's ward, for God's sake. Sent here to do exactly what she was doing. Trick him. Lure him in. Seduce him.

He must have an annulment and marry Lady Rosalind de Brissot. As soon as possible. Not just for himself, but to protect his people. The three chateaux that were now his had too great a distance between them. Separated, they were vulnerable—to Tourelle, to the simmering Flemish, to any marauding rogue who happened along. Only when he had united his holdings with the de Brissot lands that lay between could he hope to stand strong and defend them against all threats.

But first, he must rid himself of Christiane.

Gaston barely heard the whisper of the door opening.

She didn't knock. Bold little wench. One moment he was alone, and the next she was there—standing in the portal, holding a basin and soap and several lengths of linen. And a wine flask. She kept her gaze meekly lowered, but every inch of her body was taut—whether with anger, defiance, or some other emotion he could not tell.

He cursed himself silently; it had been an impulsive move, ordering her here. Witless. He had thought to prove—to her, to them both—that he was the one in command of this situation. That his reason ruled his passions. That no woman could make him lose control of his desire, least of all her.

Only now did he realize just how unwise it was to be alone with her like this. He should send her away.

But doing that would tell her how powerfully she affected him.

When he didn't speak, she finally lifted her gaze from the basin of water. "I'm here, as you demanded," she said quietly.

He fixed her with a glare. She didn't flinch. "Close the door."

"I don't know why you would trust me to tend your wound when you won't even trust me to cook—"

"Close the door."

She finally obeyed. Her hand was shaking.

His heart was beating fast, unsteady.

He purposely deepened his breathing to slow its pace. Here and now and henceforth, he was going to prove that he was a warrior first and a man second, and always would be.

"I ordered you here because I would speak with you alone, *wife.*" Casually, he leaned back and rested his weight on one elbow. The bed ropes creaked beneath his weight. "I do not trust you, but the wound is not deep and you know the King's warning as well as I: if aught befalls me, your lord will forfeit all he owns."

She set the basin on a table beside the bed, not looking at him. "You can hardly blame me for an injury you suffered while . . . while wenching."

In truth, he could. Better, though, to let her believe Royce's vivid tale. "The pain is but a small price to pay for the pleasure the lady gave me." He smiled, his most wicked grin. "And though *that* fault was not yours, if any ill befalls me now, because of your care, Tourelle will pay the price."

"I'm not in on any plot with Tourelle," she said with an irritated shake of her head.

Gaston had stopped paying attention to what she said. God's blood, she was beautiful. A breath of spring all garbed in green, warming his winter-cold chamber. She looked like an exceptionally brilliant bird that had fluttered in by mistake. She made the room look colorless by comparison, even the bright-hued silks that hung on the bed, embroidered with his crest.

It was the first time she had been in his bedchamber.

This close, he could even catch her scent: lavender and thyme and roses—

Damn and damn and damn. He willed the awareness away.

Wetting a strip of linen, she rubbed it with the soap and turned to face him at last. "I suppose it was too much to hope that a few days away would improve your mood."

"My mood will improve only when you are gone. That is why I ordered you here. Tell me, have you had time to reconsider your treacherous ways? Will you go before the King and admit the truth?"

Christiane raised her hands in a gesture of pure exasperation. "No, I can't. I couldn't four days ago, I can't now, and I won't be able to the next time you ask me, or next week, or ever."

"That is unfortunate. For you." He leveled a cool gaze on her. "I *will* be rid of you, Christiane. Soon."

"Believe me, I'm counting the days." She said it with such vehemence, it sounded like the truth.

"You make no *sense,* woman. If you wish to be gone, why will you not cooperate?"

"Because I *can't.* I'm sorry if that doesn't make sense, but I . . ." She closed her eyes and took a deep breath. "Look, do you want me to tend your wound or not? This argument is never going to get us anywhere."

"On that we are agreed," he said angrily, turning his attention to something that would rouse neither his senses nor his ire. Straightening, he unknotted the blood-soaked bandages that circled his thigh just above the knee, and tore away the remaining tatters of his legging from the area. "The wound is not deep. A scratch, no more."

She had gone completely pale. "A scratch?" she whispered, staring at the bloody injury as if she had never seen a blade-cut before. He thought for a moment that she might be ill, but instead she picked up her odd array of supplies and knelt in the rushes beside the bed.

He eyed her tools suspiciously. "What purpose has the soap? And the flask?"

"This may sound strange to you, but where I come from, we have learned that they prevent infection."

"*Wine* prevents infection?" he scoffed. "If that were true, I know a great many pickled mercenaries who never should have died of their wounds."

"Getting drunk doesn't help. You use it to clean the cut." She looked up at him, biting her bottom lip. "This is going to hurt. I promise I'm not about to make 'aught ill' befall you—but it's going to hurt."

"I am not some page who will faint at even the smallest pain. I have had many injuries far worse than this."

"Amazing that you're still here to brag about it," she muttered.

"I am still alive after seventeen years of battles because I always keep my blade at hand and my wits about me." He looked at her impassively as she began to wash the wound. "Always."

Except of late, he amended to himself in irritation. Her hands worked over him quickly, lightly; she was either trying very hard not to hurt him or trying very hard not to touch his bare thigh. Both impossible tasks. After she had washed the wound, she patted it dry, then dabbed it with the wine.

He never winced. Never made a sound. Her careful ministrations burned like Hell's hottest flames—but he was aware of the pain only in some distant portion of his mind. The rest of him had been set ablaze with an agony far worse than the wine: having her touch him.

God's breath, how long had it been since she had touched him? Had any woman's touch ever moved him like this in all his thirty years?

Her long, slender fingers felt so soft and delicate against the bristly hair of his thigh, so close and yet so achingly distant from that part of him that even now, even as he fought against it with every ounce of will he possessed, throbbed to hardness with wanting her.

Desire burned him, so forceful that it seared away all meaning he had ever attached to the word before. It was an explosive ache that consumed him even as it filled him. It flooded his loins, tormented him with insane images—

visions of pulling her into his arms, up onto his bed; running his hands over every smooth, curving inch of her; tearing her garments away and pressing her back into the sheets; thrusting himself into her deeply, and then more deeply, until they were both lost and breathless and—

Nay!

"This is the last I will see of you for some time, wife."

He didn't even realize he had spoken until she glanced up at him. "W-what?" She had just finished tying a fresh bandage around his leg. Her fingers trembled, her cheeks were flushed with color, and her eyes held a deep glimmer of heat.

Her unmistakable response to him only intensified his own arousal, which made him angrier in turn.

"I said, this is the last I will see of you."

"Why? Are you going away again?" She stood up, her expression wary.

"Nay, *I* am not leaving—*you* are the one who will be 'going away.' Since you have abused the freedom of my castle, you shall have it no more." He was practically snarling at her, but he didn't care. Damn her, this was entirely her fault. "You will be confined to your bedchamber from this day forth, until you reconsider your treacherous plans and agree to reveal the truth to the King. And since Etienne has proved unreliable, you shall have a more experienced guard: Royce, the captain of my—"

"But what about the King's warning?" she protested, her eyes flashing with sparks of anger. "If you mistreat me—"

"I am not mistreating you. You will be well fed and warmly clothed, and you may even continue your odd habit of bathing each day. But you will remain in your chamber, alone, while you think better of your loyalty to Tourelle. For however long it may take. I will not have you using my people in your scheme, distracting them with your strange foods and odd devices—"

"But everything I've created is to make life better here. Easier. People have even started coming to me with their problems, and I do my best to solve them. My devices are helpful—"

"They are part of your plans, and I will not have it. They will be done away with."

"Done away with?" she gasped. "Why?"

"Why? Because it is what I command!"

"But you can't do that! You can't undo everything I've accomplished—"

"Do you think you can defy me?" He smiled and asked it in a low tone that she should have been smart enough to recognize as dangerous.

"Yes, when you give stupid orders! The changes I've made are good for your people."

He stood so suddenly that she backed up a step.

"It is not your place to decide what is good for my people." He towered over her, clenching his fists. "They are *my* concern, not yours. They are simple folk, and too innocent to the serpent in our midst, too quick to believe—"

"I am not a serpent and I wish you would start to trust me at least a little bit. Give me a chance. Everyone else—"

"Everyone else has let their bellies run away with their reason. Now that I have returned, it will cease. Until you are ready to tell the truth, you will be treated like the enemy that you are. My people will have naught more to do with you. *I* will have naught more to do with you."

She made a wordless sound of frustration between her teeth. "You are *the* most infuriating, arrogant, unreasonable, stubborn pig of a man I have ever met!" She took one heedless step toward him, her chin raised to defiant new heights, her fists clenched as tightly as his. "You can lock me away from now until next year and I won't change! I can't! *You're* the only one around here who needs to change. I think a little defiance from someone might do you a world of good. I think—"

He encircled the nape of her neck with one hand, drew her to him, and kissed her.

Kissed her. Before he knew what he was doing. Silenced her. Crushed her in his arms.

Stunned them both with the explosive force of the heat that suddenly arced between them.

She tried to break away, stiffened, struggled, but he held her against him—one hand in her silken red hair, his other arm locked around her back—until slowly, she began to melt.

The joining of their mouths sent him spiraling downward into an abyss so wide and so deep he knew it would be bottomless. He struggled for purchase, desperate to pull away, but the blaze of desire was so huge and dark and consuming that it pulled him in until retreat was impossible, unimaginable.

Her lips opened at his urging and then he was part of her, intimately, his tongue finding her, thrusting softly, then aggressively, while he held her head still with his hand. Their tongues and tastes and hungers mingled until he felt himself shaking with the force of it, his body aflame like newly forged steel, hers a tender branch that went up like tinder. They burned one another, consumed all air, all breath, all life . . . *all.*

He broke free and thrust her away.

"Get out," he snapped, his voice ragged, his gaze narrowed with accusation. "Leave me—before I give you what you have sought from the first."

She stumbled backward, eyes wide and dazed. She did not speak, only stared at him, one trembling hand reaching up to touch her swollen, bruised lips.

He closed the distance between them in one stride. *"Get out!"*

She turned and fled so fast that she left the door open behind her. Left him alone, his body still shaking with the ferocity of his passion for her.

God help him, would locking her away be enough? Even if he banished her to the most distant, unexplored corner of the world, would it *ever* be enough?

Enough to keep him from seeking her out . . . *and giving in to the desire that burned his soul.*

Chapter 8

Two nights later, as Celine lay alone in her room, tossing and turning, she thought she could still feel the tingle of his kiss on her lips.

Which was ridiculous, she knew. Temporary insanity. Cabin fever. *Castle* fever. Brought on by two days of being locked up with nothing to occupy her time.

But whatever it was, she couldn't stop thinking about that kiss . . . about him.

Her entire body felt warm with awareness. Sensitive. Tense. As if that wild embrace had triggered some secret switch, sending a constant electrical charge through her nerve endings. Even the soft velvet of her tunic and leggings chafed. Her daily baths didn't relax her. The herb tea that Yolande and Gabrielle brewed for her didn't soothe her. Nothing helped. She felt tingly and restless all day—and it only intensified at night.

The worst part of it was, she knew her arrogant husband would be thrilled to know he had made such an impact on her.

God, what an impact.

She was driving herself crazy trying to figure out why he had kissed her. It had been so unexpected; he had caught her completely unaware. One minute they were yelling at each other, and the next . . .

Even now she couldn't stop replaying it in her mind: his mouth on hers, hot and demanding; his arms holding her fiercely; his hand in her hair; his granite-hard angles molded to her body . . . and the delicious little sizzles that had melted her muscles when his tongue played over hers.

Celine shuddered and squeezed her eyes shut, wishing it

were equally simple to shut out the vivid memories. *Why* had he kissed her? Had he merely been taunting her? Trying to show her just how useless it was to resist his will? To prove how easily he could make her respond to him?

Well, she had done a lot more than *respond*. She had practically swooned. Never in her life had she felt anything so . . . so sudden and powerful and uncontrollable. Logic, reality, the awful things they had shouted at each other, the fact that their marriage was a sham—all of it had gone sailing straight out the window. She had trembled in his arms. Felt a rising tide of irresistible pleasure. Returned his kiss. *Wanted more.*

Oh, that was the most humiliating part of it. Even when he had shoved her away, all she could do was stand there shivering, blinking at him like a fool, shocked by what he had done—and disappointed that he had stopped.

He had glared at her with a look of disgust in his eyes. Like *she* had planned it. Like *she* was the one who had grabbed *him*. Like the entire thing was her fault!

Infuriating macho chauvinist swine. She should have *said* that. Shouted it at him. Instead she had run away, mute and frightened as a deer faced with a double-barreled shotgun.

But now that she was alone and clearheaded and could think rationally, she had to admit one mortifying fact: if he hadn't forced her to leave, if he had instead taken that single step toward her and swept her into his arms again, she wouldn't have objected.

She would have given in.

To his kiss . . . and more.

He had sworn he would not consummate their vows—but he had never made any promises about kissing. Or anything else. Exactly how far might he go before it was considered consummation?

Celine sat up suddenly, getting out of bed. Tossing the blankets aside, she sent her kitten tumbling into the rushes.

"Oops, I'm sorry, Groucho." She scooped him up and settled him back in his favorite spot. "I haven't exactly been the best company these past couple of days, have I?" She scratched the bridge of his nose, but he would have none of it. With a lion-size yawn, he hopped across the covers, down the side of the bed, and rustled through the rushes until he reached the hearth.

Celine sighed, trying to calm her jangled nerves as she watched him. Little Groucho had been her only companion since she had been shut in her room, but that made no sense, either. Yolande had brought him up from the great hall that first day, just after Royce had posted himself outside the door.

The odd thing was, Yolande had said it was Gaston who had ordered Celine's pet brought to her room.

Why had he done that? It made no sense.

But neither had that kiss. Or anything else he had said or done, from the very beginning. He made her work like a dog; then he let her have the bath she longed for. He was furious over the changes she made while he was gone; then he kissed her. He seemed to enjoy her response; then he pushed her away as if she were loathsome. He ordered her locked up; then he let her have Groucho for companionship.

She could hardly be blamed for feeling confused.

Shaking her head, she turned to the small table beside her bed and poured herself a cup of water. She understood Gaston less and less every day.

Finishing the water, Celine went back to bed and huddled under the covers once more.

She had to start thinking rationally here. There was one thing she *did* understand about Gaston: the man was a womanizing cad. The sort who could tumble tavern wenches whenever he pleased, then brag about it publicly. If she were looking for a thoughtless, selfish, one-night-stand kind of guy, there were plenty of them back in the twentieth century.

She had always wanted more. Much more.

As if that weren't enough, she sensed he had boasted about his conquest only to hurt her.

It was cruel. And it worked.

Every time she thought of him in bed with the tavern girl—Celine pictured a toothy blonde with a buxom figure and a mug of ale in each hand—she felt a sharp ache, right in the pit of her stomach. To imagine him weaving that

masterful sensual spell over another woman, kissing someone else the way he had kissed her, using his mouth and
body and hands, making love . . .

She cut the image off abruptly. It was making her nau-
seous. And her eyes were getting strangely misty.

She blinked hard. What did it matter to her? She had to
leave. The sooner the better. He wasn't important to her,
she wasn't important to him, and this marriage was nothing but a burden to both of them. Let him do all the
"wenching" he wanted. It didn't matter.

So what if she felt a little attracted to him? It was understandable. He had a body created to inspire female fantasies, not to mention potent eyes and a wicked grin any
movie star would kill for. What woman wouldn't feel attracted to him? It was perfectly normal . . . and purely
physical.

It was also stupid. And useless. And she wasn't going to
waste one more brain cell thinking about it. She had already wasted two whole days.

She *should* be focusing on how to get home. Her annoying husband was making good on his promise to have
nothing more to do with her, and that was just fine by her.
Perfect, in fact.

First thing in the morning, she was going to start doing
a little detective work. She would need to find a way to
distract Royce for ten minutes or so—just long enough to
sneak out of here and into the bedchamber down the hall
for a closer look at her "window of opportunity." She
wanted to see if there was anything unusual about it.

She pulled the blankets closer, pleased that she was finally getting her thoughts, emotions, and plans back on
track.

She was leaving.

It didn't matter to her what Gaston did.

She didn't care about him.

Or whom he slept with.

And that *was not* a tear gliding down her cheek.

The room was still dark when she opened her eyes
sometime later, feeling sleepy and disoriented, wondering

what had awakened her. Then she felt a tug on the bed-clothes.

"Lady Celine, wake up," a small voice whispered.

Celine rolled over, startled. A child stood beside the bed, her eyes glittering unnaturally blue in the dim glow of the hearth's embers. "Fiara?" Celine whispered, squinting in the low light. "How did you get in here?"

"You must hurry, Lady Celine." The little girl glanced toward the hearth. "Aye, Groucho, greetings to you as well. I am pleased you have been such good company to your mistress."

Celine's grogginess dissipated as she tried to follow the dual conversation. "What do you mean, hurry? How did you get past Royce? Hurry *where?*"

"I am going home," Fiara said adamantly. For all her mysticism and seriousness, she suddenly sounded very much like the lonely little girl she was. *"Maman* thought I would be happy here, but I am not. If you would still like to see her, I will take you with me."

"Your mother?" Celine sat bolt upright, her heart doubling its pace. "But I thought you said—"

"She will not be happy that I disobeyed her, but I will not stay here one more day." Fiara's voice quavered and Celine heard a telltale sniff. The child rubbed at her eyes with one small fist. "Please do not worry about Captain Royce. He will not be a problem. But if you would like to come with me, I think you should dress first."

Celine didn't need any more urging than that; she was on her feet, dressed, and grabbing her cloak in two minutes flat. Gaston would be furious when he found her missing. He was suspicious and mistrustful of her as it was, and this little disappearing act was not going to improve matters. In fact, she thought with a shiver, "furious" wouldn't even begin to describe his probable reaction; it would make his mood the other day look downright gleeful by comparison.

But Fiara's mother might be the only person around who could tell her what she needed to know to get *home.* She couldn't miss this chance to meet the woman, no matter what the risk.

As soon as Celine was ready, Fiara turned and opened the door, not being at all cautious.

"Fiara, wait. Don't you think we should—"

The little girl stepped into the corridor without hesitation. Celine froze, certain her escape was about to end before it had even begun.

But she didn't hear a word from Royce. After a moment, she followed Fiara—and found her guard sitting beside the door, asleep.

"Well, some great guard he turned out to be," Celine muttered in surprise. "Asleep on the job."

"He will not waken until morning."

Celine glanced at Fiara and back at Royce, realizing only then that his position looked a little odd: his legs stretched straight out in front of him, his arms limp at his sides. It didn't appear he had settled in for a nap—more like he had been standing upright and slid down the wall.

Celine knelt beside him with a little gasp of alarm. "Oh, Fiara, you didn't *do* anything to him, did you?"

"I did not hurt him," Fiara said indignantly. "I merely looked into his eyes for a few moments and suggested he sleep until morning."

"You *hypnotized* him?" Celine hesitantly tapped Royce's shoulder, but he didn't stir. He appeared unharmed, but he was lost to the world.

"He made a most challenging subject. For some reason, he is a very suspicious person."

Celine turned an uncertain gaze on her small companion. This sweet-faced ten-year-old had a surprising array of tricks up her sleeve. It wasn't difficult to understand why she frightened people, especially the other children. Celine was more than a little unnerved herself. "Fiara, I'm not so sure—"

"Milady, we must go. There has been no snow for almost five days, so the roads will be more passable, but it will still require several hours to make our way to the village afoot."

Celine knew she couldn't afford to hesitate, but the risks involved here were starting to sink in. The two of them would be going beyond the safety of the castle gates, alone—and she had no idea what might be waiting out there in the medieval gloom. "Are you sure it's smart of us to go off through the woods at night, on foot? And un-armed? I mean, aren't there . . . wolves and who knows what else prowling around?"

"They will not be a problem," Fiara said confidently. She turned to lead the way down the corridor.

Somehow, that was exactly the answer Celine had ex-pected.

She stood up, resolutely forcing aside thoughts of wolves and cutthroats and other terrors . . . such as facing Gaston when she got back. When it came right down to it, she had no choice about this. She would just have to deal with the consequences later.

With one last, worried look at Royce, she followed her diminutive guide.

Walking through a medieval forest after midnight, Celine could easily see where tales of spooks and Hallow-een and werewolves and headless horsemen had gotten their start.

The winter wind sliced through her fur-lined garments, numbed her feet, made a white mist of her breath—which she could barely see in the pale thread of light from the night's half-moon. Darkness and threat seemed to emanate from all sides, even from the bare tree branches that clat-tered overhead like bony fingers. The moon's tentative glow barely penetrated the black woods, shimmering on the snow. She could just make out Fiara's small shape trudging forward down the trampled path.

Deep drifts blanketed the edges of the uneven road, which hardly lived up to the term. A superhighway it was not. Celine tripped on deep ruts and killer potholes more than once. In some spots the trail opened wide and straight, but in others it twisted and narrowed so tightly she doubted a horse and rider could squeeze through—though apparently several had. The snow was covered with hoofprints. And footprints and wheel marks.

And paw prints. Big, canine-looking paw prints.

Several times they heard a wolf howl, and the eerie

sound sent an icy shaft of primitive fear through Celine. She couldn't tell how far away the hungry-sounding beasts were, but once she thought she saw a pair of huge shadows moving through the trees beside them. Fiara appeared unconcerned.

It wasn't until the first rays of morning light had brightened the uppermost branches that they came in sight of their destination. Exhausted, the muscles in her legs tingling with fatigue, Celine breathed a heavy sigh of relief. The small hut, nestled in a clearing, looked as welcoming as the posh Plaza Hotel in New York. There were no other huts to be seen, but curls of smoke rising above the trees showed that the village was only a short distance away.

The humble little home had the same construction as the outbuildings at the castle: walls made of mud and sticks and a thatched roof. The straw had a few bare patches, though. A lone chicken strutted about the yard.

A woman came to the door with a startled look on her face, even before Fiara had broken into a run.

"Maman!" the little girl cried. *"Maman, maman!"*

The woman's look of surprise dissolved in a burst of tears. She fell to her knees to sweep her daughter into her arms.

When Celine caught up with them, the woman gazed up at her openmouthed. "By all the holy gods," she whispered, straightening with Fiara still clasped in her arms. She was in her late twenties, as beautiful as her daughter, with the same golden hair—and the same laser-blue eyes. "Y-you are . . . you are—"

"A moon-lady!" Fiara chirped happily. "Oh, *maman,* I am so glad to be home. I could not stay with Aunt Marithe. No one liked me, and I was so unhappy, and I do not care if we have little to eat, if only I can stay here with you!"

The woman stroked her daughter's hair, but her wide eyes were still on Celine. "From . . . from when have you come?"

The bizarre question sounded completely rational at the moment. "From seven hundred years in the future." Celine swallowed hard, weary and hopeful and above all relieved that she was finally speaking the truth to someone who believed it. "From 1993. My name is Celine Fontaine. I guess I don't have to explain to you how I got here?"

The woman shook her head, but kept staring as if she could not quite believe her eyes. Then she abruptly turned her attention back to her child. "Oh, my sweet, reckless Fiara! You must be more careful, daughter. If you were to reveal too much to the wrong person—"

"I was careful, *maman*. I always am. Lady Celine is unhappy, and she wants very badly to go home ... and I know so well how she feels. I had to help her."

Celine smiled at Fiara, touched by the depth of empathy in such a young child. "And I am *very* grateful, Fiara, that you brought me here to speak to your mother."

"Aye, come, we must speak." The woman cast a sudden, nervous look around the clearing. "But inside."

The inside of the hut looked much like the outside, clean but threadbare. It was a single room without windows. A firepit provided warmth and illuminated the sparse furnishings: a small, hand-hewn table, two chairs, a pallet bed and pillow in one corner, and a shelf with a few wooden bowls and iron cooking implements.

There was little food to be seen, nothing but two sacks of grain, though a large, ornate chest stood in one corner, bound with iron fashioned into elaborate, finely wrought Celtic motifs.

The woman took a basket from a hook on the wall and handed it to her daughter, looked at her in silence for a long moment, then handed her a coin from a pouch at her waist.

The little girl's eyes shone with excitement. She hugged her mother, then ran to Celine and hugged her, too. "Oh, Lady Celine, *maman* is not angry. She is going to make a fine meal, to celebrate my return, but first she wants to speak with you. I am going to the village to see Madame Nadette and buy some mutton." She held up the coin with a proud smile. "*Maman* says I may even visit a while with Madame and help with her herbals."

With that, Fiara hurried off on her task. Her mother followed her to the door, smiling sadly as she watched her go before turning to Celine. "I have not told you my name, have I? I am sorry. I have lived so long alone with my daughter that I forget, sometimes, the usual way of speaking. I am Brynna." She motioned Celine to a chair and took the other one herself, still looking a bit nervous. "For my daughter's sake, I beg you, whatever you learn here this day you must keep secret. Please—"

"I'll be grateful for whatever help you can give me," Celine assured her. "And I promise I won't tell a soul. But why are you so afraid? What is this *power* that you and your daughter have?"

"Power," Brynna whispered, lowering her gaze to her patched skirt. "Aye, I suppose some would think of it that way. Though it is not, in truth." She glanced up, studying Celine for a moment. "Long ago . . . centuries ago," she began slowly, "was a time of Ancient Wisdom, a time when mankind understood all—the languages of the earth and its creatures, the ways of the sea, the paths of the stars—"

"Astronomy," Celine whispered, her heart starting to beat harder.

Brynna nodded. "And more, much more. But then came a time of darkness, and the Ancient Wisdom was lost. It survived only among a few, men who were held in high esteem, sought as healers, as wise judges in disputes, as advisors to kings. They came to be known as Druids."

"Druids?" Celine breathed, thinking of tall men in dark cloaks, Stonehenge, King Arthur's Merlin. "So that's what you and Fiara are?"

"Two of the very last. You see, long ago, some who did not possess the Ancient Wisdom began to fear those who did. They hunted them down, drove them from their lands, killed them. Only a handful survived. My father was a Druid of great knowledge, but he taught me to keep my . . . *powers* secret, for fear of those who do not understand. Those who would call us witches and evil. People who might harm us."

She paused, her hands twisting in the folds of her skirt. "I did as he bade, and married an important man in the town where we lived, a silversmith. My husband . . . he forced me to leave when he learned the truth of what I am, what our daughter is. Fiara"—Brynna glanced up with a smile, her expression bittersweet—"is my greatest joy, but she is not cautious. I have tried to warn her, but at her age, she finds amusement in her powers. And her gifts are very strong. I must rely on my father's writings to assist me; Fiara's abilities seem to flow naturally. It makes me fear for her. I thought if she could lead a more normal life, among normal children . . ."

Her voice trailed off, but her eyes said it all: she wanted her child to have a better, happier, safer life than she had had herself. Brynna's loneliness, and the sacrifice she was willing to make to save her daughter from her own fate, made Celine's heart ache. She leaned across the table to squeeze the other woman's hand. "If there is anything I can do. Any way I can help—"

"You will find it," Brynna said with the same tone of certainty Fiara often used. "You have an exceptionally kind heart, Lady Celine. It radiates from you. But first, it is I who must help you, is it not? You must tell me all you know of how you came to this time. It was on the eve of the new year?"

"Yes. From what I can figure out, I think it was a lunar eclipse—"

"Eclipse? A dark of the moon?"

"Yes, I guess you would call it that." Celine barely knew where to begin. Most of what Celine knew in this area came from listening to her sister, Jackie, who loved science and studied it; she herself hadn't taken a single science course her first semester—her only semester—in college.

Boy, the little decisions that made a huge difference in life.

"I know a little bit about how eclipses work," she said. "Let's see, I guess first of all I have to explain that the world is round, not flat . . ."

They spent the better part of the day talking about astronomy and time, putting together Celine's twentieth-century science and Brynna's ancient knowledge to try to make sense of how the lunar eclipse had sent her here.

Celine used balls of wool to demonstrate how the earth orbited the sun, and the moon around the earth, and how a lunar eclipse occurred whenever the three lined up straight: the moon on the earth's far side, the sun casting the earth's shadow on the moon.

Later, Brynna opened her ornate trunk, which contained sheaves of her father's writings, to see if his papers had any useful information to offer.

Fiara returned in the afternoon, and the three of them ate a meager supper—it pained Celine to note just how meager it was. Afterward, Fiara went to bed, exhausted by her midnight walk and her day of excitement. She slept soundly, except for a brief moment when she sat up, staring drowsily at the wall next to her pallet, almost as if she could see outside, and mumbled something like "He means no harm." Brynna tucked her in again, explaining that her daughter often awakened when wolves or other forest animals wandered close to the hut.

Hours later, as darkness fell, Celine and Brynna sat with brows furrowed, contemplating drawings and star charts sketched by Brynna's father. Both were pleased that they were finally making some progress.

"So time, you see, is not so precise as many believe," Brynna was saying, lighting a candle. "It is not a solid thing, to be carved into days and hours at our bidding. It is fluid, liquid. It can change as easily as the sea changes, on one day calm and smooth, on another stormy and dangerous."

"So New Year's Eve was just a dark and stormy night, timewise." Celine muttered, studying an ancient piece of parchment with runic lettering and lavish illuminations in silver and gold.

Brynna smiled. "Aye. And just as the sea can be affected by outside forces, such as wind and rain, time can also be affected by outside forces. You have told me that it is the moon that controls the ocean tides—"

"Yes, something to do with gravity. And if the moon is strong enough to affect massive bodies of water that cover half the earth—"

"Is it not also strong enough to affect something so liquid as time?" Brynna pointed out with growing excitement. "On the eve of the new year, the eclipse must have been strong enough to cause a ripple in time . . . a whirlpool."

"And I was standing right on top of it," Celine whispered. "And it pulled me in."

Brynna nodded, eyes bright. "Like a door. A trapdoor that fell open beneath you. You are most intelligent, Lady Celine."

"Not really." Celine laughed. "At least, not compared to the rest of my family. So if that's how the moon sent me back in time, how do I get it to send me home?"

Brynna spread out the paper she had been poring over, a roll of parchment so ancient it was yellowed and cracked and disintegrating along its gilt edges. "According to my father's chartings of the stars, there will occur four more darkenings of the moon this year—'eclipses,' as you call them. First a partial one, here." She pointed to a circle on the map. "Then a complete one, several months later." She pointed to another spot. "Then two more partial ones after that. Here . . . and here."

"Did you say several *months* later?" Celine felt her heart drop to the bottom of her toes. "I . . . I don't think I have several months, Brynna. I'll have to get home on the first one. I'll *have* to. I've got an . . . injury that needs attention. Soon."

"In your back." Brynna glanced up with a concerned expression. "I thought I sensed something odd there. Something amiss."

"Yes. And it's something that can't be cured by herbals or bleeding or a barber-surgeon whose idea of sound medical care is amputation." Celine could hear her voice rising.

"Then we must send you home on the first dark of the moon," Brynna said emphatically, making a measurement on the chart with an odd little metal device that looked like an elaborate protractor.

"When will it be exactly? Can you tell?"

"A fortnight . . ." Brynna muttered, moving the tool across the chart, "then another se'nnight . . . it will occur three weeks from this night, Lady Celine. The first night that the moon begins to wane from full. And I believe that somewhere ... hmm ..." She set the protractor aside and started rifling through the sheaves of her father's writings piled on the table. "I think my father makes mention of that—how the waxing and waning may affect the time-journey."

"Come in on the waxing moon, go out on the waning moon. That makes sense." Celine tried to remain calm, but her stomach was churning. *Three weeks*. Did she have three weeks?

"Aye, if only I could find the note," Brynna said, tossing aside sheets of her father's scribbles. "Ah—here it is." She held up a page triumphantly, then leaned closer to the candlelight and began to read. "Hmm ... indeed ... ah, most interesting! Listen carefully, milady. Here is what you must do."

Chapter 9

"**W**hat?" Celine asked nervously. "What must I do?"

Brynna read the page again. "My father mentions here the Druid legends that speak of people coming back in time, and says he knew of such people himself." She lifted her gaze. "I remember him telling such tales when I was young, but I never quite knew whether he was merely making them up to amuse me. You are the first time-traveler I have ever met." She glanced back at the parchment. "He says that not all of those he knew managed to return home. Some were trapped here, and lived out their days in this time—"

"Oh, my God," Celine whispered.

"Nay, milady. It is no cause for alarm. He says it will work as you said—in on the waxing moon, out on the waning moon. But there is a secret to making the return passage successfully. A key to open the door."

"A key." Celine took a deep breath, forcing her fear to the back of her mind. "What kind of key? I've got to get it right the first time, Brynna. If I make a mistake—"

"Nay, you will not. My father says that those who were successful went out precisely as they came in. You simply must imitate, as closely as possible, the instant you were sent back in time. Stand in the same spot, wearing the same garments you were wearing, even thinking the same thoughts. The key, milady, is that you must be complete— you cannot leave anything behind. And you cannot take anything from this time with you." She glanced up again. "You have been here but a few days. Do you still have all the belongings you arrived with?"

Celine didn't need to think about it for more than a second; she remembered vividly the moment she had awakened in Gaston's bed. "Yes," she said with relief. "Yes, I do! All I had with me was my teddy—an undergarment that women wear in my time. It's considered rather indecent here. The serving women wanted to burn it, but I insisted on keeping it because it's my only link with home. I've still got it, in my room!" Her fear gave way to growing excitement. This was going to work. She was going *home*. Back to her time, her family, her life.

Brynna smiled. "Then you should have no difficulties, milady. My father says here that only those time-travelers who had lost or discarded something they arrived with could not return home."

"So I'll just put on my teddy, think twentieth-century thoughts, and if the moon will cooperate . . ." Celine smiled, hope and anticipation building within her. "I get zapped and wake up safe and sound in 1993."

"Aye." Brynna laughed. "Three weeks from this night, milady. Mark it well. The 'eclipse,' as you call it, will occur on the first night after the moon reaches full, just as it begins to wane."

Celine nodded. Three weeks. No way would she forget. Waxing in, waning out. The idea made perfect, logical sense. "Thank you. I'm so grateful for your help." She stood and picked up her cloak, realizing she had kept poor Brynna awake half the night. "I'd like to send one of the serving girls with some food and things from the castle, if that would be all right—please, for Fiara?"

Brynna looked like she was going to object at first. Hard experience had clearly made her a fiercely independent woman, not the sort to accept charity. But at the mention of her child, she swallowed her pride. "Aye, milady. I thank you for your kindness to my daughter."

Celine had every intention of sending just as many things for Brynna as for Fiara, but she didn't mention that. "She's a very special little girl." Celine smiled. "Like her mother. Thank you again. I promise I won't tell anyone the truth about your . . . powers." She glanced toward the corner, where Fiara was curled up beneath a blanket. "Good-bye, my little guide," she said softly. "If I don't see you again, be well. And be happy."

And you as well, milady. Take good care of Groucho.

Celine started at the sound of Fiara's voice; the little girl hadn't moved, she was breathing evenly and appeared to be deeply asleep . . . yet Celine had heard the words in her mind, as clearly as if the child had spoken them aloud.

"Lady Celine? Is something amiss?" Brynna asked.

Celine turned to her. "No, I . . . uh . . . I was just trying to remember how to get back to the castle."

"Oh, aye—you must not forget this." Brynna went to the table and brought over a small map Fiara had sketched earlier. "Remember to take the left fork when you come to the turn in the road."

"I won't forget."

"And do not worry about the wolves. Fiara said she spoke to them for you."

"Oh . . . good." The comment would seem bizarre in any normal situation, but this was not normal, and it made perfect sense. "Thank you."

Brynna smiled warmly, her face full of hope. "Godspeed, milady."

With a farewell hug, Celine hurried off into the darkness.

It was a bit less cloudy than it had been the previous night, so the moonlit path was a little brighter and Celine's progress faster. She stuck to the middle of the tree-lined path, ignoring the tingles down the back of her neck when she heard the occasional wolf cry somewhere deep in the forest.

It required all her concentration just to put one foot in front of the other; after having hiked miles through the snow and then been awake for almost twenty-four hours, she kept herself going only by the excitement of her plans to return home. She was not at all eager to face Gaston's wrath when she got back to the castle. He was going to be a regular Tasmanian devil by the time she showed up.

The strange thing was, now that leaving was within her grasp, now that she had an actual date and a plan in place, she felt ... odd at the thought of never seeing Gaston again.

She chastised herself for being foolish. She had to go home, and there was no way he was coming with her—besides, he was a thoughtless, heartless, skirt-chasing jerk. Exactly the kind of man she didn't want or need.

Okay, well, maybe "jerk" was a little strong.

And he wasn't entirely heartless. He *had* let her have her baths. And her kitten. And he *did* have good reason to be suspicious of her. And then there was the fact that he had given away a huge portion of his own winter supplies to the local peasantry. Not the act of a thoughtless, self-interested cad.

On a few rare occasions, he let glimpses of his kindness and softer side shine through. Given a little time—

She squashed that thought. Time was the one thing she had in extremely short supply.

And who was she trying to kid, anyway? All the time in the world wouldn't change Gaston de Varennes. He didn't *want* to change. He was perfectly happy with his tomcat ways; that was one part of his legendary reputation he definitely lived up to. One woman would never be enough to satisfy him.

Except perhaps the wealthy, aristocratic Lady Rosalind. Lady R.

The woman he would love so much, he would one day carve her initial above every door in his castle.

Celine's vision blurred suddenly. She had to leave, and Gaston would be much happier without her. Married to his Lady R. That was the way things were *meant* to be. The rest of this was nothing but a mistake that would soon be corrected—

She stopped in her tracks, realizing that she hadn't been paying attention to where she was going for some time. Had she passed the fork in the road yet?

She turned to look behind her. The woods and the snow and the twisting trail all looked the same to her; there were no landmarks. The map in her hand indicated the fork, but unfortunately, there was no "You Are Here" sticker.

She *had* passed it, hadn't she? And chosen the left fork?

Or had she?

"Oh, *damn.*" She started to backtrack. "A nice fluorescent road sign or two would be a big help right about now," she said miserably.

She ignored the cold uneasiness that trickled through her. If she was lost, she might never find her way out of these woods. Sacajawea she was not. She was used to depending on well-marked concrete highways and savvy cabdrivers to get her where she was going.

Squaring her shoulders, she kept walking. All she had to do was find the fork—

An animal made a noise, somewhere off to the right, behind her.

Celine stopped. That wasn't a howl. It wasn't wolflike at all. More like a snuffly, wet, breathing sound. Made by something very *large.* She had never heard anything like it in her life.

Whatever made it went silent a second later. She stood there, frozen, not even breathing. Maybe it was a bear.

Had Fiara thought to clear her with the local bear population?

She picked up her pace, her heart suddenly pounding in her chest, painfully hard. She couldn't breathe. Just taking a single mouthful of air was impossible. She felt like her lungs were being squeezed by a giant hand.

Oh, God, not now. She kept walking. Briskly. Almost running. *Don't panic, don't panic, don't* . . .

It was too late. The familiar crisis hit her before she could even begin to ward it off. A full-blown panic attack. The first one she had had since she got here. At the worst possible time.

Then she heard a branch break. On the path, directly behind her.

Someone—some*thing*—was following her.

Celine froze, turned, heart pumping wildly. She could sense a presence, something large and dangerous and intently interested in her.

"H-hello?" she called out, peering into the gloom. "Brynna? Fiara? Is that you?"

But there was no reply.

* * *

By nails and blood, had she seen him?

Gaston went still, standing beside his destrier, one hand holding the reins, the other over the animal's nose to try to stop its blowing. Pharaon was growing restless at the slow pace; the stallion was better suited to battle than to stealth.

Since morning, he had been on Christiane's trail, certain she meant to meet with Tourelle—though her stop at the mystic woman's hut made little sense. Could the woman and her daughter somehow be connected to Tourelle's plot? Why was the child not returning to the castle? And what was the point of Christiane's meandering path now? She was either incredibly crafty . . . or completely lost.

He was dressed all in black; she shouldn't be able to see him. Through the shifting forest shadows he could barely make out her slender form a few yards ahead, illuminated by a sprinkling of moonlight. She was trembling like a leaf in a gale, and her breathing sounded odd—short, sharp gasps, unnaturally loud in the stillness.

"Is . . . is anyone there?" she asked.

Gaston remained silent. He wasn't going to give himself away. Not after spending so many patient hours tracking her. He cursed himself for following too close; he should have kept his distance, but every wolf's howl had drawn him nearer to her, ready to protect her if need be. The woman had to be daft or desperate, wandering the forest at night, alone and unarmed.

She peered into the darkness, looking directly at him. His jaw clenched. The game was up.

But after a moment she turned and kept moving, faster now.

Allowing the distance between them to widen, he followed. Mayhap she had realized long ago that he was behind her on the path. Mayhap she was purposely trying to lead him astray in order to protect her overlord. Tourelle could be anywhere out here, waiting.

Indeed, this would be a perfect opportunity for Christiane to have some "accident" befall her new husband.

Gaston glanced around through the gloom, one hand

drifting to the hilt of his sword. He could be walking straight into a trap. Why hadn't he thought of that before setting out after her alone?

He scowled. He *knew* why, and it wasn't merely because he had been so furious when he found her missing. It was because he had been concerned for her safety when he discovered her tracks at the edge of the wood. He had not stopped to think. He had paused only long enough to grab his sword and mount his horse before going after her.

Because he had been concerned for her safety.

Concerned for *her.*

That was such a disturbing thought it stopped him in his tracks. He stared at her through the moonlit shadows, watching her hurry down the path away from him.

He had once again allowed *feelings* to overwhelm his reason. Feelings for a woman. *This* woman. His enemy's ward. It was a witless mistake, one that might cost him his life. Which would be a just reward, he thought with a grimace, for tossing all logic aside. Galloping off alone like some reckless, inexperienced page boy—

Pharaon suddenly tossed his head, taking another huge, snuffling breath. The noise rent the silent woods.

Christiane gave a terrified shriek and broke into a run.

"Saints' blood." Gaston dropped the reins, torn between caution and chasing after her. Was this part of her act? Was she leading him into an ambush? Tourelle's armed men could be waiting in the darkness to cut him down.

Swearing, he drew his sword and ran after her.

She screamed again at the sound of his pursuit. Without warning, she left the road, plunging into the impenetrable darkness of the trees.

Little fool! She would break her neck! "Christiane, stop!"

She couldn't seem to hear him. His shout only made her go faster until she was crashing heedlessly through the undergrowth.

This was no act. She was clearly terrified. Lost and alone and terrified, and she had no idea who was chasing her.

"Christiane, it is Gaston!" He sheathed his sword,

breaking through the brush, running faster as she darted away ahead of him. "Christiane!" He was only a few paces behind her now. "Good Christ, woman, stop before you kill yourself!"

She kept fleeing in a wild panic, sobbing with terror, not paying the least attention to him or where she was going. Her slim form was a blur. It was only a miracle that she avoided the low branches and huge oak trunks and gnarled roots that loomed suddenly out of the blackness.

But the trees stopped abruptly a few feet ahead. He saw the danger before she did: the edge of a knoll that dropped away sharply.

"Nay!" With a burst of speed, he grabbed for her cloak.

Her name tore from his throat as he missed her by a hairsbreadth. His hand closed on air.

She ran straight off the edge, tumbling into darkness, her scream of sheer terror shattering the forest night.

A sickening thud below cut short her cry.

For one horrible instant, Gaston stood frozen at the top of the knoll, hand still outstretched, unable to move a muscle, his heart pounding wildly. She was dead. Sweet Jesus, the sound of that impact—

Before he could take a breath, he was plunging down the hill, scrambling for purchase as the forest floor fell away beneath him, a steep drop littered with sharp rocks and branches, slick with snow and ice. Only the saplings and evergreens tearing at his garments slowed his descent.

At the bottom, he found himself in a chasm. An ice-frosted river snaked through its center, gleaming silver-white in the moonlight. He could see marks in the snow where his wife had landed and tumbled down the hillside as he had. But she was nowhere to be seen.

Then he saw the jagged hole cracked in the thin crust of ice. *She had fallen through.*

"God's breath!" He plunged into the thigh-deep water without pausing to think, driven only by the numbing thought that she must already be dead. He tore at the jagged ice with his gloved hands. "Christiane!"

He found her in the darkness almost before her name had passed his lips. She was conscious, clawing at the slippery rocks, fighting the sluggish current as the weight of her clothes tried to drag her under. He pulled her free, hauling her from the water and lifting her in his arms. He staggered to the riverbank, his wet boots slippery on the snow.

"By sweet holy Christ, woman, if you *ever* attempt such foolishness again . . ." He could not say more; he was shaking with fury at the way she had so recklessly endangered her life.

Coughing, sobbing, she clung to him weakly, shuddering with bone-deep cold. He sank to his knees, still holding her in his arms, barely noticing the icy water that soaked his tunic, just holding her, willing his heart to slow down, his breath a white fog in the darkness above her head.

"Are you hurt?" He could hear an odd, unfamiliar edge to his voice. Slowly, carefully, he set her away from him, but she was shaking so badly she couldn't even kneel without his assistance. He kept one arm around her waist while he quickly ran his free hand over her. She winced when he touched her right side; it must have been there that she had struck the snowy hillside. Fortunately, he could detect no broken ribs.

Other than painful bruises, her worst problem seemed to be that she wasn't breathing right. She kept coughing up mouthfuls of water, exhaling more air than she was inhaling.

Gaston began massaging her between the shoulder blades. "Breathe, Christiane. You are all right, but you have to breathe."

She lifted her head, staring up at him with fear-glazed eyes, almost as if she did not recognize him. She looked as if she might faint from pure panic.

"You are safe," he said firmly, taking her face between his hands. "You are all right now, Christiane. *Breathe.*"

She did not respond, only stared at him with that wide, blank gaze, taking in naught but the tiniest gasps of breath. Her skin was unnaturally pale.

"You have naught to fear, Christiane." He gentled his tone, stroking her cheeks. "Calm down."

"I . . ." She shook her head. "I . . ."

He tried rubbing her back again. "If you do not breathe, you will faint. Take a deep breath and relax."

"Ca . . . ca . . . can't," she choked out.

Gaston began to realize that her fear came from much more than her fall into the river; she was caught in the grip of a strange, unreasoning panic, an all-consuming terror that left her helpless. And having him see her in such a vulnerable state only seemed to be upsetting her more.

He drew her close again, rubbing her back in a firm, gentle rhythm, up and down. He could feel her heartbeat thrumming wildly. "Christiane, you are all right. You are with me. Naught will harm you. Take a deep breath, just one. I will do it with you."

"Can't."

It seemed all she was capable of saying.

"Try counting to two with me. One." He inhaled. "Two." He let out the breath slowly.

She tried to do it along with him. All she managed was a bit more of a gasp than before.

"Good. Keep breathing, Christiane. To four this time. One . . . two . . ." He inhaled. "Three . . . four." He exhaled.

This time she did it.

"Excellent. But let it out more slowly. Try doubling the count when you exhale."

"This . . . isn't helping," she said in a shaky voice.

A grin quirked at the corner of his mouth; it obviously *was* helping, since she had managed a complete sentence. "You are most impatient, even for a female. Try it again, with me. To four this time." He counted for her as they inhaled together. "One . . . two . . . three . . . four."

He soon had her breathing in rhythm with him: in to the count of four and out to eight, then in to eight and out to sixteen, and before she could argue with him any further, she had started to relax. He could feel her heart slowing to a more normal pace.

"Good . . . keep breathing . . . relax . . . naught will harm you . . . be peaceful . . ." He kept it up until calm seemed to restore a bit of her strength.

"You know," she said after several moments, "I think I . . . am starting to feel . . . a little better. How did you . . . l-learn to do that?"

"In the East, during my mercenary days." He set her away from him again, still holding her by the arms to support her. "Are you all right?" She was shivering badly, and her teeth were chattering, but she had some color back in her cheeks.

"Yes. Thank you for . . . for rescuing me. I didn't know it was y-you behind me. I thought . . . you were a bear."

Now that she was safe, some of Gaston's anger returned. "God's breath, woman, do you not have the sense you were born with? Did you not hear me calling your name?"

"Well, why d-didn't you . . . let me k-know *before* that you were f-following me?" she demanded through chattering teeth. "H-how did . . . you find me?"

"A blind man could have tracked you. You made little enough effort to conceal your trail. Did you think you could meet with Tourelle and I would not notice? When he chose you to carry out his plans, Christiane, he made the worst mistake of his life."

"T-Tourelle?" she spluttered. "You think that's what I . . ." She shoved at him, as if realizing only then that he was still holding on to her. "Let me go. Get away from me."

"Indeed, I shall. As soon as possible." But instead of doing as she asked, he scooped her into his arms and stood up, striding toward the steep knoll. "But first I mean to make sure you do not catch your death of cold." She was shivering badly, and it was getting worse with every second she spent in her wet garments.

"Put me down. I am fed up with your accusations!" she cried, pushing at his chest and being generally unhelpful as he carried her up the slippery incline. "I'm tired of trying to pretend to be what I'm not! I've had enough of this! You want the truth, you can have it, buster. Do you hear me? *I wish to tell the truth!*"

When they reached the top of the hill, Gaston set her on her feet, breathing heavily from exertion and exasperation.

He could not believe she would give in now after having been so stubborn for so long. "Very well, then, tell me—where is Tourelle? Why did you go to meet with the mystic woman? What have she and the child to do with all of this?"

"Absolutely nothing. My being out here has *nothing* to do with you or Tourelle. If you really want the truth, here it is." She faced him with clenched fists, her entire body trembling with cold. "I am not Christiane. My name is Celine Fontaine, I'm from the year 1993, and that woman was trying to help me get back to my own time."

For a moment, Gaston just stared at her in stupefaction. Then he threw up his hands with a laugh. "God's breath, woman, if you are going to lie, can you not devise a new tale? Do you truly think I am going to believe such madness?"

"It's the truth! I've even thought of something else that might convince you. Look! Look at this." She took a step toward him and opened her mouth, pointing to bits of silver in her teeth. "Have you ever seen someone with *fillings* in their teeth before? And that scar on my back that you noticed before—it's a bullet wound. A *bullet*. A small piece of metal, shot from a weapon called a *gun*. How can you possibly explain that?"

"As you said before, the scar is from an injury suffered in an accident. And mayhap your convent in Aragon has strange customs such as painting the teeth with silver. Religious orders are known for eccentric behavior—"

"But that's not it! I'm from the *future!* You've got to believe me!"

He crossed his arms over his chest and gave her a cynical smile. "Your teeth and your scar tell me naught, milady. Is there aught else you would show me to convince me?" His gaze lowered suggestively to the fabric clinging wetly to her breasts. "I believe I prefer the persuasive methods you tried before."

She gave him a furious glare. "Is everything *sex* with you? Please *try* and listen to me for one second. I'm telling you the truth! An eclipse of the moon caused a ripple in time that pulled me from my family's chateau and landed me here on New Year's Eve. That's how I ended up in your room. *I'm from 1993.* That's why I have a strange accent. That's why I have short hair. That's why I didn't understand any of the medieval servant-things you wanted me to do. That's why I was able to make all the different foods and 'strange devices' for your people. What do I have to do to convince you?"

Gaston turned on his heel and started to walk away. "The cold water has addled your brain, Christiane. Strip out of those wet clothes."

"What?"

He whirled on her, eyes piercing. "You heard me, *ma dame.* Even riding Pharaon, we won't be able to return to the castle for hours—and you will catch your death in this freezing air long before then. I will at least have you warm and dry before we begin the journey back."

"But what about what I've just been *telling* you? You aren't listening. You've got to believe—"

"I will never believe such insane lies. If you insist on your stubborn loyalty to Tourelle, you will at least spare me the feigned madness. Disrobe before you freeze to death."

"Damn you!" she shouted back. "What would you care if I *did* die? You'd probably celebrate. You'd be free of your unwanted wife. You don't care half a damn what happens to me."

Gaston was suddenly shaking, not with cold, but with helpless rage at the knowledge that her accusation was utterly untrue. The idea of anything happening to his beautiful, impulsive, headstrong . . . wife. Sweet Jesus, the way his heart had nearly stopped when she had tumbled over the edge of that knoll—

"Nay, *wife,* I do not care," he snapped. "But unfortunately for me, the King does. If aught ill befalls you, I will forfeit all I own, and you are not worth that price. Or any price." He turned on his heel again, tossing back a single growled word: *"Disrobe."*

Chapter 10

G aston stalked off through the trees, muttering oaths
under his breath, cursing himself, his wife, Tourelle,
the King, everyone responsible for placing him in this impossible situation. A situation that was getting worse by
the moment.

From the future, she claimed. The *moon* had caused a
ripple in time. What madness!

He would like naught better than to haul his lying little
wife straight back to the castle, toss her into the dungeon
on her shapely derriere, and let her stay there until she decided to tell the truth—the *real* truth about what she was
doing out here in the forest and where Tourelle was hiding.

But he could not do that. If she fell ill because of her
reckless river escapade tonight, he would be blamed. And
the King would happily feed him to his royal hounds. In
small pieces.

He had to at least get her warm and dry before the two
of them took to the road, though it was the last thing he
wanted to do.

Being near her, being alone with her, he had decided,
was what made these intolerable, unwanted *feelings* creep
over him. The more time he spent with her, the tighter
they seemed to twine around him; a vexing melee of desire, concern for her safety, anger at her stubbornness, and
an attraction stronger than any he had ever felt.

God's breath, he had to get this woman out of his life.
As quickly as possible.

Making his way through the darkness to the road, he
found Pharaon where he had left him; the destrier had

been trained not to move once the reins were on the ground. Gaston snatched them up and led the stallion into the forest thickets.

"Females! Naught but treacherous, untrustworthy, scheming little bundles of trouble," he complained, grateful for an audience that did not argue with his opinion. "Especially beautiful, intelligent, *reckless* females."

When he returned to the place where he had left Christiane, she was still dressed in her wet garments, still standing in the same spot—and shivering so badly in the wintry breeze, she could barely stand.

"By nails and blood, woman, must you disobey every order I give you?" He dropped Pharaon's reins and stalked toward her. "If you refuse to follow my commands, I shall—"

"You're going to believe me eventually," she said, backing away from him as he advanced, her eyes bright with sparks of defiance. "I'm telling you the truth. I'm from the future. When the *real* Christiane shows up, you'll have to believe me—"

"And when, pray, might that be?"

"Any day now, I'm sure, now that the roads are clearer."

"So you *do* know where Tourelle is," he accused.

"No, I don't! I don't know anything about him. I don't even know what he looks like. But I know that whenever the real Christiane gets here, you'll be eating your words. *That* I can't wait to see. You need a few humbling experiences in your life—"

Her back came up against a tree trunk and she seemed to forget the rest of her speech. He stopped with less than an inch between their bodies and planted a hand on either side of her head.

"Mayhap, milady, I shall be humbled someday as you predict," he said with dangerous softness. "But at the moment, I intend to make certain you are still alive to verify that I have not mistreated you, when Tourelle is found. You will take off those wet clothes, *ma dame.*"

"I'll . . . I'll bet that . . . when the real Christiane shows up," she said in a small but insistent voice, "you'll find out that she's not even involved in any plot. She's probably completely innocent. She is my ancestor, after all. We Fontaines have always been known for honesty and fortitude. She's probably just a helpless girl caught up in a stupid battle between two men—"

He started to unfasten her cloak.

"Wait!" She reached up to stop him. "I can do that."

Her hand covered his and he felt the contact strike deep and sudden, blazing through him, like a blow from a hot blade. He did not say a word. His gaze locked on hers, he stood as still as one of the massive oaks around them, his fingers resting at the hollow of her throat.

"Then see that you do," he said at last.

Shoving himself away from her, he stalked off into the black night, drew his sword, and hacked a few low-hanging branches from nearby trees. Stripping the dead leaves, he added them to what dry kindling he could find.

He kept his back to her, but no matter how hard he tried to ignore her, to distract himself, he was keenly aware of her every movement, every intimate sound she made as she peeled the wet garments from her body in the darkness.

First she slid her cloak from her shoulders. Then she kicked off her boots. Then—he swallowed hard—she pulled her tunic over her head, voicing a shivery little gasp; he imagined it must be from the shock of the cold air against her damp, nude breasts.

He shut his eyes, gripped the hilt of his sword with painful force, tried to shut out the vivid picture of her rosy nipples pinched to impudent peaks by the touch of the breeze.

Then he heard her remove her leggings. He could almost *feel* them clinging to every curve of her ankle and knee, hip and thigh as she wrestled them off.

His mouth felt dry. At that moment a battle began, there in the forest in the midst of the snowy winter night. A war against the most challenging adversary he had ever faced, fought not with cold steel and brute force, but with hot passions and ungentle stirrings.

And the enemy was himself.

A pool of heat settled low in his belly, a pulsing ache tortured his manhood, yet he knew that the gathering storm of longings must never, *never* be allowed to break free.

It was, he thought cynically, as if he were being punished for a lifetime of pleasurable indulgence. Of all the women he had ever known, desired, bedded . . . the one he wanted most, with a hunger beyond all hunger, the one who truly belonged to him by rule of Church and King, *was forbidden to him.*

Forcing himself to move, he concentrated on building a fire, his every move sharp and taut with the growing tension within him. He had a blaze burning in a matter of minutes, flames leaping into the night.

Spreading a ground covering of evergreen branches beside it, he made a soft, dry place for her to sit. Then he removed Pharaon's saddle and the padded woolen square beneath, placing the wool atop the evergreens and adjusting the saddle so she could use it as a backrest.

When he had finished all this, he finally, slowly, turned to look at his wife.

Standing just beyond the edge of the firelight, she trembled like spring's first flower in the winter wind, her sodden clothes clasped against her, her expression one of pure misery.

It softened something inside him, seeing her so vulnerable. "Come here, Christiane," he said quietly, holding out his hand.

"My name is Celine."

He frowned. "I am not going to argue your lies any further."

"And I'm not going to answer to someone else's name anymore," she said stubbornly, teeth chattering.

Gaston's jaw tensed. Normally he would not brook such defiance, but his first concern at the moment was getting her warm and dry before she caught her death in this frigid air. "Very well," he said grudgingly. "Come here to me . . . Celine."

Instead of the gloating he had expected, she simply nodded in weary gratitude. She came to him, timidly, shivering but trying to look brave.

He felt that odd, tight knot inside him loosen another notch. Sweeping off his cloak, he held it out to her.

"You can't take that off," she said, though she looked longingly at the thick lining of silver wolf fur. *"You'll* freeze to death without it."

"I am not the one who decided to take a midnight swim. And I have suffered worse weather than this for days at a time with less to wear."

"Right. The great warrior. So tough he doesn't feel anything as mortal as cold or pain or bad weather. How could I forget?"

He stepped toward her, keeping his eyes on hers. "I promise that if I feel I am starting to 'freeze to death,' I will take it back," he lied.

That seemed to placate her. Cheeks red—whether with cold or embarrassment he couldn't tell—she finally let go of her sodden clothes and hung them on branches near the fire. When she had finished, she did not turn around; she stood with her back to him, as if she could not make herself face him, arms wrapping about herself, firelight dancing over her lush curves.

She went very still when he came up behind her and gently enfolded her in the heavy mantle.

God's breath, but she felt soft and fragile and slender in his arms. Her body fitted so perfectly against his, the top of her head just brushing his chin, as if she had been made for him, made to fill his arms in exactly this way. His cloak was so large that it covered her from neck to heels and trailed upon the ground; he wrapped it snugly around her, his heart beating strangely at the small sound of relief and pleasure she made when she felt the fur, still warm from his body heat, against her nakedness.

Lifting her in his arms, he carried her to the fire. She uttered a little gasp of surprise but offered no other protest.

He meant to set her down on the soft bed of evergreens he had made.

Meant to leave her there and sit on the opposite side of the fire.

He truly meant to.

"Gaston," she muttered tiredly, "it's really not necessary to keep carting me around like this."

He settled himself before the fire, sitting cross-legged with the saddle at his back and Christiane sideways in his lap. "Walking in the snow with bare feet will not improve your health." He held her still when she tried to pull out of his arms. "And neither will getting that cloak wet. It is the last dry garment we have."

"But I . . . I don't think . . . this is a good idea."

He heard the soft, nervous waver in her voice, heard her feminine awareness of him, and it sent a new flash of desire through his body. "It is warmer," he said a bit harshly, trying to convince them both that he was acting in a perfectly logical, rational manner. "And the sooner you are warm and dry, the sooner we can return to the castle."

That made sense. Perfect sense. He tucked the cloak more closely around her and held her against his chest, adding his body heat to healthful qualities of the fur and the fire.

"I guess th-that's true," she agreed, still holding herself stiffly.

Neither of them spoke for a long time. After a while the heat seemed to thaw her a bit, for she relaxed against them. Then, with a weary sigh of surrender, as if she were tired of fighting and arguing, or simply tired, she laid her head on his shoulder. In silence, they watched sparks from the fire swirling upward into the night sky.

Slowly, Christiane's eyes drifted closed.

Glancing down at her, Gaston felt the knot of desire and concern and attraction unravel even more within him. She looked so sweet, so lovely and pale, wrapped in his black cloak, the silver fur tickling her chin, her cheek resting on his shoulder, the gesture one of . . . complete, trusting innocence.

Innocence. Was it possible that she truly *was* innocent, as she said? A helpless pawn caught in a battle between two men?

Had he misjudged her from the beginning?

"Gaston, are you sure it's safe to have a fire out here at

all?" she whispered sleepily. "I mean, there are wolves, and maybe bears. In fact, I think it was awfully dangerous of you to come after me alone—"

"Is that concern I hear in your voice, wife?" he asked softly.

She opened her eyes, and for a moment he was certain she would deny it. But she did not. "I just don't think you should take unnecessary—"

"You should be more concerned about your own health, *ma dame,* wandering through the forest alone." His voice dropped to a husky note. "Defenseless against wolves . . . and other predators."

She did not seem to catch his meaning. "The wolves won't bother *me*—it's you I'm not so sure about. How *did* you find me all the way out here, anyway?"

"When I came to your chamber this morn, I found Royce asleep. He explained what had happened. Your tracks were clear at the edge of the wood."

"You came looking for me this morning?" She lifted her head from his shoulder and gazed at him in surprise. "Why? You swore you weren't going to have anything more to do with me."

Gaston stiffened, chastising himself for speaking so heedlessly. It was damnably easy for her to make him drop his guard. In truth, he had merely wanted to see her, just *see* her, even for a moment. He had thought it best to do so while she was still asleep.

But how could he possibly explain his irrational behavior to her when he could not explain it to himself?

"I rose early to see how Royce was faring," he lied. "It appears I cannot trust my men to guard you. I am the only one who recognizes you for the viper you are."

"I'm *not* a viper," she said through gritted, perfect little white teeth, "and I'm really getting tired of—"

"Do not annoy me further, *ma dame.* I am already most displeased that your disappearance forced me to interrupt my plans for the morning."

"What plans?" she asked tartly. "Playing footsie with some little blond serving maid?"

He raised an eyebrow. "What is 'footsie'?"

"It's . . . it's what you were doing with that tavern wench a few days ago."

The jealousy that sounded so clearly in her voice almost made him laugh. In truth, he had planned to spend the day with his hunting falcons, but it was better to let her believe what she wished to believe. "I had planned to spend the morning relaxing with *several* females." He smiled wickedly. "But not one of them was a blond." He was not lying, exactly; his best falcons *were* females.

"Several?" She blinked at him in shock, then tried to get off his lap, a task made difficult by the tightly wrapped cloak. "Let me go. You are disgusting! Impossible! Absolutely unredeemable!"

"A sinner to my black depths, I confess." He tightened his arms around her. "Cease your wriggling, Christiane."

"My name is *Celine*. And I'm not wriggling, I'm getting away from—"

Suddenly her struggles brought her beautifully rounded derriere fully up against his arousal. The friction made him inhale sharply, though his leggings and the mantle separated them.

She tensed, blushing crimson, and her voice dropped to a squeak. "I knew this wasn't a good idea."

"Do not fear, little wife, I have no intention of attacking you," he assured her darkly.

"How could you be so . . . after you were planning to be with another woman—other *women*—just this morning . . . and now you . . ."

"It is a physical response, *ma dame*, common to all males when they have a female wriggling in their lap."

"Is that so?" She gave up her battle to be free, apparently realizing that he was not going to let her run off into the woods a second time this night. "So it . . . has nothing to do with me or any other woman. We're all interchangeable to you. You're just another typical male—hot and bothered at the drop of a hat."

Her words made little sense to him. "You are far heavier than a hat, and it was the forcible way you dropped into my lap that caused the problem. I do have some measure of control, however. You are in no danger, Christiane."

"Celine," she corrected, recovering some of her ire. "I just don't want to be accused again of trying to seduce you."

"I cannot accuse you of that, because no seduction is taking place. Merely a physical response, which will no doubt subside as you keep chattering."

"I do not chatter."

"You do, and it is a most unappealing trait in a wife."

"Just like unfaithfulness is most unappealing in a husband!"

She suddenly blushed and bit her lip, looking mortified that she had said that.

He quirked an eyebrow at her. "You find my behavior disturbing? You said before that you do not care."

"I don't," she said quickly. "It's—it's your *thinking* that I find disturbing. You seem to believe that men should be allowed to do whatever they please. You really think men are superior to women, don't you?"

"In all the ways that matter," he said honestly. "But I suppose that you would disagree?"

"Yes! Being bigger and stronger and taking territory and . . . and making *conquests* are not all there is to life. Women at least think before they act, especially when it comes to . . . to . . ."

"Lovemaking?" he finished for her with a mocking grin. "Do you mean to say that women do not get aroused with passion as men do?"

"Not the way you think. Maybe tavern wenches are different, but . . . but most women need to be *in love* before they make love. They don't just throw themselves at everything that moves."

He laughed. "My inexperienced lady, you must be as innocent as you claim if you still believe in so childish an idea as love."

She gazed at him blankly, her expression filled with genuine amazement. "You don't believe in love?"

"It is a woman's word, not a warrior's," he said dismissively. "It is not something a man can claim with his sword or hold in his hand or own. It is not something solid, like land and walls, to build a future upon. My brother thought it real, and he is dead."

He regretted letting that slip as soon as the words had passed his lips.

A gleam of feminine understanding came into her eyes. "Your brother fell in love with someone . . . and died because of her?"

"He allowed himself to be softened by a female," Gaston said tightly. "I'll not make his mistake, ever."

To his irritation, she would not let the subject drop.

"But haven't you ever *felt* love?" she whispered incredulously. "For anyone? Not for your mother and father? Or your brother—"

"My mother died soon after I was born. My father and brother held my respect for their honor and skill as warriors."

"So you . . . grew up without love?" Sadness clouded her blue-gray eyes. "And you've never known *anyone* who truly loved someone else?"

Gaston clamped his lips into a thin line. He thought of Gerard and Avril, who had paid far too high a price for what they had called "love."

And he thought of his friend Sir Connor of Glenshiel and his wife, Lady Laurien. They had been married for five years now, had two sons and a daughter. In letters, they, too, spoke of love.

But mayhap it was merely an extreme form of passion between them, one that a noble, honorable knight such as Connor could indulge in, without the weakness it brought to lesser men.

But that could never be true for him.

"Love is naught but a word. A false word some men use to entice gullible females into bed," Gaston said with a steely edge to his voice. "I prefer more honesty in my dealings. I do not use falsehoods, nor do I need them. Pleasure is what is real. Plcasure is enough."

That comment made her eyes fill until they were shining with such deep pain that it was almost more than he could bear—and worst of all, he could tell she was feeling that pain for *him,* not for herself. She did not argue with him, only shook her head, speechless.

"Save your pity, *ma dame,*" he snapped. *"Love* is the last thing I would want from a woman. It is a tether women use to keep their men close to hearth and home—and I have no wish to be tethered. Or so weakened that I am rendered useless."

"But that's not—"

"I do not wish to discuss it further."

"But love isn't a tether! It doesn't restrict you, it frees you. It isn't just *something* to build a future on," she insisted with the unshakable faith of a believer, "it's the *only* thing."

"You are wrong," he said simply. "Someday, when you have greater experience, you will understand that."

"Never. I'll *never* understand that. And you don't ever have to worry about me trying to seduce you, *because I would never make love with a man I didn't love.*"

"Truly, milady?" he said with soft mockery. Her stubborn, unyielding insistence ignited a need in him to prove her wrong. "Do you believe that you have such control over your passions? Are you made of ice?" He lowered his head to hers. "Have you forgotten so quickly how you responded to *this?*"

Chapter 11

Without warning, he took her mouth in a kiss that was as slow as it was deep. A ravishment that had naught to do with so childish a notion as *love*. An embrace meant to disabuse her of that naive idea and replace it with a woman's experience of unmistakable *pleasure*.

He moved his mouth over hers with relentless purpose, urgent, demanding. Christiane stiffened and struggled, making a sound of protest in the back of her throat, but her efforts to push him away were futile; he held her locked against him, and her arms were wrapped in his cloak.

And her resistance was as brief as it was useless.

After only a moment, the ice in her melted away and she stopped fighting him. Then she began to respond, kissing him back. He felt a surge of triumph, of pure male satisfaction. She obviously remembered as well as he every fiery moment of the kiss they had shared in his bedchamber, the sudden, overpowering joining . . . like this.

God's breath, like *this*.

He uttered a low groan and fastened one arm around her shoulders, bending her backward, deepening the kiss.

He had proved his point. The lesson was ended. Women—at least women like Christiane—had just as much fire and passion as any man; they required only the *right* man to teach them about physical pleasure and their surrender was assured.

He had won. He could release her at any time.

But her lips . . . those soft, swollen petals were parting tremulously at the touch of his tongue, and she was granting him entry to the sweetness of her mouth. He thrust boldly inside, wanting but one taste of her. Only one.

With feinting little strokes that left her moaning, he explored her fully, intimately. She tasted of silken heat and the most delicate, enticing innocence he had ever known. The scents of earth and water and the softer notes of thyme and lavender and roses that clung to her skin spun around him like a heady mist, drawing him in.

Deeper, closer. Until he was nearly drunk with it. With the satiny play of her tongue against his . . . so tentative, but so willing. Untutored, but ready to learn. A tremor shuddered through his body, wrenched a hungering sound from deep within his chest.

He moved, rested his weight on one elbow, shifted her to the bed of evergreens. Holding her closer, he continued the wet, hot mating of their mouths, pressing his lower body against hers until she could not mistake the forcefulness of his desire for her. Through it all, she shivered against him.

Not with cold or with outrage, but with unmistakable wanting . . . wanting for him.

He finally tore his mouth from hers. Their breaths rasped together in the darkness, louder than the roar of the fire two paces away that bathed them in heat and light. He stared down into her once-stormy gaze, found it now dark with passion.

"*Pleasure,* my lady wife," he said roughly. "The word is *pleasure.*"

He did not give her a chance to respond before his lips captured hers once again. He needed the taste of her, more than he needed life, more than he needed reason. Before either of them knew what was happening, he had slipped a hand inside the folds of the cloak, his cloak, that concealed her nakedness.

Swallowing her murmur of surprise and uncertainty, Gaston kept his eyes closed and kept kissing her deeply. Her slender body, hidden in the folds of the dark mantle like a secret treasure, felt cool to the touch. Smooth as ivory. A tantalizing contrast to the warm, rich fur that concealed her.

He must not do this . . . yet he could not deny himself the pleasure of a touch, one touch. A moment of pure sensation that he would never forget. He was in control. He wanted only to teach her the true depth of her own passions. He could stop as soon as he wished.

His thumb whisked over the taut peak of one breast, back and forth, slowly, until a small cry broke from her. The feminine sound of wonder and desire struck him like a lash; he could feel his body straining, sheened with sweat caused not by the blaze that crackled and leaped beside them.

He released her mouth, left a trail of lingering kisses over her chin and jaw, nipping her neck. He took the delicate skin between his teeth and bit her, so very gently that he left no marks. His hold on her shifted, enough that she might pull away if she wished. But she did not.

Her passion-bruised lips offered no protest, no outrage, naught but broken breath and wordless moans as he moved lower. He nudged open the fur at her throat, unable to resist the temptation to see the full, soft roundness that so tenderly filled his hand. A single glimpse, and then he would stop.

He moved the mantle aside, exposing that one perfect breast until it was bathed in the golden glow of the firelight: the pale curves, the taut crown, his hand resting there, so broad and dark and male against that exquisitely feminine part of her.

The sight left him breathless, raked his body with reckless demands, shredded all logic and reason. She was a maiden unmatched, an ivory goddess arching against him, pale innocence wrapped in his black cloak. Lips parted, eyes closed, she waited, quivering and wanting, trusting him with her untried body, sweet purity and raw passion all in one. All his.

The words slammed into him like a battering ram. She was his. *His.* And he wanted her, in every way a man could want a woman: wanted to take her, wanted to keep her, wanted to never let her go.

But he must not take her. Could not keep her. Had to send her away, as soon as he could.

This was all he would ever have of her. A moment of

pleasure, frustrated and incomplete. Stolen, as he had stolen all else of value in his life.

A fierce possessiveness gripped him, a need to brand
her, to make her his, now and forever. And he knew it was
madness.

Madness. Even to touch her was madness. He stared
down at her lush body, so vulnerable before him. How
could she trust him when he dared not trust himself? He
grasped for sanity, struggled for breath, dangerously near
the edge of his control. He should wrap her in the cloak.
Leave her untouched. But he could not tear his gaze from
her breast, could not move his hand away. He had to stop.
Had to release her. Had to . . .

As if in a fevered dream, he lowered his mouth to her
breast.

With fingers and lips he drew the taut peak into the heat
of his mouth . . . and laved the impudent little pebble with
a long, wet brush of his tongue.

"Gaston!" She shuddered, gasped.

He suckled her, groaning, unable to stop, unable to turn
back, his body rigid. A sweep of his other hand exposed
still more of her naked, trembling flesh. He needed to
watch her burn, every inch of her. Needed to see and hear
and taste and feel—

Need. Aye, it was need that he felt for her. Like none he
had ever felt before, for any woman. It was a need he
could not understand, one that had naught to do with the
straining ache in his groin. But he had no time to explore
it. There was no room in his fevered body for aught but
sensation and iron control—one swiftly giving way to the
other.

Her nipples were wet and glistening in the firelight before his mouth covered hers once more. His hand skimmed
over the tender curves of waist and belly, seeking her most
feminine secrets, and she whimpered beneath him.

He found her with one gentle finger, unable to resist
sampling with a caress what he must deny his throbbing
manhood. He wanted—*needed*—to watch her undulate in
the dancing firelight, to hear her voice swell with sweet

music as she found release, her first release. This he would take and no more.

She was already damp, the hot nubbin swollen with desire. The passionate proof of her response to him wrested a strangled sound from his chest.

She matched his cry as he began to stroke her.

He lifted his head, gazing down at her, and knew that she would haunt him the rest of his days. He would never forget the scents of smoke and melting snow blended on the cold night wind. The sweet, feminine taste of her on his tongue. The feel of her slender form arched against him like a bow, smooth and strong and elegant even in the throes of violent passion.

He would never forget her.

Ruthlessly, he tried to banish the feeling, tried to think of naught but pleasure. He handled her delicately, touching her with light feathering motions that he knew would lash her with the deepest ecstasy; he played her body the way a musician would play a beautifully made instrument, carefully, skillfully, his fingers sure but restrained. He gave her time to adjust to the unfamiliar sensations, taking her from a hush of breathless anticipation to a slow, building movement.

Yet he was the one who trembled.

He tried to force the feeling aside, vexed and annoyed, but could not. He lowered his cheek to hers and went still, closing his eyes, his breathing harsh in her hair. How could the simple act of giving her pleasure affect him so powerfully? How could *she* affect him so powerfully?

There could be but one answer.

He seized onto it and held it fast.

She affected him this way because she was forbidden to him. That had to be the reason.

Her hips lifted against his hand, her small movements and demanding cries torturing him, every thrust of her body making his engorged shaft ache and throb. He began to stroke her again, more slowly this time. Her breathing roughened and splintered into small, eager gasps.

He would never be sated until he had taken her, melded

her body and his into one, the way the scents of smoke and melting snow tangled and blended on the night wind.

He lifted his head, watching, needing. She burned and he with her, a blaze in the middle of the snow-swept forest, far brighter than any real flames. One glimpse, one touch, one taste would never be enough. He must have more of her. All of her.

And he knew of a way.

"Gaston . . ." Celine sobbed. She thought she might faint, but he made conscious thought, resistance, anything but sensation and surrender impossible.

She opened her eyes and found his gaze locked on hers, his face washed with fire and shadow, cold and heat, passion and longing. He made no sound, only stroked her tenderly, urging her on. His breathing matched hers, as it had before when they knelt by the river.

He shifted his hand slightly, slipping one finger inside her, and her breath stopped altogether. His thumb took possession of the sensitive bud hidden by her damp curls.

The slow, patient, perfect brush of his thumb against that part of her that so ached for his caress . . . and the indescribable sensation of having him touch her *inside* . . .

She cried out brokenly as she felt a tremor beginning, spiraling upward from deep within her body, tension that wound tighter . . . tighter . . .

She gripped fistfuls of the cloak, bit her lip until she drew blood, helpless against the pleasure that whipped through her, helpless against the wildness rising from some unknown place inside her, a savage, inescapable tide.

She could not fight it, could not resist the ecstasy rushing through her, could not deny him any more than she had been able to deny his kiss.

Or the feelings she had for him.

But there was no time to think, for his touch was sweeping her upward, carrying her to a high, unexplored place, lifting her free of the earth in the same strong, powerful way he had lifted her free of the water. His fingers began to move faster within her, his thumb alternating soft, teasing flicks with rough, demanding caresses.

"Gaston!"

It was the last word she spoke before the spiral broke. In a single beat of her racing heart, an exploding shower of fire and light claimed her, cascading through her with an intensity beyond anything she had ever imagined. Pleasure raked her every muscle and nerve ending and she writhed in its grasp, uttering a primitive cry of revelation and release that echoed through the trees and the night. And when it had passed, she went limp, trembling, weak, as if she had just been born.

Gaston wrapped the cloak around her and pulled her into his arms, holding her close, his embrace strong and secure as the world spun wildly. She breathed into his shoulder, feeling his heart pounding as hard as hers.

"My sweet, sweet Celine," he said roughly, holding her tighter.

Celine felt a surge of joy in the midst of her blissful light-headedness; he had remembered her name. Her *real* name. She *did* matter to him. She wasn't just another female body, interchangeable with all the rest.

She lifted her head from his shoulder, still dizzy and weak and languid. "Th-that was . . . it was . . ."

"Nay, do not try to describe it, little one." He rained kisses over her cheeks, her nose, her lips. "Saints' blood, how I want you. Damn my black soul, I want you to stay with me."

Celine was stunned. "Gaston, I can't—"

"Nay, I want you, and I know you want me. Do not deny what we both know is true." He cupped her face in his broad hands, looking at her intently, his eyes burning with reflected firelight. "You cannot deny it any longer. Not now. By nails and blood, I must have you. There is a way—"

"Gaston, I can't stay with you—"

"Nay, listen to me. There is a way out of this, for us both." He kissed her again. "If you will go before the King and tell the truth, it will release me from our marriage so that I may wed Lady Rosalind. Then we will be free. Free to share our pleasure for as long as we wish. You can stay with me. As my mistress."

Celine stared at him, her pulse roaring in her ears. She didn't know which she felt first: fury or hurt. Both ripped through her with such force, she almost slapped him.

"As your mistress?" she cried. "And what about your wife?"

"Wives arc for land and for heirs, naught more," Gaston said dismissively, stroking her cheeks gently, looking as if he thought this was a perfectly reasonable offer. "I will bed her only to get sons—but you, my lady of fire, you will have my passion."

"And what of your love?" she demanded furiously. "Which one of us gets that?"

His expression hardened. "That discussion we have already finished, *ma dame.*"

Celine felt so crushed by hurt and disappointment and disbelief that she couldn't stand to be near him. She thrust herself out of his embrace, taking the cloak with her. "If you offer me passion without love, you offer me nothing!"

"Do you refuse me?" He seemed both surprised and irritated.

"Do you really think I would stay as—" She broke off, feeling tears burning her eyes. "It doesn't matter, anyway! This is impossible. *We're* impossible! I'm from 1993 and I have to go back to my own time. Don't you understand?"

"Nay, I do not understand your lies in the least, Christiane." He reached out to cup her chin. "But you, I believe, do understand. *I* have been proved right. Despite all your naive female notions of love, milady, you have just shown how beautifully you respond to pleasure."

Celine closed her eyes, feeling more humiliated and lost and stupid than she ever had in her life. He *had* proved his point, in no uncertain terms: proved that he could make her respond to him with one kiss or a single touch, with no words of love between them.

He didn't care about her. And he didn't believe she was from the future; speaking her real name moments ago had merely been a slip of the tongue.

He felt nothing for her. Nothing but what he felt for other women, all women, any woman. Lust.

While she . . . she felt such a confusing clash of emotions for him that she couldn't begin to put a name to them.

Except, at the moment, raw hurt.

But she couldn't let him know that.

"You haven't proved anything," she said hotly, opening her eyes, blinking back tears. "There's more to life than pleasure, Gaston. More than you'll ever know. All you've proved is that we'll be a whole lot happier without each other."

He cast her an irritated expression, stood, and stepped around her to douse the fire. "Cling to your childish fancies if you wish. But it appears that you are now warm, and it is time for us to return to the chateau."

Time.

She sat there feeling alone and helpless as he went to gather her drying clothes from the low-hanging branches.

Time.

She had to go home. As soon as the lunar eclipse occurred in three weeks. Because if she stayed here, she would die.

Either from the bullet in her back, or from the pain that was slowly sinking talons into her heart.

Chapter 12

A huge hearth dominated the castle's kitchen, large enough for roasting an ox whole, the massive logs inside it generating a steady heat that made the entire room feel summer-hot, even the brick floor. Standing at the oak-planked table in the center of the chamber, Celine paused to brush a strand of hair from her damp forehead.

Her heart skipped a nervous beat when she noticed how warm she was. Was it a fever?

No. No, it was the hot *room,* not a symptom. She was fine. Her imagination had been running away with her ever since she returned to the castle three weeks ago. For a couple of days she had experienced an odd sensation in her lower back—a twinge above her right hip—but it had disappeared just as suddenly.

It might have been nothing. A pulled muscle, from the physical exertion of her run through the forest, her icy dip in the river, and . . .

She took a deep breath and exhaled slowly, to the count of eight. She was all right. She had to be. And soon she'd be even better. Because tonight was the night.

Tonight she was going home.

Her hand shaking, she returned to her task, beating a bowlful of coarse flour, eggs, salt, and sugar, using her latest secret creation: a rotary egg beater, made with a little help from the armorer.

"Lady Celine, I do not understand why you do this." Gabrielle handed her a goblet of milk, then a copper pan brimming with butter that she had melted over the fire. "I do not understand why you continue to cook when milord

161

has granted you the freedom of the castle and said you no longer need work as a servant."

Celine stirred in the milk bit by bit, then the butter, before setting the bowl aside. "I enjoy teaching you," she said a bit too brightly, wiping her flour-covered hands on her skirt. "And I like feeling helpful."

That was true, at least partly. She also wanted to keep busy, wanted to keep her mind off things.

Lots of things.

"I believe I am almost ready, Lady Celine," Yolande said from beside the hearth, where she was heating a long-handled copper skillet.

"I will see if I can find some honey for our 'midnight snack.'" Gabrielle hurried off in the direction of the larder, the cool-storage area that filled a separate room attached to the kitchen.

"Yolande, I think we should let this batch sit and thicken up a bit before we try it," Celine said.

"Mayhap that would be best," the older woman agreed sheepishly.

Most of the first batch of crepes had dripped into the fire or slid onto the floor. One had ended up on the ceiling. Celine couldn't help but smile as she looked up at it; her two French-chefs-in-training were nothing if not enthusiastic. Each night for the past three weeks, after the servants had finished their daily duties and the kitchens were empty, she and Gabrielle and Yolande had gathered for a cooking lesson.

They didn't have the faintest idea how to dislodge that sticky little pancake up there, though, so the three of them had decided to leave it for one of the men to worry about in the morning.

Celine leaned back against the waist-high table, watching Yolande at her task. Slowly, her gaze was drawn to the flickering flames. It had been nice, these past weeks, to hear everyone use her real name. Not that she had tried to convince anyone else that she was from the future; they had merely accepted her explanation that it was a nickname from her convent in Aragon, one that she preferred to "Christiane."

Gaston was the only one who refused to use her "nick-name." He wasn't buying a single word she said, and he wouldn't call her Celine. Not that he had called her much of anything lately.

He had avoided her completely since that night in the forest. That disastrous, foolish, humiliating night.

Celine's eyes burned as the firelight brought it all back in painful detail. The two of them had barely spoken to each other all the way back to the castle. Gaston had held her in his lap, and insisted that she wear his cloak, even when she had tried to give it back to him. He had been gentle and protective and she had almost thought that he . . .

That he might care about her, just a little. That he might regret what he had said. Her hope had strengthened when they arrived here and he had abruptly declared both her imprisonment and her servitude ended. Though he said he didn't believe she was innocent in Tourelle's plot, he no longer seemed to consider her a threat to his people.

But after that, he had simply avoided her. He was finished with her. Finished trying to persuade her to do what he asked, finished trying to use her to attain his goal. He had instead sent search parties out on the roads leading from Aragon, with orders not to come back until they found Tourelle.

None of the men had reported in yet. Celine was disappointed about that; she had hoped to see Gaston's face when he met the real Christiane. She wanted to hear him admit that he had been wrong. Just once.

Once before she left.

Without Christiane, nothing short of running her husband over with her Mercedes was going to convince him that she was Celine Fontaine from 1993. And until he trusted her, believed her, the cool disdain he felt for her wouldn't begin to change. The chasm between them had only grown wider.

It hurt her to realize just how badly she *wanted* to bridge that dangerous emptiness, wanted him to feel something for her. A flicker of caring, a rough, masculine shadow of the emotions she felt.

Emotions that she had only begun to admit after many

sleepless nights. Feelings that made her pulse unsteady whenever she saw him or heard his voice. Even when he kept his distance.

Feelings that ran deeper than mere attraction or physical desire. It frightened her to think about just how much deeper. She couldn't sort them out, couldn't control them, and couldn't erase them, even when she was utterly furious with him. And she wanted ... *something* in return from him. More than the cold, calculating offer he had made in the forest.

Stay with me, he had said, and her heart had swept skyward.

As my mistress, he had finished, and she had crashed to earth with broken wings.

But why had she expected him to say anything else? She knew what he was. To wish for deep feeling—or *any* feeling—from a tough, battle-hardened, macho type like Gaston, a man who had never known love from anyone and had never felt love for anyone, was hopeless. Impossible. And it always would be.

Even if she weren't leaving tonight.

She had heard Gaston's men speak of him as The Black Lion, a name that resounded with pride and courage. But she wondered whether it had been a woman who first dubbed him Blackheart.

"Lady Celine?"

"Sorry?" Celine tore her gaze from the fire, suddenly aware that Yolande had been speaking to her.

"Shall we begin with the new batch?" Yolande repeated, walking over with the skillet. She looked Celine up and down, smiling. "Before you are wearing any more of it, milady?"

Celine glanced down at her dress, realizing she had gotten carried away with her enthusiasm for cooking. She always did—but at the moment, she wasn't wearing easy-care cotton-lycra off the rack from Marshall Field's.

It was a gown of velvet in a burnished rust shade; Yvette the seamstress had specially dyed the material to complement Celine's coloring. And now the bodice and skirt were splashed with egg and melted butter and smudged with sugar and flour.

"Oh, no," Celine groaned. Reaching up reluctantly, she found her cheeks splotched with ingredients, her hair tumbling from the plaits Gabrielle had pinned in place, and her rust-colored, cone-shaped hat thoroughly speckled with batter. "What have I done?"

"Do not concern yourself, milady." Yolande shook her head with a bemused expression. "Both you and the gown will look as lovely as ever with a bit of attention. Shall we use the pan while it is still hot?"

Celine nodded with a sigh. She wouldn't have minded the mess so much, except that today was the first time she had worn this new outfit. And she had worn it with the secret hope of seeing Gaston. A silly impulse. *Naive,* he would say. *Childish. Foolish.*

She had wanted to look elegant and sophisticated and gorgeous—to knock his socks off while appearing completely disinterested in him. A final show of strength and pride before she left. Celine's Last Stand.

No such luck. They hadn't crossed paths once, and now the beautiful dress was all but ruined. *Stupid, stupid, stupid . . .*

Turning, she scooped up a spoonful of the crepe mixture. It was too late now to worry about the gown.

Too late for a lot of things.

She swirled the batter across the hot skillet. It sizzled and smelled buttery and sweet. "Careful, Yolande. Keep moving it. Just let the edges get brown . . . that's right." She stepped back. "Fill all the little holes, and then flip it. No, *wait—*"

She winced as another crepe ended up on the ceiling.

"Drat," Yolande muttered.

Gabrielle appeared from the larder, triumphantly holding up a small earthenware jar sealed with a cork. "We have honey!"

"But naught to eat with it," Yolande moaned. "It appears we shall have to scrape our 'midnight snack' from the rafters."

Gabrielle glanced up and shrugged. "No matter. It will

complement the 'caramel cream' we had to scrape from the wall yestereve."

She started laughing. Yolande and Celine couldn't help but join in, and in seconds all three fell into a fit of giggles. Celine could just picture her Cordon Bleu instructors surveying this situation with a mortified twitch of their mustaches. She didn't remember ever having heard instructions on the handling of runaway crepes. Especially runaway crepes stuck to a flying buttress in a medieval kitchen.

"Yolande," she said when she had caught her breath, "the movement is side to side, not up and down."

Gabrielle giggled. " 'Tis up and *gone* in this instance."

"I will master this yet," Yolande declared, marching back to the fire with her skillet and a determined expression on her face.

"And I will stir the batter." Celine raised her spoon in salute, a general marshaling her forces. She applied herself to the bowl, smiling at her students' refusal to quit. Definitely an admirable quality.

A second later, Gabrielle's giggling stopped abruptly.

Celine glanced up.

Gaston filled the doorway, his perplexed, slightly irritated gaze fastened on her.

She felt the spoon slide from her fingers. Had he come to see her? Her heart dropped to her toes, then started to pound. What did he want? Why would he seek her out after three weeks apart? Why *now*, when it was her last day and she had hoped to see him and then she hadn't seen him and—

Oh, God, she must look like a mess! An eggy, floury mess, from her skewed hat and tumbling hair to her dirty face and ruined gown. The one she had worn to impress him with her cool elegance.

He didn't say anything, just stood there looking . . . tyrannical and annoyed and . . . *gorgeous*. His blue tunic and leggings set off his jet-black hair and dark eyes and outlined every solid, muscled inch of him. Even with half a kitchen between them, she was aware of even the most minute details: the stiffness of his back, the darkness that his five-o'clock shadow added to his angular cheeks and jaw, the casual power of his hand resting on the hilt of his knife.

To her chagrin, Celine started trembling, thinking about the easy strength and grace of those hands. Trembling with memories of how he had touched her, so intimately, that long ago night. Vivid memories that made it feel like minutes ago instead of weeks.

She remembered, too, that he was capable of compassion and tenderness—and how he completely disdained such feelings as feminine and weak. He didn't believe there *could* be anything beyond a physical connection between men and women. Pleasure was all he wanted. All he would accept. Or give. It made her feel so confused and frustrated and angry that she couldn't speak.

"Milord?" Gabrielle asked meekly from beside Celine when she remained silent. "Was there aught that you wished?"

"I was looking for . . ." His voice trailed off. He didn't take his eyes from Celine. "Isabeau," he finished at last.

"She is weaving at her loom in her chamber, milord," Yolande supplied a bit stiffly. "As she normally does at this hour."

He nodded in acknowledgment, but kept gazing at Celine. "What are you cooking this night, wife?"

One of the crepes picked that moment to dislodge itself from the ceiling. It landed at her feet with a plop as if on cue.

"Crepes."

She kept a straight face and tried to look like this was the normal way to make crepes.

Why on earth was he always around when she was doing something embarrassing and stupid, like thinking she was being chased by a bear, or running off a cliff, or having a panic attack, or ruining her best dress and wreaking havoc in his kitchen?

He frowned down at the flattened piece of pastry. "I see."

Neither of them said anything more for a long moment. He didn't look up. She didn't move. She felt frozen—no, not frozen. *Electrified.* Stunned breathless merely because they were in the same room together for the first time in days.

Finally he turned away without looking at her again. *"Bonsoir."*

Once he was gone, logical thought returned, gradually. And with it a fresh flood of hurt and outrage.

"So it's Isabeau tonight?" Celine wondered aloud. "He's been retiring to his chamber with a different girl each night this week, hasn't he?"

She had heard some of his men chuckling about the way their lord passed his nights by "playing tables with pretty wenches." *Is that what they call it in these times?* she had thought, something inside her clenching in a painful little twist. She had tucked the term away in her mental medieval dictionary, along with "se'nnight" and "raiment" and "destrier" and "trencher."

Yolande hung her skillet on an iron hook beside the hearth. "Milady," she said gently, "it is the way he has always been, and men find it difficult to change—"

"None of his others are half so fair as you, milady," Gabrielle said staunchly. "Mayhap, in time, he will come to realize how fortunate he is to have you as his wife."

In time, Celine thought. "Yes, I'm sure," she said numbly.

Yolande came to Celine's side, her stern features softened by a warmth and sadness Celine hadn't seen before. "Lady Celine, do not let it hurt you. Men speak oft of loyalty but give little to their wives. They have naught but stone where their hearts should be. It is the way with *all* of them."

The older woman's eyes were glistening with sympathy and, Celine sensed, a pain that was both old and deep.

"It's all right," Celine said with a shrug. "He's free to do all the wenching he wants. I don't care."

Yolande shook her head. "You are most generous and forgiving, milady. Mayhap too much so. A woman with a heart so tender cannot help but have it hurt ... if she entrusts it to a man."

"I have *not* entrusted anything to anyone."

Gabrielle expressed her opinion more plainly, darting a nervous glance at the door and speaking in a whisper. "Even so, you deserve better treatment than such as our lord has offered, milady. He has not given you a fair chance."

Celine's head and heart were swirling with confused thoughts and feelings, and Yolande's and Gabrielle's support only added one more: she never would have believed it when she first arrived here, but Gaston's loyal retainers had started to give her their respect. Even their friendship.

But she didn't have a speck of either from their lord. And never would.

And the truth was that she wanted both . . . and so much more.

She felt a rush of heat prickling behind her eyes. "I'm sorry, but would either of you mind if we . . . we finish our lesson another time? I'm tired. I think I'll go up to bed."

"Of course, Lady Celine," Gabrielle said. She dropped into a deep curtsy.

It was a gesture of honor and regard that she hadn't used before.

"Sleep well, milady." Yolande curtsied as well, as low as if she were bowing before a queen.

Celine wanted to hug them, but she didn't trust herself to linger; she barely managed to make it to the door before tears started to slide down her cheeks.

And as she dashed through the darkened great hall, she realized that she had just made yet another mistake: she had thought for a moment that they really *could* finish their cooking lesson another day—but she had just seen Yolande and Gabrielle for the last time.

And Gaston.

And the lesson would remain unfinished forever.

Because tonight was the night.

Celine wished she had a wristwatch. Even a wrist-sundial would do. But that wouldn't work at night. Maybe a wrist-moondial? It was next to impossible to tell time here, and she had to get this exactly right. Down to the split second.

To keep calm, she kept busy: snuggling Groucho one last time; writing a note to Yolande to ask her to take care of him, hoping someone would be able to make sense of her handwriting; changing into her amber-colored silk-and-lace teddy. Her palms were sweating. She started breathing deeply, in to the count of four and out to eight, in to eight and out to sixteen.

Over the past few days, Celine had started paying attention to the church bells that rang throughout the countryside, marking the divisions of the working day: *prime* sounded at six A.M. to urge people from their beds for prayer and work; *nones* at noon, when the day's main meal was eaten; and *couvre-feu* at eight, time to bank the fire and go to bed.

She and Yolande and Gabrielle usually started their cooking lessons after *couvre-feu,* and she had been going to bed at about ten—not that she was exactly sure it was ten, but it felt like ten. Which was why, at the moment, she was pretty sure it was about eleven.

For someone who was used to digital clocks and watches with second hands and last-minute plane flights and thirty-minute workouts and overnight mail service and two-minute microwave meals and faxes and modems and the dizzying pace of life in Chicago and New York and Paris and London, it was frustrating and weird to never know exactly what time it was.

On the other hand, it was kind of nice.

She set Groucho down in front of the hearth, folding her note and tucking it beneath the pillow he had been using as a bed. As she stood and picked up her cloak, she felt a painful tug at her heart. It was going to be hard to leave her kitten behind. And her hats. She glanced at the lovely little collection she had gathered, stacked on a trunk at the foot of her bed, all in wonderfully outlandish shapes and colors.

And Yolande and Gabrielle. She would miss them, too. It was surprising how attached she had become to this place and its people in only a matter of weeks. She would miss Etienne, with his youthful enthusiasm and wide-eyed hero worship. And Captain Royce and his sense of humor . . .

And Gaston. Who was she kidding? Fool that she was, she would miss Gaston. More than she had ever missed anything or anyone in her life.

With a resolute shake of her head, she forced that feeling to the smallest, deepest, most secret reaches of her heart. Putting on her cloak to conceal the teddy she wore, she picked up a candle and tiptoed out into the hall, toward the guest room a few doors away—and her "window of opportunity."

Her mental clock was already ticking past eleven.

When she opened the door, the first thing she noticed was the light of the waning full moon seeping through a crack in the shutters. She blew out the candle in her hand, welcoming the darkness—because darkness prevented her from seeing the bed, remembering how she had first awakened in it, nestled in Gaston's arms; the way he had teased her; their first kiss . . .

She moved past the bed to the window, trying to think of every detail of what she had been doing in 1993 when she had been sent here: standing just a few inches from the glass, looking at the lights in the town below, when the moonlight struck her and she fell backward into—

The year 1300. She stepped closer to open the shutters, but found a trunk in her way, beneath the window right where she needed to stand. That damned trunk again. She remembered it from before; she had knocked her knee against it very painfully when she had scrambled out of Gaston's arms. Well, it was in the way and it would have to go.

She bent over and tried to push it, but it didn't budge.

"What's in this thing?" she wheezed. "Bricks?"

She decided it might be easier to move if she took out some of the heavy contents. Unfortunately, she discovered it was locked.

She muttered one of Gaston's favorite medieval curses under her breath. All she could do was throw her entire weight against the trunk, so she did, straining with the exertion. Slowly, the heavy object began to inch along the wall. The clank of metal against metal helped her guess what was in it: probably plates and candlesticks and other valuables, of silver or gold. Without banks, she had learned, medieval tycoon types relied on safe, portable investments that could be melted down.

With the trunk out of the way, she opened the shutters. Moonlight spilled into the chamber, making her blink in the brightness. The eclipse had already begun, a small slice of black eating into one edge of the moon's surface.

Breathing hard, she let her cloak slide from her shoulders, and waited for midnight. Her heart started pounding. Had she thought of everything? She couldn't afford to make a mistake.

When she lifted her hand to dab at perspiration on her upper lip, a sparkle in the moonlight caught her eye, and she realized she hadn't thought of everything.

Her wedding ring. She was still wearing the gold band Gaston had placed on her finger when they said their vows.

With shaking fingers, she took it off, stepped away from the window, and set it on the trunk. She had to duplicate exactly the moment she had been sent here from 1993. She could not let anything medieval hold her back.

Turning again to the window, she waited, breathing, thinking of home. Of all the reasons she desperately wanted to go *home*. To have her operation. To be safe again. To see her family, her overprotective mom and dad, and Jackie, and her brother-in-law, Harry, and sweet little Nicholas. She thought of her friends, her fiber-arts studio, her car. Movies. Television. *Chocolate*. Her condo with its central heating and well-stocked fridge. Was someone taking care of her cats?

Suddenly a ray of eclipsing moonlight glanced off the stained glass, showering her in blinding brilliance. The same breathless tingle she had felt on New Year's Eve swept over her.

And then came the dizzying feeling of the floor shifting out from beneath her.

Chapter 13

"**G**ood night, milord. I thank you." The dark-haired beauty picked up her slippers and delicately covered a yawn as Gaston escorted her out the door of his bedchamber.

"Nay, it is I who thank you, Isabeau."

"The pleasure was mine, milord." She smiled shyly. "Though upon our next meeting, I cannot promise to succumb to you so easily. At least not so many times."

He grinned. "I am sorry if I was ruthless with you tonight. And that I allowed the hour to grow so late. I did not realize I had kept you occupied so long."

" 'Twas a most pleasant occupation, sir. Whenever you wish another match, please seek me out. This was so much more enjoyable than an evening at my loom."

"Mayhap I shall." He nodded absently as he led her through his solar, then bade her farewell at the door that led into the great hall. "Sleep well."

"I am certain I shall." She curtsied. "Our games have worn me out completely."

Gaston closed the solar's door as she departed, resting his forehead against the smooth wood, shutting his eyes. After a moment, a low groan of pure wretchedness slipped out of him.

Day by day, hour by hour, he was slowly going mad.

No matter how many nights he spent this way, with how many different women, none of it took the edge off his restlessness. He guessed the hour to be near midnight, but he was not even tired.

Straightening, rubbing his hands over his eyes, he walked back into his bedchamber, closing the door behind

173

him. He went to the table before the hearth, picked up the wooden game board, and slid the ivory and black playing pieces back into their leather pouch, along with the dice. It was useless to keep trying to pass the nights this way.

The rounds of tables with pretty company distracted him barely a whit. None of the women raised his interest in the least. In truth, his favorite game merely served to make him agonizingly aware of what he would rather be doing, and with whom.

For three weeks now he had thrown himself into all manner of activities, but he could not wear himself out no matter how he tried. The days he spent at hunting, hawking, sword practice. And the nights . . .

The nights were unendurable.

All because of that one night in the forest snows when he had watched his wife blaze so gloriously in his arms.

That reckless encounter had set free a simmering need and an irksome tangle of unwanted *feelings* that made all the days and nights that had followed pure torment.

To his annoyance, he had discovered that even food and wine had lost their appeal. What he needed was a long, cool draught of Christiane.

He opened the trunk at the foot of his bed and tossed the game board and pouch inside, letting the lid fall with a thwack. Saints' blood, why did she have to be so damnably stubborn in refusing his offer to stay with him? It was a perfectly reasonable offer. He would take care of her, protect her. She would want for naught.

To think of the passion and pleasure they could share, if only she would relinquish her misguided loyalty to Tourelle and her naive, false notions about love. The image of her in his bed made him want to shout his longing from the parapet of his highest tower.

She was his, by God. *His.* She belonged to him in a way that had naught to do with kings or vows or laws or so foolish a female notion as love. They were a match, a pair, bound together by a far stronger force, one forged of mutual desire and a potent attraction deeper than any he had ever felt. It was the sort of bond a man could depend upon, unlike something so vague and fleeting as emotion.

And he knew she felt it, too; her response to his merest touch was proof enough of that.

Why could she not admit it?

She *would* admit it. She had to. Because their marriage was about to end, within a se'nnight, mayhap less.

He strode around the bed and took off his tunic, forcing himself to prepare for sleep, though he knew it would not come. He had charged his men not only with finding Tourelle, but also with spying on him.

They had orders not to return until they had some evidence of Tourelle's treacherous plans. That was why they had been gone so long, he knew. As soon as they returned, he would be able to go before the King, present real proof of his enemy's scheme, and obtain the annulment that would rid him of his unwanted bride.

Unwanted?

Untrue.

Sitting on the mattress, he nudged off his boots. Christiane was most definitely wanted. Not as his wife— but definitely wanted. He could not keep his body from stirring at the merest thought of her. Earlier tonight in the kitchens, he had not allowed himself to take one step toward her or linger longer than a moment, because he knew it could end in only one way: with him taking her into his arms and off to his bed.

He should not have allowed himself near her at all, but he had been walking through the great hall when he caught the rare, sparkling sound of Christiane's laughter, and it had drawn him like a thirsting man to a sweet, clear waterfall.

He snuffed the candle beside his bed and let himself fall backward onto the mattress, remembering.

The look of her had captivated him as much as her girlish giggling: that shining, wide-eyed gaze; her tousled hair; one of her many hats half tumbled; the ruined gown reflecting the sheer joy she found in cooking. The scene made him smile even now.

It had all been so arrantly unladylike . . . and so irresistibly charming. For one moment, before she realized he was there, she had truly looked *happy*.

And what would become of her, this flour-dusted, red-headed, engaging little minx of his, when his men returned and their marriage ended?

His smile vanished. He ran a hand through his hair, thinking for the first time of Christiane's possible fate after all of this was over. More than thinking of it, *worrying* about it.

It should not matter to him what happened to his enemy's ward, but he could not deny that it did. At first, he had cared only about getting her out of his life, but now he . . .

Now he was . . .

Concerned. That was the word. Concerned for her well-being. Naught more.

Yet it was a peculiar sort of concern, one he had not felt before, forceful and yet gentle at the same time, and so much a part of him that he could only yield to it.

And it made him question what would become of Christiane. Would Tourelle send her back to the convent in distant Aragon? Gaston did not like to imagine her condemned to that fate. It was hard to believe that Christiane had ever set *foot* in a convent, much less been raised in one. She bore as much resemblance to a novice nun as he did to a monk.

He could not believe that a woman like her, a woman of such passion and spirit and fierce independence, would willingly return to the quiet restrictive, celibate life of the cloister.

Which raised a second possibility. Tourelle might marry her to another man.

That thought sent a savage rush of denial through Gaston. He thrust himself off the bed and started pacing, as if he could escape the image he had conjured. The idea of another man touching Christiane, taking her to his bed, claiming her sweet secrets as his own—*nay!*

But even as that loathsome image hit him like a fist in the gut, another, still worse possibility presented itself.

Tourelle would be furious that she had failed to carry out his plans. Furious enough to punish her. The whoreson might beat her. Or do far worse.

Gaston's jaw clenched. He would *never* let that happen.

There was but one answer. She might not be willing to accept the idea yet, but it truly would be best—safest—for her to remain here with him. He would protect her.

Eventually, she would come to see that her naive ideas about men and women and love were naught but imaginings, learned from listening to too many troubadors' tales. She would leave behind such girlish fancies anon. He had given her the first taste of her true, womanly passions, and she would not be able to resist them for long, any more than he could. And once he was married to Lady Rosalind, there would be no reason for him and Christiane to resist.

She had to stay.

Every fiber of his being resonated with that thought. The sooner she accepted it, the better for them both.

Crossing the chamber in two strides, he yanked open the door and went to inform her of his decision.

Nothing was happening.

The feeling of the floor slipping out from beneath her feet lasted less than a second.

Celine opened her eyes, trembling with the beginnings of fear.

She hadn't moved one inch, much less seven centuries. Clammy fingers of stark terror closed around her throat.

Why had it suddenly stopped working? *What was going wrong?*

Her heart started pumping wildly. What was *she* doing wrong? The dazzling moonlight still bathed her, the eclipse was clear, the time was right, her clothes, her thoughts. Why had the feeling of movement stopped?

This had to work! It was her only chance to get home. Her only chance before the bullet fragment in her back . . .

"Oh, please," she cried, reaching out to touch the glass, staring up into the blinding white light. "Oh, God, please!"

The window remained as solid as the rush-strewn stone floor beneath her. She grasped the stone sill with both hands, pleading with every ounce of her heart and soul for this to work. Whispering a prayer, she squeezed her eyes shut, desperately hoping she would open them to find herself in 1993.

But she did not. When she opened her eyes, she remained solidly, undeniably, in 1300.

A dizzy rush of nausea swept over her. She felt like she was going to be sick, or faint, or burst into tears. She refused to let herself slump to the floor. She couldn't panic. She could not panic! She clung to the sill and to one fact: she *would* have another chance, in three months.

Three months.

And what if her medical condition worsened by then? What about that ache she had felt in her back for several days? What if the bullet fragment was shifting even now? What if she didn't have three months? *What if she died before the next eclipse?*

A sobbing, wordless cry of denial and doubt and fear tore out of her. She leaned against the cold glass, fighting tears.

No. Shaking, she summoned every bit of courage she possessed, refusing to give in to mindless terror. She had to hold herself together. Figure out what had gone wrong. Consult with Brynna again. Find a way to get *home*.

She heard a sound in the doorway behind her and spun around with a jerky, startled movement.

At first she couldn't tell who it was, could only blink into the darkness, her eyes still dazzled from the moon's brilliance. Then the wavering silhouette resolved itself into a tall, muscular, unmistakable form.

Gaston.

Her heart skipped a beat, then started pounding harder. She was still here, still in his time . . .

Still his wife.

The tears she had managed to hold back suddenly started flowing down her cheeks—because in the smallest, deepest, most secret reaches of her heart, some part of her was glad. *Glad that she had failed.*

A small sob of confusion and fear and despair escaped her, and she almost took a step toward him. It didn't make any sense: she wanted nothing in that moment as badly as she wanted his strength and comfort, to lose herself in the safe fortress of his arms. But the fact that she could not read his expression kept her frozen.

He stepped toward her. She could see that he held a piece of parchment crumpled in his fist—the note she had left for Yolande.

"What in the name of God are you doing?" he asked in a tone that might have been simmering rage or complete disbelief. "What is this?" He held up the note. "What do you mean by saying, 'I am going home and will never see any of you again'?"

Celine moved. Sideways, out of the light. Flattening herself against the wall. "I—I *was* trying to go home." Her pulse was roaring in her ears. Words came tumbling out in a rush. "I was trying to get back to my time just like I told you and it should have worked only it didn't work and I—"

"I cannot believe that you would try this again." He stared at her teddy as he moved into the shaft of moonlight. "Did you *expect* me to come seeking you tonight? Did you think to trick me into consummating our vows when that *garment* failed you before?"

He wasn't wearing a shirt. Or boots. He wasn't wearing anything except a pair of form-fitting leggings. And she could see his expression now.

And it made her tremble.

His dark features were etched with a hard-edged mixture of desire and disbelief. His gaze swept her body in a single swift stroke that she *felt* like a physical touch.

"Th-his didn't have anything to *do* with you," she cried, her voice a shuddery sob. "*I was trying to go home!* I've been telling you the truth all along and I—"

"If you expect me to believe that," he said roughly, his voice deep, "you are even more naive than I thought."

Celine slumped against the wall, covering her eyes with her hands, her head falling forward. It was one blow too many to find suspicion and lust and anger where she so desperately wanted understanding and compassion and comfort.

"P-please just leave me alone," she said shakily, not looking at him, not wanting to cry in front of him. "You'll never believe me. You'll never believe anything I say. Just leave me alone."

He moved so silently that she never even heard him.

Not away, but toward her.

She gasped when his hands closed around her wrists and he trapped her against the wall, between the cold stone and his bare chest, raising her arms and pinning her hands on either side of her head with slow, inexorable strength.

"What I believe, *ma dame,* is that you should be more careful in spinning your web."

His eyes glowed nearly black in the silvery light, desire overpowering all the other feelings she had seen there.

Her heart and her breath seemed to stop. "Let me go! You can't—I know you won't consummate our—"

"Nay, Christiane, but I am an accomplished lover, and there are ways I could take my pleasure of you that would leave you a virgin." He leaned into her, his body hot with arousal, his breath coming harsh and heavy. "I have lain awake nights wanting you, wife, and I will endure no longer."

Chapter 14

C eline's captive hands clenched into fists. "Wanting *me?*" She struggled against his grip, but that only pressed her breasts more firmly against his bare chest, leaving her shaking and breathless at the stunning contact. She lifted her chin, wishing she could wipe the too-obvious tears from her cheeks. "Why would you want *me?* I'd think you'd be more than satisfied after *playing tables* with girls like Isabeau night after night!"

His dark eyes burned into hers before he dropped his head to take her mouth in a hungry kiss. "It is but a game," he said against her lips, "and it satisfies me not."

Celine desperately tried to keep her senses from spinning out of control. That single kiss sent a shock wave through her body, but his cold, casual comment struck at her heart like a knife. "That's all it *is* to you, isn't it? A *game*. And one partner is the same as any other."

"Partner?" he muttered, nuzzling her cheek, nibbling a quick, searing path to her earlobe, her neck, lower. " 'Tis more an opponent."

An opponent! Celine made a low sound of frustration and hopelessness and tried again to push him away, but he held her still and kept kissing her, tracing a damp trail along her throat, over her collarbone, across her shoulder.

She burned with resentment at what he was doing to her, at the melting heat that began between her thighs, at the feel of his bare, hot skin against hers. She resented the delicious friction of the crisp hair covering his chest against the wisps of silk and lace barely covering her breasts. Resented the fact that she noticed the lean, muscu-

181

lar feel of him and the tangy spice of his scent—*and reveled in them.*

Oh, God help her, but she wanted him, needed him, wanted and needed this.

Because she cared for him. Cared for him more deeply than she had dared allow herself to admit. And *that* she resented more than anything. Because he viewed her in exactly the same way he viewed all women, as nothing but—

"An opponent?" she finally managed to choke out, though it was almost impossible to get her brain and her tongue to work together and form words. He was kissing his way to her breast, his lips and tongue and teeth blazing a trail of sweet torment. She tried to stay still, tried not to respond, because every small movement she made only brought another part of her into contact with another part of him. "That's . . . that's how you see women? All women? Opponents? Conquests? Not as friends or partners or—"

"You make too much of it, Christiane." He kept her hands trapped against the wall, kissing and nuzzling every part of her as if he meant to enjoy her one inch at a time. Nudging her teddy out of the way to expose her nipple, he licked her, long and slow.

A ragged breath escaped her and she arched against him helplessly, feeling herself swirling down into the pool of sensual fire he kindled between them. He stole away fear, anger, breath, voice, and left only longing in their place.

" 'Tis merely a game," he continued in that chiding tone, kissing her tender skin softly. "A pleasant amusement that engages both luck and strategy. Why do you wish to discuss it now?"

"Luck?" she exclaimed on a strangled breath. How could he *be* so calculating? His choice of words shredded any illusions she had about him ever having the ability to feel something for her. "Is that all it *is* to you? Luck and strategy?" *Like this?* she wanted to shout. *Like what you are doing to me now?*

"Aye, especially when played with more than one, in teams."

All the air left her body in a single shocked exhalation. "Let me go!" She tried to wrench her arms free, glaring down at him in fury. "I am *not* going to listen to another word about how you amuse yourself by having orgies with groups of women! Let . . . me . . . *go.*" She said each word distinctly, through clenched teeth.

Her outburst earned her a look of stunned surprise. He straightened, staring down at her; then after a moment an odd gleam came into his eyes. "Christiane," he said lightly, "precisely what sort of game do you think it is, 'playing tables'?"

"The sort that you're good at," she said hotly. "The sort you like to play with tavern wenches. The sort you're playing with me right now!"

For some reason, that made him laugh. "Indeed." Keeping her captive, he bent his head to kiss her cheek, then continued his tingling exploration of her bare skin, still chuckling at his private joke. "You are very quick to believe the worst of me, wife."

"You make it easy enough!"

"Aye," he admitted, "it would seem that I do."

"You're just as quick to believe the worst of *me!*"

He lifted his head, and his smile faded. He didn't say anything for a very long time. His eyes searched her face, those brown depths hot with desire, potent with longing— and swirling with a new look she had not seen before.

When he finally spoke, his voice had dropped to a lower, gentler tone. "In truth, I am not certain what to believe about you anymore, my lady wife." He released her wrists. "But mayhap we have both been too quick in our judgments."

He wasn't holding on to her anymore. He levered his weight off her and braced his arms against the wall, looming over her without keeping her captive. She could have moved away, walked out. But that deep, tender tone of his voice held her prisoner more than his hands ever could. And her heart was beating strangely.

When she made no move to leave, he lowered his head until his lips were a scant breath from hers. A lock of his hair fell forward, tickling her. He grinned. "Mayhap, mi-lady, we should begin over again."

"B-begin over again?" she whispered, her lashes already fluttering downward in anticipation of his kiss.

"Aye," he murmured. "I am Sir Gaston de Varennes, lord of this chateau. And you, *chérie?*"

"Celine." She lifted her mouth to his. "Celine Fontaine."

"Celine."

He wasn't questioning or scoffing this time, merely accepting her name before he sealed his lips over hers and accepted her kiss.

Her heart filled with hope and longing and so many feelings she couldn't begin to sort them out, couldn't do anything in that moment but moan softly when his arms closed around her; he kissed her, held her, enfolded her in his heat, his strength, his life, until she could only slide her hands across the broad muscles of his chest, along the corded sinews of his neck, until she was twining her fingers through the dark curls at his nape.

At her light caress, his arms tightened. They held each other, tighter, closer, kissing until Celine knew she would faint and didn't care, until time spun out beyond counting.

Time.

When he finally lifted his mouth from hers and allowed them both a breath, she lay her head against his chest, closing her eyes, asking the question she couldn't bear to ask. "Do you believe me, Gaston?"

His breathing was fast and shallow and she could hear his heart pounding. "I believe you are not who I thought you were. I believe you are not a woman who would give unwavering loyalty to a knave such as Tourelle. And you are too intelligent to be taken in by any lies he might tell you." His voice took on a rough, unsteady edge she had heard only once before, when he had rescued her from the river. "And I believe more than aught else that I want you to stay with me."

She glanced up to find him gazing down at her with that look of unfamiliar darkness swirling in his eyes again, and her own eyes burned with sudden tears at the bittersweet impossibility of what he asked. "And what about the game you like so much?" she asked with a pained smile, though she knew the answer made no difference. "What about playing tables with all those different, pretty opponents?"

He grinned down at her. "Does it vex you so, little wife? Do you care so much?"

She thought of keeping her secret, but didn't. *"Yes."*

His expression softened. His eyes, his voice, his very touch softened. He cupped her face in his broad, callused palms. "Then for you, *chérie,* I shall give it up. I vow to you that I shall never play another game of tables."

She closed her eyes, too late to stop a tear that slipped from beneath her lashes. "You would give it up . . . for me?"

He kissed the drop of moisture away. "Aye." His fingers wove into her hair. "I want you, Celine. And you are worth that price. Or any other."

His kiss stole her breath before she could reply or ask any more questions.

Then hunger took control of them both.

All the fire and suppressed longings they had been battling for three weeks spilled over and swept them away in one swift cascade. He walked her backward, a single step. She came up against the wall but barely felt the impact, pressing herself into the heat of his body. He didn't bother with sweet preliminaries this time. She didn't want them. His tongue demanded entry and took it, thrusting against hers. She kissed him back, long and hard and deep, her hands sliding into his hair as he lifted her, until the soft juncture of her thighs cradled the hard arousal barely concealed by his tight leggings.

She inhaled sharply at the contact, but never gave a thought to stopping him, felt herself soaring and falling all at once, drugged by his kiss as she always was. He held her tight with one arm across her back and she wrapped her legs around his hips; he slid his other hand between their bodies and she shuddered, not with fear but with anticipation.

She didn't want to think of the future or the past or any time at all but this moment. This sweet *now.* She was trapped in this place, this time, this marriage, these feelings she did not want to fight . . . and all of it urged her to give in to what they both wanted. She didn't care anymore what he called it, or what she called it; all she knew was that she could not feel so much for him and be so wrong about what he felt for her.

And this might be all she ever had of him, all that God would grant her, before she returned to her own time or . . .

She gasped when she felt his hand moving against her soft mound. He fumbled with the snaps he encountered on her teddy, then pushed the fabric aside impatiently. His fingers brushed against her, gently; then when he felt her dampness, more powerfully.

She cried out when he began to stroke her, his fingers delving into her, teasing, seeking, demanding. The sensations began to build, so quickly, so violently, spinning tight within her belly, the heat and light of a universe full of stars all condensed into one, straining toward the explosion of sheer ecstasy. Then she felt his hand shift away from her to himself. And then . . .

Then came the unfamiliar feel of smooth, hard, velvet-steel flesh pressing against her thigh.

Gaston almost lost control as he felt her soft, bare thigh against his rampant arousal. This was torture. A mistake. Sweet Christ, the worst mistake he had ever made in his life. The feelings he had for this woman were *weakness*. Letting himself feel passion for one female above all others was *madness*.

But in that moment he wanted to be weak, welcomed madness.

He began to thrust against her skin and the silk of her garment, keeping her firmly in place, not daring to let her move. Groaning, he rubbed his length along her hip and thigh, relentlessly torturing and pleasuring himself at the feel of what was almost real.

With a whimper, she tried to shift closer, but he held her pinned and kept moving his hips, faster, harder, his breath a harsh storm against her neck. Bracing her against the wall, he reached down and began to caress her intimately again.

She threw her head back against the stone, shivering and writhing against him, the spasms of pleasure making her tighten around his fingers. He choked out a groan of frustration and need but kept moving, pleasing her and himself, kneading the swollen bud of her desire until she was breathless with wanting release, and then he gave it to her and she took it so easily, crying out his name in a sweet song.

By some miracle he kept himself from making the small thrust of his hips that would have let him plunge his full length home, into her, deeply. His every muscle rigid, he pressed his head against her shoulder, undulating with her against the wall in a shameless mockery of the passionate act. And then the fever seized him, pleasure coiling, spinning tighter upon itself until it ripped loose and tore free. With a muffled shout of release, he felt himself flowing, his seed spilling over her bare hip.

They were both trembling. Spent and yet wanting. Fulfilled and yet frustrated. The mingled, hot chorus of their breathing filled the chamber.

"Merciful God," he swore softly, appalled at the risk he had taken, knowing he would do it again in a heartbeat. He let her go. Let her unwrap her legs from around his waist, let her slide down the wall until her small, bare feet touched the floor.

He stood there, unable to move, wanting to say something. But he could find no words to apologize or explain or express what he was . . . *feeling*.

He abruptly turned away.

"Gaston?" she asked in a voice soft with hurt.

He spun back toward her, capturing her in a fierce gaze. "I *will* have you," he vowed. "Not tonight, nor on the morrow, but as soon as the annulment is complete and Lady Rosalind agrees to wed me. I will have you and I will not let you go. *I will never let you go.*"

She gazed up at him blankly, the languor of their intimacy quickly disappearing from her eyes. "Lady Rosalind?" she whispered. "But I thought . . . you said . . ."

Gaston cursed under his breath. He had come here to persuade her to accept the idea of staying with him, and instead he had half ravished her and now was making her feel like a possession, a chattel. He was not handling this well at all.

He tried to remind himself of the reasons he had thought of earlier, when it all had seemed so clear and logical. "You will be safe with me, can you not understand that? Tourelle cannot harm you as long as you are in my keeping. And you have naught to return to after our marriage is finished—you cannot want the cloister, and you have no family, no land, not a blade of grass or a single coin to your name. Do you not see that it would be better to stay?"

"Better . . .?" she mumbled. "As your mistress? Is that really all you want . . . all you feel for me?"

"Celine, we have—"

"No, don't." Her eyes swirled with a sudden blue-gray storm of anger and hurt. "Don't bother reminding me that we've already had this discussion. It doesn't matter, anyway. Haven't you been listening? I'm from the future. I have to go *home* or I'm going to die. That's why I came to this room in the first place. You can see the eclipse for yourself—a dark of the moon. Just look out the window."

He was not certain how the conversation had gotten diverted from the very pleasant subject of her becoming his mistress to the unpleasant annoyance of her incredible tales, but he flicked a glance out the window to placate her.

Then he turned toward it more fully, staring into the light with an uncomfortable clench of his heart.

There was indeed a dark of the moon as she had said, a small slice of black obscuring the silver disk. His gaze narrowed.

Even as all reason denied what she had said, he found himself glancing back at her, studying her strange garment . . . looking down at the crumpled note of farewell he had dropped on the floor.

"It's true," she told him again with quiet insistence. "I'm from 1993."

He shook his head, fighting it, but at the same time a trace of uncertainty began to take hold. He thought of all he had witnessed: the way she had appeared so suddenly in his bed; the fact that Royce and his men could find no trace of how she had entered the castle; her short hair when she was so obviously not a novice nun; her strange ways and knowledge; the devices she had invented; her meeting with the mystic woman in the forest; her presence here tonight in this chamber; the fact that she did not know of a game so common as tables . . .

None of it made sense.

Unless she was telling the truth.

The facts added up to an utterly impossible conclusion. If he were to depend on his powers of logic and reason, as he had all his life . . .

I have to go home or I'm going to die.

Nay, it could not be true!

"You've got to believe me," she said stubbornly. "I came here tonight to go home. I put on this outfit because I have to go back the same way I came in. I can't take anything from your time with me. Brynna—the mystic woman—explained it to me. And . . . and look at that."

She pointed to the trunk she had pushed from beneath the window. A gold ring gleamed on top of it.

"I even took off the wedding band you gave me because I couldn't take it with me."

He stared down at the band of gold, then lifted his gaze to hers slowly, still not willing to believe it.

Not wanting to believe it.

He opened his mouth, but before he could say a word, a cry of alarm out in the corridor cut him short: the sound of someone calling his name.

"Conceal yourself," Gaston said curtly as he went to the door. When she was hidden in the shadows, he stuck his head out into the hall. "You there! Hold!"

Etienne, who was halfway down the hall and heading for the spiral stairs, turned around with a jerk. "Milord! I was sent to find you, but you were not in your chamber," he said breathlessly. "Captain Royce and his men have returned, sir—and they have the Duc de la Tourelle and his traveling party with them."

"Excellent. Tell Royce to make our *guest* comfortable. I will join you below in a moment." The news sent a shot of satisfaction through Gaston. At last, he would have this resolved. He closed the door and turned to inform Celine, but she was already hurrying toward him.

"They're finally here?" she asked excitedly.

"Aye." He eyed her warily, still unable to sort out all she had told him. "Why does that please you?"

"Because now you'll finally meet the real Christiane! And you'll have to believe me!" She rushed past him as if she were going to run right out the door.

He caught her, hooking a finger in the back of her silk garment. "Not so quickly, my headstrong lady. You are not going below garbed in that. In fact, you are not going below at all. You will stay in your chamber until I summon you."

"But—"

"Do not argue with me. I will not risk letting Tourelle within ten yards of you until I talk to my men and have the truth of his plans."

Not giving her time for further protest, he escorted her down the hall to her room and sent her inside, unable to resist a solid, possessive little pat on her derriere. She called him something most unladylike as he closed the door, and he went below with a grin; he rather liked her unladylike ways.

He entered the great hall to discover a noisy crowd of his guards, unfamiliar knights, and nuns in their black habits, all of whom were talking at once.

"Sir!" one of his men shouted gratefully from amid the melee. "We could not find you—"

"You will not believe this, milord." Royce appeared at his side, still wearing his travel garb and looking as if he had endured a hard ride. "Nor will you like it—"

"You will pay for this, Blackheart!" That was shouted above all the clamor, and Gaston recognized the voice, though he had not heard it in months. He turned to find Tourelle, his arms held by two of Gaston's men and an ugly sneer on his face. "You will pay for your treacherous misdeed with your lands and your *life!*"

Gaston gave him a sardonic stare. "Which misdeed do you speak of, Tourelle?"

"Do not pretend ignorance!" Tourelle snarled. "Tell me what you have done with my Christiane. She disappeared on the eve of the new year, in the middle of the night. Vanished without a trace!"

Chapter 15

What the heck was taking so long?

Celine needed no more than five minutes to get dressed. After that, she sat perched on the edge of her bed, waiting to be summoned below, wearing a velvet gown in deep sapphire blue with silver embroidery on the scoop neck and long, fitted sleeves. Pride and something more made her want to look especially good for this long-awaited moment. The moment when Gaston finally realized just how wrong he'd been about her.

She pictured him looking at her with understanding and trust and . . . maybe even that gleaming darkness swirling in his eyes, the expression she had glimpsed once or twice in unguarded moments. The thought made a warm glow settle through her.

Maybe he would even apologize to her, though that didn't really matter. What she wanted was his trust. Once he gave her that, he might let go of this ridiculous idea that pleasure was all that mattered, that caring and compassion were feminine and weak. Maybe he could even admit that he cared for her, at least a little.

She felt so sure that he did.

And they had so little time left together, only weeks before she had to return home. That is, if she didn't—

No, she wasn't going to think about that. She would make it. With Gaston by her side, she would be strong.

But the minutes dragged by and no one came.

Maybe he was in shock. Meeting the real Christiane and realizing that Celine had been telling the truth all along would be quite a stunner.

Several more minutes dragged by. She couldn't wait any

longer. leaping up from the bed, she started for the door, trying to think of what excuse she could offer for ignoring his orders. A resounding knock sounded just as she was reaching for the iron latch.

She pulled the door wide, unable to suppress a smile. "You rang?"

Royce stood in the dark hallway holding a torch, looking haggard and tired and not at all amused.

No doubt this was his version of shock.

"Sir Gaston would see you below, milady."

"Yes, of course," she said happily, breezing past him out the door.

He practically had to run to keep up with her as she hurried into the darkness, rushed down the spiral stairs that led below, and opened the door into the great hall.

A noisy crowd filled the room, all shouting at one another. There were a half-dozen nuns in long black robes, and Gaston's guards, and a few men she hadn't seen before, and various servants who had no doubt been roused from their beds by the tumult, and Gaston, who was having a heated argument with an expensively dressed stranger.

She glanced from one feminine face to another, trying to pick out Christiane.

Standing at her side, Royce cleared his throat loudly, twice. Everyone finally quieted and turned toward her.

A gasp went through the crowd.

Celine looked at Gaston with a tentative smile. "Well, where is she?"

The riot that erupted made the clamor before seem like silence by comparison. Before she had even finished her question, Celine found herself surrounded and practically knocked off her feet by a flock of chattering nuns, all of whom seemed intent on hugging her at the same time. They bombarded her with joyful cries and questions.

"Dear, sweet girl, you are unhurt!"

"Why did you disappear so suddenly?"

"You gave us *such* a fright!"

"How *did* you travel here?"

"How could you leave us that way without a word?"

Caught in the confusion of questions and hugs and pats and squeezes, Celine couldn't force a word in edgewise. With all of them talking at once, she could hardly even understand what they were saying—but the little she could make out made no sense. "What do you mean? Please stop shouting at me. *Please!*"

She barely managed to disengage herself from the smothering little group when the stranger Gaston had been talking to forced his way forward through the crush and pulled her into his arms, holding her so tight she couldn't take a breath.

"God's blood, Christiane, we thought we had lost you!" His voice shook. "Are you all right?" He set her away from him, holding her by the shoulders and looking her up and down. "This cur has not harmed you, has he? How did he spirit you away from us? Tell me what happened!"

Celine stared at the man. A sick dread twisted her stomach.

He had called her Christiane.

But how could they think *she was Christiane?*

"W-what are you talking about?" she choked out. "I don't know you! I've never met you before!" With his red hair and blue eyes, he bore a striking resemblance to one of her uncles. She guessed he must be the hated Tourelle.

He clasped her to him again. "Poor, sweet maid. Was he telling the truth of it, then? Did you suffer some sort of blow to your head that stole your memory?"

Celine wrenched herself out of his embrace, backing away from him, from all of them, shaking, the fringes of panic starting to close in. "What . . . what is this? Some . . . some sort of . . . awful joke? Where's the real Christiane?"

She looked to Gaston for an explanation, but he only regarded her with a hard stare, not a sliver of emotion showing on his rigid features. He stood apart from the crowd, watching them. Watching her.

One of the nuns began to explain. "You disappeared, *ma chère*, just after the great blizzard we encountered. We were bringing you here for your wedding when the storm struck and forced us to take refuge in a forest. We last saw

you on the eve of the new year, when you went to sleep
in your tent. The next day, when Arlette came to fetch you
for morning prayers, you were gone. There were only your
footprints in the new snow, leading a few paces from the
opening—and there they stopped. It looked as if a great
bird had swooped down and carried you off."

"You frightened us terribly!" another put in.

"We spent days searching for you, milady," one of Tourelle's men added. "We feared that you had become lost in
the snows. What happened to you?"

Celine couldn't answer. She just stared at all of them,
thunderstruck. Her shock quickly gave way to fright as the
unbelievable truth sank in. Disappeared. Christiane had
disappeared on New Year's Eve. The same night she had
been brought here from 1993. Which meant . . .

What? What did it mean for her chances of getting
home? Would the two of them have to switch back the
same way? At the same time?

Was that why the eclipse hadn't worked?

Her mind reeling, she turned blindly to Gaston, instinc-
tively seeking comfort and safety in the one place she
might find it with the world spiraling out of control. But
the little group around her had closed in so tightly that she
couldn't move toward him.

And he made no move toward her.

"Gaston, you . . . you have to believe . . ." Celine began,
though she barely believed it herself. "She must have
been . . . struck by the light from the lunar eclipse. Just
like I was. She must have been . . . sent to the future. I
don't know how this happened, but we . . . we've traded
places somehow!"

His rigid features shifted only slightly, his lips tightening into a hard, cynical line.

He didn't believe her. He would never believe her. Not
now. His expression revealed exactly what he was thinking: that she was Christiane and had been all along. That
everything she had told him up until now had been one
enormous lie.

"No!" She whirled back to the strangers gathered
around her, desperately turning from one concerned face to

another. "I'm not Christiane! Can't you tell? Don't I look different? Don't I sound different? I'm *not* Christiane!"

A couple of the women looked at each other, shaking their heads sadly. They clearly thought she had lost her marbles.

"Did Christiane speak English?" Celine demanded. She proceeded to tell them who she was and where she was from and how she had gotten here—all in her best Chicago-accented American English.

"She speaks in tongues!" one nun said, crossing herself.

Another came forward cautiously, as if approaching a wild animal that might bite. "All will be well, Christiane," she said soothingly. "I have cared for people with terrible injuries and strange brain-fevers before, in the convent's infirmary. It is possible your mind will return in time."

"There's nothing wrong with my mind!" Celine yelled at them, shifting back to French. She clenched her fists, shaking with helpless frustration. "Don't you see that this doesn't make any *sense?* How could I possibly have gotten all the way here from wherever you were camped? And how could I have done it so fast? Even if I *were* Christiane?"

"But you *are* Christiane, dear," one of the women insisted. She came to stand right in front of her, speaking loudly and distinctly, as if Celine were half deaf or mentally impaired. "Your . . . name . . . is . . . Christiane . . . de . . . la . . . Fontaine."

"I'm *not* crazy! Look! Look at this!" Celine opened her mouth and pointed to her teeth. "Did your Christiane have fillings? Did she have a scar on her back?" She was tempted to tear off her dress and show them the mark. Instead she spun to face the crowd, looking for her friends. "Ask Yolande and Gabrielle! Ask them about my scar. And about the strange foods I've been cooking and the devices I invented for them and the fact that I've had everyone calling me Celine and that I don't know anything about your way of life in this time. Ask them! Ask Gaston!"

She looked at him again, silently begging him to believe her, to help her.

In return she got only that stoic stare.

His eyes condemned her as a liar. A cunning, skillful liar. The cool contempt in his dark gaze hurt worse than any words, worse than a physical blow. It ripped through her with the same agony and numbing shock as the bullet she had been shot with so long ago. Whatever tiny, fragile spark of trust and caring he might have felt for her was gone.

Gone.

Snuffed out. Destroyed before it had ever had a chance to burn a little brighter and cast even a small light into the black shadows that cloaked his heart.

He stood there, judged her, and found her guilty. He looked at her the same way he had when she first arrived here.

As an enemy.

A sound of pain escaped Celine's lips. One of the nuns put an arm around her. "You are overwrought, poor lamb."

"Aye, it would appear you *are* suffering some strange brain-fever," Tourelle concurred in that same patronizing, infuriating tone everyone else was using. He stroked her short hair. "But you are most definitely my ward, Christiane. It is true that I do not understand how you came to be here so quickly, though. Do you not remember?"

Celine hung her head, looking at the rush-strewn floor, feeling all the staggering events of the past few hours crushing down on her. The eclipse had failed, Christiane had disappeared into the future, and now she herself was trapped in the past. Trapped in the identity of her ancestor. Trapped in a marriage with a man who looked at her like he hated her.

And she might never be able to get home.

A choking wave of defeat and despair rose in her throat. "No, I can't," she whispered. "God help me, I can't explain what's happening to me." She covered her face with her hands.

At the first sign of tears, she was instantly surrounded again by clucking nuns, who patted her cheeks and offered comfort.

"You must be honest with us, my dear," Tourelle said quietly. "Has Varennes hurt you in any way?"

Had he hurt her?

Celine was so racked with pain that she could not even speak.

But she knew that wasn't the kind of hurt Tourelle meant, and she would not give him any ammunition to use against Gaston. She shook her head silently.

"There is no shame in admitting the truth," Tourelle urged. "The fault would not be yours. He claims he has not forced himself on you, or bedded you even once. Is that true?"

The nuns made little exclamations of shock at the question. Celine simply raised her tear-streaked face, looking at her husband. "He told you the truth," she said softly. "Our marriage has been nothing." Her voice broke. "Nothing but a mistake."

Tourelle put his arm around her, tucking her close and turning her away from Gaston. "I would speak with her in private, Varennes," he said over his shoulder. "To be certain that my ward is not merely saying what you have instructed her to say, out of fear of you."

"She is no longer your ward," Gaston said, finally breaking his stony silence. "She is my wife."

Celine stiffened at the taunting edge in his voice. He wasn't claiming her as his own; he was getting in a dig at Tourelle.

"That," Tourelle snapped, "is a temporary situation which will soon be remedied."

"Indeed. Temporary," Gaston agreed with a humorless laugh.

It tore at what small shreds were left of Celine's heart.

"Will you allow me to speak with her or nay?"

"By all means," Gaston replied casually. "Speak to her in private. Visit with her as long as you wish. I am certain the two of you have much to discuss. Your long journey here. The weather. Plans for seduction and murder."

Tourelle's arm tightened around Celine. "You are mad, Varennes, if you think this sweet innocent would partake in such treachery. But then, that is what you have always been—a mad barbarian. Completely lacking in honor. As you always shall be."

Gaston didn't respond to the gibe. "Etienne, escort them to my solar and post yourself outside the door. Make certain that the good and honorable Duc does not raise a hand against my *wife*. Royce, Matthieu, I would speak with you."

Without so much as one word to her, not one word, he turned and stalked away with his men.

Celine listened to them go, feeling a pall of desolation settle over her as their boot steps rang through the hall. Now she would never be able to convince Gaston she wasn't plotting with Tourelle. Or that she was from 1993. Or that he must let her go meet with Brynna again. Oh, God help her ... was she ever going to be able to get home?

Or was she going to die here?

She wanted to curl up into a ball and sob out all the shock and hopelessness she felt, but Tourelle had taken a firm grip on her arm and was leading her off to the solar, following Etienne. A sharp word stopped the nuns when they started to tag along.

As she moved with Tourelle into the small chamber, Celine glanced at Etienne, but he would not meet her gaze, stiffly taking up his post outside. Tourelle nodded politely at the lad, escorted her in, and closed the door behind them.

Once they were alone, he flung her away from him. Any trace of kindness or concern vanished from his face.

"You are far more intelligent than I had given you credit for, my sweet," he said, carefully keeping his voice low.

Celine stumbled backward, coming up against the stone hearth, startled by the sudden change in him. Beneath his mild words there was something threatening in his tone, something almost ...

Evil.

"I—I suppose it's useless to tell you that I've never seen you before and I don't have any idea what you're talking about?"

Tourelle took a step forward and grasped the back of

one of the carved chairs that flanked the room's trestle table, a storm of anger gathering in his face, his voice a harsh whisper. "There is no need to keep pretending, Christiane, though your performance in the hall was most inventive. That madness about not being Christiane is an excellent way to keep Varennes off the scent. I must congratulate you on the cleverness of your scheme. And appearing here so suddenly on the eve of the new year and in his bed was truly inspired. I only wish I had thought of it. *And* that you had informed me of what you were about. You will not be so careless again!"

"I—I didn't—"

"Nay, do not try to explain it now. It matters naught. What I would know is why you failed. Varennes told me you *fled* when the moment was at hand." Tourelle's grip on the chair tightened in white-knuckled fury. The massive piece of furniture shook. "How could you *run* when you had him within your grasp?"

Celine pressed herself back against the hearth, her heart in her throat as she began to understand. "My . . . grasp?"

"Cease your playacting!" he hissed. "You have been here more than a month, damn you. Why have you not bedded Varennes? It does me little good to kill him if you have not secured your place as his widow!"

Celine stared at him, wide-eyed. Christiane—her ancestor, her innocent, convent-raised ancestor—*had* been in on some murderous plot with Tourelle! Celine had been wrong about her.

And Gaston had been right in his suspicions all along.

Tourelle shoved the chair aside and stalked around the table. "Tell me the truth, Christiane. Have you used any of the alluring tricks we discussed? Have you at least *attempted* to seduce him?"

Amnesia. That was her only hope. She had to make him believe she really did have amnesia. It might be enough to get a little information out of him.

Precious information that might save Gaston's life.

"M-milord," she said shakily, "I truly don't know what you mean. I have no memory of you, or of any plans." That should sound believable. It was true.

Tourelle had been advancing toward her, but he suddenly snapped around, fists clenched, every inch of his heavily muscled, six-foot-tall body taut with anger. "Damn you, you impudent girl!" He exhaled through his teeth as if trying to calm down, then turned back, frowning at her. "You have always known better than to defy me this way," he murmured almost to himself. "Mayhap you truly did suffer a blow to the head."

"I . . . I think that may be it," she agreed. "I don't remember. But some . . . some of it is starting to come back to me, now that I've seen you and the others." She closed her eyes and shook her head. "But it is still . . . foggy. Per—mayhap you should explain it all to me."

She opened her eyes to find Tourelle glaring at her, his arms folded over his broad chest. "You had better start remembering quickly, Christiane. I have no patience for mistakes." A suspicious gleam came into his blue eyes. "Or disloyalty. You have not started to develop some ill-advised *affection* for Varennes, have you?"

"No. I don't care about him," she said blandly. "He hates me." She tried to keep her voice steady as she said that. "And . . . the feeling is mutual. It's just that I can't remember what it is I'm supposed to do. Tell me and . . . I'll do it."

"Your part is simple enough. You are to lure Varennes into your bed so that he consummates your marriage. Since he is the last male heir of the line, when he dies, all he owns will pass into your hands." He paused, as if relishing the thought. "Our hands."

"But I don't think that will work. He's too suspicious of me. And h-he's really not attracted to me. Besides, what about the King's order? If anything happens to Gaston, you'll have to forfeit everything *you* own. Maybe you should reconsider—"

"I have taken care of that," Tourelle insisted mysteriously. "Do not worry about the King's order. You have only to manage your part."

"But how do you intend to actually kill him?" she prodded carefully. "Are you going to try and make it look like an accident? Even if you—"

"The less you know of that, my sweet, the better for you." He stepped closer and gave her a hug of reassurance that made Celine feel sick. He obviously wasn't going to reveal any of the most important details to her.

Setting her away from him, he tucked a stray strand of her hair behind her ear. "Keep your attention on your own task, Christiane. It seems you have made at least some progress already—Varennes's people have told us how intelligent and kind you are. You have done an excellent job of making them drop their guard and accept you as one of their own. You will not be a suspect."

Celine's stomach turned. Her mouth felt dry. He clearly had this all planned out, and she had unwittingly played right into his hands.

"But what if my part . . . fails?"

It was one last hope. If she never made love with Gaston, Tourelle would find no profit in killing him.

The Duc smiled, and somehow there was more threat in that smile than if he had fastened his hands around her throat and squeezed.

"Ah, but you will *not* fail, my dear. Or has your memory loss made you forget what I told you before? About the Moorish traders who deal in women? They would pay well for a pale beauty such as you, a virgin fresh from the convent. Do you wish to spend the rest of your days as the amusement of some Saracen desert lord . . . or as the wealthy widow of Sir Gaston de Varennes?"

Celine pulled away and turned her back quickly, hoping he couldn't see the color draining from her cheeks. "I understand."

That was an understatement. She had judged her ancestor too quickly. A threat like that, used against an innocent, convent-bred girl . . . Poor Christiane had been forced into this.

"Excellent, my dear." Tourelle stroked her hair, as if he were caressing a favorite pet. "I shall return home at once, then, and leave you to your task. My chateau is but a few hours' ride from here—in case you do not remember." He started for the door. "I will expect to receive a missive from you before a se'nnight is past, Christiane. Send it with one of the nuns. Send word that you have succeeded in bedding your husband."

The cold gray of dawn chilled the air as Gaston stood leaning against one of the trees in his apricot grove, casting blistering mental curses upon whatever cruel trick of fate had thrown Christiane into his lap.

He had spoken to Royce and Matthieu, and their report was not heartening. They had not been able to find any proof of Tourelle's plans; the Duc had apparently been looking for Christiane, exactly as he had claimed. After following him for days, they had finally confronted him and brought him to the chateau.

They had no proof. No evidence. Which left Gaston exactly where he had started: trapped in this marriage, shackled to one of the most incredibly treacherous women he had ever had the misfortune to meet.

When he thought of the way she had so easily confused him, cloaked herself in lies, planted small clues here and there to mislead him, almost made him believe. Made him *want* to believe. Made him want *her*. God's blood, she had come so close to succeeding.

But which was better? To mistakenly believe that she was a woman from seven hundred years in the future, intent on leaving him and returning to her own time?

Or to know the truth, that she was in fact Tourelle's ward, intent on seducing him?

Neither alternative eased the churning pain that knotted his gut.

He looked up through the barren branches that scraped the iron-gray sky. He was not sure what had drawn him out here in the dead of winter. The trees were barely taller than he was; he was probably killing this one just by leaning on it.

He glanced down at the snow, remembering how hard he had laughed when Gerard had ridden up with the cartful of tiny saplings, just after Gaston had taken possession of this castle. What was a knight doing with that collection of sickly-looking sticks? he had chortled.

His elder brother explained that he had brought the apricot trees back from Crusade and wanted to give them to his brother as a gift. Tending an orchard was a true nobleman's calling, Gerard had said, and Gaston was a true nobleman now that he finally had a castle of his own.

A true nobleman. The words had cut Gaston's laughter short, made his throat tighten even now. Gerard had never known exactly *how* he had taken possession of this castle. How he had won it in a tournament, by cheating. With the help of a potion dropped in his opponent's drinking water. He had unhorsed the poor fool quickly, and claimed this prize.

Stolen it.

Gerard had never questioned. He had simply insisted that his younger brother take the trees, and Gaston had accepted, telling himself they would probably not survive the winter.

But somehow they had. Somehow they still did, every year.

Two years ago, he had given in and started tending them. Not because he felt any noble calling, he had told himself, but because he liked sweets. Dried apricots in the winter were a—

"Gaston?"

The feminine query from behind him cut through his thoughts like a knife. A knife in his back.

He did not turn to look at her. "It is unwise for you to be here with me, *wife.*"

She came closer. "Etienne told me you were out here. I know you may not believe—"

"Aye, there you have the truth of it, Christiane. I may never again believe a word you say. Tell me, what did you and Tourelle decide upon? Poison? That would be easy enough to disguise in one of the odd dishes you cook. Or mayhap you chose a less cowardly method. A quick blade at my throat some night? Nay, too difficult to disguise as an accident. Mayhap a saddle with its cinch loosened just so?"

He spun on his heel, startling her so badly that she stepped back and almost fell.

"But of course," he continued coldy, "all would be for

naught unless you had first lured me to your bed. And that is why it does not matter what method of murder you have chosen. Because your plan will never succeed."

She stood there staring at him with wide eyes, shivering. She had come outside without a cloak. He set his jaw, cursing himself for noticing her discomfort.

And then she said the last thing he expected.

"Yes, Gaston. That's exactly what he has ordered me to do. He wants me to seduce you."

He slanted her a wary glance. "What is it, *wife?*" He said it like an epithet, the way that always made her wince, as if he hated the very word and all it stood for. "Do you come here to tell me you have developed such *affection* for me that you cannot carry out your overlord's fiendish plans?"

"Yes."

The answer was so simple, and spoken with such feeling, it struck him dumb.

"Yes, that's what I've come here to say," she went on, slowly, calmly, as though she had given this some thought while rushing outside without her cloak like a reckless little fool. "I know you'll never believe me now, but I'm exactly who I told you before, Celine Fontaine from 1993. But because Tourelle believes I am Christiane, I was able to get him to tell me what he's planning—"

"And you have come straight here to share it with me," he scoffed.

She didn't react to his sarcasm. "It's exactly like you've suspected all along. He wants me to trick you into bed so that our marriage will be final and I'll inherit everything when . . . when you . . ." Her voice broke and she suddenly took a step toward him, a flood of emotion glistening in her eyes. "He means to *kill* you, Gaston—"

"What a surprise."

"Stop being so damned sarcastic! Listen to me. I couldn't get him to tell me *how* he plans to kill you. He just insisted that he and I wouldn't be suspects and that he wasn't worried about the King's order. You've got to get out of here before something terrible happens to you!"

Gaston glared down at her, his heart beating hard. So

hard he could hear it as well as feel it. She looked so earnest, as if she were truly concerned for him, as if she . . .

Nay, he would not be drawn into her web of lies and seduction again. He shook his head, laughing at his own gullibility. "Do you expect me to simply believe all that you say?"

"No. No, I don't care *what* you believe anymore. Just save yourself. Get away from here. Away from me. Far away. Until he gives up this stupid plan."

Suddenly there were tears on her cheeks. Gaston went rigid, hating how easily she made him react to her, utterly despising the urge to hold and comfort and protect that welled up unbidden. He hated as well the suspicion that had taken hold, upon hearing that Tourelle was not worried about the King's order.

The good and honorable Duc had one clear way to kill him and appear completely innocent, and it was exactly the sort of thing that whoreson would do.

Kill Christiane as well.

Tourelle could hardly be a suspect if his beloved ward died in the same accident as her husband. And with the last male heir of the Varennes line *and* his wife out of the way, Tourelle would have the closest right to the Varennes lands—using both the marriage tie and his ancient claim through his mother's line.

It all flashed through Gaston's brain in the span of one rapid heartbeat. He nearly took a step toward his wife, driven by the maddening, deepening urge to keep her close and safe. He was not sure how he held himself in check. "Christiane, how did—"

"Celine," she insisted.

"Christiane," he repeated just as stubbornly, "how did Tourelle first persuade you into his scheme? Was it loyalty on your part . . . or did he force you into this? Has he threatened you in any way?"

She shook her head. "There's no time to argue about that anymore. None of it matters. He's planning to kill *you.* You've got to leave and I've—"

"It does matter," he said flatly. "You will tell me."

"If there's one thing I hate about this century, it's the

way men order women around! Do you have any idea how annoying that is?"

He closed the distance between them in two strides and caught her chin on the edge of his gloved hand. "Do not attempt to change the subject, my lady wife. Is Tourelle threatening you?"

She trembled at the contact and jerked away from his touch, turning her back. "Something about Moorish traders and desert lords," she muttered in an irritated tone.

A steel edge of fury lanced through him. So that was Tourelle's threat—to sell her to slave traders. And to think that the Duc called *him* Blackheart, when he was using so savage a tactic against his own ward, a convent-raised innocent.

If that was truly what—who—she was, this maddening woman he stood staring at; he still could not believe that she had ever set foot in a cloister. But the nuns were certain she was Christiane, and Tourelle as well, and they had known her all her life.

Who was he to dispute their certainty?

Damn him, whoever she was—Christiane or not, liar or not, insane or not—he had to keep her safe. He could not abandon her here, and he could not send her away alone. Not because the King had ordered him to ensure that no harm came to her, or even because he was concerned about Tourelle's threat of slave traders.

It was because of the accursed concern that he felt for her, that gentle yet unyielding *feeling* that would not be banished. It made leaving her behind impossible.

It also made him resentful.

And furious at his own weakness.

He would not make his brother's mistake. He would never be softened by a woman. Any woman.

"We will leave on the morrow," he said abruptly.

"We?" She spun around. "But *I* can't go anywhere! I've got to stay here. I need to—"

"To stay near Tourelle?" he finished for her. "Nay, Christiane, I'll not leave you here to weave further schemes. I mean to put as much distance as possible between you and your overlord." It was the only explanation he would allow himself to give her.

She looked exasperated. And angry enough to chew steel and spit rust. "It's too risky to take me with you," she pointed out. "Aren't you afraid I'm going to try to lure you into bed? You'll be better off without me. It makes more *sense* to leave me here."

Aye, it did.

But he knew he would ignore all sense, all logic, all reason when it came to keeping her safe.

"We leave on the morrow, as soon as supplies can be readied." He pinned her with a determined look. "And if you think this will make it easier for you to trick me, you are wrong. You will never again lure me into your lies, Christiane. Or your bed."

Chapter 16

Celine huddled in the darkness between a sack of rye flour and a cask of wine, and knew all along this was never going to work.

A mad impulse had led her down here, to the *bouteillerie*, a basement beneath the kitchen where wines and staple goods were stored. Gaston had ordered her to be in the bailey, ready to leave, by the time the morning bells rang at six—and that had been well over an hour ago. She had thought if she could just hide, if it took him too long to find her, maybe he would give up out of sheer annoyance.

Ever since Tourelle had declared her to be the one, true, real Christiane yesterday, her husband had done nothing but growl orders and glare at her. Even the nuns, who were staying to rest and gather supplies before beginning their long journey home to Aragon, had kept out of his way. Since he was so furious with her, maybe he would give up and leave her behind.

But as she knelt there, trying not to sneeze on dust and pepper, she realized this impetuous tactic was useless.

He would find her. He might hate her, but he also didn't trust her one bit, and he wasn't going to leave her here to "scheme" with Tourelle, as he had put in. She had tried reasoning with him all day yesterday, but he hadn't listened. He had remained adamant about taking her with him.

Even though they both knew it was a mistake.

Stubborn, pigheaded, tyrannical male! Why couldn't he see that he had a much better chance of staying *alive* if the two of them separated and kept as far apart as possible?

Celine huddled deeper into her cloak, shivering in the clammy, musty air. She had to remain here. Not just to save him, but for her own reasons as well. She had to stay near that window upstairs. Had to find some way to get home when the next eclipse took place in three months.

And if she didn't have that long . . .

Either way, it made no sense for them to stay together, to risk the desire that ignited so easily between them.

To risk making a mistake that might cost Gaston his life.

Suddenly she couldn't breathe.

Oh, no. She tried to take a deep mouthful of air, but ended up choking on dust. Her breath started coming in short, shallow gasps. *Oh, God.* Panic seized her with an iron grip. She jerked to her feet, sending the pile of sacks she had hidden behind tumbling. Closing her eyes, she tried to calm down, too late. Her heart was already racing. The familiar, uncomfortable chills chased down the back of her neck and over her shoulders.

No, no, no. Reaching out in the darkness, she grasped the top of the nearest wine barrel, something solid to hold on to. All she had to do was breathe deeply. All she had to do was . . .

Telling herself that did no good. Terror had already taken hold. She knew this was stupid. Knew there was no reason to panic. Knew this was the worst possible time for another anxiety attack. And knowing that did no good.

She was shaking badly. Gripped by mindless, all-consuming fear. *Run.* That was all she could think of. She had to run. Run, run, *run.*

She stumbled forward, shoving past the wine barrel she had huddled next to, but it was impossible to find her way in the dark. She had purposely chosen the least-used corner of the *bouteillerie*—and now she couldn't remember the way out. Right or left? She whirled, blind. She couldn't see the stairs. Right? There was no way out. Left? She couldn't breathe. Her heart was pumping. Her muscles tensed painfully. She had to run. But it was impossible to see. Panic and indecision held her paralyzed.

Then she heard footsteps on the stairs. Boots. She tried

to cry out. Not even a sob would pass her constricted throat. She could only stand frozen in the middle of the room in the darkness, light-headed with stark, unreasoning fear, wishing for ... wanting ...

"God's blood, woman! Where are you?"

Yes!

No! She didn't want him to find her. Yet that deep, furious familiar voice sounded as sweet as anything she had ever heard in her life.

A moment later she saw the glow from his torch, flickering along the stairwell as he descended from the kitchen. Then his boots came into view. Then all of him, clad in black. With an equally dark expression on his face.

He stopped on the bottom step. Glowering at her. "God's breath, but you defy all belief, wife. What new ruse is this?"

All she could utter from her dry throat was a wordless croak. Then, to her utter mortification, she started to cry. It seemed to be all she did in his presence anymore. Cry like a helpless little fool. And this was a particularly humiliating sort of sobbing—tiny, panicky gasps of air and tears.

He shoved his torch into an iron wall sconce and came to her. "What has happened? Are you hurt?" He almost looked like he was going to touch her, but checked the motion even as it began.

Celine could only shake her head. "I ... I ... c-c ..." She began hyperventilating.

"You cannot breathe?" He looked down at her in puzzlement. "Is this some strange seizure that comes over you—or another trick?"

Her heart was beating too hard, filling her throat, making it impossible for her to speak, or to do anything but stand there in tears, shaking. She looked at the floor. She didn't want to look at him, didn't want him to see her like this. And she couldn't bear the cold mistrust in his eyes.

And then he took her in his arms.

Oh, God.

"Have you forgotten what I taught you before?" he asked a bit more gently. "Breathe." Slowly, almost reluctantly, he started to rub her back. "You know that you can do it. Calm yourself."

Celine stiffened at the first touch, trembling with more than panic now. She shouldn't let him do this. Not here. Not now, when they were alone in the torchlit darkness. This wasn't what she had intended at all! He was supposed to be leaving without her—not comforting her, helping her.

But he held her tighter, and after a moment's resistance she let herself be wrapped in his embrace, in his warmth and strength and confidence.

"Shhh. You are safe, *ma dame*. Breathe in. With me." He started counting for her, as he had before. This time the exercise began to work almost from the start. In to four and out to eight . . . in to eight and out to sixteen . . .

The rhythm was familiar now, and comforting, and bit by bit she began to feel in control of herself again.

She pulled out of his arms the instant she was feeling even a little better. "Th-thank you."

He let her go, turned away stiffly, retrieved his torch. "These attacks seem to come over you whenever you try to run from me. Mayhap it would be better if you stayed close." It sounded like he was trying to be sarcastic . . . but it didn't quite come out that way. His voice lost its bite as he said the word "close."

"I—I can't. I shouldn't. You know I shouldn't."

"I will not begin that discussion again. Not after enduring it yesterday from dawn until dark." He glanced around the small chamber as if he had developed an intense interest in his wine collection, looking everywhere but at her. "What exactly did you think you were doing down here?"

She dropped her gaze to the dirt floor, feeling foolish. "Trying to hide." The idea sounded even more ridiculous spoken aloud, but she was not going to lie to him anymore, even to save her pride. "I thought maybe you would . . . leave me behind."

"And now that you realize your mistake, wife, it is time to go. You have caused your measure of trouble for the day." He motioned for her to proceed him up the steps. "And you have cost us a good deal of daylight."

With an exasperated sigh, she walked past him and

started ascending the spiral stair. If she kept fighting him, he would no doubt haul her out of here like one of the sacks of grain. "You haven't even told me where we're going," she complained.

"To the chateau that belonged to my father, in the north."

Celine stopped and turned. "But that's not safe for you! Tourelle will guess where you are before too long."

"I am not running from him, Christiane—I am getting *you* away from him. The fact that you hid from me makes you look all the more suspicious, *ma dame,*" he said ominously. "Do you truly wish to remain here so badly? To stay near him and plan further treachery?"

Celine just stared at him, mute with chagrin. He wouldn't believe the truth. He had already jumped to the wrong conclusion and found her guilty.

"If Tourelle comes seeking a fight," Gaston continued in that same tone, "he will get it. Chateau de Varennes is much larger than this keep, and far better defended. And it is more than a month distant from here and his murderous schemes."

"A *month?*" she cried. "But that's—"

"I had planned to move there permanently in the spring. But the worst of the season's snows are past, so there is no reason to delay. We shall leave with a few guards, and the servants will follow when they have packed the furnishings."

Celine's jaw fell inch by inch as he said all this. *Permanently?* She remembered overhearing a few servants talking about moving in the spring, but she hadn't paid much attention to it.

Since she had expected to be long gone by then.

"But . . . you mean we won't be coming back here at all?"

"Nay." He gave her a nudge.

She remained rooted to the step. "But I can't—I mean I have to—"

"Move, *ma dame.*"

His granite-hard tone left no room for argument. She turned and started upward again, feeling like she was be-

ing marched off to her own execution. "Gaston, please, I
know you don't like me to keep saying this, but I'm not
who you think I am, and—"

"I know."

Startled, she stopped and turned again, unable to believe
her ears. "You know what?"

He shifted the torch to his other hand and leaned one
muscled shoulder against the stone wall. "I spoke with the
sisters from Aragon after supper last night." His voice was
mild, but his eyes were piercing. "They said they knew
naught of you ever being called Celine by anyone. Or of
the silver on your teeth. Or the strange foods that you have
been cooking. They said you had always been useless in
the convent's kitchen, unable to so much as boil a chicken.
And I showed them some of the odd devices you have invented. They had never seen aught like them. In the convent or anywhere in Aragon."

Celine felt hope well inside her. "So you know that I—"

He cut her off. "But all of that could merely have been
a ruse, intended to mislead me and make me drop my
guard. The nuns are of the opinion that it is all somehow
related to your supposed brain-fever, but I tend to believe
that you deliberately planted these clues to make me think
you were someone other than Christiane, Tourelle's ward."

She made a sound of frustration through her teeth. "You
are *the* most suspicious, mistrustful man ever to set foot on
the face of the earth."

"A virtue that has kept me alive through many years
and many enemies."

That sounded like his last word on the subject. Celine
would have turned and started climbing the stairs once
more, except that his eyes held her captive.

His potent gaze burned into her as he spoke again, his
voice dropping low and deep. "But they said that you had
no scar on your back. There was no accident. No mark.
Ever."

Hope blazed through her heart all over again. She could
see him struggling with it, see him almost believing the
unbelievable, his face cast into harsh angles, his jaw rigid.

He stared at her, as if he could know her true thoughts once and for all if he just looked long and hard enough.

She swallowed with effort, whispering, "My scar couldn't be related to any sort of brain-fever. And it's not something I could have faked. It's not a clue, it's the truth. It's a bullet wound—from a weapon in the future."

Her voice broke whatever spell held him there. He tore his gaze from hers, glancing upward as if pleading with God, then down at the stone beneath their feet. "Madness," he muttered under his breath. Stepping around her, he led the way up the stairs. "We are leaving, wife. Follow me. Unless you wish to be carried."

Celine followed. There was nothing more she could do to fight him. Or convince him. She had said all there was to say. He would have to believe her or not, trust her or not . . . care about her or not.

But he would have to make those choices for himself.

She caught up with him and they walked in silence to the bailey, side by side. Celine squinted in the blinding light of the winter morning as they left the keep. Two dozen well-armed men awaited, some mounted, some leading packhorses. Etienne stood holding the reins of a dappled gray mare.

"I have made certain all your belongings are here, milady," he said, patting the bundles tied to the saddle. "Gabrielle finished packing for you."

"Thank you, Eti—oof!" Celine was caught unaware by Gaston's hands closing around her waist. He lifted her into the saddle without looking at her; his touch didn't linger a second longer than necessary. As soon as she was securely seated, he turned and stalked to the head of the line, leaving her to deal with a flush of sensual heat that warmed her body and a wildly erratic pulse. He swung into the saddle of his huge black destrier.

Royce saluted him from beside the gate. "Farewell, milord. Godspeed."

"Keep a sharp eye upon your neighbors," Gaston suggested dryly. "I am entrusting this keep to you, Royce—and I expect to find it in the same condition when next I see it."

"The same or better," Royce assured him with a rakish grin.

Acknowledging his captain's salute, Gaston nudged his mount forward. The clatter of hooves and the jangle of weapons created metallic thunder as the riders crossed the drawbridge.

Just on the other side, Gaston turned in the saddle, taking one last, quick backward glance at the keep.

Celine felt a tug at her heart. Even from her position a few horses behind his, she could see in his eyes, in the tense set of his jaw, that he did not want to leave this place.

She had seen almost the same look moments ago, when he had gazed up at her on the stairwell.

But it lasted only a second before he turned forward and set his heels to his horse, his back rigid.

As her mare trotted along in the middle of the line, Celine noticed a sound coming from one of the baskets tied to her saddle. She unlaced the top and made a little exclamation of surprise when Groucho batted at her hand.

She bestowed a grateful smile on Etienne, who rode beside her. "Thank you, Etienne. That was very thoughtful of you."

He nodded toward the head of the line and spoke in a whisper, as if revealing something he was not supposed to reveal. "It was not I who thought to bring along your kitten, milady."

Celine followed his glance, warmth tingling through her as she studied the dark knight who was leading them into the forest, his black hair glistening in the sun.

But even while his unexpected, kind gesture pleased her, she couldn't shake the certainty that every mile they were about to travel would not take them farther from trouble, but deeper into it.

And God only knew what Tourelle was going to do when he found out they had left.

Trying to supervise both the preparations for supper and the moving of furnishings, Yolande had her hands full. Especially since a holiday mood had descended upon all and sundry once word came that they were moving to their grand new home earlier than expected.

At least the upper chambers were almost emptied. She bustled through the door of the last one, at the end of the corridor, past a man who was carrying out the footboard from a bed.

"Step careful, there," she instructed. "I will not have any marks on milord's fine goods."

"Yolande, have you the key to this?" Gabrielle asked from the far corner of the chamber. She was kneeling beside a trunk that had been pushed against the far wall.

"Oh, aye, that is a heavy one, is it not? We shall have to take out some of the silver before it can be moved below." Yolande walked over, looking for the key among the dozens on the iron ring that hung at her waist. "I think this is the one."

She inserted the small key, opened the trunk's lock, and lifted the lid.

But silver was not all they found inside.

"My oath, what is *that?*" Gabrielle asked in wonderment.

"I do not know. I have never seen aught like it in my life." Yolande picked up the odd object that sat atop the pile of plates and goblets and candlesticks.

It was like a leather pouch, but square in shape, and made of a very strange sort of leather—with a texture like fish scales, in a garish pink color Yolande had never seen before. And it had no drawstrings, but handles. And what looked to be a seam on top, with a scrap of metal attached.

"Why would someone make a pouch and then sew the top closed?" Gabrielle wondered, lifting the bit of metal to examine the seam.

"I do not think we should—"

Even as Yolande pulled the odd pouch away, Gabrielle's hold on the metal scrap caused the seam to open with a soft ripping sound.

"Fie, Gabrielle. Look at what you have done."

"No, Yolande, I think it is *meant* to open in that way. Look!" She pulled on the bit of metal again and the seam closed, making the same sound. She opened and closed it again and again. "See how quickly and smoothly it works? How clever!"

"This must be some strange treasure that milord purchased."

"But why would he place it in here? He has trunks for valuables in his own chamber."

"Aye," Yolande agreed, puzzled. "We keep only dented or damaged pieces of silver in here, the ones not fit for display. And I have not opened the trunk in months. I thought I had the only key."

"So how could this have come to be in a locked trunk?" Gabrielle toyed with the fastening again. "And what *is* it?"

She opened it, peeked inside, glanced up at Yolande. Then curiosity got the better of them both. They could not resist examining the contents.

The pouch contained a jumble of wondrous strange things that made them gape in astonishment. There was an elongated square of the same pink leather, wrapped about a neatly trimmed sheaf of the whitest parchment Yolande had ever seen. A hat, made of unfamiliar slippery-shiny material, blue with a red letter on it. A small book, bound in paper rather than leather, with no illuminations—but it had impossibly tiny, neat lettering on its pages. A ring of small, flat objects that almost could have been keys. Two circles of what looked like black glass, joined together, with long, slender side pieces that folded in and out on ingenious tiny hinges. A heavy black box no larger than Yolande's hand, impregnated with shaped bits of glass, with a strap attached. And a number of things she could not even begin to identify.

At the bottom of the pouch was another elongated square of the same pink leather, fatter than the first. It had a simple gold fastening rather than the seam-that-was-not-a-seam.

Gabrielle picked it up and opened it, eyes alight. Inside, tucked into slits, were neat rows of flat, elongated metal squares—except that they were not metal. They were hard and flexible and shiny, but they were not metal. They had more of that impossibly tiny, neat writing on them. One had a silver square in the corner—with a rainbow trapped inside it!

"Mercy of Mary, Yolande, what *are* these?"

"I do not think we are meant to be looking at this," Yolande said, trying to take it from her friend's hands.

"But look at this one!" Gabrielle pulled out one of the squares, thinner than the rest. It had a miniature portrait in the lower left corner—a miniature smaller than any Yolande had ever seen, of incredible lifelike detail, painted with such skill that it was impossible to see the brush strokes.

And although the painter had made his subject look too pale, and her hair was in disarray, and her garb most unusual, her identity was unmistakable.

It was Lady Celine.

Chapter 17

He did not wish to stop here. He would not be welcome. Nor did he welcome the memories this place held. Gaston slowed Pharaon to a walk, shifting uncomfortably in the saddle as he caught sight of the sprawling chateau that loomed out of the forest an arrow's flight away. He had planned never to set foot here again. But he had someone other than himself to think of, and no other choice for a place to rest.

He reined his stallion to a halt, waiting for the others to catch up with him, shrugging out of his cloak. The evening was unseasonably warm; the setting sun cast the keep's turrets and battlements in shadows and darkness, a brooding contrast to the pleasant breeze that rustled through the trees, carrying the first scents of spring and rebirth: wet grasses and melting snow and swollen streams.

That there should be such life in this place of death seemed a bitter jest. Even the towns and fields they had passed through, so ravaged by Tourelle's forces last autumn, had been swiftly rebuilt, repaired, renewed. All was as it had been.

Yet it would never be the same again.

The injustice of it gnawed at his gut. The cold indifference of fate galled him. All his life he had indulged every whim, emptied every cup, tumbled every willing wench, fought for every greedy lord willing to pay his price. Never had he given one thought to the future. Not one. Profit had been his ruler, pleasure his muse. By all rights, he should have been killed two dozen times over.

Yet here he was, hale and hearty, sitting before one of the finest new chateaux in all of France. As its lord.

While the one who had built it, invested every year of his life and every fiber of body and soul in creating it, the one who had earned it, his brother, Gerard . . . was gone.

Pharaon whickered softly and turned his head, ears pricked. A moment later, Gaston heard the sounds of hoofbeats, of tired horses blowing, and the creak of saddle leather as weary riders stretched and yawned. He moved his mount to the side of the familiar path in the gathering darkness.

Matthieu rode in the lead. Gaston spoke to him briefly, then sent him and the rest on ahead. He waited while they rode slowly past. He would bring up the rear, in case the keep's lone occupant was harboring more hostility toward him than he guessed.

Riding in the middle of the line, his wife kept her eyes straight ahead as she passed. She did not glance at him, did not even acknowledge his presence—as had been her habit the entire month they had been traveling. She ignored his very existence.

He should be pleased about that, should find it a welcome relief from the arguing and defiance and chattering he had been subjected to for so long.

But he was not pleased, and it was not a relief . . . and he missed her chattering. Her indifference bothered him almost as much as the bone-tired, fragile look of her: she hunched over her palfrey, clinging to the saddle with one hand, to the horse's mane with the other.

The grueling pace he had set had taken far too great a toll on her, though she had never complained. Like an idiot, he had not noticed for the first few days. He had been too angry with her, determined not to look at her, determined to keep at least one vow in his life—that she would not confuse him further with her mad tales.

But his will had weakened, and his gaze had wandered to her once . . . twice . . . constantly. He had seen her fatigue. The way she rubbed the small of her back after the long days in the saddle. The way she shifted uncomfortably on her pallet at night, when they had to make camp in the open because there was no inn or abbey nearby. She would lie awake, unable to sleep because of her sore muscles. He lay awake a few paces away, unable to sleep because of a far different sort of ache.

As soon as he had noticed her discomfort, he had slowed their travel to avoid tiring her. With four weeks' riding behind them, they should have already reached their destination, but Chateau de Varennes was another five days from here. At this pace, the servants would reach their new home before their lord.

As the last of the little caravan rode past him, he nudged Pharaon back into line, and found his gaze again lingering over his wife. She was so tired that she swayed in the saddle, practically asleep. He had to fight an urge to sweep her from her horse and carry her the rest of the way. The thought of touching her . . .

He gripped the reins so tightly that the leather cut into his gloved hands. He had not touched her since the morning they had left his castle. Not even a casual brush of his fingers over hers, or an accidental contact as they passed each other.

Though he had considered that. Plotted it. Imagined it until his body and his brain were fevered with wanting it.

She sighed, her slim shoulders rising and falling beneath the soft outline of her cloak. She pushed back her hood and turned her face to the right, closing her eyes at the touch of the breeze. He almost thought he could see the outline of every dark lash resting on her ivory cheek. Her lips parted as the last rays of the sun caressed her coppery hair with golden light. The breath-stealing vision lasted only a second before she turned away again.

Just long enough for Gaston to feel something inside him wrench painfully. Questions clawed at him again, as they had during too many tormented nights while he watched her sleep: *Who are you? Why are you here? Who has sent you? What do you want with me?*

What had she intended when she came to him in the orchard that day of Tourelle's visit? Was revealing her orders a daring act of bravery, in utter defiance of her overlord, or a smoothly cunning trick?

Did she seek to save him, or to trap him?

And what of her strange attacks of panic, which had become more frequent as they had left his castle farther behind? Were they reality or ruse?

He had no answers. She had led him in such circles that it was impossible now for him to sort truth from lie. And more difficult still to untangle any of it from desire.

His throat was dry, even as he looked at her and thought the word. Desire. *Need*. Night by night, hour by hour, he had constructed a wall of defense against it, refusing to think of her as aught but *she* or *her* or *wife*. He had told himself that she was merely a woman, no more and no less attractive than any other he had known.

But when he looked at her, even the briefest glance, the others he had known merged into naught but a vague memory of curves and smiles and silken hair and fleeting pleasures.

She was more than that. So much more. She was the stormy clash of gray and blue in sea-deep eyes. The scent of thyme and lavender and roses. And a troublesome kitten, and odd hats. The mutinous tilt of a feminine chin.

She was a blaze of sweet passion in his arms.

She was the sound of giggles in his kitchen.

And she had entwined herself through his life so deeply that he could not tell where the connection between them began or ended.

Or whether he wanted it to end. For in a way that no other woman ever had been, she was important to him. He should want her out of his life, more than ever, yet he wanted her with him. More than ever.

And it was because of her, because he was concerned for her, that he found himself at this keep that he had never wished to look upon again ... steeling himself to face a woman who liked him even less than his wife did: his *belle-soeur*, his sister-in-law, who might well greet him with an arrow through his throat.

If she was in a good mood.

Lady Avril's brown hair hung down her back, unbound and tangled; it made her look younger than her nineteen years. Gaston found her where the servants had said he would: in the solar, seated before the window. In Gerard's favorite chair.

She was staring down at her needlework, though her hand rested upon it unmoving and the sun's light had long since faded. The fire on the hearth had burned low.

She had been in here the entire day, they had said, but even from where he stood, Gaston could see that she had worked only a few stitches.

"Avril?" he said softly.

She did not reply, or acknowledge him at all, and he did not know what else to say. Her guards and retainers had been overjoyed to see him. Their mistress, they revealed, was still deeply depressed over her husband's death, she had not been eating well, and they were most concerned. Especially since she was with child.

Gaston could still barely believe that stunning news, but beneath the folds of the loose-fitting black gown she wore, he could see the roundness. She was well along. Her maid had said the child was expected in another three months.

His brother's child.

The idea brought a strange, tight feeling to his throat. What was it he had thought? *Life in the midst of death.*

Yet he had stepped into this chamber expecting to be greeted by an earful of curses, not by this wan, silent ghost. Looking at her now, he found it impossible to picture the fire-tempered lady who had so captivated his brother. So changed him.

"Avril?" He took a step toward her. "Why did you—"

"If you ask me whether the child is Gerard's, I swear to God I will strike you dead."

She had not moved, or even lifted her gaze, but her words stopped him in his tracks. And made him feel a bit better. Though the tone was lifeless, the threat was pure Avril.

"I do not question the child's parentage," he assured her immediately.

"Ah, but you cannot claim it did not cross your mind, *beau-frère*. Is it not what you have demanded that I do? Replace him? Find another man?"

"I have *encouraged* you to marry again," Gaston corrected quietly. "For your own sake. Have you not given thought to what I suggested when I saw you last?"

"Nay. Have you given thought to what *I* suggested?"

"Since I am standing here before you, it should be obvious that I have not thrown myself into Hell's deepest pit to burn for all eternity."

She lifted her gaze to his at last. There was only the smallest spark left in her green eyes. "The suggestion stands."

Gaston held his temper in check. "Avril, why did you—"

"Have you come to tell me that I must leave here?"

That struck him like a blow. How could she believe him capable of such cruelty? Did she actually think that he would throw her out? In her condition? "Nay," he grated out. "We are on our way to Father's keep. This is your home, and shall be for as long as you wish. As I told you before."

"You will pardon me, *beau-frère,* if I doubt you." A haunted look misted her eyes and she dropped her gaze back to the unfinished tapestry. "It would not be the first time you have broken your word."

Her whispered accusation knifed through him, stabbing into an unhealed wound hidden deep inside. The pain made him clench his fists. He quelled the feeling, the guilt, tried again to pose his original question. "Why did you not send word that you were with child?"

"Because I did not think you would care."

That knocked the breath from him. She said it without ire, as a flat, certain statement of fact. How could she think that her pregnancy would not matter to him? She was the last of his family, she and the child she carried.

Had he truly been so harsh with her? So cold and heartless? He had merely offered suggestions as to her future. Perfectly logical, reasonable suggestions. Avril needed a stern hand. Someone had to look to her best interests.

"Regardless of what you thought my *feelings* might be," he said tightly, "you should have sent word. I am responsible for you now."

"Aye, you have pointed that out many times, *beau-frère.*

Along with the fact that I am to follow your orders." She
returned to her needlework and took a stitch. "Will you allow us to stay here or not?"

"I have given you my word." He was rapidly losing his
temper. "I have three chateaux now. I certainly cannot live
in three places at once."

"Then I shall stay here. Where he is."

"Where he *was.*"

"And I shall stay *alone,*" she continued as if he had not
spoken. "I do not intend to remarry. Ever."

Gaston slanted a grimace heavenward. Was it not
enough for God to plague his life with *one* stubborn, unreasonable, emotional female? Did he truly need two? Precisely what had he done to deserve such women in his
life?

"Avril," he said patiently, "you clearly do not understand your situation. You are but hours from the Flemish
border, and the skirmishes have become more serious.
Mayhap you cannot imagine what will happen if enemy
raiders sweep through this region—but I can. You are directly in their path. And this keep would make an irresistible prize. What do you plan to do? Don armor, take to the
battlements, and defend it yourself?"

She shot him a flashing emerald glance.

"God's breath," he groaned, rubbing a hand over his
eyes. "You would."

"I have defended myself before."

"By nails and blood, you are a *woman!* A woman alone.
It is dangerous for you here—and do not boast to me
about your skill with a crossbow. Killing a man is far different from shooting a partridge."

"I have my guardsmen. And I am confident that you
will protect me, *beau-frère.* Killing and destruction have
always been among your finest skills."

He swore vividly. "Having guardsmen is *not* the same
as having a husband to see to your lands and your safety.
And I shall be five days distant—this entire chateau could
be in ashes before I ever received word that the Flemish
were at your door."

"I will not remarry," she said simply.

Her calm made *him* sound like the one who was being unreasonable, which made him all the more angry. He gave up trying to argue that women needed male protection, from the violence of the world. Reason was clearly doomed to failure here. Instead he tried another tactic. A new one. "Think of your child."

She straightened as if he had slapped her. "I *am* thinking of the child!" she said furiously. "I will not have Gerard's son or daughter grow up with a stranger for a father. I cannot simply replace my husband because you tell me that I need a new one. Take your practical reasons and be damned! I *love* Gerard! You are incapable of understanding that, but *I love him.* As I will never love any man again!"

Gaston winced. There was that female word again. The one that had driven more poor fools to commit more mindless mistakes than any other. "You are not yet twenty, Avril. The rest of your life is a very long time to spend alone."

"Do you not think I know that?" She thrust herself out of her chair, her eyes suddenly bright. "Gerard and I were married little more than a year and a half. We had but a handful of days of happiness, *and you ask whether I know how long I must live without him?*" She choked on the question, then whispered, deadly calm, "I count the hours with every beat of my heart."

She turned her back, and after a moment Gaston realized she was crying.

He stood paralyzed. He had never seen her cry before. Had never even thought of Avril—strong, independent Avril—in such a vulnerable state. He did not know whether to reach out and comfort her, or walk out and let her grieve in private.

And so he stood there and felt awkward and did neither.

She leaned her forehead against the window, pressing her hands against the glass, staring down into the darkness of the empty courtyard. "He would not allow me to say farewell, that morn when he left." Her voice was hollow. "He made light of my concern. He said, 'It is but a tourney, Avril, an amusement. I will be home before you have

time to miss me.' " Her hands slid down the glass. "Before
you . . . have time . . . to miss me," she repeated softly.

Gaston took a deep breath, swallowing hard against the
cold lump of pain that filled his own throat, closing his
eyes against the strange burning in them. "Avril . . . a
memory cannot protect you. Or hold your lands. Or be a
father to your child."

"You blame me," she said suddenly, tearfully. "Do not
deny it. I know that you blame me somehow for his death!
But ask yourself this, *beau-frère*: Where were *you* when he
most needed you? You with all your battle-skill? Why
were you not there that day? *Why did you break your
word?*"

Celine let out an exclamation at that. She had been there
for several minutes, standing just inside the door of the
darkened solar, unsure exactly how to interrupt the shouting match; the servants had suggested that she play peace-
maker when it became obvious from the volume that
things were not going well between Gaston and his sister-
in-law.

Poor choice on the servants' part, she thought miserably.
Because she made a lousy referee, and Gaston and Avril
had both just turned to stare at her.

"How long have you been standing there, wife?" Gaston
demanded angrily.

"I . . . I'm sorry. I thought . . ."

He took a step toward her. "I trust you have found it all
entertaining," he snapped.

"It's hard to ignore you when you can both be heard
halfway into the great hall," she replied hotly. "The servants thought they'd better send in someone to raise a
white flag. They wondered whether the two of you might
not care to continue your conversation over supper. I don't
know about you, but some of us are starving."

"You are the Fontaine woman?" Avril asked curiously.
She nodded in Gaston's general direction. "His new
wife?"

"Yes. I'm sorry about all this, Lady Avril. I didn't mean
to listen in. My name is Celine."

"You have my condolences, Lady Celine."

"Uh . . ." It took a moment for Celine to understand that Avril was not offering condolences on her name, but on her marriage to Gaston. "Thank you."

Avril laughed at Celine's response, then dabbed at her eyes. "Tell me, how *do* you withstand this irksome tyrannical streak of his?"

"Actually, it's only irksome some of the time. The rest of the time it's almost tolerable." Celine paid no attention to Gaston's quelling glower. "It's his opinions of women that are really annoying."

"Indeed, I have always thought so," Avril concurred, ignoring the glower when it was turned her way. "It would seem you have come to know him well already. Have you any advice on how I might better manage?"

"Well, the first thing you have to learn to deal with is his arrogance," Celine offered with the beginnings of a smile. "His main problem is that he thinks he's always right. Then there's his temper—"

"And his suspicious nature," Avril added, warming to the subject. "We must not forget the way that he refuses to trust people."

"Yes, that, too. And then there's—"

"Enough!" Gaston thundered. "Mayhap the two of you would prefer to be left alone to amuse yourselves over my countless faults?"

Both of them gave him looks of wide-eyed innocence.

"Actually, that might not be a bad idea," Celine said.

"Aye," Avril agreed. "Off with you, *beau-frère*. I am certain there is something somewhere that needs to be hacked or trampled or shouted at or boiled in oil, or that would otherwise benefit from your attentions."

Gaston scowled at each of them in turn, muttering a mixture of oaths and adjectives that Celine was grateful she couldn't quite make out. As he turned on his heel and stalked past her toward the door, though, she thought she caught a mumbled prayer that Avril's baby be a boy.

"Good eventide, wife," he said coolly. "And to you, Avril. I am certain the two of you will enjoy yourselves to no end. No doubt you will understand one another far better than I understand either of you."

He slammed the door behind him with such force that the hinges rattled. Celine found herself still gazing at the spot where he had last been, feeling a little sheepish and sorry that they had teased him so mercilessly. But mostly she felt relief.

Relief from the strain of having to hold herself so icy and uninterested in his presence, when she was burning inside.

"Do you love him so much?" Avril asked quietly.

Celine spun around with a jerk, surprised by the unexpected question. "No! I . . . I mean, I—"

"You may be able to deny it to him. You may even be able to deny it to yourself." A bittersweet smile crossed the younger woman's pretty features. "But it is clear in every small glance you give him, when he does not know that you are looking."

Celine's stomach knotted. She stared down at her toes, misery piling upon misery. Was it so obvious, this love she had barely begun to admit, even to herself? "I . . . I can't love him."

She thought of the eclipse that was growing closer with every passing week. And of the pain in her back, the recurring ache that she prayed was caused only by the long days of riding, though she knew better.

Of what might happen to her before she had time to return to Gaston's castle.

Of Tourelle's threat about what would happen to Gaston if their marriage was ever consummated.

And none of that changed the way she felt about him.

"I *can't* love him," she repeated, not sure which of them she was trying to convince. "I can't stay with him. It's . . . it's very complicated."

"He does not return your feelings?"

Celine shook her head. "No. Not in the least. But that's not it. Even if he did, we could never—"

"Nay, you cannot think that way, Lady Celine. When you find love, you must catch it close and hold it tight. Do not let it go so easily."

Celine lifted her head just in time to see a new tear slide down Avril's cheek, and she felt a wave of sorrow for what the younger woman had lost.

And for what she herself would never know.

"He . . . doesn't believe in love," Celine whispered, swallowing hard. "He can't even see it when it's right in front of his eyes. That's why he keeps making that infuriating suggestion that you remarry—he can't see that you obviously loved Gerard deeply. He thinks husbands only exist to manage and protect, and wives only exist to provide land and heirs."

Avril sighed heavily, nodding, her lashes drooping. Suddenly she looked very young and very tired and very pregnant.

"I'm sorry, Avril," Celine said, walking over to help her back into her chair. "Here I am chattering, as Gaston puts it, and you must be exhausted. And hungry. Would you like me to bring you something to eat?"

"Nay, it is I who must apologize." Avril refused to sit down. "I have been a poor hostess. You have had a long, fatiguing journey, and you will want to retire early. And you said you were starving. Mayhap we should go and see to supper."

Celine's stomach growled as if in agreement. She was pleased to hear Avril mention food, since the servants had said their lady hadn't been eating. "That's a good idea. Do you suppose I could stage a bit of a mutiny and take over the kitchen? Cooking is one of my passions and I'd love to make something special for you."

"A mutiny?"

"An uprising," Celine clarified.

Avril raised an eyebrow. "Lady Celine, I like you more and more. Off to the kitchens it is."

They started to walk toward the door. "I suppose," Celine said, "that Gaston is going to be in a foul mood all through supper. We probably shouldn't have teased him that way."

"Fie on it. We shall send one of the servants to his chamber with a tray and a game of tables. That always takes his mind off most anything."

"A game of tables?" Celine squeaked, stopping in the middle of the room.

"Aye, it is his favorite."

"And you . . . encourage him?"

Avril looked at her strangely. "Should I not?"

Celine frowned, growing suspicious as bits and pieces of the discussion she had had with Gaston on the subject started coming back to her. "Avril, what exactly is 'tables'?"

"Merely a game." Avril pointed to a trestle table and chairs in one corner. "I've a set there."

Celine walked over and looked down at the objects Avril had indicated. "I see." Her frown deepened. "Avril, I think that after supper, I am going to have to have a conversation with my husband about one of his favorite subjects." She turned and moved toward the door with a new snap in her step. "Lies."

Chapter 18

Backgammon.
     Celine had planned a truly satisfying scene around that word. A virtual festival of righteous indignation. Gaston had led her to believe he was sleeping with every pretty girl within arm's reach, when the whole time he had been playing *backgammon*.

She paced the length and breadth of the spacious bed-chamber Avril had given her, fuming over the issue alone. Which wasn't nearly as satisfying as letting her husband have it with both barrels. For a man who put so much importance on truth and trust, he had been misleading her thoroughly. How did he dare accuse *her* of being dishonest and manipulative? She was the one telling the truth about who and what she was.

Why had he let her believe the worst of him? Why hadn't he just corrected her about what "playing tables" really meant? The only reason she could think of—that he had been getting a good laugh from her stupidity—made her both furious and hurt.

She had spent the better part of the evening plotting an after-supper ambush: thinking of ways to bring up the subject, and all sorts of brilliant, witty things she might say. But her plans had been thwarted by Gaston's disappearance. He hadn't shown up for supper.

Avril had been unconcerned, saying it was his habit to go off by himself, especially if he was upset about something. Insisting there was no cause for alarm, she had coaxed Celine into a tour of the unique chateau: from the fountain in the kitchen to the marble pavilion in the gardens to the unusual tile floors in some of the upper chambers. Avril explained that Gerard had become fascinated with the East while on Crusade as a young man, and had included Moorish touches everywhere when building this chateau for the two of them.

There were Persian rugs instead of rushes in the great hall, blown-glass goblets at the table, and damask curtains and canopies on the beds. Most of the rooms were downright luxurious compared with the Spartan simplicity of Gaston's castle. Celine, however, had barely admired the architecture, focusing more on looking for her husband, her righteous indignation mixed with worry and thoughts of Tourelle's threats.

Gaston was nowhere to be found.

Standing in the middle of her chamber, she finally stopped pacing, rubbing her back. He was probably trying to worry her on purpose, to repay her for teasing him earlier. Well, she wasn't going to let him ruin another night's sleep; he had already kept her awake too many times on the trail, every small movement he made on his pallet making her feel all tense and restless and tingly-hot inside.

It should be a relief to have him nowhere in the vicinity for the first night in weeks. It *was* a relief, she corrected herself. Kicking off her slippers, she went over to her bed on its large, round dais, looking up at it with an appreciative sigh. She started unlacing the back of her gown, struggling to do it herself because she didn't want to waken one of the maids Avril had assigned to her.

The bed would be quite a treat after so many nights spent in cramped inns, sparsely furnished abbeys, or on the forest floor. It was a huge, heavily carved four-poster, with soft white sheets, tasseled silk pillows, and several finely woven Arabic coverlets in cotton and wool. Definitely lavish by medieval standards. She pulled her gown over her head, let it drop in a pool on the floor, and climbed up to slide between the almost-silky sheets.

What she needed most right now was sleep; too many long days of riding had left her with zero energy. Not to mention a dull ache in her lower back that she was too afraid to think about.

Curling up on her side, she closed her eyes and tried to relax. Which was almost impossible with all the disturbing thoughts chasing through her head. Such as the odd little fact that Avril had revealed earlier while they were talking in the kitchen.

Celine had been whipping together a decent version of pasta while Avril discussed one of *her* personal passions: languages. There had been a renewed light in the younger woman's eyes as she mentioned her collection of poems and manuscripts in Latin and Greek. She also spoke fluent German, Castilian, and a smattering of Arabic. One of her special interests was the study of word origins. "Avril," for example, meant "spring." She had puzzled over the name Celine for a while, never having heard it before; then she had gone to look it up.

When she had come back and happily announced the meaning, Celine had dropped an earthenware jar of dried sage from numb fingers, not even hearing the crash when it shattered on the floor.

Even now, opening her eyes, she still felt a little queasy and weird because of it. Celine was a name that had been in her family for generations. Centuries. Her mother had named her after her great-great-grandmother. The meaning she had always heard was downright boring: "sprig of parsley."

Avril said that Celine meant "daughter of the moon" in ancient Greek.

An eerie tingle chased down her neck and shivered through her. She sat up, pushing aside the covers, rubbing her arms in the darkness. *Daughter of the moon.* It was almost as if her destiny had been decided even before she had taken her first breath. Like all this had been meant to happen, from the day she was born.

But that was ridiculous. It couldn't be true. She wasn't meant to be here. Not with a bullet in her back. Not with a husband who didn't trust her, or care for her.

Or even like her very much.

Him again. Invading her thoughts at every turn. With a groan of frustration, she got out of bed and put her gown back on, not bothering with the laces. A breath of fresh air might do her some good. The night was warm for March. She crossed to the far side of the room, toward the door that Avril had said opened onto a terrace.

She peeked out, then stepped outside. An actual terrace. Definitely odd-looking in a castle, but there was an entire network of them, encircling the chateau's tallest tower, one outside every bedchamber. They were supported by massive buttresses, but otherwise looked surprisingly delicate, with onion-shaped roofs, gracefully sweeping arches, tile floors, and walls and ceilings inlaid with ivory and lapis sparkling in the light of the full moon.

It was one more bit of Moorish influence—an especially romantic touch that Avril said Gerard had included to surprise her. Celine ran her hand over the smoothly curving edge of the rounded, waist-high stone railing. This was not the work of a rigid, unfeeling man.

How could two brothers be so different?

From what she could glean, Gerard hadn't always been that way. Avril said their marriage had been arranged, and at first he had been very much like Gaston: high-handed and arrogant and coolly unemotional. They had had terrible arguments, and she had spent most of her first weeks as a new bride crying and wanting to go home.

And then slowly, so subtly that neither one of them had realized it was happening, he had fallen in love with her, and she with him. It had been, Avril whispered softly, mostly a matter of time.

Time. Celine leaned out over the railing, looking down at the castle walls far below, the bailey, the moat, the moon-silvered treetops beyond, bare branches that would soon be green with new buds. She felt very close to tears.

Time. She was just exhausted. That was all it was. She should go back inside and at least try to get some rest, even if she couldn't sleep. Pacing and wandering and trying to come to terms with her troubling thoughts were making her feel worse, not better.

She turned to go in but stopped in mid-stride when a small object fell past her terrace, right out of the sky.

She rushed to the far railing, just in time to see whatever it was land in the moat with a splash. Puzzled, she glanced up to see where it had fallen from—then gasped.

Gaston sat perched on the onion-shaped roof of the terrace adjacent to hers. From six feet away and ten feet up, he glanced down and gave her a lopsided grin. His beard had grown in during their weeks on the road, and it made him look all the more like a complete rogue and a disheveled reprobate. "Good eventide, wife. Come to enjoy the view as well?"

Her throat had closed off so tightly that she couldn't say anything for a moment. He was wedged precariously between the curving roof and the tower. One wrong move and he would fall. "What do you think you're *doing* up there?" she shouted at him, terrified.

"Enjoying the view," he replied, as if it should be obvious, his words slurring. "And a flask or two of my brother's excellent Castilian wine." He lifted the object in his hand.

"You look like you've had a flask or *ten* of your brother's excellent Castilian wine." Her words were angry, but it was fear that made her fingers tighten around the wide stone railing. However in the world he had gotten up there, there was no way he could get down safely. Not drunk.

"Two. Ten. No matter." He let his head fall back against the stone tower, making a sound that wasn't quite a laugh. "In truth, it is *my* excellent Castilian wine now."

The liquor that muddled his voice couldn't quite hide the sadness that lay beneath his words. Celine felt his pain so suddenly and so deeply that it made her hurt inside. How could she not have recognized it before? She hadn't given a thought to his grief. It had to be torment for him to stay here, in this place so full of memories of his brother.

"Gaston," she said quietly, trying to keep his mind and her own on the problem at hand, "how did you get up there?"

He made a vague gesture with his free hand. "Up onto the ledge. Then a leap, then a twist, then a bit of a pull." He moved his shoulder uncomfortably, mumbling, "I think I may have strained an old wound."

Celine bit her bottom lip to stifle a groan. "And did you have any plan for getting back down?" she asked, trying to remain calm.

He slanted her a glance, his head tilted to one side, his tousled hair falling over one eye. "You sound worried, she. Are you worried?"

Celine didn't know why she was being called "she," but she didn't care at the moment. "I just don't want you to break your neck—if you don't drown in the moat first!"

She shouldn't have said that, because it made him look down at the moat. Which made him lose his balance. She covered her mouth with both hands, too horrified even to scream, seeing it in slow motion as he started to slide.

He recovered almost instantly, probably more from the instincts of a lifetime of training than from any conscious thought. Regaining his precarious seat, he gave her a reckless grin. "You are right, she. This may be dangerous."

Shaking, Celine slowly lowered her bloodless fingers. "Gaston, don't move. *Please* don't move. Stay right there. I'm going to get some help."

"Nay, do not leave, little wife. I will come down if you are so concerned."

"No!"

But even as she shouted it at him, he was already moving, sliding down the side of the roof with all the caution of a kid in a playground, only to stop himself on the decorative, upswept edge with his booted heels. He tossed her his last remaining flask as he swung into a movement—so quick she couldn't see it—that involved grabbing the roof and twisting himself into a midair somersault.

She didn't realize she had shut her eyes until she opened them, as soon as she heard the solid sound of his boots hitting the tile floor inside his terrace. He stumbled but straightened, then negligently rested one hip against the wide stone railing, not even breathing hard. Still wearing that cocky grin, he held out his hand. "May I have my flask back?"

Celine slumped against the nearest arch, hiding her face in the crook of her arm, unable to speak. Even drunk, he had the physical ease of an athlete. Thank God.

"Wife?"

"No, you may not have your flask back," she choked out, though she was tempted to aim it straight at his reckless, unthinking head.

"But my shoulder hurts," he grumbled. "Did you not once tell me that wine is most effective on wounds?"

"Not on *old* wounds. And drinking it doesn't do anything for you." She lifted her head and gave him a glare. "Except turn you into a daredevil lunatic."

He frowned, his eyes glassy, his lids half drooping. "I have suffered all the female deef . . . defli . . . deli . . ." His tongue stumbled over the word until he finally got it out. "Defiance that I mean to brook for one day. If you will not give it, I shall come and take it."

"Oh, no, you don't, buster." Celine whirled to go inside. "I'm going to lock my door right now."

It took her one second too long to understand his meaning.

From the corner of her eye as she turned, she saw him backing up to jump from his terrace to hers.

"Oh, my *God!*" She spun toward him, flinging the flask away as she raised both hands. "No, *don't!*"

Her plea was about as effective as shouting at an oncoming train. She heard the flask splash into the moat as she saw him making a running vault with awful clarity: two quick steps, then his hand coming down hard on the railing, lifting him over with enough force, she hoped—enough speed, she prayed—to let him clear the distance. It seemed he hung suspended in the air for an instant that felt like all eternity.

Then some miracle brought him through the wide arch on her side without cracking his head on the stone. He landed in a running, staggering crash that plowed straight into her and carried them both into the wall.

The impact knocked from her what little breath was left in her lungs. His weight crushing her, she couldn't draw in enough air to shout and curse at him as she wanted to. She could only grab onto him, barely able to believe that he was still in one piece, her fingers grasping handfuls of his tunic as she buried her face against his chest with a sob.

His arms went around her and he pulled her close, laughing into her hair. "You are trembling, wife. And you dropped my flask into the moat."

She stopped hugging him and tried to push him away, shoving at his chest. "You lunatic! You reckless maniac!" She pummeled at him with her fists. "You could have killed yourself! You could have—mmphh."

He kissed her in mid-pummel. A swift, teasing kiss that cut off her tirade before she could even get warmed up. He ended her tiny blows as well, leaning into her and capturing her between the hard muscles of his chest and the hard ivory- and lapis-inlaid wall. Celine struggled, barely able to believe she could be more furious than she had been seconds ago.

She twisted and fought and finally managed to wrest her mouth away from his. "Stop that!" she cried breathlessly, shivering with the impact of his kiss and the feel of his muscular body pressed against her. "It's not going to work. You can't kiss me into not being mad at you!"

"Can I not?" He chuckled with inebriated humor, dusting kisses over her forehead and temples and nose. "Mayhap I am not yet doing it correctly." His head dipped and he nuzzled the soft skin exposed by her gaping bodice. "Mmm. I like this new way you have of wearing your gown, wife."

He rubbed his cheek against her there, his beard sending little shivers rippling to her most sensitive places. Celine held her breath and cursed herself for not retying the gown's laces. "I—I wasn't expecting company to swoop in! And I would appreciate it if you would swoop right back out again. Preferably through the door this—"

She inhaled sharply when he nudged her bodice out of the way just enough to expose one breast, the soft peak pinched to instant hardness by the touch of the night air, the attentions of his tongue, and the roughness of his whiskers.

"*Gaston,*" she gasped, squeezing her eyes shut. "D-don't do that. You're not thinking—"

"I do not wish to think," he said thickly, raising his head to kiss her again, muffling her protest. He made it a much deeper melding this time, a tender assault that sent her senses reeling. His lips moved over hers slowly, sampling and tasting her, not demanding a response but asking for one. He ignited a firestorm of dazzling light and heat, pulling her nearer to him until she felt herself melting, and him with her, until they were both nothing but a pool of warm, sweet rain.

A wolf howled somewhere in the forest below, a sound of wild longing carried on the wind, echoing the feelings set free deep inside her. The kiss tasted of exotic Castilian wine and unmatched hunger and an unspoken need that called to Celine more deeply than any touch. Without conscious thought, she relaxed her clenched fists, still trapped between their bodies, until her fingers were splayed against his chest, not pushing him away but feeling the corded muscles beneath the rough cloth ... and deeper still, his pounding heartbeat.

All her thoughts and objections unraveled, *no* and *yes* tangling until she couldn't tell one from the other. It had been so long since she had touched him, felt his strength and power, known the fierce glory of his arms locked around her.

And his hands ... oh, God, his hands, so sure and yet so gentle, caressing her in that simple, extraordinary way that sent ribbons of fire unfurling through her. For so many sleepless nights, in so many uneasy dreams, she had longed for this: his mouth over hers, his hands on her body, all of it hot, sweet heaven.

Her anger and fear for him were tumbling away, like the empty flasks they had tossed into the moat. She struggled to hang on to those feelings, knowing they were her only defense against this exquisite ache he stirred within her, the swirling, dizzying need that she so wanted to drown in.

Anger and fear. Her only weapons against all the other feelings: the ones that threatened to make all sense, all caution, all the world fly away.

She tore her mouth from his. "Gaston, please ..." she begged, not sure what she was pleading for, trying desperately to remember. All she could think of was that her lips felt swollen and bruised and wildly sensitive, her chin rubbed raw by the silken abrasion of his beard. "You . . . you don't know what you're doing. We *can't*—"

"You are so beautiful by moonlight," he muttered in that wine-thickened tone. Keeping her in place against the wall, raising his hands to her shoulders, he slowly pushed her loosened gown to her waist. He lifted one of her breasts in his broad hand, cupping the softness with an expression of almost innocent wonder. He ran his thumb over the tightened peak, drawing a ragged cry from her lips.

She tried again to wrest herself free, but be held her pinned. "P-please! Go back to your room! You don't want to do this. It's a mistake—"

"You are too late," he slurred. "Too late to save either of us, she. You are mine and I will have you." He moved his thumb again, making her whimper at the heat coiling in her belly. "Have you not heard?" he muttered. "I am an unfeeling knave. I care naught for my mistakes. I take my pleasure where I find it—and I have found you, my lady wife." He pulled her to him with one arm, his other hand suddenly at her waist, pushing her gown past her hips. "By all the blessed saints, I have found you."

"But you're not a knave! That's not the truth and you know it. You don't—"

She lost her voice and her mind when his callused fingers slid into the hot silk at the apex of her thighs. He uttered a low, masculine sound of pleasure and anticipation and caressed her deeply.

"Oh . . . ah . . . oh, God. Oh, *please,*" she sobbed, feeling the blinding passion and bright ribbons of sensation wrapping tighter around her, every motion of his fingers pulling her downward into that hot, sweet heaven even as she clawed for sanity. "G-g-go . . . go away. Go and sleep it off. *Please.* Before you do something you'll regret in—"

"Regret?" he echoed hollowly, his hands shifting, his arms flexing around her back. "Do you wish me to tell you of regret?" He lifted his gaze to hers, his dark eyes dazed and glistening with more than desire or the effects of the Castilian wine. "You never had an answer to what Avril asked earlier. Have you not wondered, wife, where I was when I was supposed to be at Tourelle's tourney? What great purpose it was that kept me away?" His voice took on a hard edge. "What I was doing while my father and brother were dying?"

"Gaston—"

"I was playing at dice, at the autumn fair in Agincourt. In the company of a pair of comely peasant wenches. I promised Gerard that I would join him and our father at the tourney and then I changed my mind. Broke my word. Because a bit of gambling held more appeal than spending the day with them. I was throwing dice *while their throats were being cut.*"

Celine choked back a sob, hurting for him, hurting for all the pain he was holding inside, the grief and guilt that shone in his eyes. "Gaston, I'm . . . I'm so sorry—"

"Nay, do not offer me your pity, *ma dame*. It is not your pity I want."

His mouth captured hers again and he made a sound deep in his throat. It might have been pain or desire or something else, but she didn't have time to sort it out, because he didn't give her time. He simply sealed his mouth over hers and swept her into his arms.

She struggled and fought, but his hold on her was solid, and that kiss stole her breath and any chance of talking sense to him. He stumbled a bit as he turned to carry her into the room, but he kicked the terrace door shut with his heel—and his steps were sure and purposeful as he headed straight for the bed. He mounted the dais and deposited her on the tangled covers, not even pausing to pull back the blankets.

The fine wool coverlet was soft beneath her, compared with the rough cloth of his tunic when he lowered himself over her. He gave her no chance to scramble away, setting her entire body aflame with his touch and the reckless intoxication of his kiss. She tasted the potent liquor he had drunk and the unique masculine tang that was Gaston until her blood was filled with fire and her every muscle shook with long-denied wanting.

Resistance slowly became a distant, foreign, fading idea

that seemed to belong to another woman in another place. Another time.

Bracing his forearms against the mattress on either side of her head, he moved against her, until both of them were breathing deep and unevenly. Though he was still fully clothed right down to his boots, she felt his rigid masculine hardness pressing against her with unrelenting, impatient purpose, and a small muffled cry of hesitation and uncertainty escaped her.

His kiss changed, his lips moving over hers with a far different intent than mere silence. The gentle force of it left her helpless and hungering, and when he opened his mouth and touched his tongue to her tender lower lip, she could only open her mouth to receive him.

The first satiny brush of his tongue against hers wrested a shiver of need from her, so intense it went through her whole body like glittering ice and flame. He deepened the kiss, but still did not plunge fully into her offered dampness; instead he kept teasing her with a rain of tiny wet kisses that barely touched his tongue to hers.

When she made another small sound, knowing as he must that it came from impatience and not protest, he lifted his mouth from hers, just long enough to tear off his tunic and kick off his boots and leggings. His naked, muscular body was a stark silhouette in the moonlight. He poised over her only for a moment, tense and still, the size of him daunting even cloaked in shadow.

And then he lowered himself over her, pressing her back into the mattress. "Gaston . . ." she whispered helplessly, even as she arched beneath him.

She couldn't do this. Musn't do this. Musn't let him do this. *Reasons.* Hadn't there been reasons? She tried to remember one. All she could think of was him; all she could remember clearly was one overpowering truth that had imprinted itself on her mind with such simple, heartfelt words.

When you find love, you must catch it close and hold it tight.

With a wordless cry of denial, she grasped fistfuls of the blanket to keep herself from wrapping her arms around his neck. He began to slide down her body, his bristly beard and the crisp hair covering the flat planes of his chest unbearably arousing, a prickly contrast to the smooth, wet sorcery that his lips and tongue worked over her breasts and belly.

He moved lower and she went rigid, unable to breathe as she realized his intent, stunned by the rush of shocking anticipation that flooded through her.

His hands circled her waist, slid lower, grasped the rounded cheeks of her bottom . . . and then he lifted her to his mouth.

And kissed her in a most intimate way, beyond anything she had experienced before.

A shuddering moan escaped her as the very tip of his tongue found the satin bud hidden in her damp curls, and touched it.

Celine writhed in his grasp, knowing she should stop him, knowing she could not stand the savage pleasure that raked through her at that single, incredible flick of his tongue—and needing more. More of his touch. More of him. All of him.

He did it again, with exquisite care, a slow sampling that brought a sheen of fever to her entire body and left her undulating beneath him. The ribbons of bright fire wrapped around her closer, tighter, and a trembling began in her belly.

Then he took the delicate bud more deeply into his mouth, drawing her in with his tongue. He suckled her gently.

His groan of pleasure made her sob as much as the intense sensations that clenched taut deep within her. Her eyes were open, but she could no longer tell dark from light, reality from dream, body from soul, so violent were the pleasure and emotion arcing through her, need that went beyond all description. Breath, thought, heartbeat all raced wildly, her head tossing on the silk pillows, wordless pleas tumbling from her lips in French, in English.

Then he tugged at her ungently and all the world flew away.

It was like an explosion. Like being surrounded by a

hundred walls of the clearest crystal that all shattered at once, bathing her in a thousand shards of feeling so powerful she thought for certain she was dying. The trembling that had begun low in her belly tore free and radiated outward in wave after wave, one ribbon after another unraveling and snapping within her.

The crystal firestorm still gripped her in its shuddering fury when he moved to cover her in one smooth glide, his body all heat and hardness and smoky-dark intoxication. He kissed her, letting her taste her own arousal while he rubbed his rigid shaft against her, rampant heat against yielding, honey-soft silk.

"I want you," he muttered roughly against her mouth. "Tell me you want me. *Tell me.*"

She was still drifting to earth, still dazed by the intensity of the pleasure he had just given her, and yet his voice touched her even more deeply than his most intimate kiss. Suddenly there were tears in her eyes. He might consider himself a coldhearted knave, a scoundrel who took his pleasure when and where he wished and felt nothing—but he had just proved himself wrong. Because he would not take her unless she gave her consent in no uncertain terms.

It was one last chance to save him.

"You'll hate yourself in the morning." She whispered her thoughts aloud. *"You'll hate me."*

Poised to enter her, every muscled inch of him rigid with desire and slick with sweat, he went still. "Then tell me you do not want me and I will go," he ground out.

She sucked in a broken breath. "I . . . I do not."

"Nay," he said, low and confident, kissing her, lowering himself over her. "You cannot lie, she. Not now. Not anymore. Your body speaks to mine too clearly."

"You're drunk. You'll be furious in the morning. Because you're *not* a knave."

He nibbled her lower lip. "How is it, wife, that you can believe that when all the facts"—he rubbed his arousal against her soft dampness—"tell you otherwise?"

Celine held her fists clenched against the coverlet, wanting so much to wrap her arms around him. Could he really not know? She wouldn't say it, knowing that once the words were out, she could never take them back.

When she didn't speak, he lifted his head and looked down at her in the moonlit darkness. She couldn't hide the feeling fast enough. It must have been shining through in her eyes.

"Mercy of God." He lowered his head, breathing into her shoulder, a shudder going through his taut form. "Not that. Nay."

The words spilled out on a breathless whisper. "I love you."

She felt him wince. "Ah, my sweet innocent. You should not. You should not believe that. Nor should you say it. Not to me. Have you not learned yet? Your husband is a Blackheart and will only use such foolish words against you."

She shook her head in silent denial.

"Ah, but I will. See how quickly." He lifted his head, his smile returning, though this time it held more sadness than humor. "I want you, sweet wife. Do not make me go. If you love me, do not make me go."

Celine turned her face away from him, looking at the silvery light that spilled in through the window.

He nuzzled her throat. Ice and fire. Silk and savagery. Sweet gentleness and rough promise. She wanted all of it, all of him. But it was the pain haunting him that most overcame her; she wanted to soothe it, to take him into herself and her love and ease all the torture in his soul. She had no promise of tomorrow, only this night. This now.

Just as he had hung suspended in the air between his terrace and hers moments ago, their lives hungs suspended precariously between his time and hers. And what waited below was not dark water, but the bottomless unknown.

She lifted her mouth to his, wrapped her arms around his neck. *"I want you."*

And tumbled with him into the abyss.

He shifted his weight. She moaned beneath his mouth. He seemed to be everywhere at once; his hands, his kisses, and then the blunt hardness of him, where it must not be, where she most wanted it to be.

He molded himself to her, hardest where she was softest, and he lowered his cheek to hers, whispering through clenched teeth, "Hold tight, little one."

She held him close with all her strength. "Gaston, I love you."

She said it again in that mind-shattering second when he joined his body to hers. One swift stroke drove him home, embedded him deep inside her. She felt only a moment of pain before the feeling became a hot, pulsing fullness. He uttered a groan—whether regret or pleasure—and then he began to move, his hips arching and pressing against hers, driving him deeper. Thrusting hard and fast, he sent a building wave of pleasure spinning through her senses.

And almost as quickly as it began, it was over. Racked by an explosive spasm, he cried out, as if in pain, and collapsed atop her, his weight pressing her down into the soft wool beneath her. He muttered a curse.

She stroked his perspiration-slick back, feeling him trembling, and she kept her eyes squeezed shut, not sure why she was blinking back tears. Anguished, burning tears. It wasn't because it had hurt; the pain had been less than nothing. It wasn't because she was disappointed that it had ended so quickly.

She held him while their breathing and hearts slowed and their taut muscles went slack, and still she did not understand. He slid out of her, rolling onto his side, gathering her close without a word.

He mumbled an apology, brushed a kiss through her hair, and a moment later was asleep, there beside her in the crumpled bedclothes, the light of the full moon falling across them both.

And then she knew why she was crying.

It all reminded her of the first night she had arrived, on New Year's Eve—in his arms, in his bed, with him drunk and the moonlight surrounding her, as real as his strong arm around her waist.

Destiny. God help her, it seemed like destiny. Like they

had been doomed to play out this scene until it came to this end.

Just as they were doomed to be torn apart—by time or by death or by the hatred she knew he would feel for her when his head cleared in the morning.

Crying silent tears, she curled closer into his arms, stealing this one sweet moment of glory, feeling whole and complete for the first time in her life.

Knowing it would be the last.

Chapter 19

Hellish did not begin to describe the agony in his head. A hulking Teutonic battle-lord with a war hammer could not have inflicted a more unrelenting pounding. Gaston had long suspected that somewhere in the brimstone depths of Hades, Satan had a special pit reserved for arrant sorts like himself—and the splitting pain between his temples told him that he had arrived.

He dared not move; to lift his head even an inch promised tortures beyond any in his vast ale-soaked experience. That fact held him prisoner, there on the threshold of awareness. He wished fervently that he could slide back into blessed unconsciousness. Wished a pox upon all Castilian wine makers. All Castilians. All wine makers. He groaned, then stopped because even that mild sound of misery struck his head like a spiked mace.

His mouth felt like someone had stuffed a crumpled ball of sackcloth into it. He opened his eyes slowly, one reluctant lash at a time, for he could tell from the touch of warmth at his back that his chamber was already flooded with daylight. The glare bit into his bleary eyes like a blade.

And then he realized two facts at once:

One, he was not in his own chamber.

Two, he had yet to truly taste the depths of Hell.

She lay beside him, her soft body curled into his, as naked as the day she was born, exactly as he had dreamed it so many times: her buttocks nestling his morning arousal, his arm draped possessively around her waist, the morning sun shimmering on her hair like dew on an innocent flower.

The pain in his head was suddenly naught compared with the dread and denial that raked his gut.

Holy Mary, Mother of God, what had he done?

He could not move, even as his stomach lurched threateningly. Some part of his addled brain clung to the word "innocent." Mayhap he had wandered into her room in the grasp of a drunken dream. Mayhap he had merely lain beside her . . .

He carefully lifted his arm and moved away from her, rising from the bed one slow inch at a time, ignoring the stabbing torment that exploded through his head. Even before he stood, his rapidly awakening senses told him that his wish was hopeless.

For there on the woolen coverlet was the proof of what he had done, the stain of her lost virginity. Burn him, he had not even bothered to pull back the blankets and ease her onto the sheets before he had taken her.

He staggered backward a step, stumbled from the dais, almost tripped over his boots. They lay discarded atop his garments. He stared down at them—and the night's folly came back to him one drunken drop at a time. Most of it. Some of it. Enough of it. He had barely taken the time to undress before plunging his straining manhood into her body.

Groaning a curse, he raised both hands to his head in a futile effort to either stop the relentless thunder or crush his own skull. He could not blame her; she had used no tricks or lies. He remembered that much. He had been the one who had come to her. She had told him nay, pleaded with him to leave, but he had pressed on. Run her to ground like a hunter after a sleek doe.

He squeezed his eyes shut, loathing every heathen impulse in his black soul. He had wanted her and he had taken her. In a stupor so deep that he barely remembered the act itself. He had brought her here to rest—and instead had ravished her. With no thought for her and all for himself. He should have known better. Should have known that he could not be trusted near her without a score of attendants to hold him at bay.

God's breath, *had he hurt her?* The sounds tangling in

his muddled memory were only cries that might have been pain or pleasure.

He heard a rustling of the bedclothes, a small yawn that became a sigh. He forced himself to straighten, to face her, to look at her, despite the bright, painful glare of day. She rolled over, blinking sleepily.

Then her eyes widened when she saw him.

She did not speak. And he was unable to summon even one syllable. He searched her eyes for some sign that he had not made her loathe him—and then another scrap of memory snapped into place.

I love you.

She had said that to him, even as he had been doing the unthinkable. *I love you.* She had welcomed him into her bed and her body because of her feelings for him.

Damn him to Hell and back again, he wished he did not remember that.

He stared at her and she at him until the chamber felt very small and far too hot, although the fire on the hearth had burned almost to embers. When he could stand the silence no more, he finally asked the question, dragging the words from his parched throat in a dry rasp.

"Did I hurt you?"

Her stormy blue-gray gaze still on his, she shook her head. "No." She repeated it, firmly. "No."

Her assurance was small solace as the greedy maw of what he had done opened wider to swallow him whole. For no sooner was he relieved of that first concern than a second struck and nearly sent him to his knees.

He had broken his vow. Broken his word. Again. Tossed aside any good intentions for a moment's pleasure. Exactly as he had done all his life—but this time would cost him dearly.

He had played directly into Tourelle's hand.

There would be no annulment. No marriage to Lady Rosalind. No way to reclaim his stolen family lands. No justice for his murdered father and brother. It was not enough that he had failed them in life; now he had failed them in death as well. And endangered his own life in so doing.

And his wife's.

Something inside him twisted and tore asunder. Tourelle was no doubt hard on their trail already ... and if he found out that the vows had been consummated, he would be rabid for blood. Their lives would not be worth one sou.

Gaston had betrayed them all. His father. Gerard. His wife. Betrayed them as only he could.

The sunlight glimmered around him, around her, bright, cleansing sunlight, and its purity showed all the more clearly the thoughtless act he had committed. The dark stain on the coverlet marked mayhap the most unforgivable sin in his entire unholy life.

And he had done it here, in his noble brother's chateau.

Some of his horror must have shown in his face, because she hurried to console him, sitting up, trying to cover herself, apparently not noticing the mark on the coverlet as she drew it in front of her.

"Gaston, don't look at me that way. You didn't hurt me. It was ... you were ..."

"Drunk and witless," he finished sharply, his gaze on the splotch of red.

"Caring and gentle," she corrected, then blushed crimson. "Well, not ... not all of it was gentle, but it was still ... I mean it was—"

"Whatever it was, it is over." He clenched his jaw, ignoring the pain the motion brought. Then he stalked to the side of the bed, snatched up his garments, and started yanking them on. "It is over and Tourelle has what he wanted."

"I am *not* plotting with Tourelle!" she said defensively. "And I have no intention of trying to kill you, so don't you dare try to accuse me of seducing you. I wasn't the one who jumped onto your terrace!"

"It matters naught. Whoever you are, I am shackled to you now—till death do us part. All because I allowed wine and desire to overwhelm my reason and render me witless."

"Shackled?" she repeated breathlessly, as if he had struck her. "But last night, you ... you said ..." She closed her eyes. "Don't you remember any of it?"

He jerked on his boots. "Do not remind me of aught that I may have said last night, *ma dame*. I would have told you anything to have you hot and willing in my bed."

She inhaled a sharp, pained gasp, still trying to cover herself with that damnable blanket. "I told you that you would feel this way," she accused softly. "I warned you that you would hate me."

He spun away from her with a low sound of frustration, the pain in his head redoubling at the sharp movement. Hate her? By nails and blood, that was as far from the truth as the moon and stars above the world. Hate did not number among the multitude of *feelings* he had for her.

Guilt, he felt. And regret. Need and desire, more fierce than ever before. And above all else, that soft, unfamiliar, unwanted concern that tightened around his chest, making his heart beat unsteadily. It was almost like . . .

Nay, he would not call it caring.

"May I have my dress, please?" she asked tonelessly when he did not deny her accusation. "It's . . . it's out on the terrace."

Not looking at her, he stalked to the far side of the room and thrust open the terrace door, wincing in the full, bright daylight that slashed his eyes. He snatched up the gown from where it lay, a pool of lush fabric on the cool tile. Seeing it there cleared more of the haze from his mind, brought another torrent of memories—the way he had slid it off her shoulders, nuzzled her breasts, pinned her against the wall. Given her no choice as he swept her into his arms.

Aye, he had allowed her to *think* he was giving her a choice; but, truth be told, he did not believe he could have walked away from her even if she had refused him.

He crushed the velvet in his fist. Blackheart. Never had he earned that name more than last night.

He walked back to the bed and handed her the gown. "Get up."

"There's no need to be surly," she said hotly. "I'm not—"

"Get off the bed."

She scrambled up, releasing the blanket and holding her

gown in front of her. He yanked the wool coverlet from atop the rest and carried it to the hearth.

"What are you doing?" she asked. "You can't burn Avril's—"

"It is mine to do with as I wish." He stuffed it into the huge hearth and stoked the embers. When the sparks became flame, he straightened and turned to look at her. "Mine to keep . . . or to destroy."

His emphasis on that last word made her flinch. "Gaston, don't. You're not what you think you are. Avril was *wrong* when she said destruction is what you're best at. You proved that to me last night. You proved that you can be . . . more gentle and caring than you know."

He did not reply, nor did he allow himself to stay one moment longer. Anger and self-disgust and something more drove him to the door.

It was fear. Fear of the words that even now choked up in the back of his throat and threatened to spill forth. He had given in to unguarded words and sweet passions last night—and the result had been disastrous.

Only when he had closed the door solidly behind him did he allow himself to go still, leaning against it in the cool darkness of the corridor, his pulse rushing and his head throbbing, his breath coming sharp and shallow.

He could ill afford to be weakened by feminine words like "caring," and that other one which he did not even allow to take form in his thoughts. Especially now. They had to leave here, and quickly. If it was the last thing he did, he meant to save her from Tourelle. Her and Avril both, for if the bastard learned that Gerard's widow was with child—another Varennes heir—he would not hesitate to take her life as well.

Gaston forced himself to walk away from his wife's door. He had failed those who had counted on him in the past; he would not fail again. He had too many lives depending on him. Too much to protect. Too much to lose.

Never again would he take advantage of the naive feelings his wife had for him. He could not be both lover and warrior. Not now and not ever.

* * *

For once, Celine didn't argue when a servant came with husbandly orders from on high. She had barely finished getting dressed, only minutes after Gaston left, when he sent word that he wanted her to gather her things and be ready to leave within the hour. No explanation. No word of why it was imperative for them to leave so suddenly. Just do it. Typical.

But she didn't complain. She simply thanked the servant and sent him on his way, then found her slippers where she had kicked them off the night before. That was all the "readying" of her things she needed to do. All the rest was still packed, since they had arrived only yesterday.

Then she sat on the bed and waited for the servant to come back. She had no emotional energy left for arguing with Gaston's orders.

When she had wakened this morning to find his warmth no longer beside her, she had felt disappointment, only to have it instantly replaced by hope and uncertainty when she saw him. He had not run from her room at the first opportunity; she dared think that what they had shared might have affected him, as strongly as it had affected her. That it might have unlocked something inside him.

But when she had blurted her fears, any flicker of optimism she might have felt had been ground out. *I warned you that you would hate me.* God, some vulnerable, naive part of her had actually thought he would deny it. But his leaden silence had said far more than words ever could.

And all she had been able to do was sit there going numb, thinking, *I love you.*

Did he even remember that she had said that last night? If he did, it obviously didn't matter. For a man of so few words when it came to emotions, he had expressed himself quite clearly. He thought himself trapped. How had he put it? *Shackled.*

He didn't feel anything about what they had shared last night. Except regret. So much regret that he had burned the evidence. The fire still blazed and crackled in the hearth, turning their passion to ashes.

She sat on the bed, blinking, still dazed by her own stupidity. How could she have deluded herself into thinking that he cared for her? That he had had any other goal last night than pure male lust?

He had been right about her; she *was* naive and foolish. And he didn't care anything more for her than he did for the countless other women he had taken to bed. The awful truth of it brought an actual, painful ache to her chest. She choked on a humorless laugh. That was all he had left her with: an ache, and a throbbing awareness of him, in that soft place between her thighs where his hard body had briefly become part of her.

Someone knocked at the door, but the sound barely registered. She didn't respond until the knock was repeated twice.

"Come in."

She expected the servant, coming to help take her things below.

Instead it was Gaston.

She inhaled sharply, her gaze fastened on his, her fists crumpling the bedclothes on either side of her. She hastily erected an iron gate around her heart; she wasn't going to keep hurting herself by declaring her feelings for him. Not when he didn't return them in the least.

His eyes were glazed with an odd look; she thought it must be the effect of his hangover.

"The servants . . . they are—are arrived," he stuttered.

"Fine. I'm ready to go. Why didn't you just send one of them up to fetch me?"

"Nay, not Avril's servants. Our—*my* servants." He lifted his hand. She finally tore her gaze from his face long enough to look at what he had carried in with him.

She stopped breathing.

"They arrived at . . . Chateau de Varennes some days ago," he continued in that stumbling, disbelieving tone, "and when they did not find us there, Yolande and Gabrielle rushed here, to give me this. They arrived this morn. They . . . thought it might be important . . ."

Celine barely heard what he was saying. There was a ringing in her head that blocked out all other sound. She could only stare at the bright pink object he held, something so out of place in his hand, in this time, that it took a dizzying moment for her to identify it.

And then she was up off the bed, running forward. "My purse. My *purse!* Where—how—my God, have they been *hiding* it all this time?" she asked incredulously.

He let her take it. "Nay, they found it while moving furnishings. In a trunk." He exhaled a harsh sound, as if he were having trouble breathing. "A locked trunk. In the room where—"

"Where I appeared in your bed on New Year's Eve!" Celine said breathlessly, clasping it to her. "But how did it . . ." Her mind raced back to the moment she had tumbled through time. "I was standing in front of the window. Looking for an aspirin. And I had my purse in my hand. But then the moonlight hit me and I *dropped* it . . ."

As the pieces started fitting together, her heart soared.

"But I dropped it *after* the light hit me! I was falling backward, and it fell from my hand—and it must have come back in time with me. I ended up in the bed and this ended up in that trunk!" She spun around, clutching the purse like a priceless treasure. "That stupid, wonderful trunk!"

She felt like dancing. Relief and joy and hope all whirled inside her, so overwhelming that she didn't give Gaston a chance to get a word in edgewise.

"This is *it!*" she cried. "This has to be why the eclipse a few weeks ago didn't work! I pushed that trunk out of the way so I could stand in front of the window—oh, God, if only I had left it where it was!" She turned to him, waving the purse. "I didn't have this before, so I couldn't go back through time. But I've got it now. Don't you understand? This is the key that'll open the door! I can go *home!*"

Not waiting for a reply, she ran to the bed, unzipping her purse and spilling the contents. "You'll have to believe me now!" she said triumphantly. "You want proof that I am who I say I am, Sir Suspicious? Well, you've got it! Absolute proof. I've been telling you the truth all along!"

She started tossing things onto the covers. "Checkbook. Wallet. Look at this—credit cards. My driver's license!

How about a calculator? Or my camera? Or a chocolate bar!" She was tempted to take a bite, but didn't dare. She had to keep everything exactly as it was to get home. "Passport. Sunglasses. Plane tickets—God, I couldn't even begin to explain to you what those are for. My keys." She held them up and jangled them. "This one's to my condo. This one's for my Mercedes—boy, talk about losing your car keys big time." She tossed them into the growing pile, laughing, and pulled out her Chicago Cubs baseball cap. "You think my other hats are weird, how about this one?"

She put the hat on and faced him with an ecstatic grin. "See? Fits perfectly. My name is Celine Fontaine, buster, and I'm from 1993!"

He didn't smile. He was still standing near the door, unmoving, looking at her with that dazed expression. Like someone who had just been run over by a car.

"Gaston?" Celine's smile faded. She hadn't realized, until that very second, what finding her purse really meant. She would be all right; she would be going home.

But she would also be leaving Gaston.

And he wasn't saying a word. No emotion. No regrets about her leaving, or the way he had doubted her for so long. Nothing.

"Gaston . . . you do believe me, don't you?"

"I believe you," he said quietly, still looking at her in a way someone might look at a three-eyed, green alien that had just landed in a flying saucer. "I . . . examined the contents of the strange pouch before I brought it to you. There is no other explanation but that you . . . are from the future."

His voice was hollow, almost wooden. She had never heard him talk that way before. She left her purse where it was and moved toward him. "Are you all right?"

"We have to leave here," he said abruptly, walking away before she could reach him. "I will . . . take you back to my chateau. That is what you wish, is it not? That is the only way you can return . . . home?"

"Yes." She stopped in the middle of the chamber, still wearing her Cubs hat. "Yes, everything I told you was true. I've got a bullet fragment in my back. I have to have surgery to remove it, so I've got to return to my time. The next eclipse is in just a few weeks. And it'll work this time. I'm going to be all right. I . . . I can go home." The confusing mix of relief and regret and sadness she felt left her shaking.

"Then we shall leave at once." He stopped before the hearth, looking down at the crackling flames. "But I must warn you that the journey will be dangerous. Tourelle will be searching for us—and I do not wish to take my men with us. I would leave them here, to protect Avril."

"Yes," she agreed dazedly. "Yes, of course. I'm sure we'll be fine on our own. I'm . . ." She spun around and looked at the small pile of things she had dumped on the bed. One was a new travel guidebook, *Chateaux of the Artois Region,* that she had picked up while shopping with her sister, Jackie, a few days before New Year's Eve. "In fact, we might not have to wonder. I might be able to tell you right now what happens."

He shot her an annoyed glance. "If you know what will happen in the future between me and Tourelle, why did you not tell me before?"

She grabbed the brightly colored paperback. "Because I didn't have my purse. And *I* don't know what's going to happen—but this might." She flipped to the page that described her family's chateau. "Here it is. Manoir La Fontaine . . . it probably mentions you in here somewhere. Maybe it'll talk about what happened with you and Tourelle."

She scanned the small print, weighing whether it was wise to tell someone of his own future. Especially someone as headstrong and reckless as Gaston. But she could not bear to see him worry needlessly, not if she could reassure him that everything was going to be okay.

"Here you are," she said, reading. "It mentions that you were one of the original owners of the chateau . . . and that you were married, and it says here that—" Her voice choked. "Uh-oh." Her fingers gripped the book as she read it again. "Oh, no. Oh, my God, *what have we done?*"

Chapter 20

"What do you mean?" Gaston demanded, walking over to her from the hearth. "What is it we have done?"

Celine didn't look up at him. She couldn't tear her eyes from the book, from the painful words spelled out in inescapable black and white.

"What does it say?" Gaston asked impatiently, looking over her shoulder. "Has it aught to do with Tourelle? Tell me the truth of it—even if it is the worst."

"No, it's . . . it's not the worst at all. There isn't anything here about Tourelle." Celine flipped to the index in the back of the guidebook, her heart beating strangely. "He apparently wasn't important enough to merit a mention . . . his name isn't even listed."

"Then what does it say about me?"

Celine didn't want to tell him. She wished she had never thought of looking in the damned book. The black ink dots swam dizzily before her eyes, but she couldn't lie about what they said. "It . . . it isn't so much what it says about you. It's what it says about your . . . family." Her voice shaking, she read the section aloud. " 'Seldom did the chroniclers of the medieval period record the names of—' "

"The 'medieval period'?"

Celine glanced at him. "The Middle Ages. The time between the Dark Ages and the Renaissance—your time. I'll explain it to you later." She started reading again. " 'Seldom did the chroniclers of the medieval period record the names of women, who were not seen to be as important as men when it came to the matter of making history—' "

"As indeed they are not."

"Would you please stop interrupting?" she snapped. " 'Seldom . . .' Oh, to heck with it. I've read that three times already. Here's the important part: '. . . and that is the case with the wife of Sir Gaston de Varennes. History has recorded her only as Lady R, but the couple provides one of the most interesting and little-known footnotes in this period in the Artois region. Not for their own accomplishments, but for that of their son, Soren, who saved the life of King Philippe VI, founder of the Valois dynasty, in a bold maneuver at the Battle of Cassel in 1328 . . .' " She let the book slide from her trembling fingers. It fell onto the pile of her things on the bed. "That . . . that's all it says about you. It goes on to talk about how important the Valois dynasty was."

When Gaston didn't say anything, she looked at him.

He was standing there with a peculiar expression on his face. "I am going to have a son?" he murmured. He started to grin. "Not only a son . . . but a *bold* son."

"Don't you get it?" Celine choked out. "You're supposed to have that son with Lady R. Doesn't that ring a bell? Lady *Rosalind*. You're supposed to marry Lady Rosalind!"

Gaston's smile faded and his dark eyes locked with hers. "But that is impossible. The King will never grant me an annulment, now that we have—"

"Exactly! That's just it. We've changed history—I mean the future. I mean . . ." She raised a hand to her forehead. "Oh, God, I don't know *what* I mean anymore. But we've changed what was supposed to happen. If you can't marry Lady Rosalind, your son will never be born. Which means King Philippe VI might *die* in that battle, and the Valois dynasty might never be founded, which will alter the entire course of history." She sank down onto the bed, mortified by the impact of it. "Everything will change because of . . . what we did last night."

One small event, one night, one moment in each other's arms that had seemed so *right*. Like it was meant to be. But that single fragment of time touched dozens of others.

No Valois dynasty. What else might change? The

French explorers who had helped open up the New World? The fact that the French had lent the Americans a big hand during the Revolutionary War? France's own Revolution a few years later? Different kings, a different dynasty ... a different future.

With a groan, she leaned over, propping her elbows on her knees and burying her face in her hands. "We've got to undo what we did. Before it's too late. You've got to marry Rosalind."

"Milady, lest you have any illusions on it," Gaston said sarcastically, "allow me to inform you that it is not possible to undo what we did last night."

"But maybe it will work out all right, anyway." Celine spoke into her palms, utterly miserable. "I mean, I'll be gone. Maybe you could just marry Rosalind after I disappear."

"Nay, the Church will still consider us wed. It will not matter that you are missing. I will be unable to remarry anyone."

"You're kidding." She lifted her head, blinking in disbelief. "Couldn't you have me declared dead? Or just divorce me?"

"Are marriages so easily undone in your time?" he asked with a disapproving frown. "Nay, wife, here in what your chronicler called 'the medieval period,' we have laws. Without an annulment, it truly shall be till death do us part."

Celine groaned again, hid her face, tried to think.

"In truth," Gaston continued slowly, "the matter is worse yet than that. When you return to your time, I will no doubt be accused of causing your disappearance. Tourelle will claim that I killed you and disposed of the body. He will not have to go to the trouble of murdering me— the King will give him what he seeks. I will be forced to forfeit all I own."

"No!" Celine shook her head and stood up, fists clenched. "I won't let that happen. We can't let any of this happen! We ... we'll have to get an annulment before I leave."

"But that is im—"

"There's no evidence!" She gestured to the fireplace. "Who knows about what happened last night, other than the two of us? Unless you have been downstairs boasting to your men about—"

"Celine," he said warningly.

She turned her back and paced away from him, not letting herself enjoy the fact that he was finally calling her by her real name. There wasn't time. "Fine. So you haven't told anyone. And I haven't told anyone. No one knows but the two of us. We'll just . . . we'll have to pretend that last night didn't happen. Act as if nothing has changed between us. And get an annulment."

"You mean to lie? To the King? To everyone?"

She spun around to face him. "I can live with one lie if it means saving the entire future!"

"And why would the King suddenly grant me an annulment?" Gaston leaned a brawny shoulder against one of the bedposts, folding his arms over his chest. "When he has so adamantly refused thus far?"

"He would believe *that*, wouldn't he?" She pointed to her purse and the jumble of her belongings on the bed. "Once we prove that I'm not Christiane, and explain everything, he would have to let you get an annulment and marry Rosalind. Especially if it means saving a future king. One of his own heirs."

Gaston tensed his jaw. "Aye," he said with a slow nod. "He is at heart a reasonable man. I believe he would agree to it."

Celine folded her arms over her chest, in imitation of him, trying to steady herself and her voice. "Then that's what we'll have to do."

"The King is in Paris." His gaze captured hers. "It will cost us five days at least to travel that far south of my chateau. Have you . . . have we that long?"

"According to what Brynna said, the next eclipse is still six weeks away."

"You are certain?"

"Believe me," she said shakily, "I wouldn't want to take a chance of missing it. I've been keeping track of the days."

He kept staring at her. "We will still have Tourelle to think of. He will be searching for us. I had planned to take lesser-used roads to avoid him."

"Then we'll just have to ride as fast as we can. Day and night if necessary."

"But that will place too great a strain on you." A muscle flexed in his beard-darkened cheek. "And on this injury you have in your back."

"It's a risk I'll have to take," she insisted quietly, dropping her gaze, unwilling to let herself believe that what she saw in his eyes and heard in his voice was concern. "I can't think just about myself. I can't go home knowing I've mangled history. Who knows *what* my time might be like if everything changed because of what I . . . because of what we did."

"And you will leave me here to wed Lady Rosalind?"

Celine glanced up at him from beneath her lashes. She wasn't sure what answer he expected. Or why he had even asked that question. She had to leave. And he couldn't go with her to the twentieth century; she couldn't believe the thought had even crossed his mind.

She considered blurting out the complete truth: that he was going to fall in love with Rosalind, so much so that one day he would carve her initial with his above every door in his castle. Gaston and his Lady R were going to have not only a bold son, but *love*. A legendary love. The kind of love people would still be talking about centuries later.

The kind of love Gaston did not and never would feel for her.

Fighting tears, unable to say any of it, she shrugged. "I don't see that I have any choice. I'm sure you'll be very—" Her voice broke, but she wrestled it back under control. "happy married to Rosalind. You'll forget me before you know it."

That muscle in his cheek flexed again. "You can say that, after what happened in this bed last night?"

Celine felt her composure slipping. "Can we please not talk about that anymore?" she asked a bit too quickly. "In fact, I think it would be better if we just declare the entire subject off limits. And we should probably think about taking some escorts with us when we leave, in case it's necessary ... t-to prove ... to have witnesses that we didn't—"

"To verify our lie that we have not touched each other?" Celine felt her cheeks burning. "Right."

"Fear not, milady," he said sardonically. "None will ever guess our secret. I will leave my men here to guard Avril, but Etienne can accompany us, and young Remy. They shall be escort enough."

"Then we're agreed," she said lightly, crossing to the bed to put her things back in her purse. "We'll do what we have to do."

He stood watching her for a long moment, intent and silent, before he echoed softly, "We will do what we have to do."

"Milady, Sir Gaston will have my head for this," Etienne whispered plaintively, pacing the room. "And whatever else is left of me after he finishes beating me to a pulp."

"Don't worry, Etienne. I told you, he'll understand after I explain it to him."

Celine rubbed her arms, feeling a chill, though the room they had been shown into was quite warm, with a fire blazing on its huge hearth. The keep, larger than any she had yet seen, was everything Avril had said it would be.

Avril was the one who had given her directions here, without asking questions; the chateau lay along the winding route Gaston had been following south for the past two weeks, and it was no more than a few hours out of the way.

A few hours Celine thought absolutely necessary to spend on this little mission.

"I do not know why you could not have explained it to him *before* we left camp," Etienne muttered. "He will not be pleased that we snuck way into the night. Like a pair of outlaws."

"I left a note," Celine said with a sleepy yawn. "Besides, I couldn't tell him where we were going, because he never would've let me leave. I didn't have to bring you along, you know, Etienne. I could have ridden off by myself. But I probably would've gotten lost."

"Which is why I agreed to accompany you at all," the young man grumbled.

"Very kind of you," Celine said cheerfully.

He scowled at her, looking every bit like the threatening knight he would become someday soon. Celine's tentative smile faded; she didn't feel as cheerful as she was trying to sound. She had told herself that she needed to come here, for the sake of future history.

But deep down she knew her real motive: an illogical, emotional need to meet her rival face-to-face.

To see the woman who would so completely steal Gaston's heart.

A brief conversation with Avril had already uncovered a positively nauseating list of glowing attributes: Lady Rosalind was so beautiful that poems had been written about her; so intelligent that scholars came from throughout the region to discuss matters of the day; so rich that she would soon inherit all the lands that lay between Gaston's chateau and Avril's. The lands it had taken *four weeks* to cross on the way north.

"Rich" was too small a word for it. In this time, Celine was a pauper compared with Rosalind. Even in her own time, she would be a pauper compared with Rosalind.

To top it all off, the lady was apparently gracious, too— because she didn't keep her unexpected guests waiting more than five minutes before she came into the room to greet them, despite the early morning hour.

Etienne uttered a gasp and suddenly seemed to develop a breathing problem, not to mention difficulty keeping his mouth from hanging open.

Celine had to bite back a *Wow!* of her own. Lady Rosalind was everything she had been told and more. She stepped gracefully through the door in a slim swirl of topaz velvet, her white-blond hair neatly plaited, her eyes a luminous color that could only be called gold. Celine was willing to bet her last centime that those ruby lips had never once muttered a defiant word. Or chattered.

She was young, no older than Etienne. She was smiling at them with genuine warmth. She was petite. She was perfect.

She was Lady R.

Of course Gaston would love her. He wouldn't be able to *help* falling in love with her.

"My greetings to you both," Rosalind said in a light, musical voice that suited all her other perfections. "My servants tell me that you are friends of Lady Avril?"

Celine had memorized a speech. A very calm, reasonable speech. A persuasive speech.

Instead she blurted out one sentence.

"I've come here to ask you for a favor."

Chapter 21

Threatening clouds hung low in the late afternoon sky as thunder rumbled in the distance. The coming downpour was naught as yet but a cool, silver silence, heavy in the air; the day's waning light lanced through the gloom now and again, illuminating the trees with sudden brilliance, cutting long shadows along the forest floor.

Gaston was certain that he must have felt this worried and uneasy before, at some time in his life. At the moment, however, he could not remember when that might have been.

The entire day had near passed, and his wandering wife had not yet returned. He felt like a loaded crossbow: taut and dangerous and ready to explode at the slightest touch. But all he could do was wait. His hands felt sore from clenching and unclenching; he had been doing little else the entire day, from the moment he had awakened to find Celine's folded note propped on his chest.

He would throttle her. God's teeth, he would throttle her for taking such a chance with her life. Disappearing without word of where she was going. Concealing her trail so that he could not follow.

"I am certain she is unhurt, milord," Remy said. The lad sat beside the fire, his dark head bent as he sharpened his knife with a whetstone; he was the youngest of Gaston's guardsmen, little older than Etienne. "If they had encountered trouble, Etienne would have—"

"Shh." Gaston held up a gloved hand to cut him off. Beneath Remy's voice and the scrape of the whetstone, he thought he heard the distant rhythm of hoofbeats. He turned to look along the path, and the sound grew louder and separated itself from the thunder. Riders were approaching, from the south.

At a damned leisurely pace.

Within moments, Celine and Etienne appeared through the trees at the far edge of the clearing. As they drew near, Gaston could see that both looked flushed and tired, but unhurt.

He folded his arms over his chest to still the fury—and the relief—that vibrated through his every muscle. *"Bonjour,"* he said, his tone dangerously mild. "I trust the two of you enjoyed a pleasant day meandering about the land?"

"Milord, we had planned to return sooner," Etienne said quickly, "but milady's horse came up lame and—"

"What excellent news," Gaston drawled, glancing at the mare's injured foreleg. "That will no doubt speed the remainder of our journey."

Celine reined her limping horse to a halt and started to dismount. "Before you get angry, let me expl—"

"I fear you are too late, milady. I am several hours past angry." He walked over before she was completely out of the saddle and lifted her to the ground. "Not only has your foolishness cost us time that we could not spare, but now it has cost us a horse as well. A fine day's work, *ma dame.*" He glanced at Remy and Etienne. "Gather our supplies. I would speak with my wife alone. Ride ahead and we will catch up to you anon."

"Aye, milord." The young men hurried to carry out his orders.

"Gaston," Celine whispered, "I don't think that's a good—"

"Remy, take milady's horse as well." Gaston fastened his hand around Celine's arm and led her over to the fire. "We will trade the mare for another at the first opportunity. For now, my wife will ride with me."

"Gaston." Her voice was a high squeak this time. "That's *really* not a good—"

"Silence." He pointed to the rock that Remy had just vacated. "Sit."

She clenched her teeth and did as he bade—with a

flashing, indignant glare. Ignoring the unladylike words she started muttering, he turned his attention to helping gather the supplies and securing them to the horses. He tied Celine's belongings to her lame mount, except for the bundle containing her pink pouch, which he fastened securely to Pharaon's saddle.

"Do not favor the mare overmuch," he instructed the two lads. "If she slows you too greatly, move these bundles to your horses and leave her."

"Aye, milord," Remy said, mounting his stallion.

"Sir? I am sorry that I—"

"Nay, Etienne, we have no time now to discuss your peculiar ideas of carrying out your duty—but we *will* speak of it later."

The young man nodded, looking as if he wanted to sink into the forest floor. "Aye, milord." He lifted himself into the saddle.

"Ride with all speed. The light is waning already, and we will have a storm to deal with before this night is out." Gaston sent them away with a slap to each horse's rump.

They trotted down the path into the deepening afternoon shadows. Even as the sound of hoofbeats faded, Gaston kept staring after them, not trusting himself to turn around and look at his wife.

Because he was shaking.

By nails and blood, he could not stop shaking; it seemed to be beyond his control. *Everything* seemed to be beyond his control. He had not been in command of himself or his life since the moment Yolande and Gabrielle had handed him that accursed, outlandish pink pouch and he had been forced to realize the truth.

Not only about Celine's identity, but about himself.

He had been avoiding it all along. From the beginning, he had convinced himself that he would be able to keep his defiant lady with him somehow, and he had rigidly believed that he wanted only pleasure of her. But his unshakable conviction had begun crumbling even before he knew who she was.

And her disappearance today, that brief, bitter taste of

what was to come, only served to make the truth agonizingly clear.

How could he not have seen it before? Even after they made love, while he felt guilty and furious at his carelessness, some part of him—some hidden part buried so deep that he had not recognized it at the time—had been pleased.

Pleased that she was truly his. Pleased that she was bound to him in that most elemental way, in every way. In ways that had naught to do with pleasure and far more to do with whispered words and the unsteady rhythm of his heart. Some secret corner of his soul had reveled in it: consummated vows could not be broken. She would be staying with him. She was *his*.

But all that had changed now. She was not his. She was leaving, and there was naught he could do to stop it. He had to let her go. It was beyond his control, and that infuriated him.

But what infuriated him even more was that it pained him. More deeply than any wound he had ever endured.

"Gaston, are you going to stay mad until nightfall or are you going to turn around and talk to me?" Celine's voice sounded soft beneath the distant growl of thunder.

He remained where he was, staring up at the storm clouds, letting her believe he was refusing to look at her because he was angry. "Tell me, wife," he said, fighting to keep his voice even, "what did you do today? That is to say, other than waste several hours and nearly break your mare's leg?"

She was silent for a moment. "Don't you think that sending our escorts off without us kind of defeats the whole purpose of having escorts in the first place?"

"Do not change the subject. Answer my question."

"I left you a note."

"Which was more infuriating than informative. What precisely was your 'important mission'?"

"Please don't say it that way. It *was* important."

"So important that you rode off with only a squire to protect you?" He clenched his sore fists. "So important that you risked your *life?*"

"You sound as if you care about that."

He jerked around and glared at her. "You act as if you do not!"

"I went to see Lady Rosalind."

That blunt statement struck him dumb. If she had said she had visited a Saracen princess in the distant East, he could not have been more surprised. "Saints' blood, woman," he choked out on a suddenly dry throat. "Why?"

"Because you said once that she didn't want to marry you. You said she had so many suitors you weren't sure she would wait for you. I . . . I had to make sure. For the sake of . . . for the future."

Astounded, Gaston stared at her blankly. "And did you accomplish this important mission?"

Celine glanced away. The wind had strengthened, heavy with the promise of rain, and it played through the red-gold strands of her hair. "I told her that our marriage was going to be annulled, and that she was the one you really wanted—"

"I cannot believe I am hearing this."

"She's very beautiful, Gaston. And sweet and demure. Actually, I think she's a little young for you," she whispered, "but I didn't think you'd mind that."

"Pray, do not stop. Tell me more of this bride you have secured for me."

She didn't seem to catch his sarcasm. "She's exactly what you want. She isn't outspoken or independent. She'll never defy you or even question you. Or argue. Or chatter." Celine tucked in her chin. "And she agreed to wait."

Gaston exhaled a sharp sound of disbelief. "This I must hear. How in the name of God did you persuade her?"

"It wasn't all that difficult. I . . . I told her . . ." She looked up at him, and even in the gathering shadows he could see tears glistening in those stormy eyes he had come to know so well. "I told her that you don't deserve the reputation people have given you. I told her that you're . . . a good man, and strong and generous and kind and—"

"You should not have lied."

A peal of thunder roared overhead, and the rain began

to fall, a gentle patter. "I didn't lie." She looked away from him, shaking. "I told her that despite your . . . th-that beneath your . . ." She raised a trembling hand to wipe the moisture from her cheeks, staring down into the fire, the flames hissing and steaming in the drizzle. "I told her that if she could look beneath that tough exterior, she would find a man worthy of all the love she had to give."

Gaston felt like a rope had been closing around his throat all day, and her words had just tightened it one final notch, choking off his very life. Words failed him. Strength failed him. He could not even raise his hood to ward off the rain. He struggled to regain the power of speech, fought the fate that was being forced upon him. "And if I do not wish to—"

"She's perfect for you," Celine said quietly. "She'll make you happy. She's everything you want in a wife." With a pained little smile, she added, almost to herself, "I'll bet she even plays backgammon."

The anguish in her voice matched the rending feeling within him, a wrenching tear that left him numb and powerless, an unfamiliar, vulnerable sensation that sent him off-balance. Which made him angry. "Celine—"

"Sorry, I forgot you don't know what that word means. Try 'playing tables.' Your favorite game. Avril showed me what it was." She wrapped her arms around herself. "I never really had a chance to ask you about that, not that it makes any difference now, but just out of curiosity, tell me—the whole time you were misleading me about what 'playing tables' meant, were you laughing at me behind my back?"

"Nay!" His anger slipped its tether at her bitter accusation. "I allowed you to believe what you wished to believe."

Her gaze snapped up to meet his. "Spare me. There's no need for us to be dishonest with each other, Gaston. Not anymore. Just so I don't go home with any foolish, *naive* notions and spend the rest of my life wondering about how you really felt, I'd like to hear you say it. Just once. Tell me the truth. All I've ever been to you is an annoyance, or an amusement." Her back stiffened and her eyes narrowed. "Or a one-night stand. Do you want me to define *that* for you?"

He pierced his maddening little wife with a stare. She was doing this to him on purpose. Making him feel this way. Making him admit what he did not want to admit. He spoke through gritted teeth. "I allowed you to believe what you wished because it made it easier, that is all. There is no time to waste on this foolishness. Though it may have escaped your attention, I am attempting to save your *life.*" He turned away, heading toward the spot where Pharaon grazed in the clearing.

"Made what easier?"

"I do not wish to discuss it."

"Made *what* easier?"

He spun on his heel. "Made it easier to convince myself that you mean naught to me!"

She gaped at him. That clearly was not what she had expected him to say at all.

"You wished the truth, milady? That is the truth." He was breathing hard. "I did not correct you about the meaning of 'playing tables' because I did not wish you to know that *there have been no other women since I met you.* I tried to use the game to distract my thoughts, but it was of no use. *You* are all that I could think of. I have bedded no other woman since we said our vows." His voice roughened. "Because I wanted no other as I want you."

"B-but . . ." she stuttered, pushing herself to her feet and wiping her wet hair out of her eyes. "But that's not true! What about the day you followed me into the forest? You told me you had planned to spend the morning with *several* females."

"Hunting falcons."

"What?"

"Female hunting falcons," he snapped, his harsh breathing forming steam in the cold air. "You never asked what sort of females."

She blinked at him, raindrops falling from her lashes. "But . . . but there was still that tavern wench. When you and your men went hunting, and you came back injured, and—"

"I never bedded her. Royce leaped to the wrong conclusion and I did not correct him, because I could not admit that I had tripped on my own accursed sword because my mind was so befuddled with thoughts of *you!*" He swore, shaking his head, his arms tensing at his sides as he fought the desire to stalk over and kiss her senseless. "There have been no others since you. I do not want any others. I do not want Rosalind." He let the heat he felt blaze through in his eyes. "Not as I want you."

She almost tripped over the fire as she stumbled backward. "Gaston, you can't . . . you don't . . ." With a small sound of distress, she turned away, lifting her hood and huddling into her cloak. "I-I don't think we should be talking about this. It doesn't matter what you want. Or what I want. Nothing we say can make any difference. We know what has to happen. You and Rosalind are meant to be together."

Cursing, Gaston shut his eyes and lifted his face to the sting of the rain. For once, she was being practical and reasonable, and he knew she spoke the truth. Burn him, he *knew*. They could not change what was meant to be. Why did some impulse within him keep fighting it?

Celine must return to her time, where she would be safe and well. Where she belonged. He must stay here, where he belonged. With his intended wife, and all the power and influence any lord could want, and a bold son who would one day save a king's life.

And in that moment all the wealth and promise of his future seemed so unappealing that he would have gladly traded places with a peasant . . . if it meant he could keep Celine.

He dropped his head, raking one hand through his dripping hair. "If you could stay," he said, his voice almost lost in the wind and rain, "would you?"

An explosive crash of thunder made her jump.

"Gaston . . . don't." She hunched her shoulders. "Don't ask that. It doesn't make any sense even to think of that. Don't you understand? It doesn't matter what I want."

"Is there so much in your time that you could not live without?"

"I-I used to think so. When I first got here, I thought I would just die without electricity and hot showers and my car and central heating and . . ." Her voice faltered and she turned toward him, her lower lip quivering. "And my family. Sometimes I miss them so much it . . . it's like part of me is missing. I have a brother and a sister, and my parents, and lots of aunts and uncles and cousins . . ."

He could hear neither *aye* nor *nay* in her broken reply. He started to walk toward her.

She did not move away. "But now I . . . I think that when I go back, part of me will still be missing. Because I've never felt this way about anyone." Her lashes brushed her damp cheeks, and though her eyes were closed, she swayed almost drunkenly on her feet as he came to stand before her, as if she could sense how close he was. She whispered, "I've never loved any man the way I love you."

His heart pounding, he reached out for her, his gloved hands slipping inside her hood to cup her face. "If you stayed . . . if you could stay . . ." He brushed wet strands of hair from her ivory skin. "I would take care of you, Celine. And protect you, and keep you with me all the days of my life."

There was no sound save the spattering of the rain through the trees, no movement save the slight parting of her lips.

Then she suddenly withdrew. *"No."* She backed away, lifting her gaze to his with an expression of stinging accusation, rubbing her cheeks as if she could wipe away his touch as easily as water. "It's impossible, Gaston. And what you're saying to me now isn't any different from what you said to me once before. When you returned from your hunting trip. You locked me in my room to keep me prisoner because you wanted me to tell you the truth—and you promised to keep me safe and feed me well and clothe me warmly. For you, nothing has changed!"

"God's breath, woman, everything has changed! I want you so badly that I burn with it. You set me afire from the time I awaken in the morning until I fall asleep at night. And then you invade my dreams. You have taken possession of every moment of my life. What more would you demand of me?"

"If you don't know, I can't explain it to you." She shook her head as if he were incapable of understanding. "You don't love me. You'll never love me."

"Would you wish me to say words that have no meaning to me? Would you have me lie to you?"

"No," she said forcefully. "Because I'd always know it's not the truth. You're going to fall in love with *Rosalind.*"

He swore a short, vicious oath. "By all that is holy, I wish I had never heard her name!" He turned on his heel, then turned back again. "I will never love her."

"You don't know that. You don't know what you might feel for her. It's like . . ." She lifted her hands helplessly. "Oh, God, how can I explain something to you that you've never felt and don't even believe in?" She made a bitter, humorless sound that could not be called a laugh. "Think of it this way: if you had never seen a destrier or a trencher before, you wouldn't know exactly what one was when you saw it, would you? You might be able to make a good guess, you might be able to describe it, but you wouldn't use exactly the right word." Her eyes melted into his the way the rain soaked into the ground, lush and deep. "Until someone who knew, someone who had maybe a little more experience, told you the word."

Gaston scowled at her, unable to follow the maze of her female reasoning—especially when he was feeling such a rush of pure male possessive fury. He wanted to shout at her, at the storm overhead, at fate, at the fact that control of his life had been wrested from him.

Instead he spoke very calmly. Too calmly. *"Ma dame,* you have spent this day persuading Lady Rosalind to accept my proposal of marriage. You assume that I will offer for her after you are gone."

Celine went very still. "You have to," she gasped. "It's in the book."

"Damn the book."

"But the future—"

"I make my own future." He flicked a glance heavenward, repeating it to the thunderous clouds. "I make my own future!"

"Gaston, you can't change what's meant to be!"

He lowered his head, his hair falling over his eyes, and pinned her with a gaze that made her flinch.

Then he closed the distance between them in one stride, taking her in his arms, pulling her to him.

"Stop it. Gaston, stop it!" she demanded, twisting and struggling in his embrace.

"You are my *wife*," he said roughly, his voice sharp with all the ache that filled his soul, all the fury that God would dare take her from him. "You are the only one I want." He lowered his head to hers. *"You."*

She pushed at his shoulders, but she might as well have been trying to move an entire keep. He kissed her deeply, pouring out the impossible longing he felt with ungentle motions of his mouth and hands. Caught in the grip of feelings stronger than any he had ever known, he sank with her onto the damp leaves and soft grass beside the dying fire. They had no blankets, no furs, naught but nature's own bed beneath them, earth wet with the promise of spring, of *life*.

Her tongue was rough velvet against his. A sound began in her throat, protest ... that became need. Her movements beneath him changed. She uttered a sob and her fingers speared through his tangled hair.

Rain pounded down on them as they consumed each other, mouths mating, her arms wrapping around him, his fingers tearing at garments, one hand lifting her hips against him. He ripped off his gloves. He had to feel her. The silk of her wet skin. The soft, strong grace of her legs as she arched beneath him.

Sweet violence swept them both as he drove deep in one smooth, clean stroke. Ravening, sighing, groaning, they moved. Sensations he had felt uncountable times before astonished him with their fresh intensity, so real he must have only dreamed of them before. The lush petals of her mouth. The feel of her fingertips at the sensitive nape of his neck. The clinging feminine heat of her. She was a burning flame, all glittering contrasts, strong yet vulnerable, stubborn yet giving, and she whispered words of love and wanting as he plunged harder, faster.

She was his, all his. She was not Tourelle's ward, not Christiane, not a liar, not insane. She was exactly what she had insisted all along: Celine Fontaine, from seven hundred years in the future. And she was a part of him.

And he was going to lose her.

Water from the heavens washed over them. Thunder was a drumbeat that could not drown out the pounding of his heart over hers. As their bodies entwined on the grass, steam from the dying fire swirled around them, mere mist compared with the heat they made. A blinding stroke of sunlight broke through the clouds, danced over them, winked out as the storm consumed it once more.

For all the years of his life he would remember her this way: crying out his name as she found fulfillment, there among the earth and the thunder and his ungentle giving.

He wanted to make it last, on and on until now became forever and they both forgot the meaning of *time*. Embedded deep and potent inside her, all he could think of was that he would remember her. His sweet Celine. All rain and tears. And he did not wish to remember.

For as release rushed through him, he knew he did not wish to live without her.

Chapter 22

❦❦ **A** nyone who would step into a metal box and let it be flung into the air is a half-wit."

"Not a box. It's called a plane." Celine laughed. "And it isn't flung through the air. There's no catapult involved. It *flies.* Like a bird flies."

"A metal bird filled with people?" Gaston asked dubiously.

"That's right. And if we had one now, instead of having to ride Pharaon here, this trip that's taken four weeks would have taken less than an hour."

"You are making this up."

Celine laughed again and shook her head, resting a little closer to Gaston, letting herself enjoy the strength of his hold on her, the way he made her feel secure in his arms even though Pharaon moved at a swift trot. The weather had been clear and warm since that rainy afternoon in the clearing two weeks ago, and they were making good time.

Etienne rode just a few yards behind them, but Remy had ventured so far ahead they couldn't see him. Though Gaston had traded her lame mare for a sturdy little plow horse in a village, the poor animal had been pressed into service as a supply vehicle; it trailed behind Etienne's horse, tethered to his saddle.

Celine had expressed concern that riding together would give an impression of closeness they shouldn't give, but Gaston refused to take no for an answer. He had insisted, assuring her that his men would not find their merely riding or talking together worthy of mention to the King.

She rested her head on his shoulder, looking up through the trees, where the first green buds were just visible.

Gaston hadn't let her out of his sight, or out of reach, since they had made love. Something had changed in him that day. In the past two weeks, she had seen a side of him she had only glimpsed before, a caring and gentleness and humor that made her fall a little more in love with him every day.

Which made every step of their journey all the more bittersweet. The eclipse was just eleven days away now. They were within hours of Gaston's chateau; they would spend the night there, then go on to Paris to see the King.

And get an annulment.

They hadn't argued over it again. They had come to an uneasy truce about it, a reluctant agreement that it was what must be, a silent accord not to speak of it anymore.

"Gaston, when we leave for Paris tomorrow, I probably should have my own horse."

"Nay." His arm tightened around her waist. "This is better for you. Using me as a pillow causes less strain upon the injury in your back."

She wasn't sure that was entirely true, but she wasn't going to be stubborn about it. She was selfish enough to enjoy the chance to be near him during the day, since they were so careful to stay away from each other at night. "I just thought this might be . . . uncomfortable for you."

He lowered his cheek to hers, the scratchy silk of his beard rough against her skin. "Because I want so badly to make love to you?" he murmured.

A rain of heat melted through her. "Because I don't want to torment you . . . or me."

He made a hungry sound that she could feel vibrating through his chest. "I fear we shall need to take our escorts with us when we leave for Paris. It would look suspicious if I asked them to stay behind."

Her breath caught as he sneaked a nibble at her earlobe. "Yes."

"Yes, it would look suspicious? Or yes to this?" His tongue teased the sensitive skin behind her ear.

"I can't th-think when you're doing that."

"I cannot think at all. Except of how to steal a moment alone with you." He nipped her neck, wringing a little moan from her. "I have tried to devise some excuse to send our loyal shadows away for even a quarter hour. It is all I think of. Us together. You all soft and hot and open beneath me."

"*Gaston,*" she pleaded.

"Aye, like that. The way you say my name like that. When I sink into you so deep . . . so hard . . ." He punctuated each word with a flick of his tongue in her ear. "And you turn into sweet honey all around me."

His hand shifted upward slightly, his thumb caressing the underside of her breast through the velvet of her gown. Her heart was pounding. "Etienne is right behind us," she whispered in warning.

"Hmm. Mayhap the solution lies in a few alterations to your gown," he murmured, his voice a low growl. "A secret opening in the skirt, and I could shift you just so . . ."

A tremor shuddered through her as he moved her more tightly against him. Breathless, she gripped his arm at the feel of his rampant arousal straining against his leggings.

"And mayhap another opening, in the front." His hand slid downward.

"And buttons," she added, shivering. "I think it's time to introduce the idea of a buttoned opening on men's pants."

"An excellent suggestion. You can make a new pair of leggings for me as soon as we arrive at my chateau."

She giggled nervously, realizing that he had gone from kidding to serious about this. He wanted to make love to her on horseback. Out in the open. "Gaston, this is crazy. We'd never get away with it. They'd *see* us."

"Pharaon's gait will conceal our movement," he assured her, kissing the curve of her jaw. "The only difficulty I foresee is in silencing the sweet music you make, wife, when I am inside you. How shall we accomplish that?"

She bit her lip, moaning softly, barely able to believe the outrageous suggestion he was making, or the reckless excitement pulsing through her veins. "I don't think we can. I can't hold back what I feel for you. Not when you're . . ."

"Joined to you, so fully that we are one?"

"Yes. Yes, when you make me feel so complete and whole and . . . perfect."

He groaned. "My sweet Celine, I am going to make love to you," he promised hoarsely. "By this time on the morrow, we shall invent a new way of riding. I mean to make you feel perfect until you faint with it."

She made a small, hungry sound, holding tight to him as he pressed her close. Glittering needles of sensation, arousal, anticipation showered through her, making heat pool low in her belly.

"But until then . . ." He chuckled dryly and straightened, loosening his steely grip just slightly. "Mayhap you should tell me more of your time. It seems to make an excellent distraction."

She had to wait for her heart to slow down a bit before she could catch her breath enough to talk. "Have I told you about telephones yet?"

"Aye, you did mention them. The devices that enable one to speak and be heard across great distances. And you spoke of the lights that burn without flame. And the cities, with their gray buildings stretching into the sky without a blade of grass to be seen. And the fact that ale is stored not in wooden casks but in small round metal objects called 'cans.' "

Celine laughed. Even without looking, she could tell he was making a face. "You make it all sound so awful. Actually, we've made a lot of advances. There's education and medical care. And people are free to live as they choose in most countries, whether they were born noble or not. Everyone has an equal say in how things are run. And people live a long time, some a hundred years or more—"

"And there are few kings. And no knights. And everyone works hard because they wish to buy many things, but homes are so stuffed with these things that some pay to have the excess stored elsewhere. And knaves steal goods, and kill, and bring terror to your cities, and go unpunished. And mothers give their babes to the care of strangers, and see them but a few hours each day. And your people so abuse the land that in some places the air is unfit to breathe and the water unfit to drink. The more you tell me of your century, the less I find to recommend it."

"You liked the idea of cars."

"Aye, the carts that race without horses. That I would like to see."

"If we had one now—"

"Is it possible to make love in a 'car'?"

Celine groaned. So much for distracting him. "Yes, actually, it is."

He nodded in understanding. "Then I can see why men invented such a conveyance."

"*Men* aren't the only ones who invent things. In my time, men and women are considered equal. Women go where they want, and do what they want, without having to ask permission from husbands or fathers or brothers."

"Even in France?" he asked incredulously.

"Even in France."

"On the whole, I do not like the sound of the future."

Celine grinned; he was incorrigible. And perhaps she liked him best that way. Persuading him that the twentieth century was a better place was a lost cause.

She didn't know why she kept trying.

"If there are no knights in your time," he asked curiously, "who keeps the peace? Who administers the laws?"

"We have people called lawyers and judges who administer the laws. But the police are the ones who keep the peace. They have special cars, and uniforms, and . . ." Her smile faded. "Guns."

Gaston's arm flexed around her waist. "That is the sort of weapon that injured you?"

"Yes."

He was silent for a moment. "How did it happen?"

She hadn't told him about that night, not in detail. She had repeated the story so many times to so many cops and lawyers and reporters that she had done her best to put it out of her mind ever since. But somehow, with Gaston holding her so close, she wanted to talk about it. She felt safe talking about it. For the first time. "I was in Lincoln Park—it's a place with trees and grass in the city, in Chicago. I went there with my fiancé—"

"You are *betrothed?*" Gaston stiffened so suddenly that Pharaon jerked to a stop.

"No, not anymore. We ... he broke it off. After what happened."

Gaston relaxed and nudged his stallion forward. "If he deserted you when you were injured, he was a cur and you were better off without him."

Celine's smile returned at that completely unbiased opinion. "His name was Lee. Leland Dawber III." She was surprised and pleased to discover that she could speak his name without hurt or regret or embarrassment. "And I think 'cur' is a pretty good description. Anyway, we went to the park because I wanted to celebrate New Year's Eve by making snow angels. That's, uh, something children do. You lie down in the snow and move your arms and legs and make it look like an angel."

"Children?" He chuckled, dropping a kiss on the nape of her neck. "It sounds to me like something you would do. I have always found you most charming stretched out in the snow."

"Yes, well ..." She shivered at his kiss and the memory of the fiery encounter he was referring to. "Lee proposed to me that night. And I accepted." It was hard to believe now, that she could have ever thought herself in love with a man like Lee. "But when we got back to his car, there was a gang of teenagers, and they—"

"Teenagers?"

"Oh, sorry. Teenagers are young people, around Etienne's age. These boys had guns, and they wanted to steal Lee's car."

"And where were these guardsmen—these 'police' who are supposed to keep order?"

"Well, unfortunately, they're not always there when you need them. Lee should have just given up the stupid car, but instead he argued with them. There was a scuffle—a skirmish, you might call it—and one of them fired his gun. But he missed Lee and hit me instead."

"And this weapon, this 'gun' "—Gaston's voice took on a rough edge—"could have killed you?"

"It almost did. I spent weeks in the hospital, having surgeries. There was one bullet fragment they couldn't get, so tiny I can't even feel it. The doctors—physicians—thought it best to leave it in place. They said it would probably never bother me. But less than a year later, it started to shift. They told me it was getting too close to an artery— those are the largest veins in the body, the ones that carry the most blood. They said if I didn't have it removed . . . it would kill me."

Gaston's hand shifted from her waist to her back, touching the spot where the scar was concealed beneath her gown. "And they will be able to save you, these physicians of your time?"

"Yes. The twentieth century might not be better in every way, but our level of medical knowledge and skill is a definite improvement."

He made a sound in his throat that might have been assent, or worry. "And this 'bullet'—does it cause you pain?"

"No, I've been fine. I had a few twinges right after we got to Avril's, but they went away."

He was silent for a time; then he wrapped his arm around her waist again, and pulled her closer than ever, tucking her head beneath his chin. "I do not like the idea of sending you home to this century of yours, where there are such dangers and no knights."

She blinked back a sudden hot rush of tears at the softness in his voice. "But we both know that I've got to go home, Gaston," she whispered. "We can pretend all we want. We can avoid the subject as long as we want, but we both know what I have to do."

He didn't reply. She leaned into him, closing her eyes, and they rode in silence. Was this what the rest of her life was going to feel like? Celine wondered, swallowing hard. This ache of loneliness and loss and helpless desire, this longing for a love like none she would ever feel again?

The minutes stretched into an hour, time ground to dust beneath the steady rhythm of Pharaon's hooves.

She was almost dozing when a flight of birds suddenly burst out of the trees ahead of them, an eruption of beating wings and shrill cries. Gaston yanked his stallion to a halt, a spray of pebbles and dust scattering across the path. Celine had to grab Pharaon's mane and Gaston's arm to keep her balance. "What—"

He clamped a hand over her mouth, his entire body taut and still. Etienne reined in beside them, his expression grim, his crossbow already in his hand. Gaston drew his sword.

Celine's heart jolted. What was wrong? What could possibly *be* wrong? They were almost to Gaston's castle. The birds were just startled. They—

Remy's voice sounded ahead, shouting a high-pitched cry of alarm.

Which was suddenly cut short.

Gaston burst into action. Celine found herself lifted to the ground before she even knew what was happening.

"Guard her with your life, Etienne," Gaston ordered in a harsh whisper. He cut the bundle from his saddle, the one containing her purse, and tossed it to her as he pinned his squire with a steely gaze. "Do you hear me, lad? *With your life!* Run!"

"Gaston!" Celine caught the bundle, but she never had a chance to question him or call out more than his name before he wheeled his horse and galloped off in Remy's direction. Etienne vaulted from the saddle, holding his crossbow in one hand, grabbing Celine's arm with the other.

"Etienne, no!" Celine struggled. "We can't just let him ride off alone like that!"

"Milady," he hissed, "this is for your own good—"

"I don't *care* about my own good. He's—"

"Shh!" Keeping a firm grip on her arm, he smacked the horses—his stallion and the little plow horse—sending them galloping back down the path the way they had come. Then he darted into the trees at a dead run, tugging her behind. Celine didn't have any choice but to race with him into the shadows, her mouth dry, her heart hammering.

She didn't understand at first why they were fleeing on foot. Then she realized that any pursuers would follow the horses first before they thought to search the woods. The trick might buy them time. She stumbled as she tried to keep up with Etienne's agile stride. He still held the crossbow in his hand.

Behind them, she heard the sound of riders pounding down the path, right where they had stood seconds ago.

They ran until the trees were nothing but a blur and every gasp of air hurt her lungs. Finally Etienne stopped and pulled her behind a thicket. They crouched there, both breathing hard. Celine was shaking, her pulse pounding. What had happened to Gaston?

"Rest a moment, milady," Etienne whispered. "Then we must keep—"

"Christiane?"

The angry male voice was a thin, distant sound that came from the direction of the road.

Tourelle's voice.

Celine almost leaped to her feet in panic, but Etienne yanked her back down beside him.

"Nay—if we break cover now, we might be seen," he whispered. "Wait until he moves on."

"Christiane!" Tourelle shouted again, the name carrying eerily through the trees as he rode slowly along the path. "Do not vex me further by hiding! Show yourself. Your husband is not yet dead, but he will be if you do not come out. *Now.*"

Etienne fastened a hand over her mouth to stifle her cry and locked an arm around her waist to hold her still. She struggled against his grip.

"Milady, nay," he hissed in her ear. "It is a ruse."

Trembling, she forced herself to stop fighting him. Logic told her she couldn't do Gaston any good by obeying Tourelle's demand, but not knowing what had happened made her want to scream. *Where was he? What had they done to him? Was he hurt?*

Tourelle was getting closer: she could hear the steady clop of his horse's hooves on the dirt road now, and his voice, louder, icy with fury.

"You have betrayed me, you willful, ungrateful girl. You have driven me to desperate acts. I cannot be responsible for what may happen next if you anger me further.

Already the boy who was riding ahead of you is dead, Christiane. He would not come along quietly. He tried to warn his lord—a foolish choice. We were forced to kill him."

Celine flinched and closed her eyes, remembering the sound of Remy's voice cut short so abruptly. It made her feel sick inside. She could still see his easy smile and the pride he had felt at being chosen as one of their escorts. She heard Etienne swear beside her.

"Let his blood be on your hands," Tourelle shouted, his voice terrifyingly close now. "All of this unpleasantness could have been avoided, Christiane, had you carried out my orders. But instead you repaid my trust with treachery, and you fled with Varennes."

The sound of his horse's hooves stopped. Celine felt a cold trickle of fear down the back of her neck; though she and Etienne were concealed by the thicket, she almost believed that Tourelle was looking right at them. He stopped talking. She held her breath.

He continued along the trail.

"You know it is useless to defy me," he said coaxingly, his voice fading as he moved on. "It was inevitable that I would find you. I have had my men looking for you on every road north for weeks, but Varennes was too careful. *You*, however, my dear, were not. You were sighted on one of the main roads, riding a lame mare near the chateau of Lady Rosalind de Brissot. It was easy enough for my men to follow you and guess your destination."

Celine bit her tongue to hold in a sob. This was her fault! Gaston had been so cautious, but her impulsive side trip had led Tourelle right to them! Remy's death *was* on her head. And if anything had happened to Gaston—

"Once my men reported back to me, I knew I need not even trouble myself giving chase." Tourelle laughed. "Far simpler to lie here in wait and let you gallop straight into my arms. It was most thoughtful of you, my dear, to make this easier for me. Almost as if you had planned it." His voice hardened. "Though I know better now. I grow weary of this, Christiane. Show yourself!"

He was so far away that they had to strain to hear him.

"A moment more," Etienne whispered, rising to his feet, half crouched so he couldn't be seen, pulling her up beside him. They stood poised, listening for Tourelle to move far enough away that he wouldn't notice them when they left their hiding place.

But they were so focused in the direction of the trail, they failed to pay attention to what was behind them.

A rustling whoosh of air was the only warning as a sword came slashing straight down at Etienne's head. He dodged, dropping and rolling. The blade tangled in the bushes. The man who held it yanked it free, snarling curses.

"Run, milady, run!" Etienne cried as two other burly swordsmen closed in. From his prone position, he whipped up his crossbow and fired at the nearest attacker.

Celine screamed, paralyzed with shock and horror as the small, deadly arrow found its mark. The man staggered back with a high-pitched cry and fell to the ground.

Etienne scrambled to his feet. *"Run!"* He swung the crossbow with both hands, connecting solidly with the jaw of the second man, sending him reeling.

Celine couldn't move—even when she heard horses galloping toward them through the trees. It was like she was trapped in the middle of a movie, everything happening too fast, the sounds so loud they drowned out her own terrified screams.

Etienne turned to face his third opponent, but the swordsman was already thrusting forward with his blade. From where she stood, Celine saw with horrifying clarity the point sink into Etienne's side. He crumpled to his knees, jaw slack. The man pulled the sword free, bright with blood, and Etienne tumbled face-first into the leaves and grass of the forest floor, not making a sound.

The other man, the one Etienne had hit with the crossbow, lurched to his feet, holding his jaw and swearing. He kicked Etienne over onto his back.

Etienne was gasping for air, his eyes wide and staring—then one long, shuddering breath escaped him. His lashes closed slowly. He didn't breathe again. The two left him there in a pool of blood and advanced on her.

With a cry of rage and anguish, she dropped her bundle and threw herself at them, fists raised.

Someone caught her from behind before she could take a single step. He spun her around, grasping her shoulders.

"What a pleasure to see you again, my dear," Tourelle said cheerfully. "But look at the measures you have made me resort to. One dead lad will be hard enough to explain away to the King—but two?"

"You *bastard!*" She tried to hit him, but he caught her wrists easily.

"Poor, overwrought Christiane." He subdued her with a bruising grip. "Wherever have you learned such language? From your beloved husband?" He jerked his head to the left, where several more of his men stood with their horses.

Celine followed the direction of his gesture. She could see Gaston. Slung over Pharaon's saddle. Unmoving.

"No!" she shouted, trying to tear herself away from Tourelle. *"No! What have you done?"*

"Calm yourself, my dear. He is not dead. Not yet. I have no intention of killing him—at least not until you answer one simple question for me." He shook her, hard, forcing her attention back to him. "Tell me, Christiane, have you bedded him yet?"

Celine stopped struggling. A sudden icy calm took hold. "No. No, we haven't—"

"Do not lie to me, my sweet *innocent.* It will be simple enough to have a physician examine you and tell whether your maidenhead is intact." He shifted one hand upward, his fingers tightening around her neck, his thumb pressing painfully into her jaw, forcing her head back. "Or mayhap I will simply examine you myself!"

Celine felt a rush of fury and fear. But instead of panicking, she did something that surprised even her: she brought up her knee, fast and hard, straight into Tourelle's groin.

With a strangled curse, he released her, staggering back. Swearing and spluttering, he fell to his knees with an agonized groan.

She glared down at him. "Go to hell," she said evenly.

His men closed in on her, but he gestured them away with a savage wave of his hand. One tried to help him to his feet, but he pushed the man aside, a venomous stare fastened on Celine.

"You ... *bitch!*" he rasped out, staggering to a half crouch. Celine stood her ground. "You traitorous little bitch, you will pay for that!" Still gasping for breath, he straightened and hit her so hard, he knocked her off her feet. Her head ringing, her cheek numb, she lay there on the forest floor, dazed. The shock and pain of it left her dizzy; she had never been hit in her life.

"You are dead!" he snarled, towering over her. "You have been dead from the beginning! I had it planned perfectly. You were going to fall through the ice on Lac du Clermont. Your husband was going to die trying to save you. It would have appeared completely believable— loving husband attempts to save his new bride, but both tragically drown in the freezing lake. No one would have found your bodies until spring! There would have been no evidence by then that you had both been strangled."

He yanked her to her feet. "But you have ruined my plans for your 'accident,' Christiane. The snows are past and the ice has melted—but I shall devise something else. Something better." He spun her around and shoved her toward his horse. "And until then, you and your husband shall live out your last few days in my dungeon."

Etienne felt the blood beneath him. His blood. Everywhere. And pain. Layers of it. Wrenching, blazing pain. It felt like his left side was on fire. Darkness tried to drag him downward again, even as he struggled to find enough strength to open his eyes. He did not know what had awakened him.

Until his stallion nudged him.

He would have laughed, except that it was agony just to breathe. Damned loyal horse. He opened his eyes. Only tiny pinpricks of starlight and a glimmer of moon penetrated the dark forest. He felt cold. Unnaturally cold. And too weak to move.

Guard her with your life.

He had failed Sir Gaston. Again. But he had at least done one thing right: he had had sense enough to play dead. Lying there, he had held his breath and kept still, knowing he could not fight them.

He had heard enough before he passed out; Tourelle had taken Sir Gaston and Lady Celine to his chateau.

Guard her with your life.

Somehow—he was not sure exactly how, because he fainted once during the process—he ripped a length of cloth from his sleeve and bound his wound as tightly as he could, biting his lip at the pain. Then he made it to his knees. Leaning against his horse's leg, he pulled himself forcibly to his feet. He rested there for a moment, his stallion twitching nervously at the smell of blood.

"Nay . . ." he croaked. "Easy."

The night-draped forest danced crazily before his eyes. He had to get help. Had to . . .

Trying to steady himself, he glanced down, and noticed Lady Celine's bundle. He bent over and almost fell as he picked it up; it had seemed important to her, and he did not wish to leave it behind. After several tries, he managed to get his foot into the stirrup and heave himself into the saddle.

Groaning, leaning over his horse's neck, he urged the stallion forward. Sir Gaston's chateau was still several hours away. Captain Royce would be there; he would know what to do.

Etienne was going to either get help or die trying.

Chapter 23

A wakening only traded one darkness for another. Time passed in a hazy blur, hours of cold and blackness sliding one into the other until Gaston was not sure how many days he had spent in the small cell, with no heat or light, no food or water, and no idea why he was still alive.

Mayhap Tourelle meant to leave him here until he slowly starved to death. The hunger gnawing at his gut was matched only by the ache in his head from the blow he had suffered when Tourelle's men attacked him; he had killed one of them before they overpowered him, but that fact was small satisfaction.

Most painful of all was not knowing what had happened to Celine.

He could only hope that she had escaped with Etienne. Unless she was being held elsewhere. He had called her name, but there had been no reply from the darkness. No sound penetrated the dungeon save the echo of his own voice.

His efforts to escape proved just as useless. Digging at the clammy stone floor and walls was futile, and the solid wooden door did not give way no matter how hard he kicked it or how many times he threw his full weight against it. Despite all the noise he made, no guards came to subdue him. He was left utterly alone in the darkness.

Left alone to worry about whether Celine was safe and well.

It was a torture worse than any other Tourelle could have inflicted. Gaston almost would have believed the bastard was doing it apurpose, except that he could not know.

Could not possibly know how much Celine meant to him. How much he cared for her.

He had not known it himself, before now.

Left with naught to do but sleep and think, he found himself unable to sleep ... because all he could think of was her. He did not care what happened to him, as long as Celine was safe.

The feeling took him by surprise, yet it was undeniably true. If he never left this cell alive, if he died here without seeing her again, if all his hopes for vengeance and justice for his murdered father and brother were thwarted and Tourelle triumphed, he would not care ... as long as she lived.

Never in his life had he had such thoughts. For as long as he could remember, his own plans and desires and needs had been foremost in his mind; now, for the first time, someone else mattered more.

The realization made his heart beat strangely, made him pace the cell restlessly, made him do something he had not done in many years.

Alone in the darkness, he knelt on the cold stone floor and began to pray.

He prayed that she had escaped with Etienne. That she would go to his chateau and await the eclipse. That she would return to her time—and not waste precious hours she could not spare trying to save him.

Never in all his years on the battlefield had he prayed so fervently. And never had he made the offer he made now: his life for hers. He would give up all he had, all he was. He would die willingly, if only God would save her.

He was still kneeling there, head bent and eyes closed, when he heard a sound. At first he thought he had only imagined it, that he was delirious from hunger and thirst and fatigue. But then it grew louder, closer, inescapably real.

Footsteps. In the corridor outside. Four men, mayhap five.

Gaston rose and flattened himself against the wall next to the door, poised to make a bid for freedom if the chance presented itself.

A key turned in the lock. The portal opened a bare inch. Torchlight flickered in the gloom. Squinting, he tensed, ready to strike.

"Hold, Sir Gaston," one of the men said urgently, pushing the door open only a crack. "Allow us to speak."

Gaston remained mute, started to lunge—then froze when they stepped inside: four men, three wearing the royal blue and white of the King's guard.

"Milord," one said, bowing low as if they were at a courtly feast rather than in a dank dungeon, "his Majesty wishes to see you."

They brought food and water with them, and a change of clothes, and they waited outside while Gaston washed and donned the garments and barraged them with questions.

He did not bother with the food when they informed him that his wife was waiting above with the King.

She had been captured when he was, they explained as he hurried with them down the corridors, emptying the flask of water as he walked. Nay, she was not hurt. It was his squire, Etienne, who had gone for help; wounded, he had managed to make it to Gaston's chateau before slipping into unconsciousness. Nay, they did not know the lad's present condition, but the captain of Gaston's guardsmen, Royce, was here—it was he who had sent riders to fetch the King.

Above, in Tourelle's great hall, royal guardsmen milled about, along with Tourelle's men and several of Gaston's own. His escorts accompanied him to the solar at the rear of the chamber, where the others waited, all standing in separate areas of the room, like combatants awaiting the call to battle: the King, Tourelle, Royce . . . and Celine.

As the door closed behind Gaston, it did not even occur to him to kneel before the King; he went straight to Celine, meeting her halfway as she rushed into his arms.

"Are you all right?" He gathered her close with a mixture of relief and concern, feeling as if he had not truly taken a breath since the last time he saw her, days ago.

"I'm fine." She hugged him back just as hard. "What about you?"

"Sir Gaston, I would have an explanation," the King said impatiently, standing before the hearth, his jaw set. "The Duc has given me his version of events, and Lady Christiane related a most inventive tale, but I fear I have yet to hear the truth of what happened in the forest. Mayhap you would care to tell me?"

Gaston released Celine, just enough to belatedly bow to the King. "Aye, my liege." As he straightened, he glanced down at his wife with a raised eyebrow. "Lady Christiane?"

"I *tried* to explain to King Philippe who I am," she whispered, "but I don't have any proof."

"Where is the bundle?" he asked with a frown.

She shook her head, her eyes dark with worry. "Lost in the forest somewhere. Royce says that Etienne mentioned it when he rode in, but he didn't have it with him."

"The lad was still feverish when I left him," Royce put in. "I am not certain if he even remembers where he dropped it."

Gaston swore softly. He narrowed his gaze, running the backs of his fingers over the trace of a bruise on Celine's cheek. "And who gave you that?" he asked darkly, slanting a murderous look at Tourelle, fury sizzling through him.

Tourelle glanced away, turning to Philippe. "Sire, as you can see, Varennes is unharmed. As I told you he would be. I merely imprisoned him here because he and his men attacked us without warning—"

"It is too late for lies, Tourelle," Gaston said derisively. "The King will not believe you. One of my men is *dead*. A mere lad, and you cut him down—"

"And two of *my* men are dead," Tourelle countered, still addressing the King. "Varennes killed one, and his squire another. It was an ambush, my liege, just as I said. My men managed to subdue Varennes, and I brought him here, with my ward. I was forced to strike her when she tried to attack me, and I have had to keep her locked in one of the tower bedchambers. He has turned her against me, sire.

She would say or do whatever he tells her. I thought merely to hold them both here until I could send for you. I dispatched a rider to Paris days ago—"

"That's not true at all," Celine cut in angrily. "You were holding us here until you could think of some way to *kill* us while making it look like an accident." She turned to Philippe. "He told me everything, sir. He was originally going to make it look like I fell through the ice on a lake and Gaston drowned trying to save me. He had it all planned. But now the ice is melted and he needed to think of something else."

"Dear Christiane, how can you *say* that?" Tourelle gave her a wounded look. "Do you see how Varennes has twisted her mind, my liege? You cannot believe that I would kill my own beloved ward. It makes no more sense than her mad tale that she is from the future! The poor child suffers from some strange brain-fever, and this knave has taken advantage of her enfeebled mind to feed her all manner of lies."

The King gazed at Celine with an expression of pity; he was clearly having difficulty believing anything she told him. Gaston realized with frustration that the truth would avail them naught here; it was simply too unbelievable without the proof of Celine's odd pouch and its contents. Until Philippe saw that, all she claimed about herself—and about Tourelle and his treachery—would remain in doubt.

"Sire, my wife does not suffer from a brain-fever," Gaston said flatly. "There is proof of what she says. I have seen it."

"Saints' breath," Tourelle exclaimed, "they are *both* mad!"

"And where is this proof?" Philippe asked incredulously.

"My squire had it with him, but it seems he lost it in the forest—"

"Most convenient," Tourelle sneered.

"Etienne *did* speak of a bundle," Royce said. "He seemed to think it important."

"But you said yourself that he was feverish," the King replied.

"Sire, you cannot listen to this madness." Tourelle raised his hands in a gesture of exasperation. "I am the one telling the truth of what happened. Varennes attacked me. He broke the truce. He should be forced to forfeit his holdings—"

"This cur is a liar and a murderer," Gaston retorted, "as I have said from the beginning. It was he who ambushed *us*, when we were on our way to my chateau. Had I been planning to attack him, would I venture out with naught but two lads? And bring my wife along?"

"An excellent ruse to cover your true purpose," Tourelle spat.

The King exhaled slowly, as if trying to hold his temper in check. "Alain, it was Gaston's men who reached me in Paris first. How do you explain that?"

"Part of his scheme," Tourelle replied quickly. "He *knew* he was planning to ambush me, so he had his men at the ready to leave for Paris. He knew that sending word of what happened would make him look innocent in this."

"By nails and blood, *that* is an inventive tale," Gaston scoffed, furious at the way Tourelle tried to slither and coil around the truth. "Sire, you have proof enough of the *good* and *honorable* Duc's guilt: he has kept me imprisoned in his dungeon for days without food or water—"

"Small punishment for what you did," Tourelle said.

"Lying whoreson—"

"Enough, both of you!" the King demanded.

His voice rolled through the chamber like a peal of thunder, leaving silence in its wake. Gaston could feel his liege lord's anger radiating outward like waves of blazing heat. Celine shivered, and almost unconsciously Gaston tightened his arm around her shoulders, drawing her protectively closer.

After a taut moment, Philippe continued in that same tone. "It is apparent that I may never know the truth of this! But one thing is clear: you have *both* ignored my commands once more. I decreed that neither of you would raise arms against the other, but blood has been spilled anew, on both sides. How many more men must die before the two of you accept the peace that I have declared shall be?"

The fury of his voice matched his expression as he glared from one of them to the other, his eyes forbidding further argument.

"God's blood, I have had a bellyful of this." He shook his head in disgust. "I have used peaceful means and failed. I have tried to negotiate a truce between you, but you will not accept it. This poor maiden has been driven mad, and that is not yet enough." His voice turned frosty. "We will settle this once and for all upon the field of honor. You will decide it with single combat, my lords. A joust, *armes à outrance*. To the victor the spoils. Is that acceptable?"

Tourelle gave Gaston an assessing glance, then smiled. "Acceptable," he agreed.

"Aye," Gaston said with relish, anticipation burning through him.

"No!" Celine turned to the King with a look of dismay. "No, you can't let them—"

"Milady, the choice is not yours. The challenge has been made and accepted."

"But it's not fair! Gaston was injured in the battle with Tourelle's men, and he's been locked up without food and water for five days. He's not in any shape to fight anyone."

The King raised an eyebrow, then glanced at Gaston. "You shall rest a day and we will meet on the next day at dawn. Will that be acceptable?"

"Aye, my liege."

"Gaston!" Celine pleaded, turning back to him. "That's not enough time—"

"There is no choice." He softened his tone, raising a hand to her cheek. "There are but six days left."

It was obvious she understood what he meant, though no one else in the chamber might. They had but six days to find her missing bundle and return to his chateau in time for the eclipse. Five, if he rested a day; he dared not take longer than that.

"But I don't *care* about that," she whispered.

"Then it is well that one of us is thinking of your future." He gave her a grin, but she apparently didn't share his confidence.

In fact, she looked ready to joust with him herself. "Damn it, you stubborn, reckless—"

He pulled her into his arms again and looked over her head at the King. "My liege, I would ask that my men be allowed to leave, that they might search for this bundle we have spoken of."

Philippe shrugged. "As you wish."

"Then we meet on the day after the morrow." Gaston shifted his gaze to Tourelle, and smiled. "At dawn."

Celine stood beside Royce, trembling with a chill that didn't come from the morning mist curling around the hem of her cloak. The King had chosen a neutral field a few miles from Tourelle's chateau, and a sizable crowd had gathered by the time the first pale rays of light had broken over the horizon. The King stood at the center of the spectators, flanked by his royal guards, who formed a blue-and-white neutral zone between Tourelle's supporters and Gaston's.

Celine barely glanced at anyone. She couldn't tear her gaze from the two pavilions that had been set up on the right edge of the field, a few yards apart, their brightly colored pennants fluttering in the breeze. Her heart fluttered almost as wildly.

She kept telling herself there was nothing to worry about; this was just a joust, a ceremonial duel, not one of those insane tournaments like the one in which Gaston's father and brother had been killed.

But she couldn't shake her fear that Gaston might get himself seriously hurt.

She had seen him only briefly since their meeting with the King; his idea of "resting" had been to spend all day yesterday preparing for this moment. He and Royce had taken hours selecting and preparing weapons and armor. It had all been very grim and determined and efficient, with no time for feminine interruptions.

Pharaon had been readied as well; the stallion stood outside Gaston's pavilion, decked out in chain mail and quilted padding and black silks. Someone had even strapped a metal faceplate on him, with a unicorn-style horn in the middle. Prancing and tossing his head, he looked absolutely ferocious. A small boy nervously held the reins, and one of Gaston's guardsmen stood on the other side, ready to act as squire since Etienne was not available.

Her throat dry, Celine glanced at Tourelle's pavilion.

The Duc was already outside, strutting around, laughing with his squire. His confidence made Celine uneasy. She wouldn't put anything past him. Even with the King's guards supervising all the preparations, he might attempt something underhanded. And it only increased her anxiety to realize how evenly matched he and Gaston were: Tourelle might not be as tall or broad-shouldered as Gaston, but he had a muscular build, several years' more experience in battle—and he hadn't spent the last few days in a dungeon.

And there was something Gaston had said once before that kept haunting her.

What if her love proved too great a distraction? What if she had weakened him, made him less of a warrior . . . as he insisted had happened to his brother?

Gaston stepped out of his pavilion and a murmur went through the crowd. He looked strong and confident, moving easily despite the chain mail and pieces of plate armor that covered his chest, back, arms, and legs. He wore a great helm topped by a black plume, and mail gauntlets, and black silks over the armor . . . and a strip of red velvet tied snugly around his left arm.

Her vision blurred, but she blinked rapidly and forced a smile. He had come to her last night after supper and gruffly asked for that: a favor from his lady, a bit of cloth from her gown. It was traditional, he had said.

She had given it to him with shaking fingers, and tried to ask a few questions about exactly what this joust entailed—was it like the ceremonial, colorful events she had seen in the movies?

He had laughed and asked what a "movie" was, and before she could bring the conversation back to her questions, he was gone; he'd assured her he would be all right, thanked her for the lady's favor, given her the briefest kiss, then left to continue his preparations.

She knew him too well by now. He had been purposely hiding something from her. It had made her so nervous, she hadn't been able to sleep all night.

Now, as she watched, Gaston and Tourelle mounted their horses, and their assistants handed them their shields and weapons.

Her stomach started churning. The weapons included evil-looking steel-tipped lances. And swords.

Celine turned to Royce, a chill dancing down her spine. "I don't understand—why do they need those?"

"It is to be *armes à outrance,* milady."

"What's that mean? I thought they were just supposed to try to knock each other out of the saddle."

"Aye, the object is to unseat the opponent, with the lance." Royce nodded. "In *armes courtois,* blunted weapons are used, and the joust is ended when one is unseated, or when three lances have been broken. But this battle will continue on foot. It is to be *armes à outrance*—sharp points."

Celine felt all the blood drain from her face. She turned back to the scene before her with gathering horror.

"Milady? Did you not understand before now?" Royce took her elbow when she swayed dizzily. "It is to be a battle to the death."

Chapter 24

Gaston could feel Celine's heart beating as one with his, as vividly as he could feel the bit of velvet fluttering around his arm. But he did not allow himself to look at her. He did not dare. Not now. For a vexing uncertainty crouched within him, a nagging suspicion that his feelings for her, and hers for him, might have changed him somehow. Weakened him.

But as he sheathed his sword, a familiar calm descended over him.

The day became this moment; the field became these scant yards that separated him and Tourelle. It was an almost hypnotic sensation of the world narrowing to a single point. As if his weapons and armor wove a spell around him that blocked out all else—all fatigue, all questions, all feelings, all fear.

He had waited too long for this. Since that anguished day when word reached him that his father and brother had been killed, he had burned for it: his blade against Tourelle's. No truce. No talking. No interference. The simple, inescapable justice of combat. Sinew and steel.

In the light of the rising sun, he became the lethal edge of the sword strapped to his side, the weight of the shield fitted to his left arm, the length of the lance gripped in his right hand. He was no longer man but warrior.

And he would either kill or die this day.

His heart pumping, his blood running hot, he glanced at Tourelle, then touched his spurs to Pharaon's flanks and galloped to the far edge of the field.

The crowd, the pavilions, the mist faded from his vision. He turned and braced the wooden lance across his

304

body, the deadly metal point angled to the left. His stallion pawed the ground. Gaston felt equally restless, eager for the signal to charge.

The King came to stand apart from the crowd. They would have none of the usual flourishes and formalities. No heralds to recount their past deeds, no trumpets blaring before each charge, no tilt fence between the horses to prevent them from crashing into each other. Naught but the essentials: power and prowess. Sinew and steel.

"If it is blood that you want, my lords, then you shall have it," Philippe declared simply. "The match ends when one is dead."

He stepped back to his place, and after a brief murmur, silence descended over the spectators. Gaston had the eerie sensation that he could hear the mist curling over the grass.

His hand tightened around the lance. The mail of his gauntlet was cold against his palm.

"*Allez!*" The King's shout shattered the morning air.

A flick of the reins sent Pharaon charging across the field; he did not need the spurs. A battle cry tore from Gaston's throat as his destrier galloped at full speed toward Tourelle's bay.

He kept his body balanced in the saddle and stirrups, his strength united to the stallion's, gathering behind the lance. The pounding of hooves was like thunder before a storm.

Shields raised, the opponents clashed with a deafening clatter of metal, guttural oaths, and the horses' screams. Gaston threw his weight forward to force his lance into Tourelle's shield even as he absorbed the blow to his own, shifting at the right moment to avoid losing his seat. Both lances shattered.

Their speed carried them onward, past each other. Gaston's chest and arms ached from the force of the impact. He and Tourelle dropped the damaged weapons as they turned at opposite ends of the field, and their assistants ran forward with replacements.

They paused only long enough to take up the new lances before they launched themselves forth again, racing headlong across the field.

They slammed together in another clash and scrape of

metal against metal, strength against strength. Tourelle's lance missed the mark this time, but Gaston's blow struck cleanly. His enemy almost tumbled from the bay horse. A rush of triumph sizzling through him, Gaston galloped to the end of the field, tossing aside the broken lance and signaling impatiently for another.

Only then did he feel the sticky warmth running down his side.

He glanced downward and realized that Tourelle had missed the shield apurpose: the sharp point of his lance had opened a gash in Gaston's side, sliding between the breastplate and backplate of his armor and making short work of his mail tunic.

Pain flooded in, and fury at Tourelle's cowardly tactic, but he forced both to the edge of his awareness. Ignoring the blood, he snatched up his third and final lance and moved into position.

And charged again.

He poised low over Pharaon's neck, aiming at the bottom of Tourelle's shield, the very center of his balance. But at the last moment, Tourelle's lance suddenly tilted upward. He struck another coward's blow—straight into Gaston's *gorget,* the collar of metal that protected his throat. It sent Gaston sprawling and almost tore off his helm. A cry rippled through the crowd.

His head ringing, his wounded side afire, Gaston forced himself to his feet, drawing his sword even as Tourelle dropped his lance and dismounted. Too late Gaston realized his helm had been knocked askew, half blocking his vision. There was no time to set it aright. Tourelle was on him. He warded off the attack with his shield and they threw themselves at each other, fighting savagely even before the horses could be led from the field.

The metallic clang of blade against blade rang out, heavy and hot as the noise in a smithy's forge. They hacked and slashed with brutal force, using the shields to both fend off blows and strike at each other. There was no grace to their combat, no strategy. They bothered not with taunts or jeers; there was naught but ruthless, deadly purpose. *Kill.* Sinew and steel.

Gaston felt every blow vibrate through his arms. Straining, swearing, they battled almost in place, neither gaining nor yielding ground. Gaston wounded Tourelle, a glancing blow to the shoulder. Tourelle feinted and opened a line of red along Gaston's thigh. He did not feel the pain. His heart beat like a war drum. The sun rose higher, burning down on them until their breathing came harsh and loud, and still they fought on. Gaston felt sweat pouring down his body. His muscles tensed and dodged a little more slowly with each thrust and parry.

In a sudden burst of violence, Tourelle struck a rain of blows that shattered Gaston's shield. Gaston tossed it aside—but before his assistant could reach him with another, Tourelle closed in. Gaston fended off the attack with his sword, but Tourelle had the advantage. He slashed sideways, a cut that Gaston could not ward off without a shield.

Leaping backward, Gaston barely avoided being sliced in half—but the weight of his armor made it impossible for him to keep his balance.

He slipped on the grass and went down, flat on his back. He heard a single feminine scream from the crowd as the point of Tourelle's sword stabbed toward his exposed throat before he could roll aside.

"Die like a dog!" Tourelle snarled, eyes wild.

Gaston twisted his head—and his skewed helm blocked the deadly thrust. The blade dented the metal but slid off the curved side. Before Tourelle could draw back, Gaston brought his legs up in a savage kick.

Tourelle went sprawling, his weapon flying from his hand. Gaston lunged to his feet and closed on his opponent, sword raised to deliver a death blow with all his strength behind it. Suddenly a small knife appeared in Tourelle's hand.

Treachery. Gaston's full weight carried him forward. He could not twist out of the way quickly enough. Tourelle flung the knife. Gaston evaded it the only way he could: diving to one side. The blade missed his throat and buried to the hilt in his shoulder. He landed heavily on his side, his breath knocked from him, his head swimming in a haze of pain.

Tourelle was on his feet, running for his sword. But the

knavery of the hidden knife had snapped something inside Gaston. It was precisely such murderous treachery that had killed his father and brother. Whatever last shred of control he possessed vanished. With a wordless snarl, he thrust himself to his feet, attacking Tourelle before he could reach his weapon.

Tourelle was forced to defend himself with naught but the shield. He began to retreat. Gaston pursued mercilessly, striking blow after blow, backing him across the open ground.

"I yield," Tourelle cried. "I yield!"

"You have fought a coward's battle," Gaston said. "Die a coward's death!"

His next thrust knocked the shield from his enemy's grasp.

Tourelle raised his hands. "Let us strike a bargain!"

"You offered no bargain to my father and brother when you murdered them." Gaston reached up and yanked the small knife out of his shoulder, not even flinching. He advanced for every step Tourelle retreated, a weapon in each hand.

"I will admit it!" Tourelle shouted. "I will admit all."

"Admit it, then!" Gaston lifted his sword until the point was but an inch from his enemy's face.

Frozen, Tourelle opened his mouth as if to speak.

But with a sudden move, he dove for the knife in Gaston's hand.

This time Gaston was faster. He whirled aside and back, his sword arcing in a savage thrust just as Tourelle's momentum carried him forward.

Instead of the knife he sought, Tourelle came away with the sword—buried deep in his belly.

He staggered, mouth agape, eyes wide with disbelief. He gripped the gleaming steel as if he might pull it free. Instead, with a gurgling cry of denial, he fell, his last breath a bubbling of blood on his lips.

Gaston stood where he was, shaking, breathing hard; his every muscle hurt, and he could feel the full, searing pain in his side and shoulder and thigh, now that the battle was done. Finished. Vengeance and justice. Sinew and steel.

The killing fever that had burned through his veins began to clear, like the morning mist that had vanished from the ground.

It was over. He suddenly felt tired, more tired than he had ever felt in his life. Wrenching the dented, twisted helm off his head, he threw it aside, then pushed back the mail coif and padded leather he wore beneath. Sweat poured down his face, his body. Sweat and blood. Only by sheer force of will did he keep from sinking to his knees.

He raised his head to look for Celine, but the crowd of men had gathered round, a crush of warriors. He could not see her. The King came to stand by his side, and took the knife Gaston still held in his hand. He turned it between his fingers, looking at it with a frown of disgust. "Treachery. Knavish, cheating treachery." He lifted his eyes to Gaston's. "I fear I am in the awkward position of having to admit that I was wrong."

Before Gaston could even begin to form a reply to that, or catch his breath enough to say a word, one of Tourelle's men spoke, his expression troubled.

"Sire? Sir Gaston . . . is our lord now."

"Aye. To the victor the spoils," Philippe confirmed. He addressed the gathered warriors in a stern tone. "All of you owe your homage and fealty to Varennes now."

The man who had spoken glanced nervously at Gaston. "Then the vexing secret we have kept must be kept no longer. My liege, what the Duc said before he died . . . it was true."

"Aye," another of Tourelle's men said. "Sir Soren and Sir Gerard were killed by treachery, not by accident. The Duc hired mercenaries from the south to carry out the deed. The rest of us were not to know . . . but we heard rumors of what he had done."

"And why have you kept this to yourselves for so long?" the King demanded angrily.

"The Duc threatened that if any one of us but breathed a word," the man explained, "some among our wives and children would meet with untimely 'accidents'."

"And there is more, my liege," a third warrior added. "The ambush in the forest—that was our lord's doing as well, not Sir Gaston's. The Duc told Lady Christiane of his murderous plans. He intended to kill them both."

"I was there," another admitted. "I heard him say it."

There were murmurs of assent from others in the crowd. His frown deepening, the King turned to Gaston.

"It would seem I have been the only one who did not recognize the real Tourelle," Philippe said dryly. "What say you, Gaston? These men knew of the truth and concealed it. Their fate is in your hands. It is within your rights to order them stripped of their spurs and horses and banished from your holdings."

His breathing steadier now, Gaston drew himself up to his full height, his gaze meeting those of Tourelle's men, one at a time. They could have kept their secret forever, protecting themselves; instead they had admitted all before him and the King, risking much.

"Nay, my liege," he said after a long moment. "I shall need men of strength and courage to keep safe my lands. The past is the past. All who will swear loyalty, all who are honorable from this day forth, will have naught to fear."

A murmur of surprise went through the gathered men. Then, silently, one after another, they dropped to one knee, heads bowed in a gesture of fealty.

Watching them, Gaston felt as if a great weight had just slid from his shoulders. He finally had the truth of what had happened to his father and brother. Spoken aloud, for all to know.

And he realized another truth as well in that moment, accepting it more deeply than he ever had before: it would have made no difference had he been at Tourelle's tourney. *He could not have saved them.* Had he been there, he would have been killed as well.

Mayhap it was not wise to question God's plans; mayhap he had been meant to live, to seek this justice, to serve some other purpose. *The past was the past.*

And the future . . .

He turned to speak to Celine, only to find that she had yet to make her way through the crowd to his side.

"Where is my wife?" he asked with sudden concern.

"I fear she fainted," the King said with a rueful grin, "when you fell and Tourelle's blade was at your throat. Royce carried her to your pavilion. Come." He slapped

Gaston on his uninjured shoulder and turned to walk back toward the tents. "You must have your wounds tended, and we must speak."

Gaston was almost knocked to the ground once again, as soon as he stepped into his pavilion.

"You're all right!" Celine threw herself into his arms. "Thank God. Oh, thank God, you're all right! Royce wouldn't let me watch the rest after I fainted. I could only hear it and that was almost worse, because I couldn't tell anything from the noise and—oh, God, you're all right!"

Her arms tightened around his midsection. Gaston winced, but stifled a groan and gathered her close. "I did not mean to frighten you."

"Frighten me?" she sobbed, stepping back. "You could have been killed!"

"But I was not."

"But you *could've* been."

"But I was not," he insisted with a gentle grin.

"Milady," the King interrupted, holding aside the tent flap as the barber-surgeon, summoned from among Tourelle's men, entered with his instruments. "Mayhap you would wait outside with Captain Royce? There are matters I would discuss with your husband, and he must have his wounds stitched."

"Wounds?" Celine repeated in a suddenly small voice, looking Gaston up and down.

Gaston felt grateful that the tent flap had just fallen behind his assistant, who stepped inside to help him out of his armor. The only light in the darkened pavilion was provided by a candle on the trestle table in the center. He would prefer to spare Celine the sight of three deep blade-cuts.

"Naught to worry about," he assured her, taking off his mail gauntlets and tossing them on the table with a casual air. "But mayhap it would be best if you waited outside with Royce. I would not wish you to faint again."

"I am *not* the fainting type," she insisted with a mutinous tilt to her chin. "Except when my husband is almost getting himself killed."

He placed his hands on her shoulders, smiling down at

her. "Milady, your husband may become 'the fainting type' if you do not cease being stubborn. Allow us but a few moments with the surgeon." He turned her around and sent her toward the exit. "And then you may return."

With a muttered protest, she gave him a last worried look and went out.

"I congratulate you on your victory, milord," Royce said with pride before he followed her.

"My thanks, Royce, for all you have done."

As soon as the tent flap had closed, Gaston gave in to the pain, settling heavily onto the nearest stool, unable to grit back a groan. His assistant set to work quickly, unfastening the various plates of armor, removing the chain mail and padded leather beneath. Gaston felt relief as each heavy piece came off, not only because it made it easier for him to breathe—but because it was almost as if his past questions and doubts and guilt were being removed with them.

The King sat on a stool across from him as the barber-surgeon began laying instruments on the table. "You were right about Tourelle from the beginning, Gaston. Much trouble could have been avoided had I taken your word from the start. You have my apology."

Gaston gazed at his sovereign in astonishment; never had he heard Philippe apologize. To anyone. For anything. "A king must make difficult decisions," he said with a shrug—regretting the gesture when it pained his shoulder.

"Aye, but a king must also know enough to judge men wisely, and I have been most unwise."

"My liege, it is over now."

Gaston's assistant left with the armor, and the surgeon stepped near, applying a stinging, wet compress to Gaston's raw shoulder that made him flinch.

"Pardon, milord," the young man said. " 'Tis wine, to cleanse the wound. It is a method of preventing infection."

Gaston glanced at him, a wry grin tugging at his mouth. So Celine thought all the important advances had not been made until *her* time. "Has my wife been offering you advice?" he asked curiously.

"Your wife?" The young man looked at him in puzzlement. "Nay, milord."

"Gaston." Philippe flicked an impatient glance at the barber-surgeon, who quickly swabbed the other cuts, turned back to the table, and began tearing lengths of linen for bandages, leaving the two men to their discussion. "Gaston, all that was stolen from your family is now returned to you. Along with Tourelle's considerable holdings as well." The King leaned forward, his face sober, as if he were only now getting to the subject he truly wished to address. "It makes you, in truth, a most wealthy man. Lord of a vast portion of the Artois region. I am not certain I can grant such wealth to a mere knight."

Gaston regarded him warily. Would Philippe take back what he had only just granted? All of it? Part of it? He held his tongue.

"And so," the King continued, his features breaking into a smile, "I suppose I shall have to make you a *duc.*"

Stunned, Gaston could not speak for a moment. "Saints' breath," he sputtered at last. "Sire! I . . . it is—"

"Nay, do not thank me. When I make a mistake, I admit it—and I make amends."

"Amends?" Gaston choked out. "But a *duc.* You have me leaping over more ranks than—God's blood! Baron, *viscomte,* comte—"

"Aye." Philippe laughed. "It is good to be King."

Gaston couldn't help but laugh as well, though it hurt his side. "Sire . . ." He shook his head in disbelief. "It is too generous. Too—"

"Noble? Gaston, today on this field, I saw more nobility than I have seen in all my years in battle. You fought honorably, even with all that lay at stake, even while Tourelle acted the knave. I see now that I accepted what others said of you too easily in the past. Mayhap that is why I was so slow to judge whether it was you or Tourelle who was telling the truth."

"But that does not mean that I deserve—"

"You are more deserving than most who inherit such a title," Philippe insisted. "You have earned it. Far more than you earned the name Blackheart. Aye, mayhap you committed some regrettable deeds in the past, but a man can change. Nobility is not in titles, Gaston, or even in deeds." He rose to leave. "It is in the heart."

Gaston dropped his gaze to the ground, uncomfortable with such words. *Change ... nobility ... the heart.* He had resisted change for so long. Thought he must stay as he was to survive. Believed he could never be truly noble, that he did not wish to be.

That he could never give in to his heart.

It was difficult to accept all at once.

"Mayhap, my liege."

"I believe it is true, and I should know. I am a king." Smiling, Philippe clapped him on the shoulder. "I leave you to the surgeon, my good Duc." He turned to go, then stopped before the tent flap, turning back. "Ah, but I almost neglected to address the other subject I meant to speak to you about. The request that you made of me so long ago—the annulment. I believe I know what your answer will be, but it is yours if you wish. Do you still want it?"

Celine waited until the King had left Gaston's tent. She wasn't sure it was acceptable for a mere woman to address a king, but someone had to ask the question that needed to be asked, and she wasn't sure Gaston would think of it, after all he had been through today.

But as soon as she raised the question of an annulment, the King cut her off.

"I have already discussed it with Gaston, milady. Speak to him."

The abrupt way he said it, and the look in his eyes, told her more than she wanted to know. A sinking feeling began in the pit of her stomach. She knew it was inevitable. Knew it had to be.

But realizing that her marriage to Gaston had been ended still hurt.

Hurt as if someone had run her through with one of the metal-tipped jousting lances.

"Thank you, sire," she muttered numbly.

The King bade her farewell and left, gathering his men in his wake. The others were busy cleaning up the field and taking down Tourelle's pavilion; the body had already been carried away for burial. Royce was occupied removing all the hardware from Pharaon.

Standing by herself outside Gaston's pavilion, the wind tangling her hair, she waited. Waited until the barber-surgeon left. Waited until Gaston was alone.

Then she still waited.

She didn't want to go inside. Didn't want to say what had to be said. But she finally squared her shoulders and forced herself to walk forward, stopping just outside the tent flap. "Gaston?"

"Come in, Celine."

She stepped inside. He was sitting on a stool beside the trestle table, wearing nothing but a length of linen draped around his lap. Fresh white bandages covered his thigh, circled his ribs, bound his shoulder. The dim firelight bathed his skin in flickering gold.

Her stomach tight with concern, she shifted her gaze to the candle on the table. "Are you really all right?" she whispered.

"A few scratches, no more."

He sounded almost cheerful. Maybe he was a little delirious from the pain. "I . . . I came to say good-bye," she said softly. "I think it's probably best if we . . . I mean, there's really no need for us to—"

"You came to say good-bye?"

He wasn't going to make this easy. "Yes. It's best if we just part now, don't you think? You've probably got a lot to do here. I could go back to your castle for the eclipse. It's impossible for us to . . . I mean, we shouldn't . . . we can't . . ."

She lost her voice. He didn't say anything.

"Oh, God, Gaston." She wrapped her arms around herself, feeling miserable, forcing her gaze to his. "There's no sense postponing the inevitable! Let's just make a clean break, right now. It's really better that way, now that the King has agreed to the annulment."

"But, my lady wife," he said in a deep, steady voice, "there is not going to be an annulment."

Chapter 25

Celine's heart skipped a beat. She had the unnerving feeling that she was in a dream, her senses unnaturally sharp, making her vividly aware of Gaston's eyes gleaming with dark heat as they held hers; of the glimmer of candlelight playing over the angles of his face; of their shadows dancing on the side of the pavilion, undulating together as the silk fluttered with the wind.

She blinked in disbelief. She was definitely awake. But she certainly couldn't have heard him right.

"What did you say?"

"There is not going to be an annulment," he repeated in that same tone, his voice and body both as solid and unmovable as granite.

"You mean you turned it *down?"* she cried.

"Nay, I told the King that I wanted the annulment."

She shook her head, squeezing her eyes shut, half dazed with confusion. "Gaston, you're not making sense!"

"I told him I wished to have the annulment—but I asked him to wait a few months in granting it. He agreed, though he was not pleased. From what he has seen, he believes we should stay married . . . and he has a difficult time believing that we have not consummated our vows."

"But he agreed to it—so we *are* getting an annulment."

"Nay." Gaston shook his head, his eyes locked with hers, potent. "We are not."

"Would you please stop contradicting yourself?" She was shivering despite the heavy velvet gown and cloak she wore. "What in the world is going on? Why did you ask him to wait a few months?"

"Because I have a plan." He stood, his muscular form

slowly unfolding until his dark hair brushed the roof of the pavilion and he seemed to fill the small space. The linen knotted around his waist slid low on his hips.

The rhythm of Celine's pulse shifted, fast and unsteady, and an all-too-familiar heat tingled through her. She backed up a step, turning. This was no time to let him distract her from the very practical and painful matter at hand.

"Gaston, there's no plan that could possibly let us stay married," she said quietly, moving away until the table was between them.

He followed, advancing for every step she retreated. "The King has made it possible." He faced her across the table, leaning forward to brace his arms on the scarred wood. "He was in a most generous mood. He made me a *duc.*" He shook his head, a wry grin playing about his lips. "Me. A *duc.*"

She smiled, sharing his happiness. "Congratulations," she said softly. "That's wonderful, and you deserve it. But it . . ." Her voice faltered. "It doesn't change anything between us. It can't."

His gaze held her captive, and made her tremble. He was still sweaty from the battle, his hair and beard damp with perspiration; the bandages, stained with his blood, a glaring reminder of the violence and danger he had just taken part in. She could see that he was still burning with aggression, his hard-muscled body tense with the adrenaline.

His breath guttered the candle when he finally spoke. "I want you as my wife, Celine. Now. Tomorrow. Forever. I will not lose you. I will not surrender. I will not yield."

"Do you think I want to surrender?" She clenched her fists. "Do you think I *want* to leave you here? In Lady Rosalind's arms? In her bed?"

"I do not want Rosalind, and now I do not need her. With all the King has granted me this day, I possess more lands and wealth and power than any lord could want—"

"But you *still* have to marry Rosalind. What about the important son you and she are supposed to have?"

"I have thought of that. We have the advantage, you and

I. We know what must happen in the future. We know how my son is to save this future king—the time, the place. We need simply to make certain it happens."

He came around the table, so swift and determined she didn't have a chance to move away. He reached for her, his hands taking her in that strong, sure way that made her knees weak. He held her still, tilting her face to his.

But what stole her breath even more than his touch was the raw longing in his eyes. The need.

"You could have my son." His voice shook, the urgency of his words matching the intensity in his eyes.

That stark, unguarded emotion, stronger than any she had known from him before, flowed through her like the spring wind that stirred the silk of the pavilion, sending warm longings rippling through her. Fantasies from deep within. Wishes. Dreams of how much they could share if only God granted them more time.

But her dreams were of tomorrows that could never be.

And children who would never be born.

She inhaled sharply, torn by bitter pain. "I won't be *alive* long enough to have your son if I stay! When the eclipse happens in five days, I have to—"

"You have to go," he said firmly, drawing her closer, his fingers tangling through her hair. "You have to leave me. Go to these physicians in your time and let them make you well. *But then you must come back."*

His fierce command took her completely by surprise. She had been so focused on getting home that she had never thought of that possibility.

Come back.

She could come back!

Once she had the surgery, once the bullet was out, she would have no reason to stay in the twentieth century. None. Not when she could return to him. Share his life, his future, his love. Have his children. It all swirled wildly through her mind, images of years of joy—not days or weeks, but *years.* The idea made her heart beat crazily.

"Yes! Yes, I could. I could come back. And I could even bring things with me, wonderful things! I . . ."

But even as hope swelled in her heart, reality invaded.

Questions. Problems. She shut her eyes, willing the concerns away, but they tore apart his glorious plan with sharp, unrelenting claws.

Gently she raised one hand to his chest, feeling his heart thundering beneath her palm. She opened her eyes, aching. "Gaston, I'm . . . I'm not sure it would work. If there's one thing I've learned, it's that time-travel isn't an exact science. There's no way of knowing if I could get back to this year again. What if I missed? What if it fails? You can't wait for me forever."

His fingers moved restlessly over her cheeks, her jaw, her throat. "I can," he said hoarsely. "Forever."

His declaration made tears spring to her eyes. She lifted both hands and laced her fingers through his. "But we can't take the chance that it might not work. Even if we could, even if it did work, we can't play Russian roulette with history—"

"Russian what?"

"It's a game of chance. A *deadly* game. And that's exactly what we'd be doing if I came back, if you stayed married to me instead of marrying Rosalind. The book says you're supposed to have a son with Lady R—not with me. Who knows how the future might change if it were *our* son instead of yours and Rosalind's?"

She started to pull away, but he captured her wrists, his callused palms rough against her skin. "I will not wed Rosalind."

"But you—"

"I will not wed her. I do not understand these feelings in my heart, but I cannot deny them any longer—"

"Gaston, don't do this! Not now. Not when we have no time left. Don't make me wish for what can never be. You've got to stay here and marry Rosalind, and I've got to go *home.*"

The last word came out as a breathy sob. She realized in that moment that the twentieth century was no longer her home. And never would be again.

Her home was here, with him, the man she loved.

And any other place in the world or in time, without

him, would never be anything more than a bleak, cold shell.

His face was lined with strain, his fingers flexing around her wrists as he pulled her against his body. "I care for you, Celine." His voice became rough. "Deeply."

She tucked in her chin as her tears began to fall, and rested her forehead on his bare chest. She had thought she would never hear those words from him, the ones she had waited for, wished for. "But we were never meant to happen," she whispered raggedly. "And I'm going to spend the rest of my life thinking of you, remembering you, every hour of every day. And I don't want to think of you here alone, Gaston, waiting for me. That would kill me just as easily as the bullet in my back. I want you to *live,* the same fierce, reckless, passionate way you've always—"

"Naught will be the same for me." His hold on her shifted, his arms sliding around her back, pulling her in tight. "Naught will ever be the same without you. There will be no passion left. No life."

"But there has to be," she said just as fiercely, raising her head. "You have to find it. Fight for it. I want you to find happiness, with your son, with your . . . family. I . . ." She could hardly speak through her tears. "I want you to have *love.*"

"I want no love but yours." His own eyes were glistening. "And I will love no other but you."

"Gaston—"

He crushed her close as his mouth swept down on hers, his kiss branding her, claiming her, the rough penetration of his tongue sudden, possessive, deep. A low, sobbing breath echoed in her throat, her hands sliding through the thicket of hair on his chest, her lips opening to him as his words shimmered through her, magnificent and unbearable. *I will love no other but you.*

He loved her. This warrior knight who had fought the idea with all the strength he possessed, who had deflected every bit of feeling as if it were a lethal sword stroke, *loved her.* He had once scoffed at the word, but now he used it.

With tears in his eyes.

And it ran wild through her, like a fever, engulfing her heart and body and soul. She twined her fingers through his damp hair and returned his kiss, taking his mouth as he took hers, her tongue plunging, tasting, curving around his. But even as they came together in scorching need, a wrenching thought tormented her.

Five days from now, she would never be able to touch him again. She would be robbed of these kisses, torn from this heat of love and longing, wrested from the soul-satisfying wholeness of being his.

Shattering images of countless years alone sliced into her thoughts, all the cold days and colder nights alone stretching out before her, her heart as empty as her body. This might be the last memory they could share, their last moment of stolen glory.

As if he read her mind, he moved suddenly, backing her toward the table, lifting her onto it. She cried out into his mouth, twisting in his arms, wanting him even as she resisted. They *couldn't*. It was too dangerous. There was nothing between them and the men outside but the flimsy silk walls of the pavilion. Someone could walk in on them at any moment. And if they were caught, there would be no annulment, not now, not in a few months, not ever.

But there was no stopping him. He tore the linen he wore from around his hips and gathered her in, holding her as if he meant to make her his until day and night and all time spun out and they were still one. One body, one breath, one love, united against the forces that threatened to tear them apart. Defiant in the face of time, fate, death, destiny.

She could feel his heart pumping, his hunger and force-fulness and love all mingled in his touch, his kiss. She could feel the hardness and heat of him, the sweat on his body—and the blood from his wounds. She knew he had to be in pain, and made a sound of protest. How could he think of making love when he was hurt?

But he never even flinched. His hand left her just long enough to knock the candle out of the way, sending it tumbling to the dirt floor. It sputtered out, cloaking them in darkness as his fingers pulled at her bodice and his mouth covered her bare breast, suckling hard.

Celine's bruised lips parted and she gasped for air, the center of her body tightening as his rough kisses lashed her with wild, sweet sensations. In his fierce embrace, questions and worries went spinning into the distance; she was alone with him in the dark, her body arching into his as they raced headlong together toward a heaven where all dreams came true, all wishes were granted, all fantasies ignited into reality. She wanted all of it, all of him, every inch, every breath. She wanted to be his. Now. Tomorrow. Forever. *Forever his.*

He pushed up her skirts, his hand parting her thighs, opening her to the heat of him, the naked masculine power. He slid her closer until she was poised at the edge of the table, the throbbing steel of his arousal pressing against her softness. His blunt fingers stroked into her, quick and demanding, until she was shaking with longing and dampening his hand.

"Yes," she whispered with a small cry, her fingers digging into the corded muscles where his neck met his shoulders. "Yes, my love, take me," she demanded huskily, her blood running hot, her breath harsh as need swept through her like jagged lightning. "Take me and don't stop. Don't ever stop."

A growl tore from deep in his chest. He caught her wrists and pinned them behind her, taking both in one hand with an iron grip. With his other hand, he fitted himself to her, the velvety steel of him entering her the barest, most tantalizing inch. Then he speared his fingers through her hair, dragging her head to his.

He took her mouth, thrusting his tongue against hers, and joined them fully with one stroke that left them both groaning with the sweet violence of it.

He was part of her, all the length and weight and thickness of him. She kissed him, hard and hot, burning with his intensity as he locked her against him and began to thrust, deep, hard, fast. He ravished her, making love to her the same way he had fought for his life on the battlefield, with the same volatile power. It was rough and fierce and overwhelming and it swept her away and drew all her awareness into him.

She reveled in the strength of his body as he moved. The massive lines of his chest and shoulders. The raw scent of him, mingling with the softer note of her own muskiness. The wet, gliding fullness of him inside her. The tingle of her skin rubbed raw by the roughness of his beard.

He groaned and she made the same sound, her throaty growl a more delicate echo of his. Passion wiped away all awareness of pain, of danger, of anything real—how many days were left; the future; the past.

All she cared about was him. All she loved in the world was this one man. Her warrior knight. Her Black Lion. Ravenous and untamed. Tender and loving. They were together, they were alive—closer than they had ever been before, more alive than they ever would be again.

He released her wrists, his arms catching her close as her hands twined around his neck. She wrapped her legs around his hips, taking him deeper, clinging to him, her hips arching into his with each stroke. The tension that clenched deep in her belly began to unravel. He was so hard and powerful within her, his rhythm so ancient and primitive and glorious as he drove into her, mercilessly sweeping her toward the peak.

Their joined bodies heated the tent, the pounding of their hearts the only sound in the silence. Surging, straining, uncontrollable, uncontained, they moved together until all their differences vanished. Hard and soft, male and female, taking and taken, medieval and modern—all blended and melded until the world spun away and there was only the two of them and what they gave to each other. Love and passion. Two made one.

Celine clung to him, her body tightening around his as the tremors began sweeping through her. Her whispers of pleasure came out as his name and urgent pleas for him to make it last. *Now. Tomorrow. Forever.*

But neither of them could make it last. The world exploded around them in a sudden burst of brilliance as he emptied himself into her in a fierce flood, flowing, pouring deeply as she surrendered to her own release. He lifted her right off the table and she was soaring with him, far from this place, this dark pavilion. Flying in his arms, washed with hot needles of pleasure that left her shattered and whole. She felt it to the depths of her heart, just as she felt him embedded to the depths of her womanhood. Love and joy that banished all else.

Banished even the small, nagging fear that she harbored about the bargain she had made this morning—her secret bargain with God.

Chapter 26

Moonlight and night air flooded in through the window in Gaston's bedchamber. Leaning out through the open shutters, gripping the stone sill, he glared up at the blue-white orb that so dominated the tiny stars glimmering around it, the cold, distant sphere that scribes and troubadors always praised so lavishly. He wished he could rip it from the sky.

It had brought her here to him. Celine, a sweet and sudden and unexpected gift. But soon it would wrench her away just as abruptly.

In a mere four days.

That damnable, almost-full moon. He had come to think of it as an enemy, one he must battle for the greatest prize he had ever set out to win. But the shimmering silver glow was not an opponent he could fight with muscle or blade; it eluded and defied him, shining across the bare floor of his empty chamber, as if mocking how equally empty his life would soon be.

Gaston thrust himself away from the window. He stalked about restlessly, rubbing his sore shoulder, staring at the bare walls and floor. The room had been swept clean of rushes; his furnishings and belongings had been taken to his new home in the north weeks ago. Royce kept his own chamber on one of the upper floors, saying he did not feel right taking the lord's chamber when he was not and would never be a lord.

This place where Gaston had lived for more than nine years felt empty and strange. Not merely his bedchamber, but the entire chateau. Most of his servants and guardsmen were in the north, preparing their new home for their lord.

And his lady.

Who would never see it.

She would not be coming back to him. And he must marry Rosalind.

Four days. That was all they had left. Even now Celine was above, in the chamber where she had first arrived, talking with Brynna. He had sent Royce to fetch the mystic woman, to bring her here so that she and Celine could make certain all was in readiness before the dark of the moon. Gaston would take no chances with Celine's life.

Though he did not wish to be separated from her for even a moment, he had left the two women alone for their discussion. He could not listen to them plan every detail of how his wife was going to leave him.

And they did not need his help. All was proceeding vexingly well. Etienne's fever had broken, and he had been able to describe the path he had followed through the forest. Gaston's men had soon located Celine's bundle. With her garish pink pouch and her garment of topaz-colored silk, she had all she needed. To leave him. Forever.

Growling a frustrated oath, he exited the bare chamber, slamming the door behind him. He felt angry and irksome, and all the pacing and thinking he could do would make him feel no better. The two women had been planning long enough; they could continue their accursed discussion on the morrow.

He had other plans for his wife this night, and they did not involve talking.

On the floor above, he opened the door to the chamber without knocking. Celine and Brynna were having such an animated conversation, standing at the window examining the panes, it took a moment before they seemed to realize he was there.

As they turned, Gaston felt suddenly out of place, like a bull charging into a display of delicate perfume flasks at a trade fair. He remained in the doorway, his hand on the latch. "I did not wish to interrupt."

"You're not interrupting." Celine crossed the room with a bittersweet smile.

He met her halfway, wrapping an arm around her shoulders, pulling her close with a low sound. "I lied. I did wish to interrupt." Staring into the blue-gray depths of her eyes, he almost kissed her, but was mindful that they had an audience.

Then he kissed her anyway.

"By all the holy saints," Brynna gasped.

Gaston raised his head to find the mystic woman gaping at them with a look of wide-eyed astonishment.

"I'm sorry," Celine said, color rising in her cheeks. "Brynna, we didn't mean to embarrass you—"

"Nay, milady, I am not embarrassed . . . it is merely that I have not seen you and Sir—I mean you and the Duc . . . together before." She stood frozen, as if in a hypnotic daze. "Oh, sweet Mary, I may have had it wrong all along," she said breathlessly. "How could I have overlooked this?"

"May have had what wrong?" Gaston demanded.

"Overlooked what?" Celine asked at the same time.

Brynna gestured absently to Celine's belongings, stored neatly in the corner. "We thought it was the missing pouch that held you here, milady. And it . . . it may have been. Or it may have been something else. Something I never *thought* of before. But I did not know . . . I had no idea . . ."

"Of what?" Gaston asked impatiently, his gut tightening with concern.

Brynna moved closer to them, hands raised as if to make a measure, or as if she were warming her palms before a fire. "Lady Celine, you must take with you everything that you arrived with . . . you cannot leave *anything* behind."

"Like my purse?" Celine asked in confusion.

"Or your *heart.*" Brynna stopped a few feet away, squinting as if in a bright light, while her hands moved in a graceful pattern through the air. "Oh, milady, the feeling . . . it is so strong between you, I can *see* it. It is like . . . like the light and the heat of the sun. Of a hundred suns. I did not know . . . I never realized! All along we have been concentrating on the physical elements—your garment, your pouch—when *this* may be far more important."

"Not things," Celine whispered in amazement, "but emotion?"

Brynna nodded, looking worried. "I had no idea that you and your husband were so much in love."

Gaston felt as if the floor had been snatched from beneath him. His arm flexed around Celine's shoulders. "Are you saying that she cannot return home?"

"I do not know, milord. Lady Celine is the first time-traveler I have met. My father knew of dozens, but I have not his experience. All I can say is that this may be important. Never have I witnessed so strong a link between two people." Brynna shaded her eyes with one hand, as if Gaston and Celine were emitting a blinding glare. "Mayhap it was this emotional force which pulled your lady to you across time . . . and now the bond has grown so *strong—*"

"So strong that it might be unbreakable," Celine finished for her.

Gaston stared at Brynna, unable to move, unable to speak, shaken to his core by what she had said—that it might be *him* holding Celine in this time. That his love might cause her death.

But Celine seemed strangely calm.

"Celine?" He finally moved, drawing her in, tilting her face to his with one hand. Mayhap she was dazed with shock.

"It's all right, Gaston." She gazed at him, her eyes clear, her voice steady. "I'm fine."

"Milord, there is still hope," Brynna said helplessly. "It may hold her here—or it may not."

"We'll find out in four days." Celine slid her arms around his ribs and hugged him. "One way or the other."

Gaston felt like shaking her. How could she be so calm, with her life hanging in the balance? "Brynna, if you would excuse us," he said, fighting to keep his voice even, "I would speak to my wife alone."

"Aye, milord." Brynna walked around them, still gazing at them with a look of awe. "I am late in attending to

Etienne—I promised that I would make an herbal for him, to help him regain his strength more quickly. Milady? We will speak again on the morrow?"

"Yes. Thank you for all your help, Brynna."

The mystic woman curtsied and went to the door. As it closed behind her, Gaston took a deep breath before he could speak.

"Help?" he said sarcastically. "Celine, do you not understand what she has told us? What it means? If you cannot return home, you will—"

"I know," she said calmly. "But I'm not afraid."

He could not voice his reply to that.

I am.

He released her and turned away, battling an emotion unlike any he had felt before. Not in all the times he had nearly lost his own life in battle had he known the cold, bitter taste of fear on his tongue. But he knew it now.

"By nails and blood, I will not accept it so easily," he growled. "I will fight. We will find a solution. We shall stay away from one another. Bury our feelings."

"Shut down all the emotions we have for each other? Pretend there's nothing between us? Like we were blowing out a candle?"

He jerked around. "Aye! And I will leave here. Ride as far as Pharaon can last. In four days at a fast gallop, I—"

"Gaston." Her lashes dusted her cheeks, then lifted. "Do you really think that would work?" she asked softly.

He clenched his jaw, fought for breath against the iron bands of fear closing around his chest. He knew the truth of it: once, weeks ago, such pretense might have succeeded, but not now.

"Nay," he choked out in agony.

She moved toward him, her lips touched by a gentle smile. "We'll know whether the eclipse will work when the eclipse happens. In four days. Until then there's no sense in worrying about it. Worrying won't change anything."

He watched her draw closer, her movements strong and graceful, her slender form showing not even the smallest whit of a tremor. He could not help feeling a surge of love and pride at her courage. "You truly feel no fear, my brave lady?"

"You've taught me a lot, my brave knight."

They came together in a tender embrace, not speaking for a long moment.

"You really *have* taught me a lot, Gaston," she whispered after a time. "I was just thinking this morning that I haven't had a panic attack in weeks—and it's not just your breathing techniques that have helped me. It's something else."

"Pray tell, what great wisdom have I imparted?" he asked with a pained laugh.

"That when you have something important to do, you should simply do it. Because fear is a useless emotion that doesn't change anything." She rested her cheek against his chest. "And life is too short and too precious to spend any of it being afraid."

He found it difficult to speak past the lump in his throat.

"Gaston, we only have four days left, and I don't want to spend them being afraid."

He tilted her chin up on the edge of his fist. "Then we shall feel no fear, my lady of fire. We shall take this time and seize it with both hands and make it ours."

"Pretend that we have all the rest of our lives."

"With naught to keep us apart."

"No bullet," she whispered. "No eclipse. No Lady R."

"Naught but the two of us." He slowly lowered his head. "Forever."

His mouth closed over hers and she responded with a hungry sigh, and they melded and became one in a deep, gentle joining. Not breaking the kiss, he bent and scooped her into his arms.

"*Gaston,*" she protested against his mouth. "If you keep picking me up, you're going to tear out your stitches, and I don't think the barber-surgeon would appreciate—"

"Burn the surgeon. I care naught for the ache in my shoulder, wife—it is the ache elsewhere that requires swift attention." He nimbly opened the door. "And I will not make love to you in this chamber."

He shut the portal solidly behind them.

Chapter 27

They needed naught more than a makeshift bed and a fire in the hearth. As he stoked the roaring flames, Gaston thought that his barren chamber had never felt so comfortable, so complete, even when it had been filled with rich furnishings and tapestries. Celine knelt beside him, on the thick pile of sable and wolf and marten fur throws he had gathered, gazing up at him. Awaiting his touch.

She wrought a spell on his room, on his life. Astonishing, the magic a wife could weave, simply with her presence. Her eyes sparkled with wonder and love, as if he were more worthy of worship than a god, more desirable than all the jewels and riches she might ever possess, more important to her than breath.

Had he once feared that she would make him less of a man? he wondered as looked down at her, his hand straying through her hair. She looked at him as if he were the light of sun, moon, and stars all in one. Never had he been more aware of his masculine strength, his warrior's body, his muscle, hardness, experience, power. He saw it all, and more, reflected in her eyes, as the hearth flames made shadows dance around them in the darkness.

He knelt in front of her, sliding his fingertips over her temples, her cheeks, her neck . . . lower.

Celine closed her eyes as he eased the velvet gown off her shoulders. "Every time," she whispered, "you make me feel brand new."

His throat closed. Had any king, any Saracen desert prince, any emperor of the East ever possessed such a treasure? She was sweetness and innocence. Pale as snow, del-

331

icate as spring's first petals. And she was flame and intoxication. More potent than wine in his blood, hot as a blaze when she burned.

He kissed the bared hollow of her throat, inhaling the scent of lavender and thyme and roses that lingered from her morning bath. "This time, I want to make it last, *ma chère*. All night."

"All night," she agreed in a sultry whisper.

He slid her gown lower, gently pulling it down her arms, letting the jewel-bright fabric fall to her waist. She was glorious. Half nude yet unashamed of her nakedness, her hair shimmering flame-red in the firelight, the tresses grown longer in her time here, curling beneath her shoulders. Her breasts trembled before him, full and taut, the rosy tips puckering to hardness even as he watched.

He could see her breathing deepen, felt his own match hers.

"I would tell you that you are as beautiful as a goddess," he said reverently, touching her, running one finger slowly from the kiss-dampened hollow of her throat, over one breast, to the other. "But it would be a lie, for you are more beautiful. Even a goddess would envy you. Even a poet could do you no justice . . . and I am no poet."

For the first time in his life, he wished that he were. Wished that he had skill with words rather than with weapons. That he could describe the shy smile that his compliment brought to her lips, the sweep of her lashes as they lifted, the blush that colored her cheeks so charmingly. The beat of his heart became heavy, demanding.

He continued his slow path, down her ribs, lower. She felt like honey and cream. Sweet. Smooth. He rested his hand at her waist, caressing and kneading the flare of her hip as his eyes lingered over her. He longed to taste her, to take one of those trembling, proud peaks into his mouth, to hear her small gasps and cries of pleasure, leave the nipple glistening and hard from his kisses. Fighting the throbbing urgency in his groin, he held himself in check. This would last, even if he died of it.

He grasped a fistful of the velvet piled about her slender

curves. "Let me see you, Celine," he commanded softly. "All of you."

He held the gown as she rose. The heavy fabric slid down her legs, revealing each enticing inch in slow splendor. She left the garment at her feet, stepping out of it, truly a goddess of elegance and grace. Hearth fire and moonlight battled to bathe her skin in gold and silver.

She stood before him, ran her hands down her sides and up again, not brazen, but comfortable in her body; the curve of her lips told him she found pleasure in the way he looked at her. His shaft felt almost painful as it pressed against the restriction of his leggings.

His every muscle rigid, he caught her hand and pulled her down until she was kneeling before him again. She exhaled a small sigh at the feel of the furs against her nakedness, the sound like a warm caress all down his body.

He stopped touching her just long enough to remove his tunic, but before he could pull it over his head, she covered his hand with hers.

"Let me," she asked softly.

He released his hold on the garment, and allowed her slender fingers to do the work. She lifted it, sliding her palms up over his chest, his arms, as slowly as he had undressed her, her touch a glittering heat that warmed his skin more than the fire.

She dropped the garment to one side and reached for his leggings, pausing, her eyes meeting his, the color in her cheeks deepening. He swallowed hard, controlling himself ruthlessly, though the feel of her hand there, so close to that part of him that throbbed with awareness of her, was almost more than he could endure.

Keeping his gaze fastened on her face rather than her fingers, he braced his arms behind him to balance his weight, and allowed her to continue disrobing him. She gently peeled off the leggings, careful not to jar his bandaged thigh. He closed his eyes and groaned when his arousal sprang free. He heard her quick intake of breath.

And her feminine murmur of appreciation.

It almost undid him.

But before he could sit up and reach for her, intending

to turn her murmurs into sighs with his mouth and hands, she placed her palm firmly on his chest and gently pushed him down into the furs.

He stared up at her with a quirked brow and a growl of surprise; he was used to being in command of every encounter . . . but the way she was smiling down at him, her hand stroking his chest while her gaze swept slowly, hungrily along his prone body, made him lie still, intrigued.

"My lion," she whispered. "My Black Lion."

He caught her hand and nibbled at her fingertips. "Beware, lion's lady, for your predator is hungry tonight. He may not wait long before devouring you."

"Devouring me?" she asked, challenge gleaming in her eyes. "What if I devour him first?"

Her husky tone made his blood run hot. And the suggestion she was making—if that was indeed what she meant—but nay, it could not be. The thought of his sweet Celine, her soft, full lips . . . the shocking image burned him like a brand, seized him with violent desire.

She bent near, rubbing her cheek against the hair of his chest. *"Please,"* she whispered, kissing him, her silken red tresses cascading over his body.

A hundred searing tendrils of pleasure whipped through him. The idea of relinquishing control over their lovemaking was new to him, but he began to find the thought as arousing as it was unfamiliar. Never had he lain passive beneath a woman's hands, her mouth, allowing her hunger, her feminine demands, to determine what would happen and when.

Deciding to explore the possibilities, he lay back more fully in the furs, folding his hands behind his head, knowing that control could be his once more the second he wanted it. He returned her smile with a slow, lazy grin of his own, his shaft pulsing. "Have your way with me, lioness."

Her breath came out as a low sigh. Her tongue ran over her bottom lip.

He clenched his teeth to stop a groan, fighting all the instincts that urged him to take her in his arms and pin her beneath him; this new passiveness might prove more difficult than he had thought.

He managed to hold himself still for the moment, while she curled her fingers through the thatch of black hair covering the flat muscles of his chest, her eyes fascinated.

"My lion . . . yet in some ways, you are a lamb."

"Lamb?" He scowled with mock ire.

"Yes." Her smile widened. "Would you like me to show you what I mean?"

Keeping a tight leash on his hunger, he granted her permission.

"Show me."

Her fingers slid lightly over the bristly hair and muscles beneath her palm. "Here, you are most definitely lion. All strength and power." She quieted when she came to his nipples, teased them with her fingertips.

Then she bent her head and flicked them with her tongue.

He sucked in a breath, speared by a hot blade of pleasure that went straight to his groin. She nibbled at him, suckled, and the heat of her mouth, the wet brush of her tongue, drew a ravenous sound from his throat. He kept his hands at his sides only with fierce effort.

"You even sound like a lion," she murmured approvingly, her warm, moist breath impossibly arousing over his heated flesh.

She stretched out more comfortably at his side, snuggling up against him. Gaston thought he would go mad at the feel of her pearl-tipped breasts pressing into his ribs, the triangle of curls below rubbing against his hip.

"Celine . . ." he warned with a low, rumbling sound, deep in his chest.

"Mmm, I like to hear you roar," she breathed, running her hand up over his shoulders, to his neck. She paused to trace the muscles there, as if she took deep pleasure in every inch of him. "No lamb to be found here. Very much a lion." She caressed his bearded cheeks. "And here . . . I love your mane, Gaston. So thick and dark, and very rough. And very handsome."

He tried unsuccessfully to nip at her fingers. "You would not have me shave it?"

"No," she said with a firm shake of her head. "I like how it feels when you kiss me."

"When I kiss you . . . where?"

Her eyes met his, smoldering. "Anywhere," she said softly. "Everywhere."

The spear of pleasure went through him again, hot and sharp. Never had he encountered a woman who could blush with innocence, yet enjoy her own sensuality so fully, speak of it so openly. She was a maze of contrasts, his Celine. A jewel with a thousand precious facets. If he spent a lifetime with her, he would not discover every one.

But they did not have a lifetime.

He forced the thought away, remembering their promise to each other.

Her hands kept moving on their tantalizing path. "I believe I have found a lamb spot," she said triumphantly, tickling the sensitive skin behind his ear.

He grinned, giving in to a small shudder of pleasure. "One," he conceded. "No more."

"No, two." She lowered her head and kissed his other earlobe, nibbling.

He found it an incredibly arousing sensation, her small teeth sampling him. Without conscious thought, he touched her, unable to resist the urge to slide his arm around her back, pull her close.

"Aha, another lamb spot," she declared, wiggling free of his hold. "Two, in fact . . . here." She ran her fingers down his arm until she reached the softer skin on the inside of his elbow, where the veins pulsed closest to the surface. She watched his lifeblood throbbing, then slanted him a sidelong glance, her eyes large and melting.

Taking his hand in both of hers, she kissed his callused palm. "And here. Here you are both lion and lamb. It's here that you hold a sword or a lance . . . yet it's here that you're so tender when you touch me. Fierce . . . and gentle."

Her words were like a warm rain that flooded his soul. *Fierce and gentle.* Warrior and loving husband. Two in one. He never would have believed it possible, that his softer side could exist at peace with his battle-skill. That he could give in to one without risking the other. But she had made it true.

When she released his hand and lowered her head to his, he met her lips in a ravenous, demanding kiss, but she barely allowed him a taste of her before she lifted her mouth.

And began to taste him.

"There is one part of you," she whispered, leaving a path of wet, openmouthed kisses down his neck, his chest, "that is undeniably lion."

His breath came in sharply. He grasped fistfuls of the wolf pelt beneath him, the only way he could prevent himself from pulling her astride him. He was rampantly hard by the time she followed the narrowed path of hair over his belly, teasing him with her lips and tongue. Her words and kisses left no doubt as to what she intended, and the thought alone almost brought a spasm of release.

His body went taut with strain beneath her. "Celine . . ." he rasped on a dry throat. Control threatened to slip from him.

She skipped over the bandage at his waist and followed the dark hair to the throbbing part of him that so ached for her sweet attentions. She lifted her mouth from him, not touching him, silent.

The waiting stretched out, racking him with fire-tipped needles of pleasure, on the very edge of pain.

Her hand found him first, gliding along the hard length of him, gently, tentatively.

A groan rent from deep in his chest. She stroked him with the lightest, petal-soft touch, and his hips thrust upward.

"Here," she said reverently, wonderingly, "here you are very much lion."

He could not reply. He had no voice, no mind, no breath. There was naught but the drumming of his heart and the explosive ecstasy of her touch as she rubbed the velvety tip, making a small, intrigued sound at the drop of moisture there. She explored him, tracing the throbbing veins, circling him with her fingers, so curious, so sensual and yet innocent. When her hand tightened, sliding slowly up and down, he knew he could bear no more.

But then she shifted beside him, turning.

And he knew there was more to bear. Too much more. He could feel her breath fanning over him, the heat more arousing than aught he had ever imagined in his life. He went rigid beneath her, dangerously close to release. *"Celine!"*

"Shh, my lion," she urged. "I wish to know all of you. *All of you.*"

And then she kissed him.

A tentative kiss at first, a cautious brush of her lips, sampling the tip. A strangled oath tore from his throat.

Then she took him into her mouth. Drew him in to that hot, wet satin. Took him deep, sighing.

Gaston gasped for life, for air, unable to breathe in that intense, mindless, reckless moment. The sensations of her lips and tongue giving him such carnal pleasure ... so shamelessly, so fully, a giving that was simple and joyous ...

He felt the gathering forces within him tighten and rise. *"Nay,"* he choked out, trying to sit up, blindly reaching for her.

Too late. With a last, laving brush of her tongue, she lifted her head, eyes sparkling like smoky jewels, just as he felt his body jerk with an uncontrollable shudder. He fell back, letting the spasm take him, feeling the rush of heat and pleasure rip through his body, flowing outward in a wave of savage release that swept him almost to the edge of unconsciousness, his ecstasy doubled a thousand-fold by the way his shameless lady sat watching him, her glistening lips parted and her voice a soft moan.

When he finally came back to himself, spent, gasping, she was beside him, smiling at him like a satisfied cat ... like a lioness.

"You even taste like a lion," she whispered wickedly. "All salty and hot and wild."

His response was a low roar as he pinned her in the furs, his mouth ravishing hers, his hands hungrily grasping her fire-warmed curves while she shivered in pleasure. His fingers flicked over her breasts, tugging the tips to erect hardness. He kissed her ear, biting the tender lobe. His hand slid down her belly to the soft petals below, parting her, finding her wet and welcoming merely from having pleasured him.

"Aye, my lady lioness," he growled. "And you are lamb as well."

She made broken little cries as he touched her. "Isn't it . . . wonderful that . . . I'm so very much lamb where . . . you are so very much lion?"

"We fit together perfectly." He pressed his hips against her, already hard for her again.

"Yes, my lion." She wimpered as he caressed her. "Yes, now, please. *Please.*"

He withdrew his hand, smiling at her hungrily. "Not so quickly, my demanding lady. I mean to enjoy every inch of you first."

With a sound of disappointment, she arched her hips against his, her hands sliding down his back to his buttocks. He moved out of reach and sat up, kneeling on the furs.

"I want you on your knees, *ma chère,*" he ordered huskily.

Her heavy-lashed eyes were languid as she looked up at him, reaching for him, trying to draw him back down.

"On your knees. *Now.*"

She inhaled at the sudden command, eyes wide and dark. He could see the flush of excitement that went through her body at the way he took control so aggressively.

Shivering, she obeyed, rising to kneel before him.

He edged closer, leaving a scant space between them, his eyes never leaving hers.

Touching her with only one hand, he ran his fingers downward from her breast to her hip to her thigh, over her knee, back along her leg until he felt the round hardness of her heel, the sensitive sole of her foot. Her toes. She wiggled them and he subdued a smile.

"Be still," he whispered, drawing his fingers along the return path.

When he reached her thigh, he let his hand rest there for a moment, his gaze dropping to the red curls that concealed her tender core. He looked up slowly, and drank in the storm of desire in her eyes, the glittering gray and blue. The anticipation.

He withdrew his hand, letting her wonder, for a moment, what he might do, how he might pleasure her. Letting the need coil tighter within her.

"Part your thighs, *ma chère.*"

With a breathy little moan, she obeyed, the color in her cheeks deepening. She separated her knees, spreading her legs just wide enough to admit his hand there, the rise and fall of her bosom quickening.

"More, my sweet lioness. Wider," he ordered in a deep, quiet voice, not yet touching her. "Let me see all of you. Aye, like that. *Aye.* Now lean back. Lean back and open for me."

She submitted to his every command, her pale body trembling; she moved her hands behind her in a way that thrust her breasts forward. Gaston felt a tremor deep inside him, felt his shaft swell with his lifeblood. She was a vision, kneeling before him, a smooth arch of ivory, head tilted back and eyes closed, thighs parted. The sight of her so vulnerable and trusting dazzled him, filled him with desire and love and sharp blades of need.

He reached for her with one hand, slowly, slid his fingers into the rough silk of her soft mound, groaning even as she did. He gazed at his dark hand possessing her tender womanhood, and thought he had never seen anything more beautiful.

She gasped, a sharp little inhalation as he penetrated her dampness.

"Hold on to the furs," he ordered in a low, deep voice. "Hold tight."

She did as he bade, gripping the wolf pelt beneath her. He stroked into her deeply. Her tiny white teeth closed over her bottom lip, but she could not hold back a moan as he began exploring her at his leisure, sampling her depths with gentle care. He listened to her small cries, feeling each one all the way to his soul, experiencing as much bliss as he was bestowing.

He was patient and relentless, fondling and teasing until she writhed helplessly, her body undulating, her breath broken, her hands tearing at the furs beneath her. He felt his own muscles strain with longing, but he did not allow himself to touch her with aught but his hand, knowing he would be lost the moment their bodies came together.

All night. It was a promise he meant to keep. He wanted to love her for hour after sweet hour. Wanted to watch every cherished inch of her catch fire as he lavished all his power and passion on her.

When she was panting and pleading with wanting, he found and captured her small, delicate bud between two fingers, urging it to fullness. She uttered what sounded like an oath, opening her eyes, gazing at him with a demanding, feminine look, her lashes half lowered, her lips parted. It was almost more than he could bear, that expression, the pleading, the scent of her desire, the musky feminine perfume of her that mingled with the woodsmoke from the fire.

He almost gave in to both of them, almost pressed her down into the furs and buried himself in her tight heat; his body shuddered, but he held himself back. He had known many pleasures in his life, but this feeling of desire mingled with love was still new to him, and he wanted to explore it fully, slowly, giving them both time. *Time.*

Her hips began to move, helpless little thrusting motions, as he delved lightly into her, the pad of his thumb gliding over her sensitive petals. He alternated his tender caresses with sudden, deep thrusts, echoing the joining that would soon take place.

Soon. So very soon.

He plucked gently at the throbbing bud, drawing it forth from her curls, teasing it, stroking the tip with his slick fingers. She groaned his name, her body stretching taut. He released her but for the pad of his thumb, flicking at the swollen nubbin with a butterfly touch, fast and light.

She cried out, a sharp, short gasp. Another. Another. He watched, entranced, as a shudder of release went through her and a flush of heat swept her body, tremor after tremor cascading along her slender limbs as she gasped his name over and over. He caught her close, still kneeling.

She threaded her fingers through the hair at the nape of his neck and covered his mouth and cheeks and bearded chin and jaw with kisses. His hands slid down her back to her hips, pressing her against him as he whispered words of passion.

He lifted her, still kneeling but moving himself into position so that his rampant arousal barely parted her soft heat. She uttered a low moan of longing.

"I was made to be here," he groaned, sliding into her a mere inch, into the honey-sweet tightness of her sheath. "Here forever."

"Yes. Forever. *Yes.*"

It was the last word she managed before she closed her eyes and opened her lips for his kiss. He took her mouth with fierce desire, clasping her against him as his body joined to hers . . . slowly . . . so slowly.

He thrust partway into her, then pulled back . . . almost all the way . . . then pressed forward, not quite as far, before he withdrew again.

She made a small cry of objection. He went still and she writhed against him, her hips shifting, trying to take him deeper.

"Nay, Black Lion's lady." He chuckled wickedly, sliding forward a pulsing, tormenting inch. "I mean to discover just how long I can make this last . . ." He withdrew again. "How many times I can bring you to a glorious, fiery peak . . ." He sheathed half his length, then pulled back just as far. "Before this night is through, I mean to make my lioness roar."

It was a very long time later before he thrust himself fully, deeply within her, there in his empty bedchamber, on their bed of furs, with the fire bathing their sweat-sheened bodies in molten gold.

But he made good on his vow.

He lightly kissed her hair, her cheek, letting her sleep. She lay curled next to him, her head pillowed on his arm, his hand at her waist. He had pulled one of the fur throws over them to keep her warm, firmly tucking her close.

He had kept her awake most of the night, loving her in every way he knew, exploring every inch of her body, every secret longing of her heart, every sensual facet of her soul. She fit his body so perfectly. Fit beside him so perfectly. Fit his *life* so perfectly.

She made him feel as if each day were his first. Made him feel . . .

He knew he was but a man, higher than some, lower than others, more familiar with sin and violence than most—yet she made him feel noble and good and whole. And loved.

Why had God chosen him to be blessed with such a gift, only to steal it away?

The anger flooded in, the resentment. He had done his best to banish the question, but it raked his heart now. What cruel ruse was it for God to have deposited Celine Fontaine in his bed? To have allowed him to fall in love with her stubborn spirit, her intelligence, her beauty, the way she so boldly defied him, the way she gave herself to him so completely?

The odd hats. And strange foods stuck to the buttresses in his kitchen. And feminine giggles late at night echoing through his great hall.

The way she wiggled her toes. And the smoky gleam in her eyes when she kissed him so shamelessly.

And the fact that she fit beside him now, like she was meant to be there.

What sort of vengeful God could do this, give them this taste of heaven and hell? Bring her here, only to take her back.

Or take her life.

He felt an unfamiliar moisture on his cheeks. He could not reach up to wipe it away, did not want to take his hands from her even long enough for that.

God's blood, was this what *love* truly meant? He had had *illnesses* that had not made him feel this bad—his stomach churning, his chest aching, his heart beating painfully against his ribs. Exhausted as he was, he could not sleep. He had not eaten since breaking fast yesterday morn, yet he had no appetite for food.

Was this what Gerard and Avril had felt for each other?

Was this what Avril felt every day—the anguish, the loss? By sweet holy Christ, how did she live with it? And how could he have been so arrogant to insist that she re-marry?

He tightened his arm around Celine, knowing that what he felt now was a mere shadow of the agony he would feel in four days . . .

Three, he realized, watching the sun's first tentative rays seep in beneath the window.

Three days.

He buried his face in her hair, feeling a wrenching pain straight up the center of his body. What use was love, he thought angrily, if it would not prevent him from losing her? His wife, his lady of fire, his lioness, his love.

"I will not yield, *ma roussette,*" he whispered as dawn's light burnished her tresses to brilliant copper-red.

His little redhead. The name seemed to sum up all the others, captured her fire and spirit, her sweetness and vul-nerability, better than "wife" or "lioness" or "Lady Celine" or aught else he had ever called her.

He murmured it again, nuzzling her hair, unable to stop the tears on his cheeks. "I love you and I will not yield, my Lady Roussette."

Chapter 28

A warm afternoon breeze wafted through the apricot grove, playing leafy music in the branches overhead. Celine sighed and kept her eyes closed, almost dozing, enjoying the feeling of the fresh air on her cheeks almost as much as the glide of Gaston's fingers through her hair. She sat curled up beside him, her head on his chest, while he leaned back against a tree trunk.

It felt like one of the lazy, summery days she had spent at her grandparents' sprawling country estate as a kid. Snoozing on a grassy hillside. Nothing to do and plenty of it. Nothing to interrupt the perfect blend of peace and sun and endless time.

She wasn't going to let anything ruin this day. Or the two more that were left.

Not even the dull, throbbing ache in her lower back.

She had first noticed it a couple of hours ago; it was similar to the nagging pain she had had once before, when they had been at Avril's. Since that feeling had gone away after a couple of days, she wasn't going to let it worry her this time.

No fear. They had promised each other that.

The pain wouldn't have occupied her mind at all . . . except that it reminded her of the secret bargain she had made with God. Her desperate prayer when Gaston's life had been in danger.

"Are you enjoying your 'ride,' wife?" her husband asked with a soft chuckle, interrupting her thoughts.

"Very much," she replied, eyes still closed. Their plan to test Gaston's theory of lovemaking on horseback had changed as soon as Celine stepped outside and caught the scent of the apricot blossoms. Once in the grove, she didn't want to leave.

Just sitting here with him as evening descended, amid the lush green scents of spring that carried on the gentle wind ... it was as exquisite, as wonderful in its own way, as making love to him. She found happiness in simply being here with him, listening to the steady beat of his heart, feeling the rise and fall of his chest.

This, she thought sleepily, was love: that they found the same satisfaction in sharing the afternoon in quiet, companionable silence as they found in sharing their bodies with fiery, intense passion. That they were equally comfortable with silence or words, peace or excitement. That each hour seemed sweeter than the last.

Gaston had been in an exceptionally good mood all day, smiling, laughing, teasing her. Happy. She had never seen him quite so at ease before. After waking up very late, they had taken breakfast in his room; then he had left for an hour to see to some important business which he said couldn't wait. He had returned as soon as he could, and after lunch, had whiled away an hour teaching her the finer points of backgammon.

Celine had introduced a new twist: strip backgammon.

He had taken to it with a roguish grin and a gambler's skill, winning easily. As she had known he would. Her heart had skipped a beat when he insisted on claiming the brazen prize she had wagered ... as she had hoped he would.

It was one steamy bathtub and a long time later before she noticed that the castle had become rather noisy. Stonemasons, Gaston had explained; they were making some much-needed improvements on the upper floors. That was when he had suggested a ride in the peace and quiet of the warm April afternoon, and they had ended up here in the apricot grove instead.

"I believe the craftsmen should soon be done for the day." Gaston stretched and yawned.

"That doesn't mean we have to go back inside, does it?" She reluctantly opened one eye.

"Aye, it does," he said, grinning down at her, an odd

gleam in his dark gaze. "I would like you to see their work and offer an opinion."

Celine sat up and let him draw her to her feet, sighing, reluctant to leave their little garden paradise. It really did feel like a Garden of Eden—not just this grove, but this place, this time. Felt as if they were the first man and woman, as if no one else had ever loved this way before.

But soon, she would be cast out of paradise.

She forced the thought away, ignored it as she ignored the steady, throbbing ache in her back.

The moment they entered the castle, she could hear the workmen still hammering away upstairs. "I think you spoke too soon," she said over the din, covering her ears. "They sound like they're going to demolish the entire place."

"Wait here." He had to sign it as well as say it before she understood.

He bounded up the spiral stair, and a few minutes later, the noise stopped. A short while after that, he reappeared and took her hand. "Come," he insisted, smiling broadly. "I think you will like this."

Celine doubted that; she had little knowledge of medieval construction, and no idea what opinion of value she could possibly offer. She went along to humor him. What *was* it about tools and home repair that men seemed to find so endlessly fascinating? Apparently it was a male trait that held true through the ages.

A half-dozen sweaty, dusty stonemasons passed them, carrying their tools in bundles on their backs, as she and Gaston ascended the steps. They bowed to her, smiling. She became even more puzzled upon reaching the floor above: the torches had all been extinguished, leaving the corridor in darkness, except for one that still burned at the far end of the hallway.

One last craftsman was there, standing on a crude ladder, a cloth in his hand. From where she stood, it looked like he was polishing whatever it was he had been working on. The floor around him was littered with heavy-looking iron hammers and chisels.

"Why are all the lights out?" she whispered to Gaston,

not knowing why she was whispering, just that it seemed appropriate for the mysterious atmosphere. They walked forward and she could feel stone chips beneath her slippered feet. "How am I supposed to offer an opinion if I can't *see* anything?"

"It is to be a surprise."

He led her down the hall until they were directly beneath the man on the ladder.

"Milord." The stonemason nodded politely as he climbed down. "Milady."

"Thank you for your quick work, Perrin," Gaston said. "You and your apprentices have done a fine job."

"We shall be finished within two days, milord, if not on the morrow."

"Excellent."

Celine barely heard their conversation. She was staring up at the wall the man had been working on—realizing only now that it was the arch over the door that he had been polishing. A chill shivered across her shoulders. She felt stunned. Frozen.

He had been carving letters. Two letters.

G and R, entwined.

And every curve, every graceful swirl, looked exactly like it had the last time she had seen the initials—in 1993.

"W-what . . ." Her mind and heart reeling with confusion, Celine turned to face Gaston as the master craftsman left them alone. But her husband had taken the torch and was walking down the corridor, lighting the others. As the flames illuminated the hall, she could see the same letters over every arch, every door.

"What h-have y-you . . ." she stuttered. "H-how c-could you . . ."

"The idea struck me last night." He smiled as he came back toward her.

"But how could you *know?*" she gasped, whirling to stare at the engraving over her head again. "I never described the initials to you. I never even told you about them! But they look exactly the same. Every detail!" She glanced at him as he drew near, her surprise turning to hurt. "Gaston . . . why would you do this *now?* For you and *Rosalind?* Why—"

"It is not for her. It is for you," he said firmly. "You, *my Lady Roussette.* I thought of you by that name last night while you slept, and I knew that was how I would always think of you." He put the torch back in its bracket and stepped closer, tilting her face up to his with one hand. "But it was not until this morn that I realized the import of that name. I summoned the craftsmen to have them mark the letters over every arch—because as they are part of the stone, and will be forever, you are part of me. It is *you* who are meant to be my wife, Roussette. *You* are my Lady R."

"But I can't be! The book said—"

"Nay. Do you not remember?" He went down the hall to the guest room, and returned with the guidebook from her purse. He handed it to her. "Read it, my love. Tell me again what it says."

Celine took the guidebook with trembling fingers. "This can't be true. I can't be Lady R. It's *Rosalind.* It has to be." She opened to the page that talked about Gaston and his wife and their important son. "Here. It says right here—" She pointed and started reading. " 'Seldom did the chroniclers of the medieval period record the names of women, who were not seen to be as important as men when it came to the matter of making history, and that is the case with the wife of Sir Gaston de Varennes. History has recorded her only as Lady R, but the couple provides—' "

"That is the line. Read it again."

"The couple provides one of the most interesting and little-known—' "

"Nay, the one before."

She frowned up at him, still not understanding, then looked down at the book again. " 'History has recorded her only as Lady R.' "

"Again."

Celine's heart began to beat fast. " 'History has recorded her only as Lady R.' "

"Lady R. It does not mention Rosalind at all," he said

triumphantly. "We assumed that your chroniclers meant that I was to wed Lady Rosalind, but that is not what it says. It is *you*, my love." He buried his fingers in her hair. "You and I who are meant to have a son who will one day save a king's life. You, my Roussette, whom I will love as I love no other."

The book slipped from Celine's numb fingers and fell amid the stone chips and dust on the floor. What she had pretended as a child, had dreamed of all her life when she looked up at those entwined letters . . . of a dark knight on a charger who would sweep her away . . . of a love so strong, so legendary, that it would still be talked about centuries later . . .

She sank into Gaston's embrace, held him with all her strength, her pulse racing wildly with joy. "It's all true," she sobbed. "Oh, my God, it's all true."

"It means that you *must* come back to me." His arms tightened around her, his breathing rough and warm against her hair. "You must find a way, Roussette. Whether it takes months or years matters not. You must find those in your time who might help you. Scholars or—"

"Scientists," she said into his tunic. "My family knows plenty of scientists. People in astronomy and physics and—oh, I'll talk to all of them! I'll talk to whoever will listen. I'll find a way. I'll come back! Gaston, it has to work!" She was trembling with a surge of hope that would have sent her to her knees if he hadn't been holding her so hard.

"You will find a way. You will be able to return home, and your surgeons will make you well, and then you will come back. Because that is what is *meant* to happen, my Roussette." He lowered his mouth to hers, and kissed her deeply. "We are meant to be together."

She melted into his kiss, feeling the strength of his conviction and the power of his love warm her, feeling certain, for the first time, that *nothing* could keep them apart.

"Your book says that we are to name him Soren." Gaston stood before the huge kitchen hearth, staring down into the flames with a goblet of wine in one hand. "It was my father's name."

"I like that idea," Celine said, stirring onions, vinegar, and pepper into the salsa she was improvising. With most of the servants gone, including the best cooks, she had decided to commandeer the kitchen and make dinner. With a little meat and some cheese, she could do a decent imitation of enchiladas. "It's a nice tribute to your father. Soren de Varennes. A good, strong name."

"Aye, for a strong, bold son."

Gaston's wistful voice made Celine smile. She could already picture their son, as tall and handsome as his father, growing up in a home filled with love.

"For our second child," Gaston said indulgently, "the name shall be your choice."

"Dweezil, maybe," she offered, hiding a grin. "Or how about Moon Unit?"

He turned, looking a bit less indulgent. "These are common names in your time?"

"Oh, very common," she assured him, trying to look serious. "Then there's Whoopi. That's very popular. And River, and Rumor. Or maybe Zowie, if it's a girl."

"My daughter . . . *Zowie?*"

"Or we could combine a couple of those into one. Whoopi-Zowie de Varennes," she mused thoughtfully, stirring. "Hmm. I like that. Lady Whoopi-Zowie."

He looked appalled.

She had to stare down into the bowl and bite her tongue to restrain a giggle.

"Lady Whoopi-Zowie?" he echoed.

She focused her attention on stirring vigorously. "Yes. Or maybe Whoopi-River. Or Whoopi-Cushion?" She glanced up, fighting to keep a straight face.

He was speechless.

"Or . . ." She let herself smile, let her love for him shine through in her eyes. "We could always go with something simpler. Like Jacqueline. After my sister."

A grin slowly curved his mouth. "You are jesting about the other names," he accused.

"Yes," she admitted, laughing. "I am jesting."

He walked over to her, a smile lighting his features and making his eyes crinkle at the corners. "It is good to hear you laugh, Roussette." He leaned one elbow casually on the tabletop, watching her work in silence for a moment. "Do you know, I never noticed before, but this table is precisely the right height for a use other than cooking."

"Oh, no, you don't." She ducked around the corner of the table to evade him before he could make a move. "A *duc* can't live on lovemaking alone. At least let me feed you first."

He made no effort to pursue, lounging where he was. "Very well, feed me if you must, *ma chère.*" He sipped his wine, heated promise glowing in his gaze over the edge of the goblet. "But I mean to feast on you later."

She snagged a small iron cookpot from the other side of the table and poured her makeshift salsa into it. "You'll have to catch me first," she challenged softly.

"A hunt, my sweet vixen?" he drawled. "I believe I can rise to such a contest."

She caught the way he emphasized the word "rise"—and could feel the temperature rising in the kitchen as heat sizzled between them. "A contest? One that might last all night?"

"Nay, it is to be a short one, Roussette. When I have captured my prey and carried her to my lair, I mean to subdue her quickly. Beginning with kisses. The first on her soft—"

"Keep this up and we'll be going to bed hungry."

"I am already too hungry to wait for bed." He stroked the tabletop with the flat of his hand.

She picked up the cookpot and her spoon, flashing him a bold look. "But the longer I make my predator wait," she teased as she crossed to the hearth, "the *hungrier* he will be."

He growled in reply and she could feel his gaze following her every step. She hung the pot from one of the hinged hooks embedded in the stone wall of the fireplace. Positioning it over the flames, she started stirring.

After a moment, he exhaled slowly, patiently, his voice taking on a softer, deeper tone. "You will be even more beautiful than you are now, Roussette, when you are round with child."

Celine opened her mouth to reply—when a sudden, sharp pain struck her lower back.

Like she had been stabbed.

She stopped what she was doing, so startled she simply froze with an agonized little gasp. Gaston couldn't have heard it, because he was still talking, telling her in that tender voice how lovely she would be when she was pregnant with his baby.

The pain was intense, jagged, worse than anything she had felt before. She waited for it to pass.

Her right leg started to feel tingly and numb.

Oh, God.

She gripped the spoon hard, trying not to shake. Everything was going to be all right. They had only two days left. Two days until the eclipse. Two days and she would be back in 1993 and the doctors would take out the damn bullet fragment and then she could come back to her husband.

Two days. There was nothing Gaston or anyone could do to stop the pain; she just had to hold out against it until she could get home and go to a hospital.

She forced herself to keep working, stirring. "Beautiful? Round?" she asked lightly, trying not to let him see that she was breathing in short, shallow gulps. "I'll be . . . fat."

"Nay. Beautiful," he assured her. His voice dropped to an even deeper tone. "And I shall make love to you very, very gently."

"You sound . . . hungry again," she teased.

Oh, God, it hurt.

"Aye, I am," he growled. "Mayhap I shall eat . . ." He let the sentence hang for a moment. "Some of these."

She could hear him walk to the table in the far corner and experimentally munch the flour tortillas she had fried earlier.

"Stop that," she protested. "Or we won't have any left to eat with this. Gaston, would you bring me the—"

A stabbing, searing jolt of agony went up her back. She tensed, held her breath.

"Roussette?" he asked, still munching. "What is it you wish?"

The pain wasn't quick and sudden this time; it was steady, and it got worse. She dropped the spoon into the pot, raising a shaking hand to the stone wall of the hearth. Her vision misted to gray at the edges. She didn't even have the strength or the breath to turn around and ask for help.

"Roussette?" Gaston's voice had an edge of concern this time.

She opened her mouth, but no words came out.

Her legs went weak, limp, refused to hold her. Everything seemed to tumble around her, the stones of the fireplace spinning before her eyes. She crumpled, heard him running toward her, his boots striking hard against the stone floor.

And then she was aware only of the blinding agony that wrenched her lower body and tore a cry from her lips. She could hardly feel it when he caught her in his arms, easing her down, holding her. A confusing, foggy haze closed in over her mind, her sight, her hearing.

His voice seemed to come from far away. "Nay! Sweet Christ, *nay!*"

She clutched at his muscular arm, staring up at him, barely able to see him through the gathering darkness. *"Oh, no,"* she whispered.

It was the last thing she said before blackness closed over her completely.

Even the glow of the candle at Celine's bedside could not add color to her cheeks.

Gaston truly thought his heart would stop beating, if not from the shock of what had happened, then now. Now as she lay unmoving beneath the blankets, so pale and fragile among the heavy coverings. Her skin, her lips, were so pallid it looked like she had lost a great deal of blood, though she had no wound—at least none that could be stitched or bandaged or healed.

He grasped her hand, his grip bruising, as if he could hold her here by sheer physical force.

But he knew that with every passing moment, she was slipping away from him.

He clenched his jaw, eyes burning. He had no memory of lifting her in his arms and carrying her here, to one of the upstairs chambers. All he knew was that she had not made one sound. Not when he had laid her in the bed, nor when he had summoned Brynna, nor when the mystic woman had used a strong-scented potion to try to rouse her. It had only made her drift in and out; she had not strength enough to awaken.

"Milord," Brynna said softly, glancing at him as she pressed a cool cloth to Celine's forehead. "There is little we can do. She has no wound, no fever, naught that can be aided by my herbals or healing skills."

Gaston had no breath for words. He kept staring at his wife, unwilling to accept that this was happening. Her spirit and fire and laughter could not be quelled so abruptly. Sweet Christ—it was like some unseen arrow had struck her. In the span of a heartbeat she had gone from vibrant and alive to silent and helpless. Defenseless against this bit of metal inside that was killing her.

Killing her.

Desperation and frustration and fury clawed at him, ripped an animal sound of pain and rage from deep in his chest. She was dying because of this future-weapon that had wounded her so long ago, *and he could not stop it*. Could not protect her. Could not help her. Could not fight for her.

All his life he had conquered opponents by physical prowess, battle-skill, sharp wits. But now all his years of hard-won experience availed him naught. His strength was useless. Guile, power, force—all futile. There was no way he could vanquish this unseen enemy. Even his love was not enough to save her.

He lifted her hand to his cheek, finding her skin so cool . . . warm honey and cream transformed almost to ice. He fought a cry of grief and denial that threatened to tear him to pieces. Only moments ago, she had been teasing him, his Roussette; her smile brilliant, eyes sparkling, her body strong and graceful as she moved.

They had spoken of names for their children.

He had relished the sound of her laughter.

And now one small, hidden piece of metal had silenced her. Mayhap forever.

He exhaled a shuddering breath, could no longer hold back the tears, buried his face in her hair, in the pillow. By holy Christ, this could not happen. *Why?* Why now, with the dark of the moon so near? Two days, and she would be safe and well. Could God not grant her two days?

Brynna's voice was a bare whisper on the other side of the bed. "Milord." She held one hand pressed to the slender column of Celine's throat. "Her heartbeat grows weaker."

Gaston remained where he was, numb.

Roussette, do not leave me.

His shoulders shook with that silent, futile plea. She could not leave him. Not this way. Not when there were but two days left and their future held so much promise.

This was not meant to happen.

He pushed himself upright, still grasping Celine's hand, clenching his other hand into a fist. He wrenched his gaze from her long enough to look at Brynna, heedless of the salty wetness on his cheeks. "We must find a way to keep her alive until she can return home."

Brynna shook her head, her own eyes bright with tears. "Milord . . ."

"Nay, tell me no more of her weakness! She has strength. She has courage. She can fight it. There must be a way."

"But even if there were . . . I do not think there is time."

He thrust himself up from the bed, a spill of savage curses tumbling from his lips. *Time.* "Damn that word to the black depths of hell—I never want to hear it again!" He paced away, turned back, looking down at Celine, willing her to be strong, willing her to live. *Two days.*

And then she stirred, her lashes lifting.

But even as she came awake, even as he felt a surge of hope, she made a sound of pain.

He knelt at her bedside, brushed her coppery hair back from her forehead, pushing the cool cloth aside. She strug-

gled to speak, but only made the sound again: a strangled
little gasp.

"Shh, love," he whispered, feeling the hot, bitter burning in his eyes again. He thought he had endured agonies
before—but naught in his life had ever hurt him so much
as seeing her in pain. "Be strong, sweet Roussette." He
forced a smile. "You will be well."

"You're . . . not a very . . . good liar . . . my lion." Her
voice was so weak he had to lean near to hear it. Her eyes
were glazed.

"It is no lie," he said forcefully. "There are but two
days. You will return home. The physicians of your time,
with their skills—"

"Gaston . . ."

Her voice suddenly cut short in a broken cry. She closed
her eyes, her lower lip quivering.

He bent his head, clamping his teeth together to hold in
a sob, unable to bear her suffering. He took her hand.
"You will be well," he repeated in a low voice that was almost a prayer. "And you will return home, and then you
will come back to me. And we will have a son called
Soren. And a daughter, with your fire-colored hair and
your storm-colored eyes, and she—"

"It's all . . . right, Gaston . . . I'm not . . . afraid to die,"
she gasped, her lashes lifting partway.

"You are not going to die," he said fiercely.

"When . . . you were on the . . . battlefield . . . the
joust—"

"Shh, do not think of what is past. Think only of our future."

"When I woke . . . up in your . . . pavilion," she continued insistently, "I got down on my . . . knees and prayed.
M-made a bargain with God . . . that he should take me . . .
instead of you . . . if you were allowed to live, I would . . .
die willingly."

Her words sent a chill down Gaston's spine. The admis-
sion seemed to take what little strength she had left; her
lashes lowered and she fell silent, her breathing short and
shallow.

"A noble gesture, milady," he said hoarsely, "but I have

first claim to such a bargain. I offered the same prayer—when I was in Tourelle's dungeon and knew not what had befallen you."

Her eyes opened again, wide, shining, impossibly dark against her pale skin. "But you . . . survived the . . . joust," she whispered.

The chill he felt became a sleeting storm of anguish. Rage. Fear.

Could God exact so terrible a price for his victory over Tourelle?

"Grateful . . ." Her lashes drifted downward, the barest trace of a smile touching her pale lips. "Had the chance . . . say . . . good-bye."

"Never!" he said forcefully. *"That is a word I will never say to you."*

"Will . . . wait for you . . . until our . . . souls reunited. I love . . ."

She did not complete the sentence.

"Roussette?" His voice was a strangled sob.

"Lady Celine!" Brynna laid her hand alongside Celine's neck. "I cannot find her heartbeat. I cannot . . . nay, there it is! She lives," Brynna said shakily. "She lives."

Gaston tenderly stroked his wife's cheek, his tears falling, hot and unchecked. "Heaven will not be enough, my Lady Roussette. I will *not* surrender you. Not for a day. Not for one sweet hour. I will not let you die. I mean to have you in *this* life as well as the next."

Celine lay silent, still, deathly pale.

"Is there no one who can help her?" he demanded raggedly, not knowing if he was pleading with God or himself or the mystic woman. "No surgeon? No physician skilled enough?"

Brynna shook her head. "I know of none, milord. None who would dare attempt such a task. Not even the barber-surgeon who was in Tourelle's employ—the man who assisted you—and he is the most skilled I know of in all the region."

Gaston's entire body shook with helpless fury. His wife needed him. She was lying there helpless and she needed him and he could not help her.

Think. He had to think.

Brynna rose and went to the table in the corner, where she had placed her sack of curatives. "I may at least be able to ease her pain if she awakens again." She poured a cup of wine and carefully began mixing various dried herbs into it.

Gaston swore. He rose from the bed, pacing again, toward the window and back; he rubbed his hands over his eyes, trying to force his thoughts and heartbeat under control. Trying to summon all his powers of reason and logic and cunning. Herbs and wine would not help her. A barber-surgeon would not help her. Celine needed a physician of skill enough to try to save her. Where could they hope to find such a man?

It was an impossible question. There was no answer. She needed a physician of her time. A surgeon of the future.

Dropping his hands in frustration, Gaston turned on his heel, stalking toward the window. There was no way to—

He stopped dead in the middle of the chamber, in the midst of the shaft of moonlight that spilled in through the panes.

That brilliant, silver moonlight. It blinded him, dazzled him. Not an enemy, but an answer from above. Why had he not thought of it before?

The moon.

The image tumbled through his thoughts and meshed with another, one that had been prickling at the back of his mind for days. He spun toward Brynna, watched her stirring the herbs into the goblet.

The goblet of wine.

Wine. Which could be used to cleanse wounds. To prevent infection. But only by those who had the knowledge.

And he had met only two people in his life who had that knowledge.

The moon . . . and the wine.

"Brynna," he said abruptly, the idea gaining speed in his head like a charging destrier, "you said that you knew of no other time-travelers—that my wife was the first you ever encountered?"

"Aye, milord."

He came around the bed so fast she nearly dropped the cup. "But you said that your father knew of *others.*"

"Aye. But, milord, my father has been dead for—"

"But he knew of others." He grabbed the goblet from her hand, staring at the wine. "*Dozens* of others, you said."

"Aye."

"And these people from the future—if they were unable to return home, if they lost any of the belongings they had arrived with—"

"As happened often," Brynna said, her face brightening as understanding dawned, "if we are to judge by my father's notes—"

"If these people could not go back to their own time . . . would they not still be here?"

The question hung like a glittering star in the silence of the night. For one breathless moment, Gaston thought he could feel his heart and Celine's beating as one, strong and steady.

He shoved the cup back into Brynna's hands, spun to the bed, placed his hands on either side of his wife's slender form, kissed her. "Heaven will not be enough, my Lady Roussette!"

"Milord—"

He was out the door even before Brynna had a chance to begin her question.

Celine would not live long enough for a safe return to the future.

But there might be time enough to bring the future to her.

Chapter 29

❦

"There seems to be much internal bleeding."

"Progressive circulatory shock. She'll need a transfusion, Audric. By our experiments, you're type O. Universal donor. You're elected. Mrs. Varennes?"

"Give me a needle, Thibault, quickly."

"Mrs. Varennes?"

The strange voices floated in and out of Celine's dreams . . . so loud . . . so distracting. She ignored them, floating back down into the comfortable darkness, toward a light that shone so near, beckoning her. A pure white light that drew her in like a loving embrace, to a place filled with gentler voices, with peace, with—

"You have to wake up, Mrs. Varennes."

A pungent smell waved under her nose yanked her upward, away from the light. She groaned in pain, in protest, wanting to sink back into the numbing blackness. The smell forced her to awareness. She opened her eyes—into light so bright it hurt. Brilliant light, but not the same that had tempted her moments ago. This glare seemed to come from lanterns overhead.

Glass lanterns.

Someone was speaking to her. Shapes moved around her. People. Three. She could make out only their shadows looming around her, like a movie out of focus. But then her eyes adjusted, and the outlines shimmered and resolved into—

Doctors.

They wore masks over their mouths. And coverings like tight white bandannas over their hair. Aprons. And thin

361

gloves . . . like surgical gloves. She could hear the metallic clatter of instruments on a tray.

She was hallucinating. She was dead.

But she still felt the pain in her back. So intense she started to cry. She wasn't dead . . . she was in the same bedchamber she had been in before. But not in the bed. She was on a table, draped with sheets.

Where was Gaston?

The same man who had spoken before tried again, leaning closer. "Mrs. Varennes, we're going to try to help you."

He had shifted to English.

American English.

"I don't have any X-rays to go by, ma'am, and I need you to tell me something. Was the bullet fragment lodged near the lumbar artery or the radicular artery? Do you remember what your doctors told you?"

He had a Texas accent. This was a dream. *Had he said X-rays?* A hallucination. It had to be. She felt a pain in her left arm—a needle puncture. She was too weak to lift her head, to see what was happening, but she recognized the man on her left. From where? Her pain-dazed mind would not supply a name. But the face—

He was the barber-surgeon who had worked on Gaston.

"Mrs. Varennes," the Texan said insistently, "this is very important and there's not much time. I'll be able to locate that fragment much faster and easier if you can help me."

She struggled to speak. To question them. Her mind was a fog of confusion and pain. Who were they? How did they get here?

Or was she the one who had come to them? *Had she returned to her own time?*

She remembered saying good-bye to Gaston. She had said good-bye and that she loved him and then—

"Her pulse has just become very fast, Dr. Ramsey."

"Was it the lumbar or the radicular?" the Texan demanded urgently. "Did they tell you?"

Yes. Yes, of course they had told her. Her doctors had reviewed her medical condition so many endless times that she had wanted to scream at them and cover her ears.

"The radicular," she whispered to shut him up. "W-where . . . when—"

"Everything's going to be all right, ma'am." He shifted back to French. "Thibault, get ready with suction—the glass pipette there with the inflated leather bulb on the end. Put her out, Audric."

One of them put a cloth over her nose and mouth. A cloth soaked with a strong-smelling liquid.

"Count with me, milady," the barber-surgeon on her left said. "One hundred . . . ninety-nine . . . ninety-eight . . ."

She had been through enough surgeries to know what the countdown meant. Anesthetic. It was anesthetic. *No!* She didn't want it. Didn't want to sink back into the darkness, never knowing if she would awaken again. Not knowing if she had seen Gaston for the last time. Where was—

"Ninety-seven . . . ninety-six . . . ninety-five . . ."

A soft black fog enveloped her.

A snore.

The sound she heard was definitely a snore.

It invaded the sea of strange thoughts that drifted lazily through her head. Floating to consciousness, pleased that she had finally identified the sound, Celine tried to focus on it . . . grab it . . . use it as an anchor.

She felt so woozy. Light-headed. Weightless. Like she had had far too much champagne . . . like she was hanging suspended at the peak of a roller coaster, in that no-gravity moment before it plunged down the other side.

Not that the feeling was unpleasant. It was better than the blank nothing she had felt for a long time. In fact, it was rather . . . dreamy. Like she was floating around in a warm ocean, safe, letting the tide carry her where it would.

But for some reason, she felt that it was important to open her eyes. Someone had been asking her to do that. A male voice. A very deep, familiar voice, alternately commanding and coaxing softly. She hadn't been able to respond, though she had wanted to. She couldn't remember when that had been.

In fact, she couldn't remember how long she had been asleep.

Curious, confused, she fought her way through the muzzy feeling that clouded her head, up, toward that snore.

Her senses began to clear a bit. Her mouth felt dry, like she hadn't had anything to drink in a long time. She almost unconsciously braced herself, waiting for pain . . . but there was no pain. Only an uncomfortable soreness. In her back. She opened one eyelid just a bit, experimentally.

She was lying in a bed, on her stomach. That made sense somehow, but she couldn't remember why. She felt weak. As if she would float away if it weren't for the heavy blankets covering her. Why did she feel so weak?

She opened both eyes, blinking. The first thing she saw was the shaft of bright morning sunlight streaming across the room . . . shining . . . almost like a halo . . . on a tousled dark head just a few inches away.

Gaston.

She smiled. Though it seemed to require an incredible amount of effort to smile. So he was the one snoring.

Strange, she thought sleepily, that he was sitting on a chair. Only his shoulders and head rested on the mattress, one arm beneath his bearded cheek, his other hand clutching a handful of her pillow. The position looked very uncomfortable. He was going to have one heck of a kink in his neck when he woke up.

She moved her hand, reaching toward him, though that, too, seemed to take a huge amount of work. Slowly . . . so slowly . . . she managed to bridge the distance, and rested her hand lightly over his.

He looked very tired. She hated to wake him up.

She decided not to. It made her feel inordinately happy just to touch him.

After a moment, though, he stirred, his hand moving beneath hers. He squeezed her fingers, murmuring something in his sleep.

Then he went still.

His hold on her hand tightened.

After a second, he lifted his head, the movement so

gradual it looked almost reluctant. His dark hair tangled over his forehead, half falling into his eyes.

Those potent, movie-star eyes. They met and held hers.

"Good . . . morning," she whispered, wanting to sit up and kiss him, frustrated that she didn't have enough strength.

He didn't say anything for a second. His expression was one of disbelief. He seemed to be holding his breath. He looked exhausted. Haggard. From his rumpled tunic to his tousled hair to the deep lines that bracketed his mouth and eyes.

She blinked at him, still feeling confused, like her head was stuffed with fuzz. "You . . . look . . . terrible."

A grin broke across his hard features. It broadened into a smile. Then he laughed. "Aye, Roussette, I am certain that I do." Raising her hand to his lips, he kissed it soundly, laughing so hard it brought tears to his eyes. "A ride of twelve hours to Agincourt and back followed by three days without sleep oft has a most dire effect upon my beauty."

"You were . . . snoring," she accused drowsily.

"It was *that* which awakened you?" He closed his eyes, pressing her hand to his bearded cheek, breathing so hard he could barely talk. "I should have thought to try it from the beginning." He was laughing and crying at the same time; she could feel his warm tears on her skin. "Thank you, God," he choked out. "Thank you, holy, merciful God in Heaven."

She was too tired to question what he meant about Agincourt, or why he was sitting in a chair.

"Does it hurt, Roussette?" he asked suddenly. "Are you in any pain from the surgery?"

The question cut through the clouds of confusion that clogged her thoughts. Everything came back in a flood. The bullet. The darkness. The pure white light that had beckoned to her. Then the other, glaring light . . .

"No . . ." It took her a moment to really assess how she felt. There was soreness, but not pain. More like uncomfortable muscle cramps than anything else. "I'm . . . all right," she said with surprise and relief. "Gaston, I . . . had the strangest dream. There were . . . doctors."

"Nay, not a dream, Roussette." He stood, still holding her hand as if reluctant to let go. "Do not move."

"I'm not . . . going anywhere."

He released her hand for a second, long enough to go to the door and bellow into the hallway. "Ramsey! Audric! Thibault! She is awake!"

Before Celine knew what was happening, she was surrounded—by the same three men she had seen looming over her in the bright light.

Except that this time they were all grinning and clapping one another on the back, looking almost as tired as Gaston. And they weren't wearing masks or aprons; they were dressed in simple medieval clothes.

"Well, my stubborn prize patient, how nice to see those pretty blue-gray eyes of yours again," one of them said.

She recognized him as the Texan—though he wore a tunic and leggings and was speaking French this time.

"It was touch and go there for a while." He lifted her hand. "But you've got more strength than any of us gave you credit for."

"Except the Duc," one of the others said, smiling at Gaston.

The Texan proceeded to check her pulse. "Nice and steady." He nodded approvingly. "How do you feel? Do you know what year it is?"

"It's . . . 1300."

"Excellent." He bent down and gently lifted her eyelid with his thumb, peering closely at her. "I would ask you who the President is, but that doesn't exactly apply in this situation, does it? How about identifying this man for me?" He gestured toward Gaston.

"Husband," she said with a dreamy sigh that brought a round of masculine chuckles.

"Right again. Pupils are responsive. Speech seems reasonably clear." He felt her forehead. "No fever." He went to the foot of the bed, moved the covers aside, and brushed something—it felt like a small piece of wood— over the soles of her feet. "Can you feel that?"

"T-tickles," she objected, wiggling her toes.

"Good." He did it again. "Damn good." Replacing the covers, he came back to her side, running a hand through his hair, grinning. "Nice to have you back, Mrs. Varennes. You're not in a lot of pain, are you? The potion that Audric made up should take care of the worst of it, but it was a somewhat experimental synthesis. It's hell working without a good centrifuge."

She peered up at him, feeling more confused than ever, though her head had started to clear. "Who *are* you?"

Gaston moved in front of the man, reclaiming the seat next to her bed. "I fear this requires a long explanation, Roussette," he said wearily, giving her hand a reassuring squeeze.

The other men pulled up chairs, and only then did she realize that there were several near the bed; Gaston hadn't been the only one watching over her.

"Sorry there wasn't time for introductions before, ma'am," the Texan began. "My name is Dr. Carter Ramsey. From Dallas—"

"Dallas?" she echoed incredulously, wondering if she was still dreaming.

"Dallas and Boston—Harvard Med School, class of 1982. My assistants here are what you might call 'locals,' though. Audric I believe you've met before." He nodded toward the young man on his right. "And this is Thibault, one of my students from Agincourt."

"You're from 1982?" she repeated dazedly.

"Actually 1989," Ramsey said. "But I suppose we should start at the beginning. You see, ma'am, your husband rather ingeniously took a few bits and pieces of what he knew about time-travel, and put them together into a theory—"

"That mayhap there were other people from the future who had come back in time," Gaston explained. "And if, as Brynna's father said in his writings, they were unable to return home, they would still be here. Trapped in this time." He gazed down at her like he would never take his eyes from her again.

Celine felt dizzy trying to follow it all. "But . . . how did you know . . . where to find Dr. Ramsey?"

"In truth, milady, he came to me first," Audric said. "When I treated his wounds after the joust, I cleansed them with wine to prevent infection. He noticed it at the time, but I evaded his questions. I had been sworn to secrecy. And I had no idea that *you* were from the future. Then four nights ago the Duc came bursting into my chamber, demanding the truth."

"Your husband believed that poor Audric was from the future," Thibault supplied.

"And I had a most difficult time convincing him that I am not." Audric slanted Gaston a wary glance.

"I apologize for breaking the door," Gaston told him a bit sheepishly. "And for threatening you. And . . . throwing you against the wall."

" 'Twas understandable, milord." Audric laughed. "When you were fighting to save the life of your lady."

Gaston looked down at Celine again. "I rode to Tourelle's chateau to find Audric, thinking I knew where he must have acquired such knowledge. But I was wrong. When I explained to him that you were from the future, and that you were dying . . ." His voice choked out. He paused for a moment, closing his eyes and opening them before he continued. "Once I told him of your injury, he broke his vow of secrecy and revealed where he had learned these methods—from a physician in Agincourt. A physician from 1989."

"I've had to be very careful, as I'm sure you can appreciate, ma'am," Ramsey took up the story again. "Just about everything I do could get me burned at the stake as a heretic—and I only learned that after making some very arrogant mistakes in the beginning."

Looking at him, with his thick blond hair, blue eyes, and broad shoulders, Celine found it easy to believe he might lean toward arrogance. But he seemed to be doing an excellent job of blending in; dressed in those clothes, he appeared as medieval as every other man in the room. "But how . . . how did you . . . get here?"

"What's a nice boy like me doing in a century like

this?" He smiled ruefully. "I was on sabbatical in 1989, doing research at the Sorbonne in Paris. One night I was up late, pulling an all-nighter in the library, and I fell asleep over a journal article, while I was sitting at a table in front of a window. When I woke up . . . I was still in the Sorbonne, and still in Paris, but it wasn't 1989 anymore. It was 1296."

He slumped a little lower in his chair, rubbing his eyes tiredly. "It took me a while to accept that, but once I did, I started to think of all the great things I could accomplish—all the people I could help. But the physicians in Paris just about ran me out of town on a rail. They weren't exactly ready to embrace change. I was lucky to escape in one piece, and decided it might be smarter to keep a low profile. Agincourt is a nice little town, and for the past three years I've had a small, quiet practice there. I also pass along what I can to a few *very* carefully selected students." He grinned at Thibault and Audric. "It's frustrating having to be so secretive, but I manage to do some good here and there."

"Can't you . . . get back?" she asked curiously.

"I've wondered that myself from the very beginning. But I've been having some interesting conversations with your husband and your friend Brynna, and I think my problem was that medical journal I fell asleep over. It came back in time with me, and like I said, I was a little arrogant at first. Thought I would single-handedly save the medieval world. I showed the magazine to the physicians' guild, trying to get them to believe I was from 1989, and they confiscated it. I've never seen it again." He shrugged. "According to Brynna, that means I'm stuck here for good."

"Are there . . . others?" Celine murmured. "Like us?"

"Plenty, if your mystic friend is right. But you're the first I've met. Apparently, some make it home. And the others—at least the smart ones, the ones who survive—would learn pretty quick to fit in and keep quiet. We don't exactly have a secret handshake or a password or anything, so there's really no way to tell."

"But if some ... return, why ... hadn't I ever heard of ... time-travel before?"

Ramsey shook his head. "Maybe we did hear of it and just never believed it. Would anyone in the cynical twentieth century listen to some crackpot who claimed he had traveled to the past and returned to tell the tale? Sounds like something for the supermarket tabloids." He leaned forward, resting his elbows on his knees. "But think of all the people reported missing every year. All those episodes of *Unsolved Mysteries*. The faces on milk cartons. The people who vanish in the Bermuda Triangle. Maybe not all of them were victims of crimes or tragic accidents. Maybe some of them fell through windows into the past. Like we did."

Celine nodded, feeling worn out, all of it spinning through her head.

"But it looks like we've tired you out, ma'am. You should get some sleep." Dr. Ramsey stood up, along with his students. "We'll stick around for a few days and make sure everything's okay. And we should start you on some physical therapy exercises as soon as possible, to strengthen the muscles in your back. But I think I can safely predict that you're going to make a full recovery."

Gaston rose and grasped the man's forearm. "I am in your debt, Ramsey, more than all the wealth in the world could repay. If there is aught that you need, aught that you would ask, it is yours."

The doctor seemed to consider Gaston's offer for a moment. "Can't think of anything, but I'll keep that in mind. It never hurts to have a *duc* on your side. For now, though ..." He grinned. "The expression on your face when you look at your wife is payment enough, milord."

"But if ever you have need of assistance—"

"I'll be knocking on your door."

Audric and Thibault offered their best wishes and filed out, but Ramsey stopped at the door. "Oh, almost forgot." He withdrew something from his tunic, walked back, and handed it to Celine. "You might like to have this. And you might need it someday."

She peered at the object curiously: a little flask made of clear glass, with a cork stopper, and inside it was . . .

A dark bit of metal. No larger than the tip of the fingernail of her pinkie.

"That's . . . the bullet fragment?" she breathed, barely able to believe that something so tiny could have wreaked such havoc in her life.

"That's it. And if your friend Brynna is right, you'll need that to get home, whenever the next eclipse—that is . . ." He glanced uncomfortably at Gaston. "If you . . . uh—"

"You have my thanks, Ramsey." Gaston escorted him out. "For all you have done."

When the door closed and they were alone once more, Gaston remained where he was for a moment, then came and sat in his chair again. They both looked at the small flask that lay between them.

"Next eclipse?" she asked softly.

"Aye," he said gently. "Roussette, you missed the dark of the moon. It happened two days past, when you were yet asleep."

Celine didn't have any reaction at first. All she could think was that it seemed strange, to hear him say that the night they had focused all their hopes and energies on for so long was past, and she had missed it. And she felt . . .

Glad.

"It's all right," she assured him.

"Nay, it is not." He glared down at the little flask. "Brynna tells me that there will be another dark of the moon, at midsummer. Roussette, it . . ." He paused, swallowing hard. "Once, I asked you to return home and then come back to me, but it is another matter to ask you to stay forever. You would never see your family again. Never see your home."

She lifted her eyes from the flask and gazed up at him with all the love in her heart. "I *am* home."

He looked away. "You are tired. And confused by this potion Ramsey has given you. I cannot ask you to decide now. You have not thought of all you will miss. All the wondrous—"

"I *am* home," she repeated firmly, remembering what she had told him once: that love was the only thing strong enough to build a future on. Not land or power or wealth.

And not electricity or cars or central air.

Love.

She took his hand, laced her fingers through his. "My home is with you. Now ... tomorrow ... forever."

Despite his exhaustion, the smile he gave her made him look more handsome than she had ever seen him. With their joined hands, he knocked the flask aside, sending it rolling out of the way. And then he kissed her, very, very gently.

Epilogue

Celine decided to keep the Cubs hat. She wore it now, her long hair swept up beneath it, as moonlight streamed in through the window of the upstairs guest chamber, a shimmer of cool silver in the July warmth. The cap was one of her favorites, and besides, summer always made her think of baseball.

Few of her other belongings had sentimental value. Celine felt nothing but happy and lighthearted as she quickly handed over the last few items, one by one. There were only minutes left until the eclipse.

"Here's my wallet. It has all my ID in it, and my credit cards—Mother never let me leave home without them. There's a couple thousand francs in cash you can use, if you need to. And here's the letter I wrote to my family, explaining everything. I'm sure they're grieving and hopeless by now, and I just have to let them know I'm all right."

She handed over the folded parchment, sealed with wax that was stamped with Gaston's lion crest.

"They'll recognize my handwriting," she continued. "If they have any doubts, they can always have it examined by an expert and compared with samples that they have. And my sister's contacts at the university should be able to test the paper and ink with carbon dating or whatever. Once they do that, there shouldn't be any doubt that you're telling the truth. And here's the guidebook. I know the lettering doesn't make much sense to you, but there are some good maps in case you somehow get lost—but don't get lost."

"I will do my best, milady," Brynna said with a smile,

carefully placing each item into the embroidered cloth sack she held.

"According to what Dr. Ramsey and I figured out," Celine added, "the years and the time-windows *do* seem to match up. He came here from 1989 and I came here from 1993, and he landed in 1296 and I landed in 1300. Four years' difference, both ways. So you should appear in Manoir La Fontaine about seven months after I disappeared." She felt a tug on her skirt and glanced down.

"Lady Celine?" Fiara asked, her laser-blue eyes wide and a little worried. "Will it hurt?"

Celine knelt and hugged her. "No, it won't hurt, Fiara." She smoothed a strand of blond hair back into the little girl's braid. "It's sort of like a dream—you go to sleep, and then you wake up somewhere else. Somewhere strange and wonderful. Except that it's real. You'll feel a little tingly and funny for a moment, but it won't hurt."

"And I'll be a real moon-lady? Just like you?"

"Just like me."

Fiara brightened and looked up at her mother, taking her hand. "Is it time yet, *maman?*"

"Soon," Gaston said from his post near the window. "The dark of the moon has begun."

Celine handed Brynna one last item: the roll of film from her camera. The first few pictures were shots she had taken of her family's Christmas celebrations in 1993. The rest of the roll contained pictures she had snapped around the castle and grounds, and photos of an undeniably medieval wedding.

Those had been taken at the private ceremony in the chateau's small chapel in the spring, as soon as she had been strong enough to walk. She and Gaston had renewed their wedding vows, with Royce as best man and Brynna as maid of honor.

"Give this to Jackie with the letter." Celine smiled as she pressed it into Brynna's hand. "She'll have them developed. There's a saying, in the future, that a picture is worth a thousand words. If nothing else convinces my family that I'm alive and well and head over heels in love in the Middle Ages, those should do it."

Gaston came to stand behind Celine, slipping an arm around her waist and pulling her back against his chest. "It is almost time."

"Brynna, do you remember everything?"

"Aye, milady." Brynna nodded, squinting at the two of them, as she always seemed to do when they stood so close together. "I will go first to your sister, and give her the letter and your other belongings, and speak to your family. Then I will find Lady Christiane, if I can, and explain to her what has happened to her."

"Maybe she was meant to be with someone in the future." Celine leaned into Gaston's embrace, loving the feel of his strength surrounding and protecting her, his heart beating so close to hers, the little shivers she felt when he dropped a kiss on the bared nape of her neck. "The way I was meant to be here."

"Aye," Brynna agreed hopefully. "I will do my best to help her. And I will avoid the . . . medium."

"Media," Celine corrected with a laugh. "Yes, it would probably be better to keep the whole thing in the family. I'd hate to see you subjected to battalions of paparazzi and reporters and TV cameras. Or end up as psychic-of-the-week on some talk show or infomercial." She sighed. "As I said, there are going to be some things about the future you're probably not going to like, Brynna."

"But it will be an adventure!" Fiara said eagerly.

"Aye." Brynna tugged playfully at her daughter's braid. "An adventure. And we shall have a home where we can live in freedom instead of in fear. And the jewels and other items that the Duc has given us should allow us to enjoy many comforts." She beamed at Gaston. "Thank you again, milord, for your generosity."

" 'Twas naught but my thanks to you, Brynna, for all your help. Godspeed to you both." Gaston glanced at the window and began to draw Celine away. "Roussette, it is time."

"Good-bye, Brynna. Good luck!" Celine shared her friend's excitement at all the wonders waiting on the other side of that window. She hoped the two of them would find the same kind of love and happiness she had found, with the help of a little moonlight.

Brynna scooped her daughter into her arms. "Farewell, milady. Thank you, milord. Farewell!" She went to stand in front of the window, and they could see her trembling just a bit.

Celine held tight to Gaston's arm around her; he had walked her almost out the door, as if half afraid the moon might whisk her away. "I only wish everybody could be here to see this," she whispered.

"I do not think this is a secret we can share with everyone," Gaston said. "Or anyone. Remember what Ramsey told you about the importance of a 'low pro-file.' "

"I know," Celine agreed reluctantly. "The fewer who know, the better."

The castle was almost empty but for a handful of servants and guardsmen. Royce was away at the summer tourneys, intent on making his fortune. And Etienne—*Sir* Etienne, Celine corrected herself—had left for Paris, to find adventure of his own.

Gaston had knighted his squire in a surprise ceremony after their wedding, to reward him for so bravely risking his life for her. The teenager had barely paused long enough to put on his new spurs before galloping off to see the King, to ask if he might be considered a suitor for the hand of a certain beautiful and available lady by the name of Rosalind.

Celine leaned her head back and kissed her husband's bearded jaw. "I know you're right. It's better if we just let everyone believe I'm exactly who they thought I was—Tourelle's ward, from a convent in Aragon. A little strange, but definitely medieval. It's just so darned difficult to keep a secret from friends. You know how I love to chatter."

He chuckled ruefully. "Then I shall have to see that you have your fill of chatter, wife, when we visit Avril."

Celine hugged his arms against her, eagerly anticipating their trip. They were leaving tomorrow morning, finally moving to their grand new home in the north, with a stop to see Avril and their six-week-old niece, and to pick up

Groucho, whom they had left in Avril's care. "I'm sure Avril will appreciate the company. From her letter, it sounds like her little Giselle is quite a handful even with—"

The light at the window suddenly grew brighter.

"Oh, Gaston, *look!*" Celine drew in a wondering gasp as Brynna and Fiara started to shimmer, like something out of a science fiction movie. It looked as if they were caught in a whirlwind of silver glitter. Fiara smiled at them over her mother's shoulder, and raised her hand to wave good-bye.

The image froze, suspended in the beam of moonlight, like a freeze-frame. And then they were gone.

Vanished.

Leaving behind only the window, and the moonlight, and the empty room. Celine and Gaston were alone.

Neither of them spoke or even breathed for a second.

"Saints' blood." He exhaled slowly, his hold on her tightening.

"It's all right, *mon cher,*" she said a little shakily. "I'm still here."

He didn't loosen his grasp one bit. "You will have to pardon me, Roussette, if I am careful to keep you far from all windows whenever there is a dark of the moon."

She laughed. "But most of my belongings just went several hundred years into the future—I *can't* leave now. You're stuck with me, my Black Lion. For good."

His reply was a possessive, throaty growl. "Mine forever." Plucking her baseball cap from her head, he sent it sailing across the room with a flick of his wrist, releasing a cascade of red curls. "And I shall waste no time in ravishing you thoroughly." He lifted her into his arms and nimbly opened the door.

"It's our last night in your furs." She sighed in agreement, twining her arms around his strong neck, curling her fingers through his hair.

He gave her a wicked smile. "I do not recall saying aught of my furs."

He carried her outside, where Pharaon awaited in the bailey, already saddled and bridled. In a heartbeat, Gaston had mounted the stallion and settled her across his lap. "We have a bold son to make," he said huskily.

He touched his heels to the destrier's flanks and shifted her slightly, and Celine realized he was wearing the new leggings she had made for him.

The ones with the buttoned opening.

"Yes," she murmured against his mouth. *"Tonight."*

Her husband sent the black charger galloping over the drawbridge, carrying her away into the warmth of the sultry summer night, sweeping her to heights beyond heaven in the moonlight.